About the Author

Mark lives in Barrie, Ontario with his wife and two daughters.

He can be seen with his dog in all weather down on the lakeshore enjoying sunrises on Kempenfelt Bay.

NEVER OUT OF THE GAME

Mark O. McCann

NEVER OUT OF THE GAME

Vanguard Press

VANGUARD PAPERBACK

© Copyright 2020
Mark O. McCann

The right of Mark O. McCann to be identified as author of
this work has been asserted by him in accordance with the
Copyright, Designs and Patents Act 1988.

All Rights Reserved

No reproduction, copy or transmission of this publication
may be made without written permission.
No paragraph of this publication may be reproduced,
copied or transmitted save with the written permission of the publisher,
or in accordance with the provisions
of the Copyright Act 1956 (as amended).

Any person who commits any unauthorised act in relation to
this publication may be liable to criminal
prosecution and civil claims for damages.

A CIP catalogue record for this title is
available from the British Library.

ISBN 9781784656 73-7

*Vanguard Press is an imprint of
Pegasus Elliot MacKenzie Publishers Ltd.*
www.pegasuspublishers.com

First Published in 2020

**Vanguard Press
Sheraton House Castle Park
Cambridge England**

Printed & Bound in Great Britain

Dedication

For Arlene

Acknowledgements

Without the guidance of my editor, Elizabeth Bond (Bond Writing Services), this project would never have been completed. Elizabeth, your professionalism, talent and kindness were so apparent, draft after draft. Thank you.

Pegasus Publishing believed in me and that will never be forgotten, you have been in my corner from day one.

Arlene, Maggie and Emma, you have always encouraged me to chase my dream, thank you for being the most loving and supportive family one could ever ask for.

1

November 2, Present Day

"Likely at some point in your travels, you've stopped at a ball diamond. Maybe you were walking by or just chose to pull over and watch a few moments of America's pastime. And then you hear a youngster, who was no more than twelve, call out, 'whoever wins this game, wins the World Series,'... and you smile because... well... you once said the same thing. Some things don't change as much as we think."

"Tonight, baseball fans... you're in for quite a treat... none of the athleticism, showmanship or bravado will be left in the dugout, because, at the cathedral they call Yankee Stadium, someone will be crowned World Champions."

"Yes, tonight, whoever wins this game, *will* win the World Series."

"Welcome to game seven. I'm Jon Millerton and to my left, my partner, Joe Kates. Thank you for joining us on Sports Radio 66, on an evening that will chill you to the bone, literally that is, because for the last twenty-four hours Mother Nature has taken center stage and only in the last couple of hours has the snow given way to rain and now we are left with the heavy cloud cover that threatens tonight's festivities. Let's just hope that she might become a fan of this great game and allow us some relief, and who knows maybe she might just enjoy this age-old fixture."

"So, how will this play out? We've had our fair share of intrigue, trickery, misery, fury, and of course, drama, in the first six games. We could not ask for anything more from this series."

"It all began in the first inning of game one, when tonight's starting pitcher for the Yankees, Rickey Boyles, almost maimed leadoff hitter and perennial all-star Jorge Rios. This erupted into a bench-clearing brawl and we hadn't even seen an out in the series! No love has been lost between these two baseball giants. The New York Yankees, always a perennial favorite, has made it known to the Padres of San Diego that their zero World Series wins will not end on their watch. San Diego, on the other hand, would enjoy nothing more than to hand the Yankees defeat in their relatively new, grand stadium, which casts its shadow on the original 'House that Ruth Built'."

"In game four, Boyles versus Clem, a rematch of game one, we were treated to a pitching clinic like no other. Not one, but two, perfect games leading into the seventh and then a barrage of home runs. That game ended abruptly on an extremely rare triple play. Wow, what a night that turned out to be."

"Boyles and Clem are deadlocked at a win a piece in this series, and the two kingpins of the mound face off one more time."

"There is electricity in the Bronx this evening in more ways than one, as the sky is lighting up behind us, but our trustworthy meteorologist has assured us that this will pass and we will be set to begin a historic nine innings after a very short delay. Let's sit back, hunker down, and batten down the hatches for a real 'barn burner'. Get ready, ladies and gentlemen, for an evening that folklore is made from."

"Well, Joe, there is one thing for sure… one of the two cities across this great country will erupt tonight, and the other will fall into a sad slumber and question when an opportunity like this will come along again. With that I turn it over to you."

"Thanks, Jon."

And now the two great radio commentators become the voices behind the action for the next four-plus hours.

"The opening ceremonies are completed, our eyes focus on the pitching mound where Boyles, in his Yankee pinstripes, tosses down the rosin bag and stares in for the signal from his battery partner, the back catcher, Jeff Sinclair. And the first pitch is a ball way outside, and this game is started at 8:27 Eastern Standard Time after a forty-seven-minute rain delay."

"Three more tosses and the lead off runner is on first. Not exactly the start Boyles was looking for. Samuels is up and he has something to prove to both himself and all of San Diego after a horrible series to date."

"Wow, one pitch and that crack of the bat leaves no doubt. Samuels has just drove a hanging slider on a rope to left field for a two-run shot, bringing home the leadoff walk. Boy, that got out of here in a hurry."

"As the Yankee faithful are still settling into their seats for the second time this evening, they will not be pleased with that giant scoreboard showing the hometown favorites down by two."

"New York's manager, Lacoste, is already standing on the steps of the dugout with no one out in the top of the first. He just doesn't like what he sees."

"Boyles is not comfortable on the mound. He's kicking the rubber; he's picked up the rosin bag a number of times. Lacoste recognizes his idiosyncrasies and it's not good for Yankee fans."

"I know Boyles has a lot on his mind tonight, but he's a thirteen-year vet of this league and has seen so many pressure cookers; he just needs to settle down and focus on this situation. This is the biggest game of his illustrious career."

"Settle down is exactly what he needs to do, Jon, because tonight he's looking like a rookie. In fact, he looks like he'd rather be anywhere else on earth than standing on that mound."

***

Fingers stained yellow from years of careless smoking, the man they called Wolf reached over and turned off the radio broadcast. The car was appalling; apart from the rust, the cracked windshield and the vibrating tail pipe, a layer of grime covered the steering wheel and the fake leather upholstery. It was so thick the surfaces were slippery to the touch. The smell, however, trumped the vehicle's appearance: stale grease from an amassing of fast food remains, probably accumulating since the Reagan administration. Newspapers, empty take out containers and cigarette butts littered the floors, both front and back.

Wolf tapped the ashes towards the ashtray, then flicked the filter out of the small crack in the passengers' window with the precision only someone with leagues of experience could execute. Not once did his eyes leave the road.

Wolf pulled up hastily to the VIP valet parking at Yankee stadium, an imposing place if your vehicle is only a BMW or a Volvo, as McLarens and Aston Martins are more commonplace. Patrons crossed in front and behind his car, wild with excitement, as energy was seeping through the walls of the colossal sports arena. The valets laughed at the beige rust bucket and waved him to move along. One of the young suits soon changed his tune when a hundred-dollar bill was placed in his hand as Wolf burst from the driver's door, his overcoat flowing like a cape, magnificent and daunting at the same time.

Wolf slammed the door, a crucifix swinging back and forth from the rear-view mirror tapping the front windscreen. Layered in clothing, he adjusted a hoody over his head; only his deeply creased cheeks, speckled with two days of growth, and his crooked nose remained visible.

2

May 30, Five Months Before Game Seven

The end of May marked the end of term and the finish of the college year. The dogwoods and azaleas were in full bloom, and the grass a brilliant green thanks to a plethora of spring rain and the cool cloudy days that surrounded them. This used to be Clay Stoppa's favorite time of year, but that was a long time ago.

Duvall College was nestled one mile south of the village of Gremlin, a quaint town steeped in history tucked in the southwest corner of Pennsylvania, not far from Philadelphia, but far enough so as not to become a commuter town and be saddled with all of the drudgery that comes with that designation. Just over two thousand students attended Duvall, and fewer than five thousand were permanent residents of Gremlin.

Duvall College was famous for three things. Firstly, its beauty: the campus was set on a series of rolling hills and matured manicured grounds. Secondly, the horticultural school, thus explaining the sculpted lawns and finally, baseball, and that was where Clay made his mark.

Clayton Stoppa was a living legend at Duvall and someone who carried it with the utmost of humility. He single-handedly transformed a mediocre division two-baseball team into a school with a waiting list of ball players from across the eastern seaboard. Clay had the perfect combination of baseball savvy, a presence that commanded respect, a sharp intellect, and wisdom well beyond his years.

He skipped down the marble staircase attached to the grandest limestone building on campus, his dash bearing that of a professional dancer, floating with such grace and ease. The pathway descended to the common grounds and the litany of cobbled pathways. His gait suggested not a care in the world, but it couldn't be further from the truth.

The day was clear and calm, not a trace of humidity; Clay slung his navy blazer over his forearm allowing the sun to warm his back. His pace picked up and he glanced at a few students who called him by name, he nodded politely. Clay wasn't a professor, but did hold a teaching certificate from Maine. He taught American History to first year students and was known as the handsome mature lecturer with a silky voice and dreamy eyes. His colleagues gave him playful grief each fall, after the predominantly female class would file into his lecture theatre. Although he was a fine teacher, Clay wasn't employed for his comprehension of America's past; he was the engine driving the machine they called baseball, and the Dean of Duvall College *loved* his baseball.

After one of the shortest stints in major league baseball, Clay remained in the game that had consumed so much of his life. He desperately wanted to give back to the community, and over time developed a knack for teaching the game.

During a horrific one win and twelve loss start at Duvall ten years ago, he was promoted from an assistant coach to assume the managerial position. That season they marked a nineteen and twenty record. As it turned out, it was his only season below five hundred. The players followed his lead, bought into his system and slowly he turned a perennial loser into a force to be reckoned with.

Clay looked for the five tools of baseball in each player: hit for power, hit for control, running speed, arm strength, and hands. He would compare the athletes on his roster to a major league player and help each individual improve. Clay never cloned players; he worked with the individual's talent. He let the athlete excel using a combination of natural ability and smart teaching. It was just as important for his players to be receptive to learning, as it was the God given talent they possessed.

The respect he earned was immeasurable; every player would go through a wall for Coach Stoppa, and every player was honored to be a part of his team.

Clay had something special, an air of ease and confidence that resonated with his coaching staff. Clay was easy going, but somehow created a sense of urgency when it came to improving as a team. Clay cleared the way for the game. He kept it pure for the coaches and players, removing the politics, the internal griping, and the nonsense that can cloud the game. The coaches grew with his teams and his successes. And successful they were.

Clay's pace had settled into a saunter, more in keeping with the warmth in the air and the holidays set before him. He reached his beaten-up Volkswagen, the same vehicle that had seen him through college and high school, an odometer reading well over two hundred thousand miles, a vehicle whose gleam had long diminished, but its spirit was in high gear. He rested his jacket on its hood then leaned back on the faded black finish to take one last look at the main baseball diamond directly in front of him.

What a season.

This year had been the pinnacle of success. Playing in the Commonwealth Coast Conference, the Duvall Marauders qualified for the NCAA Division II Baseball Championships at Fox Cities Stadium, Appleton, Wisconsin. As one of fifty-five teams to compete for the championship in an extremely strong field, with the likes of St Thomas, Wooster, Johns Hopkins, Trinity Emory and Kean, in double elimination, two losses and you're finished, they had their hands full.

Not only did Clay out-manage his opponents, he had his players firing on all cylinders at the right time, a trait other schools were becoming accustomed to when they matched up against his team. Duvall didn't just win the tournament; they outscored their opponents forty-eight to thirteen and were humble in victory. The team celebrated on the field, a pile of players and coaches on top of one another; however, they cut their public celebration short as Clay had always preached to his players, win or lose, put yourself in the other team's shoes. Duvall was first to line up to shake hands and saved their euphoria for the privacy of the locker room. Duvall left Wisconsin with the victory and the admiration of fans, players and coaches across the continent.

Clay's locker was cleared out for the summer, his desk empty and all administrative papers distributed to the various faculty supervisors. It was shortly after the noon hour, and he had some errands to run, for both himself and Kate, his wife. Clay lifted himself from the hood of his car and took the few steps towards the driver's side door.

From the corner of his eye he noticed a woman closing in on the driver's side of her vehicle, which was right next to his. Always the gentleman, he waited for her to climb in first. They exchanged smiles as she fumbled for her keys.

The smile left his face when he noticed she was clearly pregnant. It was not that he wasn't happy for her; it was just a reminder that he didn't have the strength for, at least on that particular day. The woman sent him to another place in another time. She nodded and thanked Clay for his courtesy. For a brief second, Clay became despondent then fell back against his car, bowed his head, brought his hand to his forehead and closed his eyes.

Of all the days.

Clay's mind drifted to a spring day, now a little over thirteen years ago, a memory easily unlocked. This day would be stuck in infamy for both he and Kate. This day was so vivid in his mind that it brought instant anxiety the second it drifted to the forefront.

The young couple, Clay and Kate, were keeping pace in a crowd destined for Fenway Park, Boston, on a gorgeous spring day not unlike this one. They both loved baseball, and this was one of several events they had planned for their getaway that Easter weekend.

"Your daughter is very excited about this game Clayton Stoppa!" Kate caught Clay looking at her significant belly.

"She's kickin' up a storm." Kate pressed her thumb against a lower rib. "I swear to God; little Amanda has been kicking this same rib for a month now."

"Kicking. Oh, I don't think so! I believe that is her throwing arm."

"Oh, listen to you." Kate nudged him with her hip.

Clay smiled and pulled Kate closer. "I think Amanda will have the best of both worlds. She will be as headstrong and as intelligent as you and be graced with my gifted athleticism."

With that, Kate elbowed Clay playfully. "Okay, try this on for size... she will be as beautiful as you and have my gifted athleticism." With that, Kate laughed out loud, her legs crossed over one another as she covered her mouth.

"I just can't wait, Kate. I can't wait to be a Dad and throw myself into her world." They took a few steps in silence and then Clay laughed out loud. "Do you remember the day you told me?"

Kate laughed as well. "Of course."

"I even remember what you were wearing."

"Not much, as I recall." Kate playfully nudged Clay as they walked with the masses along Boylston Street towards the stadium.

"It was my birthday and you came running out of the bathroom in a bath towel and a grin, holding a birthday card. You were waving the card and bouncing across the room, yelling open it, open it now. Then the pregnancy test thing fell out and it was positive and I ..."

"Yah, I remember the rest quite well. I think we christened a few more rooms that evening." Kate rubbed her tummy and pulled Clay's hand over. Clay and Kate were celebrating a belated fourth wedding anniversary that weekend; they had been a couple for seven years. They smiled at one another and, for a fleeting second, there was no one else on the street.

The reactions to the gunshots were different for everyone in that crowd on Boylston. The sudden blast caused some to slump to the ground, and others dove for cover. A few people just stood there frozen in their tracks, and then there were the screams of terror. There were some who turned towards the loud resonating sound, thinking it was just a car backfiring or two cars colliding, and others who paid no attention to the blast and carried on with whatever they were doing just seconds before. When the shots were fired Clay became completely cognisant of his surroundings, as if everything played out in slow motion.

Two shots were fired from a van that was inching its way through a drive-thru bay of the Burger King restaurant on Boylston Street, just across from Fenway Park. Shocked by the sudden outburst, Kate instantaneously squeezed Clay's hand then turned slightly in the direction of the sound. Within a fraction of a second, she lost complete control of her legs and fell, twisting out of Clay's hand to the sidewalk below. Clay, confused by the frantic reaction of those who stood inches away, spun towards Kate. He reached down to her, convinced she had tripped or slipped on the drizzle-covered walkway from a recent cloudburst. In a fraction of a second, what was a peaceful harmony of people winding their way to a ball game turned into terrorized pandemonium.

Clay dropped to both knees and leaned over Kate. She was turned into an awkward prenatal position, curled with her right shoulder and hip lying on the concrete. Kate lifted her head slightly then let it fall back to the sidewalk with a thud. Clay shook his head in confusion. *Why was she just lying there, what was going on?*

During their intense love affair, Clay had seen a gambit of expressions from his wife as they shared life's ups and downs, from grief and utter despair to sheer delight; however, that afternoon on that Boylston Street sidewalk, when Kate was shot, Clay's vision became myopic. Their eyes locked; he was staring into terror and trepidation magnified a thousand times over in Kate's eyes. Clay had never seen that look before.

"You're going to be fine, Kate," Clay's voice of terror resonated to the few onlookers that huddled around the fallen victim. Suddenly the next wave of shock hit Clay like a lightning bolt. Dark red blood appeared behind Kate's blouse. The thick liquid tracked the trowel marks in the sidewalk cement, twisting in the grooves like a snake slithering to shelter.

"What is it, Clay?" Kate was trying to follow Clay's line of sight, as he was clearly distracted.

"Is she okay? Is she pregnant? Has she been shot? That's a lot of blood isn't it?" The onlookers continued to gather.

Clay looked up in desperation. "Are you calling 911?!" Clay viciously yelled at a woman who had a massive flip phone curled to her head. She panicked and hung up on whoever she was talking to and pressed the keypad three times.

"Is there a doctor or nurse here?" Clay looked around but did not get the reaction he was looking for. Finally, a woman kneeled on Kate's other side, her jeans sopping up some of the blood. The stranger rolled up her sweater and ever so gently propped it under Kate's head.

The woman drew closer to Kate. "You and your baby will be just fine, someone just called for an ambulance." The stranger with grey hair and a calm voice turned to Clay. "How many weeks along is she?"

Clay swallowed hard; there was a lot of blood behind Kate's back. "She is in her third trimester." Clay's eye's relocked with Kate's.

This can't be happening. This can't be real.

Clay lost his composure slightly, but refocused on Kate and the task at hand. He had to be the strongest person in the world, right here, right now.

"Clay, I can't feel my legs... I really can't feel my legs." Kate was clearly terrified; one could clearly see she was looking for comfort and security in Clay's eyes, but there was none. He screamed for the ambulance, but it had only been thirty seconds since the call.

"Clay? Jesus Christ, Clay, what the hell has just happened here? What about our daughter? Oh my God, Clay, our baby, this can't be happening, Clay." Kate's eyes were wider than saucers. "Jesus Christ, Clay, what are you looking at?" Kate tried to follow his eyes. Once again, he was staring at the dark stain behind her back. He looked around to get his bearings. Clay was vaguely aware of people gathering around the drive-thru window as well. Apparently, Kate wasn't the only victim, but he pushed the thought out of his mind; he only had concern for Kate.

The woman who knelt on the other side stroked Kate's hair and adjusted the sweater. She peeked a look at Kate's back and motioned to Clay to put pressure on the wound, but they both backed off when sirens could be heard in the distance.

"Kate, those sirens are for you, the baby will be fine." Clay too was terrified... his hands were visibly shaking.

Two ambulances pulled up, the first crept through the congestion and mayhem and made its way to the kiosk. The second ambulance was for Kate.

Clay recalled the sirens being unnecessarily loud and the lights unnecessarily bright: so much movement and yelling, paramedics talking among themselves and then on their cell phones presumably in contact with a hospital.

After several minutes, Kate was moved onto a board, the bleeding was staunched, and Kate was strapped in. Clay felt the ambulance door close behind him and within seconds they were in motion.

Turn on every flashing light you have and blare those fucking sirens! Let's go!!!!

The hospital was only minutes by ambulance from Fenway Park, but the journey felt like an eternity. They sped along Ipswich towards New England Deaconess Hospital. Clay sat by Kate's side jostling back and forth as the ambulance turned hard to the right and then to the left. The sirens were muffled inside the cabin. Clay was barely holding himself together. Kate looked eerily calm.

"Clay, I really can't feel a thing. I can't move my legs. I've been shot, haven't I?"

He wrapped both of his hands around one of hers and simply nodded.

"Is our baby okay? God, our Amanda, Clay?" Kate's eyes wandered around the vehicle.

"How much further?" Clay yelled far too loud. He squeezed her hand like a firm handshake.

Kate's flat board was dropped into a gurney and a team met the Stoppas at the ambulatory entrance. If there was an upside to getting shot in the back, it would be getting shot in the back four minutes away from a teaching hospital for Harvard's School of Medicine. To say Kate was in good hands would be an understatement, but to say the damage caused by the stray bullet was severe, would, too, be an understatement.

Clay was basically pushed to the rear and he followed the white coats through what seemed like an endless series of doors.

"Sir... SIR," a nurse pulled Clay to the side as the gurney and its entourage turned hard left in some kind of trauma room, maybe the ER. Clay couldn't imagine being separated from Kate at that moment. She needed him; he was there to help.

"Sir." The nurse tried to hold Clay's attention. "You must be her husband? Friend?"

"Husband."

"Okay, good. Well they need to help Kate and your baby right now and the best thing you can do is let us do our jobs. So, my job is to get this important paperwork done."

"What are they doing in there with Kate? I need to be with her."

"You will shortly; but some of the questions I'm going to ask are imperative to the treatment she needs, right now."

"What are they doing in there? You know she's pregnant, right?" Clay hadn't heard a thing she said.

"They are stabilizing her, stopping the bleeding, checking the vitals for both your wife and child." The nurse was a pro. "They will be out shortly, so let's get this done. We can do it right outside of her door so we are the first people the doctors see when they come out."

Clay had no concept of time. The doctors were taking an unusually long time with Kate behind the closed doors. The doctors knew it, the nurses knew it, the nurse charting the Stoppa's information knew it, but thankfully Clay was oblivious to the gravity of the situation.

The door was opened several times; clipboards and hospital staff traipsed to and fro. Finally, two doctors in powder blue scrubs emerged into the hallway. The male doctor sighed hard then removed his skullcap. He forgot to introduce himself.

"We have stabilized Kate, Mr. Stoppa."

"And our baby?"

"Mr. Stoppa," the female doctor intervened. "Your wife lost an enormous amount of blood, and we are very fortunate to have her with us right now. The baby, however, did not survive. We are so sorry, we did everything in our power, but at twenty-one or two weeks, your baby just could not handle the shock. The baby…"

"My daughter you mean." Clay wanted to rip something or someone apart.

"Yes, your daughter, Mr. Stoppa. We are so very sorry."

Clay turned to the wall fighting off the tears; his fists clenched every muscle in his arms stretched to explode.

"Kate was fighting for her life in there and the baby wasn't far enough along. We did an emergency C-section, but the baby… your daughter wasn't ready."

Clay closed his eyes and leaned back against the wall. He wanted to collapse, as his knees grew weak and heavy. "If the gunshot didn't kill Kate, this news will."

"Mr. Stoppa, we need to talk to you about the gunshot, and the bullet, as hard as this is right now. We have to turn our attention to Kate, and we have to do this now, as time is *not* on our side." The female doctor wiped her brow and stared up into Clay's bloodshot eyes.

"Come over to this x-ray here." Dr. J. Cooper M.D., as her lapel read, pointed at the series of images that all looked the same to Clay. "Treatment of complex injury to the spine produced by a gunshot wound like the one your wife has had is not black and white."

Clay glanced over at another doctor who stood silent. She carried a clipboard, and on the back, it read Chief Orthopaedic Surgeon Dr. Rahid Hammel. Certainly, the credentials were there, but the comments didn't exactly exude the bolt of confidence that Clay was looking for.

Clay ran his hands through his hair and leaned back against the rail.

Doctor Cooper continued, "Your wife has been shot here." She held up an x-ray of Kate's spine, and then pointed at a light colored square lodged in the lower portion.

"The bullet is between the vertebras L3 and L4 in the lumbar nerve. These control the leg muscles." Dr. Cooper pointed with the end of her pen.

A third doctor also dressed in scrubs joined in. "I am Dr. Montague, radiologist." After a strong handshake, the doctor stood silent and followed Dr. Cooper's pen.

"So will Kate need surgery?" Clay was dumbfounded, such an obvious question to someone not staring at the love of his life's x-rays.

"The decision to perform surgery depends on four main variables: neurological status, spinal stability, bullet location and injury level."

"This isn't a classroom, doctor, so dumb it down for me please." Clay was barely holding it together.

"Yes, of course, I apologize." He adjusted his glasses. "I have studied the spine from all angles, and we likely have a compressive epidural hematoma, which means the removal of the intra-canal bullet fragments may improve motor function." He pointed at the light colored area.

"So, she'll recover? She'll have the surgery and… recover?"

"The long and short of it is, Mr. Stoppa, the surgery is not life-threatening to your wife, but the bullet location is not good. We are of the opinion that our best chances for Kate's optimal recovery begins with surgery."

"Optimal recovery." Clay repeated the politically correct term. He was going mad. Clay took a deep breath, controlled his temper and continued, "And a non-optimal outcome?" Clay looked around then choked. "Dear God, she might be paralyzed?"

Affirming silence met his question.

"Mr. Stoppa, it is too early to say, but there is severe trauma." There was some compassion in the doctor's voice, but it was certainly overshadowed by the task at hand.

Clay lowered his head and nodded. "Surgery it is then." He brushed back his hair once more.

After signing a series of papers Clay picked up a coffee purely out of habit on his way to a nondescript waiting room. No one else was around. It was shortly after midnight. Eight hours had passed since the incident, but it all remained a blur. Everything had turned upside down. The nausea would come in bouts; his mind drifted from one horrific scene to the next. He really wasn't paying much attention to anything, just pacing, then sitting, then pacing again; sometimes back and forth in the waiting room then down the quiet hallway.

I should call Kate's parents. No fuck that, I will do that tomorrow. I need to call her school tomorrow. What day is tomorrow? Was the ball game today? His eyes flitted back and forth. *What if she is paralyzed? And how do I tell her the news? Kate, we lost the baby and you may never walk again. If the first news doesn't send you over the edge, the second will. How do I tell her we lost our Amanda? This will kill Kate, kill her.*

Clay finished another coffee, not tasting one sip and then leafed through a magazine, but did not grasp a word. With each passing moment, he became more anxious, his shirt was soaked through and he could barely stop his shaking.

Anxiety was taking over his body; his thought process was irrational. He stood up and paced back and forth taking deep breaths, trying desperately not to think about the length of time his Kate had been on an operating table.

This can't be good; the longer she's in there, the worse this is. I think. Maybe. Maybe it is good. I have no fucking idea what is good and what is not good. Who am I kidding? None of it is good. This can't be happening to Kate. When will I tell her the news? Her body has just been beaten to a pulp and now I am going to smile, and say what?

Finally, after more than eight hours of quiet desperation, Dr. Cooper appeared in the doorway, disheveled and clearly exhausted. Clay was never far away and he appeared at the door immediately. Dr. Cooper's eyes met his. "That was one hell of a battle in there, Mr. Stoppa."

***

Clay nearly jumped out of his skin as he straightened himself up against his VW. A pretty student apologized for startling Clay then repeated her question, "What courses are you teaching in the fall?"

Clay composed himself, wiped the sweat from his brow, then smiled and suggested none a sophomore would be interested in, as he gathered his coat and made haste to his driver's side door. He climbed into his Jetta waved politely and set his sights on home, only ten minutes north on Highway Six. His light blue shirt was noticeably saturated.

Clay glanced at his watch, only to discover he was preoccupied a little longer than he thought, even with school out for the summer, his volunteering commitments were in full swing and he still had a timeline. Between coaching little league, being on the executive of the Big Brothers Association, and the President of Gremlin Minor Baseball, his days remained busy. There was of course one other project that occupied the majority of his summer and like a black cloud overhead, he pulled closer and closer towards its watershed.

***

November 2, Present Day

"Jon that was a mammoth run, a huge answer to the marker San Diego put up in the bottom of the second. So, now its 2-1 Padres, and this stadium has erupted."

"I am repeating myself but neither pitcher looks comfortable in the early innings, a far cry from the clinic they put on in San Diego just a few days ago. The batters need to capitalize on their opportunities or one of two things will occur: the opposing managers won't waste any time tonight going to the bullpens, or the pitchers will find their rhythm and it could turn, once again, into a pitching duel."

***

"You the ticket company guy… Colt?" Wolf stared straight at him.

"No, there are hundreds of us wearing a florescent green hoody with orange reflective."

"Are you Colt?" Wolf gave a no-nonsense stare.

The scalper nodded. "Indeed, bolt with the Colt"—as he did a little jig—"I got what you want right here. Legends Section. Row 8, just behind the dugout. Not easy to come by, my friend."

Wolf scrutinized the ticket. "That's not good enough; let me read the exact seat." With lightning reflexes, Wolf's right arm shot out and grabbed the scalper's when he tried to step away.

"Easy, asshole, let go of my fucking arm."

"I suggest you don't make a scene, Colt. Let me look at it." He squeezed harder to make his point.

The scalper reluctantly handed the ticket over; a 'no-no' without the exchange of cash. Legends SEC 17B, Row 8, Seat 7 just right of the Yankee dugout, and eight rows above the playing field. Wolf seemed somewhat satisfied; it was the correct seat and he now wanted to make sure the ticket was legitimate. Together, they walked towards the entrance gate. Wolf passed over eleven thousand, three hundred dollars in a bulging soft envelope. The scalper turned towards the wall and slowly fanned the fold and nodded. Wolf slid his tongue over his yellowed teeth and sneered, "Once the ticket is scanned you may go."

The turnstile unlocked. "You may leave." He released his vice-like grip.

Wolf didn't wait for the inning to end and did not excuse himself as he moved between the patrons towards his seat. The game was of no interest to him, and the fans meant even less. He'd been preparing years for this moment. Fans mumbled, one yelled out vulgarities rarely heard in public, something about his mother, male genitals and his sphincter. Wolf eyed his empty seat, a deep navy Yankee blue oversized luxury chair. But it wasn't the size or color of the seat that had him transfixed, it wasn't the premium location or the first-class treatment he had entitling himself to, no, his only interest… his seating partner. Wolf glanced over at the gentleman who sat on his own against the rail. With his overcoat neatly tucked below him, Wolf seated himself beside his nemesis, a man who had haunted him for decades, a man who destroyed him and a man who just didn't give a fuck.

"Relax, Junior," Allan Boyles called out to the mound, "You've done enough shit in the last twenty-four hours, so get your game together." Allan was calling out to his son on the mound. He barely noticed the body that moved into the seat to his left.

Wolf stared straight ahead as he settled into his seat, all the while intentionally burying his face in his hoody.

After all those years I thought I would feel a little emotion. I guess if I don't now, I never will... all the better to focus on the task at hand. Allan Boyles shoulder to shoulder with me. What a night this will be.

"That's my son out there." Allan Boyles pointed at the mound. He turned towards the latecomer and grimaced. Allan's face matched his personality: crusty and harsh. His features twisted like that of a bulldog and his personality as unsympathetic as a sledgehammer pounding on an anvil in the cold. He was a man with a stony conscience and a short memory. Allan Boyles rarely looked behind him, and if he did, it was to make sure he left no opportunity uncovered. Allan ate nails for breakfast, drank his coffee thick and black, and was never welcome in the room. Allan Boyles had no friends and wasn't looking for any.

Wolf turned slightly, and raised an eyebrow. "Which one?" A rhetorical question indeed, Wolf knew exactly who his son was.

"On the mound. I'm Allan Boyles." He offered his hand. Wolf tapped his glove with his own.

"The prophet from our home town Rebel," Wolf threw out there, mumbling in a barely discernable tone. "He's not very comfortable, is he?" Wolf's comment was biting, delivered with a snakelike undertone. Wolf knew who he was up against; he knew everything about Allan Boyles and his prized prodigy on the mound. In fact, Wolf could conjure up some memories that would make Allan blush, or at least twitch a little.

Allan was seated against the railing, trapped by the hooded man. "Just give him some time. Rickey's the best; you can't rattle his cage."

Wolf could sense that Allan was leaning forward slightly, trying to gain a glimpse of this stranger who refused to be impressed by his big-name son. With a smirk, Wolf caught a glimpse of the shiner ringing the old man's eye. It looked like it hurt, and that made him smile.

Wolf knew how dangerous Allan Boyles was and the power a man of his ilk possessed. Wolf was never underprepared; he was a man of great conviction, and a man who was motivated by an incident that occurred around twenty years ago and looked to complete his task this evening. Wolf was truly a man possessed.

***

May 30, Five months before Game Seven

Rebecca Sterling climbed the final three stairs to street level, her steps cautious and deliberate. She turned her back to the stiff breeze, cupped her hand over her lighter, and lit up a cigarette; something that happened at least twenty-five times a day.

"Congratulations, Rebecca," A passerby nodded toward her, smiling and trying to make eye contact.

A congregation of recovering alcoholics filed out from their meeting, the solid oak doors swinging as smoothly as they did one hundred and fifty years ago. Rebecca simply nodded and turned away from the handful that followed her out, allowing her a moment to enjoy a long drag from her cigarette. Rebecca's standoffish demeanor could be misconstrued as snobbish or unfriendly, but that wasn't the case at all. Those that knew her, or thought they did, understood that shyness was her disposition. For the most part, Rebecca kept to herself, though that wasn't always the case. Today she would 'share', so her aloofness to her contemporaries would be shelved for a short period of time. Reluctantly, she passed on a second cigarette, leaning on a rail allowing all in attendance to pass by so she was the very last to re-enter.

The group reassembled in the downstairs hall of the Diocese of Saint Apocalypses, a tired house of worship located in a seedy section of Boston's downtown core, a building built in 1857, renovated in 1923, and then forgotten.

"This is my two hundred and sixtieth consecutive meeting. I am clean five years and counting." The group applauded some yelled out her name. Rebecca bowed her head; her medium-length dark hair covered her pale and pretty face.

"I thought by now it would get easier, and for those of you who think you will reach a point when you are 'cured', and it's safe or okay to drink again, maybe let down your guard and tie one on... well that will never be the case. It's a curse; we can tame it... but we can't conquer it." Rebecca glanced at some of the newcomers and then at the seasoned vets.

These were definitely words from the wise. Rebecca raised her head for the second time; she was not comfortable in front of her empathetic audience even though most were not strangers.

"Thank you to my sponsor, Tom." She nodded took a deep breath and smiled at the chairman of the group. Rebecca was wavering towards her seat.

Tom spoke up immediately upon noticing Rebecca's trepidation, "What can you tell our new friends here today?" gesturing to the new faces that appeared and reappeared. "Share your successes, Rebecca, so others can draw on your strength."

"So, what's my story?" Rebecca looked at her feet and slid her hands into the pockets of the well-worn jeans meant more for a male frame than that of a slightly underweight female. She filled her cheeks with air and released a long drawn out breath.

Her audience perked up, shifting in their seats, the old chairs creaking under the strain. They were curious to learn something, anything, about the private life of the doll named Rebecca.

"I have certainly been around the block, and in and out of treatment centres like this one for years." She crossed her legs balancing on one.

"Who here has been shot?" Rebecca stopped and looked around the room. "No one... well at least you're honest." She managed a nervous smile. "And here I thought I hung out with a bunch of hard asses."

Some clapped; others coughed and laughed all the while chairs scraped noisily on the rough and whitewashed hardwood floor.

"I was shot here." Rebecca crossed her right arm over her chest and pressed two fingers on her blouse just below the collarbone and just beside her shoulder. Rebecca looked to Tom for reassurance.

"Where did this happen, Rebecca?" Tom would guide her through this.

"I was working at a drive-thru at a Burger King in the middle of the afternoon; not exactly a firing range."

"And then what happened, move us along to the recovery." Tom continued his prompts.

"They operated. I still have fragments in me. I can only lift this arm so far, and when it's particularly cold and damp, it aches, so now I feed myself painkillers rather than alcohol."

"And what happened to your mental state?"

"Well..." Rebecca had already had enough. "Post-traumatic stress disorder, believe it or not." She looked over at Tom. "I suffer from it. So, after I was patched up and sent home I was supposed to carry on, business as usual, but I had changed... again." Rebecca paused. "Somewhat... changed I guess." She paused again, the room was silent apart for some creaking chairs and the odd smoker's cough. "I was already on a bit of a slippery slope looking for parties and a good time, but that gunshot, two shots actually, have been ringing in my head ever since. I felt vulnerable and ashamed so began to live each day like it was my last. I was looking to forget my horrible past, my horrible incidents and then add to this the gun shots, so I was living for the moment and took it too far and began to die for the moment... fun times weren't fun any more."

That was it. That was all she would give them. And with applause that grew slowly, she sat in a chair close to the exit. She no longer acknowledged the audience.

Outside again, the group was dispersing. Rebecca was the first to light up. In her right hand she held a white Styrofoam cup of day-old black coffee that she had been nursing from the first break over an hour ago.

"So, Rebecca, want to go for a coffee?" One of the members walked beside her.

"Got one." She raised her cup stared straight ahead, her usual aloof response, bordering on rude.

She perused her epitome district, this shady Boston neighborhood, a transient district that was not safe after dark, but was home to Rebecca.

Poor choices in her late teens, an unimaginable accident and then the victim of a not-so-random shooting, shattered Rebecca's inner psyche. We all make mistakes; no one is insulated from them. It is often the severity and timing of those mistakes that decides how our lives are altered. Rebecca never accepted the counseling after the shooting incident and one will never know if she would have taken a different, a less tragic path.

Sure footings and solid foundations set up life's stage. If the footings are tilted and the foundations form cracks, then proper repair is vital. If no one takes the time to assess the damage and begin to reconstruct, then at some point, the damage is irreversible. Rebecca teetered at that very stage.

'All the Kings horses and all the Kings men.'

3

Clay could drive the three miles to Gremlin's town limits with his eyes closed; after all, he grew up in Gremlin and, with the exception of a few years of school and baseball, he had lived in the community since birth.

He passed by a farm on his right known to all locals as simply 'the ruins.' It was and still likely is, a gathering for high school kids looking to party on weekends in the summer. Clay smiled to himself as he reflected on a paper he wrote about the ruins, and how folklore suggested that Scottish settlers by the name of MacTavish founded the farm and subsequently Gremlin Pennsylvania in 1814. It made for a new and interesting perspective on the clandestine party location, which was neither clandestine nor new; in fact, parties at the ruins dated back to his parents and maybe further. Clay was proud of his town, and he continued to remind his own students about the town's history. Clay was a firm believer that history makes the present more relevant.

He shook his head as the car rolled past the rolling fields, recalling that the MacTavish clan were not drawn to Gremlin; they were stranded. A canoe, loaded with all their worldly possessions, labouring upstream, was no match for a series of waterfalls. The settlers set out by canoe, paddling upstream from a temporary Atlantic Ocean village. After paddling inland for over sixty miles, the current became progressively stronger until they could progress no further. With great hardship they portaged around the first waterfall and within a mile reached the second, this one about twelve feet tall, equal in strength and height to the first. Once again, the pioneers struggled through another portage. When they reached the third waterfall, approximately two miles upstream, they laid down their paddles and called it home. They had no idea what was further west and had no desire to find out. And so, Gremlin was founded.

Clay downshifted into town, a series of quaint abodes nestled through a river valley, created in a bed of limestone dropped during the

Cretaceous period. Through millions of years of slow and relentless scraping and grading, the lateral and vertical erosion created the landscape for the modern-day Gremlin community.

Gremlin is bisected by the aggressive and angry Grange River, a water flow full of rapids and heavy currents, which have, over millions of years, carved a sixty-foot channel deep into the bedrock, leaving a menacing and picturesque limestone wall in its wake. The top of the cliffs that run east and west are almost symmetrical, with flat sections on both sides of the Grange that then climb to a second plateau extending maybe two thousand feet and finally a less dramatic lift to the plains which extend into rolling hills, forest and farm fields.

Clay drove into town at approximately two in the afternoon, his shirt still damp. He adjusted into a more comfortable position then tuned his FM dial to classic rock, The Who, and increased the volume on his upgraded sound system, the only thing newer than ten years in his old trooper. Maybe good music would change his current state of mind. He was stopped by the first set of lights just inside the town limits. Clay pulled through on the green light, then descended to the first plateau, passing Faulkner High School, his alma mater, and then turned right onto Union Street.

Clay and Kate purchased a house on Union shortly after they married. It was the perfect choice for the newlyweds: Clay living on his favorite street from childhood and Kate ending up in a house oozing in century charm and character. It wasn't long before they tore down the 1970s façade and restored the limestone abode back to its original splendor. Not the largest house on the block, but certainly ranking as one of the most superbly maintained. It was known as the house with the willow because of the gorgeous specimen on the front lawn, its branches reaching to both neighbors and standing over one hundred and twenty feet tall. A tire hangs from a low branch, welcome to all children in the neighborhood.

The population of Gremlin has grown at a snail's pace. Clay grew up in the community of three thousand and today the census would read five thousand four hundred. Originally, the lack of growth was due to a lack of industry and, thus, poor employment opportunities. However, in more recent years the lack of growth had nothing to do with demand but was mostly due to the power and influence of the Gremlin Historical Society and the town councilors that have severed spats with the growth mongers over the past fifteen years. Industry, commerce and, most recently, a casino attempted to break down the barriers of this pristine sleepy town, but the likes of Kate Stoppa turned large corporations on their heels, red faced, flustered, and a little lighter in the pocket book.

Ten years ago, Kate got involved with city hall as a community representative during the revamping of the "strategic plan". The town was moving towards annexation, and with this would come a new planned community on the outskirts of town. She just wanted to make sure the interests of the historic neighborhoods would be looked after. It wasn't long before she locked horns with the young enterprising mayor at the time and his grandiose plans to leave his mark on the community. His plan: create a regional center of commerce, a vibrant commercial sector that would attract the larger box stores, the major car dealerships, and all of the subsidiary shops and restaurants. Add to this an industrial park appealing to lighter, smaller manufacturing, wholesaling and distribution. What he did not prepare for was an extremely intelligent and focused woman with a goal and a game plan to circumvent the development.

As hard as the slick, baby-hugging, tape-cutting mayor tried, he just could not generate enough support at the critical moments. He had powerful allies, with deep pockets, but the grass roots campaigning town hall open discussions and the basis of small community partnership prevailed. Annexation did take place, two concessions north and four wide, at the northern boundary of the town. The new official strategic plan included residential, park and conservation lands, as well as a community sports complex comprised of two indoor basketball courts, a fitness and weight facility, an indoor track, and ice pad. The outside facilities include a football practice field, cinder track, four basketball courts, and two baseball pinwheels consisting of eight diamonds in total. They stopped short of naming it Stoppa Field.

Clay set his satchel and keys on the Hoosier as he entered the mudroom. He called out and got the response he expected then directed himself without delay to the basement. He knew that any hesitation might lead to procrastination, and on today of all days that was unequivocally unacceptable. So it began; Clay carried the banker's boxes up the stairs from the basement two at time, twenty-three white symmetrical boxes in all. This was Clay's Sisyphus.

He lined up the boxes along the bay window in the dining room; the transformation began. The harvest table, a 19th century pine beauty from a nunnery in the eastern townships of Quebec, became the focal point for Clay's summer as it always did. It was soon to be covered with papers and maps, stacked high and wide.

He sat down. He was beat; each year lugging the boxes from the basement became a little more taxing on his mind. Now Clay would wait.

The sound of Kate's SUV pulling into the driveway caused butterflies in Clay's stomach. She was the only adult that mattered in his world. For all of his accomplishments, his humility was the result of his deepest admiration for his soul mate; her strength of character had no bounds. From the moment he laid eyes on her, his lifeline was Kate Stoppa.

Clay stood at the end of the table, paced back and forth and waited. For a fleeting instant he wondered how quickly he could get the boxes back downstairs. The door opened, and Kate wheeled into the dining room. Her eyes scanned the room and she spun her chair straight back into the kitchen.

Clay moved to the entranceway and stared at the back of Kate's chair. With very subtle movements she oscillated back and forth. She bowed her head as if in defeat and spun her chair around. Her expression was not that of someone who had been conquered, but instead someone who was about to rip her husband's head off.

Clay was relieved in a sense. In his own twisted way, he would rather Kate be furious than sad, until of course, she opened her mouth and venom spewed out in his direction.

"Clay." She turned, bolted forward, then turned her back to him again, holding back the tears of rage. "Every summer, the same thing; I come home and hope you are resigned to our reality. I am so naïve sometimes." She rocked her wheels back and forth, looking out the series of windows that allowed a cascade of afternoon sunshine into the stoic dining room.

They had this argument too many times. Clay reopens the past, an

Easter Saturday of thirteen years ago. The day the errant bullet changed their lives, killed their daughter and left Kate in a chair.

Nothing is worse; two people who love one another more than words can describe, tangled in a collage searching for the truth, but with each passing year, the cold case dropped a few more degrees.

Kate and Clay, a rational, intellectual, deeply loving couple arguing over the most sensitive topic that forever changed their lives. The fights ripped them apart, maybe worse than the accident itself.

"Before you say anything, Clay, let me say my piece." She held out her hand like a stop sign, and composed herself. She had rehearsed this so many times. Would this be the year Kate spoke her mind?

Kate continued, "I have been preparing for this day for a while now." She held back the tears. "I know it's coming, because we avoid the topic like the plague. We skirt around the upcoming summer, our plans, where we might go, and then it starts all over again. Oh, these fucking files, they make me sick to my stomach." Kate rarely swore, so when she did, it had some impact.

"It's over, Clay." Kate caught Clay's attention loud and clear.

"What's over?" Clay swallowed hard. "What are you talking about?"

"This." She waved her hands at all of the files. "This, Clay, the files, the case, the investigation, everything." She paused and stared him down. "And, that... that look of yours. I hate the way you look at me as if I'm broken." Kate turned slightly, wiped her eyes and regained her composure.

Clay was at a loss. Her words cut right through him. "I don't... I've never thought of you as broken, Kate. It's just that so much has been taken from you."

"From me? Or from you?" Kate's voice began to lose its edge. "Look, I know how hard it was on you when we lost the baby. But this is the last summer, Clay, the last one." Her voice became calm and quiet. "At the end of this summer we burn these files, not lock them away or anything like that. We burn them. Give me that and I give you the rest of my life. Don't?" Kate stared into Clay's eyes. "Don't and you will never see me again, I swear to God." Kate's voice cracked. They stared at one another; you could hear a pin drop. "I swear to God, Clay, I have never been this serious in my life."

Clay looked around the room.

"Think about it." Kate turned and wheeled into the hallway; she could barely see where she was going. She held back the tears for as long as she could, made it to the lift and escaped into the bedroom upstairs.

Clay could hear the chair rolling around in the bedroom and then some music came on. The volume was increased so, while in the shower, Kate could sit sobbing uncontrollably, but undetected.

Kate loved Clay so much and they had dealt with more than any couple should have to, but it was time; she just could not continue to live like this. The files would not bring closure, so she had to step in.

Where do you start with the healing process? One minute a young vibrant professional couple is planning for parenthood. Next, they are picking up the fragments of a shattered life; one that went tragically in the absolute wrong direction.

At first, the couple held themselves together by teaming up and using every ounce of energy to get Kate stronger to regain her independence. They attended numerous physical and mental therapy sessions together, they worked out together, they read together, slept together, ran errands together, basically they were inseparable. Kate was dealing with massive hormonal changes and a lifestyle she had never considered. Clay stepped through waves of emotion peaking with bouts of feeling completely useless, then pangs of guilt and the ultimate rage, which almost drove him insane. Kate suffered insurmountable pain both mentally and physically, and often she would lash out with bane that would make a cobra blush and often use Clay as a verbal punching bag.

Kate would get a hold of herself and of course apologize, but they both knew that her hostility, although not intentionally directed at Clay, carried with it a darkness that neither thought they had. Kate's temper, her nastiness, her hurtful explosions, were the result of a woman being ripped apart from the life that grew inside of her, a child that was conceived in love with the man of her dreams.

For a short period of time they clung to the hope that she could undergo surgery to successfully repair the internal damage to her uterus; however, after numerous consultations, it was decided that the risk of surgery far outweighed the slim hopes of any triumph.

If the incident and the loss of their daughter wasn't enough to test their marriage, the lengthy debates over adoption and surrogacy took their vows to the brink. Adoption, for Clay, was an absolute no. Kate was furious and thought Clay self-centered. He was of the opinion that the child would always be a substitute for their own that they lost; thus, it would be completely unfair to all involved. Surrogacy was a very complicated journey that neither Kate nor Clay could recognize as the right answer.

It was at that point Kate became horribly depressed and extremely introverted. Clay feared for her life and would not let her out of his sight. These were dark, dark days; a period of time that would ultimately haunt both of them for years to come. It became apparent that Clay had to take a leave of absence from the school so he could spend every waking hour helping Kate. With the best psychological care available, Kate crawled slowly up an extremely slippery slope back to her husband and their new life together.

Kate received help; Clay was part of the solution for Kate, but not for himself. He did not grieve the loss of their daughter the way Kate did, and although it was not him sitting in the wheelchair, he never grieved the loss of his wife's mobility the way Kate did.

But for Clay, she knew, it was revenge. Clay was convinced that an eye for an eye would be his final healing and that it would bring a form of closure for both of them.

***

A laborious hour passed. Kate made no advances towards downstairs, so Clay did the manly thing; he called her cell phone, but as he expected, silence was the response. With precious few options remaining, Clay climbed the stairs in a slow and deliberate manner then peeked his head into the bedroom.

Kate sat in her chair staring out the side window. When the door opened, Kate turned her head and their eyes locked. For a brief few seconds no words were spoken.

"You didn't marry a quitter, Kate," Clay broke the silence.

"A quitter, dear God, Clay, you are many things, but never could you be referred to as a quitter." Kate shook her head in disbelief. "You've stood by me when that… that madman took away our future."

"I love you, Kate, more than anything in the world."

"I know that every day… every day."

"I will burn the files after this summer, Kate. I give you my word."

There was silence as Kate stared into Clay's eyes.

"I believe you, and, Clay," she paused, "I will give you one hundred percent cooperation to the finish line."

They sat across from one another, Clay on the bed, and once again stared into one another's eyes.

"Clay?" Kate held her breath and rocked her chair back and forth just a little. She was thinking about all of the ferocious fights they had through the years. "Clay, can you explain why you love me so much?"

Clay continued to look intently into Kate's eyes. "I can, Kate… but it will take me a lifetime to do it."

Clay and Kate remained in the bedroom and finished making up.

4

May 31

Clay peeked through the wooden venetian blinds. He smiled to himself. He was observing Kate's every move: how she wasted no energy as she dismantled the chair from her position in the driveway until she pulled herself from the chair unto the driver's seat via a temporary plank. After fastening her seat belt, she then pulled the balance of the chair up and into the back seat. Clay figured it was less than two minutes, a time they broke as a team many years ago. Clay's smile turned to a grin as he noticed Kate glance at her watch and nod in satisfaction. "Always the competitor," he mumbled to himself.

The air was cleared last evening and the reconciliation put a fresh beginning and, ironically, a closure date on Clay's investigation. She was off to teach English at Faulkner H.S., Clay's alma mater and the location of their second meeting.

When Clay had virtually wrapped up his playing career he returned home. There was no question he still loved the game and the thought of never stepping onto the field again agonized him every day. When the Independent League approached him and suggested he was what they need for their play-off run, he just could not say no. Clay Stoppa, beaten and bruised, was still leagues better than anyone who was in this semi-professional venue.

He was put out in left field, a safe place defensively as all the team really wanted him for was his major league bat.

The scoreboard at 'Little Pomer Field' was hand operated and the girl changing the score inning by inning caught his eye. So much so that on one occasion, he had a line shot roll up and hit him in the shin when he was caught looking at the most remarkable woman he had ever set eyes on.

The manager moved him to shortstop for the remaining three games of the season to avoid further distractions, and also avoid further embarrassment in front of the five hundred faithful in attendance. His short stint at the home stadium convinced him she was gone forever, as his career with this team wrapped up on the road

The day of their second meeting, a few weeks later, Clay was returning as a guest speaker for Careers Day, a pro ball player with one major league start to his credit, coming home to settle down and begin his next career. As a favor to a history teacher from his senior year, he reluctantly agreed to show up. He had mixed emotions about attending, as he was an extremely private person; however, could not say no to Mr. Sanmeya. Everyone had an influential mentor and his hailed from room 213.

Clay ambled through the familiar halls then knocked on a door he had passed through so many years ago. Kate met him at the door and introduced herself as the supply for the day. He could not believe his eyes, it was her, the girl from the scoreboard; she was genuinely the most beautiful woman in his eyes. With a breathtaking smile, she introduced Mr. Stoppa to a class of students that already knew him as 'the baseball pro that came from their school' an alumni who practically owned the trophy case. He could not concentrate; his mind was encapsulated by Kate's presence. Agreeing to participate in class on that particular day was the best thing that had ever happened in his life.

Clay was never much of a ladies' man, not because of his looks or his personality, but because he was so focused on ball and his studies. He wasn't a strong student, so in order to get his degree he really had to work for it. His parents always maintained his marks had to be above eighty percent or no ball. Even with a baseball scholarship, he abided by those rules. He never dated seriously, and every time a girl demanded too much of his attention, he simply walked away. The truth was he actually spent more time fending off women than he did dating them.

***

Clay moved to the dining room and took another sip from his coffee. He felt more relaxed about delving into the investigation than in previous years; maybe that was a good omen.

The files were organized chronologically: first the police reports, then his own personal files on each witness to the incident. Next were the cold calls, and the various individuals that Clay had dug up through years of his own investigating. Over the course of twelve summers, Clay polled neighbors, business owners and other potential witnesses; not a leaf was left unturned.

The police had stopped their investigation years ago; officially there was an outstanding file, but Clay was convinced it was buried in the archives by now.

After so many years, what more could there be.

He stretched his neck from side to side, and then opened the incident report. He always started the summer with the incident report. He was a firm believer in re-reading events as if it was the first time; maybe something was missing from the investigation. Again, hard to believe anything fresh could be uncovered after thirteen years. Clay brought his hands to his temples and rested his elbows on the aged, honey-soaked wooden tabletop. The sunshine gleaming through the bay windows gave the room a warm ambiance.

Inside the file cover was an unsealed yet unopened envelope. Before delving into the police report he was reminded of the very reason they attended the game that afternoon. It was an anniversary card from Clay to Kate that was never opened. He flipped the envelope over, and then ran his fingers along the sharp edges. He pondered opening the flap, after all it was the last summer and after this it would burn, along with the balance of the files. He tapped the corner of the card against the table almost willing the envelope to split. No such luck and he sighed and placed it, name down, in the file.

Not just yet.

The temperature on that Godforsaken day was in the low eighties, but the humidity was at one hundred percent; a cloudburst made it uncomfortable, adding about ten degrees to the already sweltering day. Clay and Kate had been married for a couple of years and were enjoying a long weekend before school started up again. They had made some tough decisions as a couple just a week prior. Clay would stay at Faulkner H.S. for another year; he had a strong group of senior ball players in their final year and thought they had a shot at the State Baseball

Championship. He would take his chances on another opening next fall at Duvall College just up the road.

After completing a dissertation in American History, thus carrying out his final step towards his master's degree, he was ready for a break. Kate was embarking upon her first full-time position at the same high school in the fall and was completing a long-term occasional assignment before taking the summer to prepare a curriculum for her very own class. She too was taking a much-needed break before a summer of classroom preparation.

They had put off a formal celebration of their wedding anniversary, so the time seemed right to make this a romantic getaway.

It was very early in the season and the Red Sox were touted as a pennant contender. Clay picked up some good tickets through a friend of a friend, and the very formidable Texas Rangers were in town. What could be better?

They were on their way to the game; it was a seven p.m. start; unusually late for a Saturday in Boston. The Stoppas parked in an expansive lot about a mile from the stadium then joined the crowds descending upon Fenway along Boylston Street. Kate wore a sleeveless blouse and khaki shorts; Clay was in his usual jeans and white t-shirt. She rested her head on Clay's shoulder in response to something whispered into her ear. He put his hand in hers and she gave him a sassy look and they both laughed.

Clay cleared his head with a shake, his reminiscing came to an abrupt stop and he brought himself to the present and reviewed the police reports more thoroughly.

They had just crossed the curb cut and vehicle access to the drive-thru for the Burger King on Boylston. At that very instant, the driver of a white van with Massachusetts's plates pulled up to the second window to pick up his order. He pulled out a .45 calibre handgun, firing a shot into the left arm of Ms. Rebecca Sterling. The driver of the vehicle jerked forward, as his foot slipped off the brake onto the accelerator and then back to the brake. A second shot was fired. The second shot missed the intended target and ricocheted off a round steel tube filled with concrete, the type used as a deterrent for vehicles getting too close to the kiosks. The bullet glanced off the steel tube and followed the plane of the ground, at height of about three and a half feet. The bullet, traveling at approximately 950 miles per hour came to rest in Kate Stoppa's spine.

It was that straightforward. It was that complex.

The assailant accelerated to Boylston Street. Pedestrians, five-deep, leaped out of the way of the charging van. The driver squealed to the left, then a sharp right onto River Way, following the straightaway to the interstate. A few hours later, a stolen vehicle was found torched under an overpass about an hour south of Boston. The description of the vehicle matched that of the assailant's vehicle. No one was arrested; no one was questioned, ever.

Best guess, there were probably one hundred potential witnesses to the crime, but through a series of circumstances, the police only interviewed fourteen. Pandemonium erupted and bodies ran for cover after the gunshots, and by the time police fought through game day traffic, most eyewitnesses were long gone.

The key eyewitnesses included Rebecca Sterling, the gunshot victim, Susie Scaloppini, her assistant at the window, Gary Lineages, the cashier at the first kiosk, Orland Banks, Loretta Depot, Allan Gregory and Carla Naomi, all seated inside in a booth against the window adjacent to the drive-thru. Joanne and Allan Carlos, Andy Biggs and Patti Riverlock were all witnesses in their parked cars along the drive-thru. Lastly, there were four sidewalk pedestrians from the thousands heading to the game that were good citizens and had the courage to give their accounts of what they saw.

All witnesses described the driver as the shooter and he had acted alone. Everyone suggested a male. He seemed to sit tall at the wheel and based on the interior dimensions of a late model GMC van, using the height of the seat in relation to the driver's window, and the top of the steering column in relation to his chest, the shooter would stand over six feet, probably closer to six feet, two inches. The assailant was white, with green or blue eyes, crooked teeth, and his face long and emaciated. He had a dirty, blondish goatee and wore a John Deer ball cap. He was wearing a lumberjack coat, which was completely out of season. All eyewitnesses were consistent on that.

Gary Lineages, the cashier at the first kiosk, said he gave the guy a second look because he was wearing long sleeves. It was ninety degrees and humid, and this guy had on a long sleeve t-shirt and a vest. The total of his order came to a little under six dollars; however, he didn't wait for his change from a ten. It looked like he had a scar on his left thumb, but Lineages could not be sure.

Fingerprints were bountiful at the busy drive-thru, but none that were lifted matched those on the crimes unit database. It was virtually impossible to discern any particulars that could be linked to the driver.

It was later discovered that the van was stolen and was traced back to a used car lot in Warminster Township, a few states over. The vehicle was reported missing Saturday morning and was definitely on the lot Friday afternoon, as one of the salesmen had considered borrowing it on the upcoming Sunday in order to move some furniture. Broken glass on both the car lot and on the driver's side floor suggested the assailant smashed the window to break in.

The driver of the van clipped a parked taxi as it wheeled sharply onto Boylston. Traces of yellow paint were found on the front passenger's corner of the van, and a match of the partial license plate was made to the vehicle set aflame hours later. Fresh boot prints leading from the van to tire tracks were discovered. Since there were no reported stolen vehicles in the Boston area, it was assumed he had a getaway car or a ride set in place. There were no credible witnesses to a vehicle leaving the scene of the torched van.

No one could give a logical explanation as to why a seemingly random act would involve a stolen van, a checkpoint, a torched vehicle and a getaway car. It seemed that a lot of thought and effort went into what looked like such an arbitrary act.

Clay flipped the page and refilled his coffee. This part of the report always bugged the hell out of him.

The first forty-eight hours of the investigation were thorough, and Clay was satisfied with the attention to detail and the manpower delegated to the case. It was during the forty-ninth hour that Kate's case came to a screeching halt.

Clay continued to read the accident file, but now his own notes on the margins became more prevalent.

The Stoppas could not catch a break. Not one, but two massive, bloody gang-related fights broke out in the downtown streets of Boston just two days after Kate's shooting. Police were forced to close down a neighborhood, encompassing a four-block area. They requested residents stay in their homes and keep away from all windows and doors; it was like Beirut in New England.

The second gang war was brewing larger than the first. Boston's finest were maxed out. Not only were they scrambling to control a very volatile situation, they had their hands full aiding in the preparation for a special guest at the residence of the Governor of Massachusetts. Arriving in less than eighteen hours was no one other than the President of the United States.

Protestors were already lining up outside the governor's home, and although the visit was postponed, the gang-related violence was enough to detour the downtown police force. A series of stand-offs coupled with the increased violence was a walking time bomb for the seedy downtown districts. The city's emergency task force was ready to explode. Some random 'whack job' firing bullets at a fast food joint, resulting in no fatalities and no concrete leads, was fading fast, becoming the lowest of priorities very quickly. Couple this with no public pressure, the priorities for the head of the crime investigation unit shifted.

The first sign of the case free falling from the front pages was the new lead investigator, Constable John Vickers, a one-year veteran of the force, transferred from traffic patrol to violent crimes that very day. Vickers was inept directing traffic, but he was blue blood three generations, so a low-profile case was a perfect fit for a union boy that could not be fired.

He was basically a one-man show, in way over his head, with no experience, and fighting a losing battle. The harder Clay pushed, the more frustrated everyone became. Vickers was going nowhere with the case; that was abundantly clear from the outset.

Vickers set out to interview Miss Susie Scaloppini, but the results were scant at best. The police report probed her immediate family with the usual questions.

'Do you know of anyone who would want to harm you? Have you ever seen this man before? Is there any reason to believe this bullet was meant for you and not Ms. Sterling?'

Susie had pre-prepared answers for her interview with Vickers. It was a random act. Later, Clay discovered, she had motive to do so. The sooner this investigation went away, the quicker an injury insurance claim for her badly sprained ankle would come to fruition. A windfall of five thousand dollars would land in her lap so the repercussions from the day's events were definitely clouded by what seemed like pennies from heaven. This onetime windfall required Scaloppini to absolve the storeowner of all responsibility for the incident and by doing so she cut off all meaningful communications with the case officer.

Clay paused and looked at his watch. Four hours had passed since Kate went off to work. He made himself a club sandwich with fresh tomato, bacon from the skillet, sliced, nippy five-year-old cheddar with mayo on rye bread, and then opened his own file on Scaloppini.

It didn't take a rocket scientist to figure that she was no angel; in fact, she came from a family with a significant rap sheet.

Clay did some digging of his own.

Susie's brother Gino, and father Vito, had a one bay garage in the back of the family home. They did simple repair work: small engine tune-ups, tire replacements, oil changes, and reupholstering side panels after filling them with bags of weed or cocaine; simple run-of-the-mill work.

Authorities turned a blind eye to the quasi chop shop, which was 'hidden' in the back yard of the predominantly Italian neighborhood, and, even though it translated into crime, the father-son team was the go between. They were the transportation specialists, not the dealers, or the handlers, and certainly not the users. They were paid a fee to do a job and that was that.

Was the bullet meant for Susie?

Among other run-ins with the law, both men were convicted of conspiracy to traffic, and neither copped a plea. Honor thy fellow criminal. They never ratted, even when offered witness protection and a much leaner sentence. Maximum security in a state prison was no picnic and both men had served their fair share. It seemed, however, that the more time spent behind bars, the more educated they became; crime school with a captive audience. As a result, Gino and Vito made stronger and stronger contacts in the drug trade industry. So much so, that they came out with clients that paid much better and ended up with a steadier and more lucrative clientele. The boys were smart, hardworking businessmen that had a good gig in the drug trafficking trade.

Still, why kill Susie? It didn't add up.

The Scaloppini family business was well respected and was used by more than one gang or family. There seemed to be no allegiance with one group over the next. They never skimmed product or money; everything was above board with their clients. Only a fool would short-change the likes of a drug cartel. The father-son team had a code of ethics that all gangs respected, which was paramount, considering the repercussions.

Although an interesting dichotomy, no leads suggested a motive to kill Susie; her location the day of the shooting was just bad luck. Clay tapped a pencil on the honey colored pine. It was settled; he would once again track down Rebecca Sterling and close the Scaloppini file once and for all.

***

With a tap on the shoulder, Kate startled Clay. He was so wrapped in the file, he didn't hear her come in.

She turned her attention to stare at the photo of Susie Scaloppini.

"So, do you think she had anything to do with it?"

Clay adjusted his posture in the chair still smiling. "No, I don't think this was revenge. The crowds that she hung around with would not wait for a busy Saturday and hire some amateur to do a professional hit. Whoever it was, if they were after Susie, they would have completed the job… quietly… without risk. And if they did screw it up, they sure as hell would come back for her. There would be no loose ends in a mob hit."

"Why is this out then?" she pointed to the file.

"I'm just systematically reviewing the files to see if I have any revelations. I have no leads to follow up on from years gone by so I just brought it back to square one. I haven't looked at this photo in a long time so…" Clay sounded dejected.

Kate pursed her lips and moved her chair slowly forwards then backwards. Clay knew something was up when she couldn't make eye contact. "We have that thing tonight, Clay."

"What *thing*." He turned to Kate. "God you are beautiful!"

"I know; so you would do this thing for your adorable wife, right?"

"I'm at a loss."

"You're being inducted into Gremlin's Sports Hall of Fame." Kate raised her arms and motioned like that of a champion.

"Oh, shit. I forgot about that. That's terrible, I love this town. Remind me of how many are in this illustrious hall."

"Including you?"

"Yes, including me."

"Sooo, after tonight?"

"Yes, after tonight."

"One."

"Great."

"C'mon, Clay they have to start somewhere, and in my opinion, they couldn't have picked a better inductee. So, let's embrace the evening. It'll be fun." She poked his ribs. "Plus, it's important for the community and me." She did that pouty thing with her lips and eyes that always made him crumble.

"What's involved tonight? You have all your cronies down at City Hall, so you must have some idea."

"Actually, I don't… they've intentionally kept this one from me. They wanted it to be a surprise for both of us."

"I don't talk about my past, Kate, you know that. I likely had the shortest stint in the majors, and I will not talk about why."

"You're not the one talking tonight. Get showered."

"Well, I have to say something."

"Clay, you and I both know that the speech you have been quietly working on is going to be awesome."

"What… what speech? What are you talking about?" *How does she know about my speech?*

***

They arrived early; Kate dressed in Donna Karan, a deep cut black dress, which showed off her beautifully toned arms and perfect skin. She accessorized with a mother of pearl necklace. Clay wore Armani, a look that suited him just fine.

After an exchange of niceties with those in charge, the Stoppas made their way to the right-hand side of the stage and were seated. Clay picked up the two agendas from his fold up chair and handed one to Kate. Clay's eyes wandered to the other chairs. They all had one agenda per chair. A nice touch he thought.

The noise level began to increase as the crowds assembled in the Duvall College auditorium, the forum often used by the town. The facility was broken into six sections to accommodate fifteen hundred at full capacity. Clay looked up from his pamphlet every so often and noticed the seats filling up. He began to shift back and forth smiling politely at those he made eye contact with. He leaned towards Kate and covered his mouth with the pamphlet.

"Was there nothing on TV tonight?"

Kate laughed, and playfully wacked Clay in the nose with her copy.

The induction ceremony began with a series of introductions, followed by a profile on upcoming events in the community and finally the attention was directed towards Clay. He was touted as a pillar of the community, a leader by example, an elite athlete and a man whose reputation preceded him: a man of class, dignity and one that countless individuals look up to. His commitment to the college and the town of Gremlin was far-reaching, and it was with honor that Clay Stoppa became the first inductee to the Sports Hall of Fame.

A ten-minute documentary followed. It was professionally edited, showing young Clay playing catch with his dad, followed by t-ball with his mates. A black and white still shot of Clay and his dad posing behind the plate stayed on the screen for at least ten seconds.

Clay sat back in his chair and put his thumb and index figure to the bridge of his nose; clearly, he was tearing up at the site of his dad. Clay lost him so early, shortly after he joined the Tigers baseball club.

There was one clip of him on skates playing some tyke hockey, and then back to baseball. As a five-year-old, he played up a year and still led the local league in hits and runs. By the age of seven he was turning double plays from short with the eerie grace of a major leaguer. Parents asked that he be banned from playing with those two years older than him as his hits were dangerous and might hurt those in the infield.

As a ten-year-old, he led the town of Gremlin to its only little league

State championship: a tournament played in Philadelphia, which included over one hundred and thirty teams.

The next year Clay was the starting shortstop for the World Little League Championships held in South Williamsport, Pennsylvania, and led the tournament in runs batted in.

His accolades continued into high school. He never played junior ball. His talent was set for the senior team in grade nine and then in his sophomore year, batting .720 with 12 HR and 73 RBIs. Faulkner won its one and only State championship. The closest they had come since: thirteen years ago, a second-place finish losing in the finals 2-1, under the tutelage of Coach Stoppa. Six 'division one' schools recruited him. He landed in Maine. They too had success with Clay, but this time it wasn't just his bat doing the damage. He was turned into a starting pitcher and had an 'earned runs against average' of .091, unheard of at any level of ball. Clay was relentless with the game and to no one's surprise he was drafted in the first round of the MLB draft by the Detroit Tigers and played his first season with their Triple 'A' affiliate, the Toledo Mud Hens. He made his major league debut that fall. They found live footage of Clay in full Tiger's garb under the lights at Tiger stadium and finally a more recent shot showing Clay leading the local college to a national championship, and seven State championships. They have not had a losing season since he joined the ranks.

The lights came up.

The audience applauded as Clay stood up, adjusted his suit, then made his way to the microphone. Usually, he was comfortable in a group setting despite his private nature. Years in front of a classroom had eased him into public speaking, but tonight was different: tonight, it was about himself, an awkward subject at the best of times. Tonight, almost fifteen hundred local citizens, most of whom he would have some association with, whether it was at the checkout counter of the local grocery store or the day-to-day interaction with colleagues from the college, sat in his audience.

Clay reached into his jacket and pulled out the cue cards from weeks ago. He flipped through them, then tucked them back in his lapel.

"Clearly there wasn't much doing tonight in Gremlin." The audience laughed.

"Thank you, this was so unexpected and so undeserved." The applause continued. "Thank you." Clay adjusted his tie and cleared his throat. "You have gone above and beyond with this tribute and I am completely overwhelmed. I see you had some visits with my wife and our photo albums over the last while."

The audience laughed as Kate shook her head no. "That shot of me and my dad was one I hadn't seen in a while." Clay paused and cleared his throat. "A long, long while."

More applause. "I have never looked at my achievements in ball as something that would mean anything outside of my own home, so this is a very self-conscious moment for me."

"The truth is, I'm not the champion here tonight, that belongs to my wife, Kate. Without Kate, I..."—he paused to collect himself and there was a roar of applause—"she is the reason we are so involved in this community." Clay joined the ovation for his wife.

"All of my life I had the easy part. I just had to play ball. I loved the game as a player, and I love coaching today, so I am truly blessed. It was my parents that made all of the sacrifices, getting me to and from practice, and the countless tournaments, weekend after weekend, then the scouts and the scholarships. They ploughed through all of the drama and politics and left the way clear for me to just play the game. And there I was just playing the game I loved."

"Kate came along and has made me the luckiest husband alive. I truly mean that. Kate taught me about life and all of its trials and tribulations. I had led such an insulated life with ball. Sometimes, I required some perspective. Kate gives me that each and every day."

"My guilty pleasure of baseball prevails thanks to all of those around me, and I continue to enjoy its accolades. I am proud to be inducted into my hometown Hall of Fame. I can think of ten or twelve others in our town's history that deserve this accreditation before me; however, that's not the way it has happened, so I accept, with all humility, this award."

Clay's voice cracked slightly. "I would like to dedicate this evening..."

He bowed his head looked over at Kate then focused his attention to the middle section, ten rows from the front, seats seven and eight. Clay knew exactly where his parents would be seated if they were alive today, close to the front, but not too close. An elderly couple made eye contact with him. His eyes watered.

"I dedicate this honor to my dad." It was all he could do to get the words out.

The crowd's applause began slowly. The volume grew as Clay waved thank you and goodnight.

The Stoppas were amongst the last to leave as they graciously accepted accolades from the long line that wished to shake his hand.

Kate drove home. Clay stared out the passenger window, and then closed his eyes reflecting on the evening but more specifically his parents.

"Did I ever tell you my first memory of baseball?" Clay continued to stare out the side window.

"No, at least I don't recall." Kate glanced over.

"I was four, maybe five years old and my dad and his buddy had me and his two kids out for a walk. The next thing I knew... we were at the ball diamond on Elsmere Street and no one else was there but us five. We started playing shadow ball."

"Shadow ball? What's that?"

"Well not to go into a lot of detail, it's the game of baseball played with an imaginary ball. You go through all the motions of real play, but without a bat and ball. The Negro league in the 30s made it famous."

"Okay?" Kate wasn't quite sure but let him continue.

"So, we are out there, my dad is yelling orders, to hit the ball, take second, steal third. We are all running around covering the bases, catching imaginary fly balls, diving, trying to prevent runs. It was a blast. Finally, it was my turn to bat and my dad was pitching, and he wound up and threw the imaginary ball and told me to swing with my imaginary bat." Clay laughed. "So I said 'What? Why does everyone else get to hit a real ball with a real bat?'"

"Oh no." Kate glanced over.

Clay turned to Kate. "I was so into the game; I was convinced there was a ball out there somewhere that night. I just couldn't understand that it was all imaginary and I started to cry."

"Clay, that is so cute! Man, I wish we had that in the presentation tonight."

5

November 2, Present day

"Morton, the rookie infielder with the Padres, was virtually thrown into the series when Marcello was injured in the division series. He now walks up to the plate facing the right-hander Boyles, at Yankee Stadium in game seven. Four short months ago he was in playing 'A' ball for the Montgomery Biscuits, down in Alabama. What a game of opportunities; you just have to seize them."

***

"Your son has jumped on all the opportunities life has presented him, wouldn't you agree?" Wolf stared straight ahead, his face hidden by his hood.

"We all have opportunities." Allan Boyles stared at the mound his face smug and proud.

"Not so." Wolf paused as he stared somewhere between the infield and the outfield. "Some opportunities are snatched away," his voice faded slightly.

"That's bullshit. Everyone has opportunities, it's whether or not you choose to seize them or not. This is America, son. Failure is just sheer laziness."

"Pull that silver spoon out of your mouth and shove it up your ass."

The verbal attack was vicious enough and seemed to come from nowhere.

"What did you just say to me?" Allan was astounded.

"You heard me loud and clear. What I should have said was 'what a crock of shit.' By the sounds of things, you have no fucking idea how the majority of America survives day-to-day. Opportunity my ass, just drive around this neighborhood. Take a good look around."

"Whatever... look...we got off on the wrong footing here." Boyles leaned forward slightly.

"Kinda like your son in this ever-precious game."

"Go fuck yourself."

"Ha, ditto," Wolf responded with equal venom.

***

"There's a called strike three and the side is retired."

"Well, Jon, it looks like Boyles has settled down here in the third."

"That's not surprising. A good pitcher will find his control; it's up to a good opposition to get to him early. Boyles is just such a professional on the mound and has, throughout his career, performed exquisitely under such clutch situations."

***

The horns were unlocked... temporarily. Wolf turned to Allan. "Your son really telegraphs his emotions out there, doesn't he? As soon as he gains confidence, he puts his head back and throws his bottom jaw forward. Then he starts twirling the rosin bag instead of bouncing it in his hand. Curious, isn't it?"

Wolf could sense the look of disbelief on Allan's face. It was simply marvelous.

Allan leaned forward. Wolf's hood continued to shade his profile. It was not unusual attire for a raw evening like this; however, it was as plain as the expression on his face that this was bugging the hell out of Allan.

"Well he's confident now, a real powerhouse." Allan caught himself. "What the hell, why am I defending my son to a..."

"A nobody? Finish your sentence. Well that's about to change, Allan Boyles."

"Excuse me?"

"You heard me." By leaning forward slightly Wolf completely trapped Allan in his chair against a rail.

"What does that mean? If you are threatening me, I will have you tossed from this establishment in a blink of an eye."

"Oh, that's just like you, Boyles. Let someone else do the heavy lifting, and make your world a safer, calmer place."

The men went silent for a moment, both watching the Padres warming up, then the pitcher kicked up some dirt like a cow in heat.

"We share a common story, Mr. Boyles."

"A story?" Allan repeated with an indignant expression. "I don't know who you are, all I know is you are trying to get under my skin, and I would prefer to watch my son pitch the biggest game of his life without you distracting me."

"Allan, this is a very special day for both of us. Why, with your son rising to the pinnacle on the mound out there, and me waiting almost as long to reach my summit here this evening." Wolf followed a ball into the stands across the stadium.

"Maybe I should call security."

"That won't be necessary, besides…" Wolf caught himself. The next pitch was sent to center field. All heads in the Legends Section turned in unison. "Did you play ball, Allan?"

"No, too busy making money. When I was eight years old, I broke Serge Cooper's nose so I could have the best corner on the street to sell newspapers. He was twelve."

"Charming." Wolf waited to be asked the same question but to no avail. "I played."

No response, no surprise. "When I was a kid, I played ball," Wolf tried again.

"Yah, most kids did." Allan was trying to catch a glimpse of his son in the dugout.

"I was a lefty."

"A lefty?" Allan turned ever so slightly. "Well shit, son, there was your opportunity we were just talking about… hell yes."

"Snatched away, remember?"

"Yah… so you alluded to." They sat in silence.

Allan wasn't really listening; he was more concerned with creating an exit strategy. However, he found himself intrigued enough to ask, "Go to a lot of major league games, son?"

"I'm *not* your son, *sir*," Wolf spat back. "In fact, my father might have been an even bigger fuck-up than you. Not that I'd know; I never met the guy." Wolf recalled the only thing his mother had ever told him about the man who'd fathered him. He'd apparently been a junkie who treated them worse than his dog. He would come home drunk and violent, and after he was too tired to either strike or rape, he would lie on the filthy couch and pass out with his bull terrier on his lap. And his mother had told him all of that when he was just six years old. It's a shame some adults don't always see it that way; some cannot get over their own self-pity and think of who they in fact might be influencing the most.

"Not my problem, boy. Now why are you bothering me?"

"Now you sound like my mother." Wolf laughed bitterly. "She took me to see my first ball game. Spent every dime she had. First time she ever bought me a present. Come to think of it, that was the last time; it was the Cardinals versus the Dodgers. I was hooked."

"Grew up in St Louis, huh? Some nasty parts there." Both men watched the back catcher and pitcher meet on the mound, covering their mouths with their gloves as if world domination was at stake. "Moved around a bit?"

"I was born on my mother's fifteenth birthday, in the back of a micro bus filled with dope smugglers and users. So, you might say I moved around… Yah."

"Yah well, still no excuse to feel sorry for yourself. Pick yourself up, dust off and get going."

"You pompous son of a bitch; and besides, the last thing I would ever do is feel sorry for myself."

Allan just trudged along; he had no regard for anyone else. "So, you're a Cardinals fan?"

"No. At the age of six I was thrown on a thirty-three-hour bus ride to Rebel, Rhode Island, so I am a Red Sox fan."

Allan's head spun like he was knocked senseless. Wolf certainly had his attention now.

6

June 2

Saturday morning, no alarm, and no plans, just the way the Stoppas liked it. On this particular Saturday, Clay was first to rise. After ambling his way downstairs, he poured a coffee that just finished its pre-programmed brewing, and then skulked around the dining room table gliding his eyes over the files. He gulped from a large plain white porcelain mug. The first taste in the morning was always the best. His intentions today were not to spend time on the case, especially with Kate off from work. He did however have a few minutes before she would stir; he allowed his eyes to travel from one police report to the next. He opened a white folder and flipped through the interviews. There was a passerby who jumped out of the way of the speeding van, the homeless man who watched the vehicle being torched under the freeway, and interviews with the owner of the car dealership where the van was allegedly stolen.

Clay shook his head in disgust. He was never convinced that the van was stolen. Clay stared out the bay windows at a dull overcast morning; he was waving the thin file like a fan.

Over time, Clay gained access to ownership papers of those who purchased vans from Don's Car Lot, the location where the vehicle was allegedly stolen. Clay had sales transactions dating back as far as two years prior to the incident; however, it seemed to be a dead end. Clay didn't take much of a liking to Don 'the businessman'. He was one of those types who immediately went on the defensive; probably a habit formed from years of shady deals. Don was always one step from spending time behind bars, with the IRS always breathing down his back.

Clay suspected he did a lot of under the table deals, one of which was with the assailant, in which case no records would be found. Don wasn't about to go out of his way to help Clay.

Clay closed the file and flipped it back in the box.

He then reached over a box of files and put his hand on the folder that had clearly drawn the most attention over the last thirteen years. The corners of the thick white file were soft, wrinkled, and torn; this file was thumbed through hundreds of times. Clay's attention turned to the front hallway.

Kate wheeled into the dining room; on her lap was the weekend edition of the Philadelphia Inquirer. She was wearing her athletic gear, and preparing for her twenty-mile ride, her longest of the week, and in this case the month. It was imperative that she remains in as good of shape as possible. There was no vanity involved; for Kate it was life and death. Kate's circulation was not the best, and as she aged, it became more of an issue. Her doctors were adamant that she not deviate from her strict diet and exercise regime, but that was easier said than done. Kate lived a very busy life; outside of a full-time teaching position, and a comprehensive volunteering regime, she was engrossed with other groups, not least of which was her weighty involvement with handicap accessibility in the town. That morning, Kate wore a black skin-tight technical top, pushing her sweat to her second layer of clothing—in this case a light grey fleece tracksuit with reflective markings. Her headgear consisted of a technical skullcap, the best bike helmet money could buy, equipped with a rear-view mirror, and lightweight amber lenses for eye wear. She adjusted a pair of baseball batting gloves over her fingers, although she preferred weightlifting gloves as they had more palm padding and cut-out fingers. The back of her racing chair had reflective markings, as did the short axles.

Clay would join her for the first eight miles, the first of three identical circuits. There was a time when eight miles was a light workout for him but not so any more.

Kate set the paper on the corner of the dining room table and completed her strength exercises. Part of Kate's routine was to sit on the floor and lift herself off the ground allowing her abdominals to quiver under the pressure. She had the core strength of a prima ballerina and the six-pack to prove it.

They moved into the kitchen, a large rustic room with exposed brick on the inner wall, state of the art appliances, and all counters fully integrated for wheel chair accessibility. The whole house had been transformed because of Kate's challenges. It would have been a lot easier and cheaper to sell the century abode on Union and build from scratch, but that would have been a form of defeat, something that never was an option for the Stoppas. The retrofit happened over a two-year period. It was paramount not to lose the integrity and charm of the historic residence. This too added to the cost. It was a labour of love; in other words, they would never get back out the money they poured into the massive makeover. In fact, they spent approximately three hundred, thousand dollars on the overhaul; a number very close to the personal insurance settlement Kate received from the ordeal.

Kate wheeled back and forth in the kitchen, mentally preparing for her ride. She had always been an athlete. Before her accident, athletics was all about the competition and winning. Today it was a lifestyle necessary for good health.

Years ago, Kate had carefully mapped out a course for her outdoor training. She required only slight undulations, a clear and smooth route with little traffic, and a route that was adaptable to the distances she wished to travel. The end result was an eight-mile circuit that could be shortened if necessary.

"Take your leg off the kitchen counter." Kate was half angry. "Are you two?" Clay pulled his muscular appendage from the ledge the second Kate bellowed.

He knew better. Never do stretching exercises on the kitchen counter… when Kate was home. Clay smiled to himself. "Ready?"

"Try to keep up." And with that Kate wheeled within inches of Clay's toes as she slipped out the door in front of him. The Stoppa residence flows onto Union, a street straight out of a Trisha Romance painting, exquisite spring colors blended from the early blooms. Trees line the street, a soft canopy of bright green vegetation unfurling on the limbs, the branches set like fingers crossed over the top of the sidewalk. Kate paid no attention to her street's beauty; rather she bolted way ahead of Clay, forcing him to almost gallop out of the gate.

"Hey!" Clay panted as he caught up.

Kate's lips curled into a sadistic smile. She couldn't keep up the pace, but it was sure satisfying to hear her husband huffing and puffing.

"So, when did this weekend ritual become a race." Clay gasped for air.

"Oh, am I going too fast... sorry... hadn't noticed." Kate glided and settled into a comfortable pace, one that Clay could manage.

They turned onto Power Court, a more modern subdivision built on the edge of the historical neighborhood. Houses shifted from turn of the century to fifty-year-old abodes, the lots downsized slightly but the trees fully mature.

Clay glanced over at a yellow brick bungalow with a low-grade roof and a double garage. "You seen Tubs lately?" He was referring to his closest friend, Michael Campbell, who also happened to be the chief of police.

"Yah, here and there, why?"

"Nothing really, I haven't seen him around much. Guess we're both busy."

"He should be out here with us."

"No doubt." They were referring to his rather rotund frame, thus the nickname.

Two miles into the run, they completed a triple rise and headed into the country. Clay learned many years ago not to push Kate up the hills. She would grunt and curse under her breath, but the second Clay motioned to grab the handles of her racing chair she would snap poison in his direction.

Clay listened to Kate's final grunts as she eased over the final crest and allowed her chest and arms to relax for a few seconds. Clay watched her determination. She was strong, the strongest person he had ever met. And beautiful, her perfect complexion and sharp angles of her cheeks and jawbones set her apart. Kate looked up at Clay and managed a smile.

"Tough as nails, Kate. I do not have your drive."

"Yah, you're just looking to get laid tonight!" She raised her eyebrows and Clay missed a step and laughed.

They ran in silence for a stretch until they reached Alora, the picturesque community split by deep gorges from merging rivers. Gremlin takes second place in the tourism department to the charming village filled with B&B's and splendid local restaurants.

They turned into the liquor store parking lot, the half way point of the first circuit then began the easier trek home as a result of the predominantly downward slope.

Children screamed on the swings in a nearby park. Clay glanced over and then down at Kate. She was watching the mom and dad push their daughter as they all laughed in unison.

Clay was struck with a familiar anger and sadness wrapped into one. Kate would have made an awesome mom. He flipped his attention to her chair and then the incident and the unsolved case. His thoughts turned to Rebecca Sterling and the direction his last summer of investigation should follow.

"Do we have any plans tonight?" Kate startled Clay.

"None that I can think of. Why?"

"Dinner and a show?"

"Sounds good."

***

It was shortly after lunch by the time they finished the circuit. They made some leafy sandwiches on pita bread and a side dish of fresh fruit, then sat quietly listening to the thunderstorm that passed overhead. Soon after lunch, Kate left for her committee meeting. Clay had full intention of completing some yard work, but the weather suggested otherwise. He drifted into the dining room. Clay always drifted into the dining room; it was like a magnet throughout the summer. His hands reached for the well-worn file again, a file with texture of silk not that of cardboard thanks to years of probing. Clay flipped to his own investigation, his own notes. The file took him back twelve years, one year after the incident.

Clay had formed a trustworthy relationship with the Burger King manager, James Albrecht. James was young, only twenty-one, but Clay related to kids his age and made him understand the importance of his cooperation. After all, how many store managers were vital in an attempted murder case? Albrecht gave Clay the information he asked for, and over time, allowed him to seek out his own paperwork in the office files.

This particular Burger King on Boylston was open twenty-four hours, so Clay would often arrive late and set up in a booth at the far corner of the seating area away from any distractions and help himself to the store files. Clay had gathered information on all forty-seven full- and part-time personnel that were employees on the day the incident took place. He even went to the extent of looking at previous employees up to three months prior to that fateful date in the spring, thus adding six names to his list.

He leafed through the employee resumes and followed the files of both Suzie Scaloppini, and the gunshot victim, Rebecca Sterling.

Clay pressed on. He flipped through the file for the hundredth time and that was no exaggeration. Rebecca certainly had the best view of the architect; she could have been construed as an innocent victim, plain bad luck, or the motive for the shooter.

Clay thumbed further into the file. His investigation into Rebecca's past was nothing short of ordinary; in fact, it was scant at best. From what he could discern, Rebecca grew up in her grandmother's home, at least that was the only address he had for her. School records suggested she started at St. Agatha's on Maple Street not far from her grandmother's in grade eleven, but no records prior to that. The school fire and temporary displacement of both students and faculty during that time might account for the lack of information.

The afternoon flew by for Clay. He was completely wrapped in Rebecca's file. He didn't hear the mechanical lift at the rear entrance to the mudroom. When Kate wheeled into the dining room and simply asked how his day was, he nearly leapt into the neighboring chair. Kate couldn't help but laugh, even though she knew he would be even angrier. She covered her mouth trying to contain herself and Clay settled himself and shook his head at his overreaction.

They shared some small talk about Kate's meeting as she rolled forward ever so slightly her eyes searching for the morning paper. She flipped through to the Arts and Entertainment section and passed the sports to her husband.

Clay perused the headlines. Texas beat the Philly's in a crossover series game, a rare tilt between a National League and American League teams. Clay set down the sports and scooped up the local news.

His eyes locked onto the headline.
DRIVE-BY SHOOTINGS SHOW NO MOTIVE
"Kate!"

Clay shared the article with Kate. They sat across from one another in some form of a 'mind meld', neither talking but communicating all the same. There was a lot to discuss.

The Philadelphia Inquirer described a drive-by shooting a few nights ago at the Chick-fil-A drive-thru on Market Street as an isolated incident, probably gang-related. A nondescript white van pulled up to the kiosk, two shots were fired, and the van calmly rolled away. There was no robbery, and one person suffered a graze to the arm.

The Stoppas were not convinced this incident should be under carded as gang violence, an excuse to bury the file and move on.

Kate's case was never given a second thought after the debacle in front of the Governor's House. The police were humiliated by the gang violence temporarily shutting down neighborhoods and getting top coverage on national news. Needless to say, Boston needed to get back on track with some positive results: some major drugs busts and locking up a few headline criminals.

Kate's case fell so far down the list it was deemed irrelevant. It was tragic, yes, but no one was killed and there was little likelihood of an arrest. As a result, the rookie cop in charge of the drive-thru shooting was loaded up with other cold cases and sent on his way to just plod along.

One of the many oversights in the investigation included the geographic territory that was analyzed. The greater municipality of Boston was scrutinized, but nowhere outside of this jurisdiction was covered. Someone convinced the officer in charge that this type of incident would have a very local domain. Clay too was sucked into that premise and the years directly after the crime, he spent a large portion of his own investigation within walking distance of the Burger King.

The Stoppas reviewed the news flash, and then turned to the Internet, picking up any other information. To the naked eye the articles were very superficial; but to the pair of them some of the bare bone facts were spine chilling. The assailant was male, tall, thin and alone. He shot the drive-thru attendant in the left arm and pulled out of the parking lot slowly then sped recklessly west on the Delaware Expressway. A torched vehicle was found under a series of overpasses on Interstate 95. No money was reported missing.

"I'll call Tubs in the morning." Clay looked at his watch, it wasn't late, but it was the weekend.

"I'm going to call Julie, weekend or no weekend."

After six hours of imaginary sleep, they both showered in order to give themselves a false sense of freshness.

Clay picked up his phone on Sunday at eight in the morning. He could not wait any longer.

"Tubs?"

"Yeah." He was still in his REM cycle.

"Can we meet?"

"Sure."

"Eight fifteen, okay?"

"See you then." Tubs had no idea that he agreed to meet in less than fifteen minutes.

Mike Campbell, known as Tubs to Clay, held the position as chief of police for the town of Gremlin for five years now. Neither spoke of a rendezvous point, however Tubs arrived at the corner of Power and Main, the Black and White restaurant at eight twenty-five, only minutes before Clay. Their meeting place had never changed.

Some friendships bond like cement. Clay and Tubs found each other on the play yard in grade four and although their interests were quite distinctive, they were always there for one another and through the years became inseparable. Only girlfriends and short stints away for an education disconnected the men over the thirty plus years since their first meeting. They knew one another instinctively and just eye contact was enough to share a thousand thoughts and a thousand words. Friendship like that takes time; it had to distil like an old age scotch and it is earned through mutual respect.

Tubs was a giant of a man, standing six feet five inches tall, weighing over three hundred pounds, and was issued size fifteen shoes by the State Department of Police Services. Clay gave him his nickname, however only Clay and Kate used the moniker. No one else dared; to his staff at the station it was sir or if you had earned his respect, Michael, but Lord have mercy if you thought you knew the man well enough to call him Tubs.

There was only one place for the two men to meet for coffee, and that was the Black and White restaurant. Now known as the B&W, an establishment their own fathers took them to in the early eighties. The restaurant was owned and operated by a local Chinese family who emigrated two generations ago. The menu included burgers, fries, Chinese, and an all-day breakfast. Clay held the restaurant in the highest esteem, not because it was best described as a restaurant for the locals, not for its vintage sixties' décor, and not for its passable food, nor its adequate cleanliness. Very little had changed at the Black and White since opening in 1963, except maybe a few additional cracks in the red vinyl seating. Clay was loyal to the restaurants' proprietor Mr. Chuck Lau, and would forever be so, for one reason only.

When Clay and Kate arrived home from Boston after their terrible accident, and before pulling into their own driveway, they traveled through downtown just to reacquaint themselves with familiar surroundings. It was late at night and the streets were deserted. They drove down Main Street and came to a complete stop in front of the restaurant. They stared out the driver's side window in disbelief. Chuck had constructed a temporary wheelchair accessible entrance, the first of its kind in downtown Gremlin. Such an act of thoughtfulness would never be forgotten.

Clay walked in and nodded at the locals sitting at the row of bar stools. He passed six or seven men all dressed in lumberjack coats, all hunched over morning coffee, and all seated in every other stool. It was a scene from a Norman Rockwell painting. Tubs sat in a booth for four and dwarfed it.

"I took the liberty of ordering, boss."

Clay nodded and stirred single milk into his chubby white porcelain mug.

"Jesus, Tubs, when was the last time you slept?" Clay stared at his friend and couldn't miss the black lines under his eyes. "You look like you've been interrogated for forty-eight hours in a Turkish prison. What's going on?"

"Just a flu, it will pass." Tubs wanted to blow it off; he was lying, and he knew that his friend could read him like a book.

Clay let it pass for now as he had an agenda. "Well you shouldn't have said yes so quickly, this could wait."

"I am here now, so what's up?"

"Listen, Tubs, thanks for meeting me. I need to get into your police files. Kate and I need to do some work. We found something last night and we both have a feeling."

Before Tubs could say anything, Chuck brought out breakfast: eggs over-easy, peameal bacon, sausage, pancakes, toast, orange juice and more coffee. Everyone smiled and bowed slightly.

"It must be summer holidays, Clay. You know I work all summer and you have the luxury of months off, and you piss them away." He paused. "You're pissing your summer away again aren't you, boss. You and Kate should be out there enjoying it, while us thugs work our asses off."

"You're right."

"I know I'm right, but it means squat coming from me."

"Maybe so."

"How long is this going to go on, Clay? For fuck's sake give it up and move on. She is nuts to put up with your stubborn ass."

"We are."

"We are what?"

"Moving on."

"It sure as hell doesn't seem that way to me; you want to get me fired?"

"I have made a promise to Kate."

"What promise?"

"I said this is it, the last summer, and in the end, we burn the files."

"I don't believe you."

"I made a promise, Tubs." Clay looked him in the eyes.

"A promise to who?"

"Kate."

"Holy shit. Well it's about time. Did she take one of your bats to that thick skull of yours?"

"Yeah, I know. So that's why I asked you here this morning."

"What's up?" Tubs began to roll through his food.

"Time is of the essence here. I am trying to figure out which direction to go."

"So why did you pull my ass down here?"

"A drive-by, at a drive-thru in Philly."

"So… there have been thousands since yours, in many styles, with many motives. So what are you thinking here, Clay?"

"I don't know, Tubs," he reflected. "Okay, here is what I know. This incident had some similarities to our case and Kate has a feeling on this one. We both agree that something could be right under our noses."

"Thirteen years later?"

Clay ignored his friend. "We want an opportunity to analyze case by case and we need access to police files and maybe more."

"How far back are you going?"

"We will start at our incident and move forward, and just take it from there."

"What a fucking stretch. There are thousands of cases, Clay. It isn't like thirteen years ago; we now have links through the Internet that give us information from any state in the country."

"All the better."

"It's a needle in a fucking haystack, Clay."

Clay was getting frustrated. "Well that's a good thing isn't it? More information?" Clay pounded both fists on the table, the coffee spilled and heads turned. Tubs didn't flinch. Clay kept his voice low. "Maybe you have a better idea and I'm all ears, but right here, right now, my reality is that the love of my life is strapped in a fucking wheelchair for the rest of her fucking life."

"Settle down. I get it, I know."

"Well I'll be damned if in the bottom of the ninth I'll give up now." He sat back.

"Sorry about the coffee." Clay turned to Chuck who cleaned up the mess and poured fresh cups.

"Who needs the access?" Tubs moved on.

"Kate's girlfriend is flying here in the next couple of days, so she needs all the info she can gather."

"Is it Julie?"

"Yes, its Julie."

"Nice." Tubs smiled in a distant manner then refocused. "I thought she was some kind of anthropologist?"

"She is."

"Shit, Clay, what do mummies and shit like that have to do with this?"

"Well that's kinda what I said about it, but Kate corrected me."

"Oh, I get it, they deal with mummies and archaeological digs, and drive-thru shootings."

Clay smiled. "Among other things they study human nature, social and behavioral sciences, and shit like that."

"I get it. She's the one who put this cockamamie idea about cross-referencing the cases into your head. So, what's her plan? Decipher all the cases and give you a lead?" Tubs laughed humorlessly. "Well shit, this should be easy after 9/11 and the increased homeland security."

"I know, I know, I was looking for a final lead and this may be my last hurrah."

Tubs could see the desperation in his oldest friend's eyes. "So you really want to try this, huh?"

"I do. We'll give it the old college try." Clay was asking again without asking.

"I really shouldn't do this, but when did you and I ever follow the rules. Have Kate call me and I'll get her set up." He leaned forward. "No one, and I mean no one, can know this, or we are all in jail."

"I know, I know." Clay paused. "Oh, one more thing. Look into this name for me and see if anything pops up in the last couple of years." He handed him the name of Rebecca Sterling.

They sat in silence for a while. Clay then asked about Tubs' son Harper and all tension was lost.

7

June 3

If Kate were any closer to her laptop, she would be wiping her nose print from the screen. It was all Clay could do to pull her attention away long enough to give her a kiss goodbye. Her farewell was half-hearted as she was buried in the state police database, trying to acquaint herself with its nuances. Where before she had dreaded Clay's annual ritual, now she was finding herself actually getting into it—both because it was the final year and also because, for the first time in years, it felt like they had something to go on. She was starting to get excited by the possibilities; this final summer would go out with a bang, not a whimper.

Clay was off to Boston. Rebecca Sterling had agreed to meet with him one more time. His intention was closure. Since she was involved in the shooting too, he felt he just needed to see her one last time before he could really close the book on this case. Close a lead once and for all then allow himself one desperate leap with the Philadelphia incident last week.

One final stop before hitting the interstate, Clay rolled into the Gremlin Police Department and parked in Tubs' private spot. Clay laughed to himself as he got out of the vehicle. Tubs had run the name Rebecca Sterling and had left an envelope. Tubs had nothing. Not even a job. No house. No car. No marriage record. No kids. But no death certificate either, so she must be living some sort of life, as clandestine as it seemed.

He hopped in his old Jetta, got comfortable, and changed the gears smoothly as he had done a thousand times before, the old engine purring, as a diesel should. Clay had made so many trips up the turnpike, the five plus hours broken by the familiar interchanges. The Band and Bob Dylan would carry him on this journey.

Clay checked into a privately-owned hotel on the outskirts of the city. The husband and wife who owned the establishment knew Clay by name and were very familiar with the circumstances of his visit. Over the years they gave him special rates, and threw in the odd free breakfast or dinner. They had him for over for dinner on occasion just so he could have a home cooked meal.

Clay sent Rebecca a text upon his arrival. Shortly afterwards, his phone rang.

"When did you get in?"

"Just a few hours ago."

"Where are you staying?"

"Newton, always in the outskirts, cheaper, you know." Clay felt uneasy. He surprised himself with his nervousness. "So it will take me a good half hour to get downtown." He paused again.

"Half hour is fine. Don't sweat it."

"You're still downtown, right?"

She paused and looked out her apartment window at the heavy pedestrian traffic. "Oh, and yeah still in this shit hole."

They agreed to meet at a neutral location and settled on a Starbucks across from Copley Square on Boylston Street, just blocks from where both of their lives had changed forever.

"I'll see you shortly then?" Clay wanted to get started.

"Fine." She closed her phone.

Forty minutes later, Clay sat with two coffees, one black and strong, almost tar like, the other his own: one milk, half a sugar. Rebecca strolled through the door wearing an open overcoat, a plain burgundy blouse, jeans and Birkenstocks. Clay recognized her immediately; she still wore a sad expression on her pretty, angular face. Naturally, she looked older, now in her early thirties, her face carried lines, too many years of neglect, worry, and sorrow.

"Still take your coffee black?" Clay pushed the cup in her direction his smile genuine.

"Why did I agree to this?" Rebecca opened her purse and popped the top of a prescription bottle like she had done a thousand times before. She kept it out of sight but was not trying to be too discreet. She put a pill in her mouth then sipped on the coffee.

Rebecca raised her cup in acknowledgment and savored the first mouthful. She seemed agitated. Clay wasn't sure if that was a natural state or one he brought on.

"I'm a recovering alcoholic, clean five years, but I still have my vices."

"Congratulations." Clay signaled a toast.

Rebecca rolled her eyes.

"No, I mean it. I have such admiration for those who fight addiction. I don't know if I would have your tenacity."

"Tenacity, that's your middle name."

"Thank you for agreeing to meet with me again."

"I'm here for your wife. Listen, Mr. Stoppa…"

"It's Clay, it has always been Clay."

"Clay," she continued, "If I had some revelation, I would've let you know. I would have reached you somehow; however, I will answer your questions if it helps. Not exactly my favorite subject."

Clay's heart sank. "I know."

She glanced at Clay then continued, "You will be able to close this file… my file after this meeting, I can assure you." Rebecca was anxious to get this meeting over with. "Right, can we walk across the street?" She pointed at the park across from the Boston Public Library.

"Of course." Clay glanced at the sky through the floor to ceiling window.

They crossed over to a small, beautifully tree-lined green space filled with planters, benches, old cobble paths and a statue marking one of Boston's many war heroes.

Rebecca could not wait to have a smoke; she lit up the second they stepped outside, her pale fragile hands trembled as she scavenged through her purse for a lighter. Clay noticed her anxiety and took the lighter, blocked the fluctuating breeze, and held the flame steady as she consumed one of the too many drags that would pass by her lips on any given day.

Clay followed a half a step behind as they crossed onto the cobblestone, her footing sure and steady. Clay on the other hand had to watch his step, as he adjusted his bomber jacket turning ever so slightly away from the light drizzle.

"It's not getting any dryer out here." Clay glanced behind him at the warm, well lit, coffee shop, equipped with a fireplace, and comfy chairs.

"I know… it's beautiful isn't it?" Rebecca angled her face towards the breeze then exhaled. "I love how the fog moves in and out."

Clay glanced over at Rebecca's thin-shelled overcoat. Threads were noticeably hanging from the bottom.

She began to veer to her left ever so slightly then gently placed herself in one of the many empty benches that bordered the wide cobblestone walkway. A willow tree drooped one of its formidable limbs over top of the bench she had chosen. It provided temporary shelter from the increasing precipitation.

She calmly slid her hands under her legs and neatly tucked her overcoat around her lower torso. Rebecca crossed her legs away from Clay, and took a long drag from her cigarette. She shook her head and sighed.

Clay tentatively sat at the end of the bench as far away as possible, leaned forward and rested his elbows on his knees.

Rebecca broke the silence. "A simple phone call, Clay, that's all that was necessary. I'm telling you now what I told you twelve years ago and again five years ago, I don't know who shot me and I never will. I have the composite; it still rings no bells whatsoever."

"I suspected nothing had changed."

"Then why the trip? Why the bother?" Rebecca shook her head again "Fuck me," she muttered.

"Maybe I just need to hear it from you in person that it's over. Maybe it's just that simple," Clay raised his voice ever so slightly then he finally made eye contact. "It would be easy for you to brush me off by email or text or over the phone, but face to face, not so much." He paused. "And maybe I care, Rebecca, maybe I do… I might just give a fuck about you." He sounded angry but was not.

"Jesus Christ, Clay!" Rebecca's voice softened ever so slightly and she shifted slightly towards him. "There would be very few things in my life… my world… that would please me more than to help you find this person… THAT you can take to the bank. Thirteen years," Rebecca's voice trailed off slightly. She brought her coffee up to her lips with both hands, now just a trace of a tremble. "I could not believe the phone call."

"My call?"

"No, the Pope's… yes your call. After all these years you still search. You are many things, Clay Stoppa, many things."

"Crazy, is what my wife says."

"I'll bet she does."

"Oh yes." Clay chuckled out loud.

"What is it you are doing here? I have to say this, as a friend or whatever the hell we are, if I'm all you got, then it's over. Your investigation is done… I know it and you know it. Don't make me feel like a failure again."

"No, God no! That's not the case at all. I know if you could help me you would. So you are helping me, not failing. Failing could not be further from the truth. It's closure time. My wife gave me an ultimatum with a date attached and I will honor it." They sat in silence for a few moments. Clay continued, "I was just being totally selfish, making you say it to my face. Somehow, I believe we were in this together. You were shot too. I have never forgotten that."

"But I can walk, so it's not as bad right." Rebecca regretted the words the second they came out but before she could continue, Clay interjected.

"That's not it at all."

"I know, I'm an idiot, I am so sorry… Fuck… I know, it was your baby, forgive me for that. I am not that crass… really."

"I know."

"Okay… shit…" she whispered, still beating herself up for her aloof remarks.

"You said failed again?" Clay picked up on her comment.

"It was a long time ago."

"None of my business."

"Correct." And she left it at that.

Rebecca turned and looked Clay in the eyes for only the second time. She looked colorless and fragile, too thin, but with striking features that lay dormant in a sad expression. "No one has ever cared about me."

Where did that come from Clay wondered. "If you knew me and my wife, you would know that I say the God's truth." Clay paused before venturing out on a limb. "What happened to you in your past, before the shooting; Kate and I care, very deeply."

"I am not telling a stranger anything."

"I completely respect that, but we are hardly strangers. A catastrophe brought us together so long ago and, well, we have been in each other's lives ever since. If you haven't opened up to anyone for all of these years then that in itself is very sad. I know some of it, Rebecca, I want to know more and offer my help; no different than you wanted to help Kate and I."

Rebecca pursed her lips and stared down at her feet. A minute passed in silence. "I grew up on Boston Ave., a working-class neighborhood, you know, row housing, a series of front steps, the corners filled in with bars and liquor stores. You don't want to hear this."

Clay turned towards Rebecca moving ever so slightly closer nodding at the same time, "I do. I should have paid attention years ago."

Rebecca sat in silence staring into space, repositioning herself on the bench. The fog was thick now; even the benches across the pathway had a murky silhouette. She covered her face with the palms of her hands then gently slid them down to her neck.

"How long did you live on Boston Ave.?"

"It was my grandma's house. My parents never had a place of their own. That I can remember."

"So, it had that grandma feel to it? Kind and warm and secure?"

"Hardly, our house kinda stood out… it was the one you would walk by staring at the sidewalk. It had an overgrown postage stamp front lawn, a collapsed fence, peeling clapboard, and I don't just mean the paint."

"Was she nice?"

"Grandma was kind, but my parents bullied her."

"Bullied is harsh."

"No, not really."

"I was in a car accident and…" Rebecca winced ever so slightly then she covered her mouth.

"It's okay, Rebecca." Clay recognized a complete round about in expression. "Was someone hurt, were you hurt?"

"It was a long time ago and doesn't really matter any more."

"That's where you are wrong. It means a great deal, you harboring all of this for all of these years." Clay shifted on the bench, the mist was more of a rain now, and he was soaked and uncomfortable.

Rebecca turned away from Clay; she was reaching into her purse for a tissue. Clay scrambled searching his pockets, but quickly realized he had nothing to offer. He felt like a complete ass.

"Eventually things went back to normal, and I moved on."

Clay shook his head. "Jesus, I won't pry, Rebecca, but I do want to help and will listen any time."

"And then three years later, I was…"

"And you were shot."

"And I was shot. Yeah"

"And then you started your road to recovery?"

"Well… I guess, yah. I rented a room, tried to stay clean."

"So who helped you out?"

"I had housemates, but no one I was close to."

"It has all fallen through the cracks for you… Fuck." Clay muttered under his breath.

"That is it, Clay. I am spent." Rebecca almost whispered, her tone resembling that of defeated person. She leaned forward resting her elbows on her knees.

"I completely understand. Let me call you a cab or something. Can I see you later today, maybe go out for dinner or a walk or something?" Clay was at a complete loss for what to do.

"I can walk, it's just over there." She pointed at three older ten-story brick buildings about two blocks away. Clay walked her home.

Rebecca managed to soften her facial expression slightly; she also managed two cigarettes in the short jaunt.

"Okay, well I can't just leave you like this. Let's grab a coffee later."

"That's sweet of you, but you aren't going to heal me over a coffee. Don't feel guilty, Clay. You did nothing wrong here. It was nice of you to listen."

After almost begging her, Rebecca finally agreed to meet at the same coffee shop at eight p.m., in six hours.

With some time to kill he drove back to his hotel, went for a run, then showered and collapsed onto his bed. He saw he had a voicemail and checked it. It was a reporter looking to interview him about his short-lived professional ball career. *Not again.* Clay deleted the message without copying down the call back number. After quickly glancing at his watch, he dialed Kate's cell phone. "Are you home?"

"Yes, I'm just retesting the link to the police network. Tubs was just here helping me get it set up. If all goes well, we are in business."

"How did Tubs look?"

She reflected for a moment. "I didn't really notice anything, why?"

"I don't know. I've just been a little worried about him lately."

"Well, he seemed fine to me. A little tired maybe, but fine."

Clay decided to take Kate's word for it. "So, is it working?" he asked, referring to the police link.

"Yes, I think we are a go. I have lots to do here. Julie has shifted her schedule and will be here on Thursday. How was your day?"

"Rough, a rough day. As you know, I just needed to hear it from her, so move on now, I guess. I really like Rebecca, Kate. She is a good person. I've never had much to do with her, but I can just sense it, intuitively."

"You have always been good at that."

"Look who I married."

"Case in point." Clay could hear her smile in the inflection. "I am meeting her for coffee before I travel home, so I will be late."

Most would not embark on a five-hour journey at ten p.m., however the Stoppas already had too many nights apart over the years with his baseball schedule then the 'quest for the holy grail'. Dinnertime was the worst for Clay. Darkness was settling in. He was eating alone and knew Kate would be doing the same. This was the situation when he doubted himself the most, the quest for truth and justice at what cost.

So many reasons to stop his search, but when he thought about Kate chained to that chair for the rest of her life and the loss of their unborn child and their inability to reproduce, his rage would scream in desperation. Clay was not the type to forgive, in fact he believed in retribution. He believed in capital punishment and believed the person who did this to his wife deserved his own wheelchair or worse. Clay's moral values of right and wrong were cast in stone.

"Okay, I won't wait up. Drive careful, I love you."

"Love you too."

***

Only an hour had passed. After another run and another shower, his nerves were no better. Clay hopped in his VW and made his way back to Fenway and the Burger King on Boylston Street. He parked at the back of the lot and allowed his stomach to settle, then strolled the perimeter of the property looking at the sight lines. He had done this a hundred times; he scanned the parking lot on Brookline, the bridge over the Muddy River, the collection of three-story walk-ups in the West Fens district, and the high rises surrounding the restaurant. Immediately to the east, a giant ten-story complex cast its shadow on the Burger King Parking lot. Although no balconies faced directly towards the restaurant, those that faced Boylston Street did have a site line of the street and a sightline to the assailant's van.

Clay knocked on every door in the course of his investigation, followed up on potential leads, and even tracked down the whereabouts of those visiting occupants of the various units, but to no avail. No one saw the incident, and if they did, they did not want to get involved. To this day, Clay can recall the eight apartment doors that he knocked on, all housing potential witnesses, all of the dashed hopes time and time again.

He sauntered the streets one last time; he had resigned himself to the fact that this chapter was undeniably closed years ago and this would be his last trip here and maybe his last to Boston.

Clay never felt so close to the end of this investigation and each passing day led him towards the deadline. Never did he have a time limit, and maybe that contributed to his lack of success. Indubitably, this was no longer a problem; Kate had his word. Clay was closing in on the end of a thirteen-year investigation, with no positive results.

Every time I leave this place, I hope it's the last. Be careful what you wish for.

He made his way downtown to the Starbucks; it was close to seven thirty. He didn't expect Rebecca to be early; in fact, a half an hour late was probably more in line. He sipped on a coffee, partially staring out the window at the pedestrians and occasionally glancing at the Boston Globe. Time passed slowly. Eight p.m. came and went, and so did eight thirty and nine o'clock. He tried calling her cell phone. No answer. He tried again. Still nothing.

Clay was getting increasingly annoyed with a hint of worry... something about the way she had seemed when they had parted had not sat well with him. He felt the overwhelming need to check on her. Clay lifted himself from the barstool, stepped outside, and stared at the apartments across from the park. He adjusted his collar and made his way three blocks north.

The initials R.S. were barely discernible on the dirt-encrusted apartment intercom system. Rebecca was registered to apartment 801. Clay startled himself when he pressed the black button; the buzzer resonated down the street. He waited and buzzed again, this time he was prepared for the blare. After a third attempt, he made his way back to the coffee shop, but there was still no sign of Rebecca, so back to the apartment he went. It wasn't long before Clay gave up on the buzzer and simply followed a tenant through the main street entrance.

The hallway was dimly lit, and it smelled like a cat's litter box that had not been attended to... ever. The floors were greasy with a trail of sludge constantly tracked into the building, particulates crunching under his feet as he made his way to the elevators.

He pressed the button with his knuckle, somehow that seemed more hygienic. The door opened with a thud and the elevator rocked up and down finally settling four inches above floor level. Clay wisely chose the stairs. Judging by the debris on the floor, the stairwell was used as a dumping ground for drug users, as there were empty vials littered everywhere. He made his way up the stairs, careful not to step on something that could be venomous and puncture the sole of his shoe. The odors changed from cat piss to dog shit and somewhere in between; the fumes wafting from the eighth floor were more in keeping with a den of wolves.

Slum land-lording at its finest.

Clay's first knock was tentative. But soon afterward he was pounding on the door anxious for an answer and hopefully to get out of the disgusting hallway. The tenant across the hall opened her door slightly, causing the door chain to become taut. An elderly woman looked at Clay, and opened her door wide. There she stood, a toothless woman in her late fifties, wearing only a large pair of bloated lacy underwear and a monster-cupped bra hanging over her multiple rolls.

It is incredible how much detail your mind can absorb in less than one second.

Clay turned away quickly, but the damage was done; he had a mental image leaving nothing to the imagination.

"You won't get an answer from that one. She was heaving her guts out this afternoon, and I'd be surprised if her intestines didn't come up too. You can come on in and I'll phone her."

"That won't be necessary, so you go back in and mind your own business."

"Suit yourself, copper."

Clay turned the handle to the apartment, the latch released and only a small chain held the door shut suggesting of course she was in there. Clay called out but got no response.

Clay had a bad feeling; was she sick or hurt? His options were the lady next door, 911—which he expected to be prioritized extremely low in this district—or push a little harder hoping to release the latch. The latter. He then put his shoulder into it, releasing the bracket out of the door trim. Clay stuck his head through the door. Her apartment was an oasis; it was clean. Fresh air seemed to be winning the battle, and although sparse, the furniture was tasteful. Once again, he called Rebecca's name and got the same non-response. Clay was now all the way into the apartment and was officially breaking and entering. He closed the door behind him.

What the hell am I doing?

He pulled out his phone and called Rebecca again. A few seconds later her phone vibrated off the coffee table, causing Clay to jump out of his skin. He was so wound up, completely out of his element; he had never done anything remotely illegal in his life.

Clay stood pressed against the door as if this suggested he was only partially in the apartment and that was a little less unlawful. The entranceway was the living room; off to the left a small kitchen and an alcove large enough for a small table that could comfortably seat two. To his right was a hallway with a door at the end of it, and a second door on the left. The door to the left was ajar and was plainly the washroom; the only room remaining was the bedroom at the end of the hallway.

Shit.

Clay cupped his hands and directed his voice toward the bedroom, "Rebecca."

He waited, still nothing.

Now what? Shit, shit, shit.

He walked down the hall then pushed the bathroom door opened far enough to see the toilet and sink. The curtain was pulled across the bathtub. Clay fell back against the wall and closed his eyes, then shook his head at his cowardly ways.

This is a sign. Find Rebecca and get the hell out.

Only five steps farther down the hall, and he knocked on the bedroom door with force strong enough to push it open.

"Oh my God."

Clay raced over to the bed stepping in a puddle of vomit causing his heel to slide on the hardwood until the area rug stopped his forward motion. Rebecca remained in her clothes from earlier that day, her head resting over the edge of the mattress, a bottle of Jack on one side and a container of pills on the other—the same bottle she'd taken out on the bench with Clay earlier that day. Clay shook her and called her name. He reached for his phone to dial 911. She grunted.

"Rebecca."

She grunted again and opened one eye.

"Rebecca, how many of these pills did you have."

She flipped her head and looked at the bottle, and made a zero symbol with her index finger and thumb.

"Rebecca, are you sure?"

She grunted yes.

"How much of this bottle did you drink?" All but the bottom two inches was emptied from a twenty-sixer of Jack.

"Yes."

"Yes what."

"All." She managed.

She was probably still drunk maybe poisoned. "Should I get you to the hospital?"

No, she shook her head. "Just sleep."

He assessed her condition and believed she was only drunk. He tucked her in to bed the best he could and found a mop. She had fallen into a deep slumber, so he wrote her a note.

'I am sorry I have caused this to happen. Please call me when you are able.'

He left his cell number. Clay walked towards his car through the park dragging his feet through the grass, the sound and sensation soothing.

He stopped and reflecting on his stupidity. *I have no idea what state she is in.* He turned around and made his way back to apartment 801, stuck his head inside her door only to find Rebecca's cadence that of a person in a deep slumber. Clay glanced around the living room grabbed the only pillow and blanket lay down on the couch, curled his knees towards his chin, attempted to make the blanket grow around his torso and closed his eyes. He visualized Rebecca on that park bench and then how he drove her to drink… after all she'd been through. He'd been so worried about his own closure; he hadn't stopped to think about ripping open her own old wound. *How selfish.* He thought about what he and Kate went through together after the incident and then how Rebecca faced her own demons completely alone.

His cell phone lying on his chest vibrated and once again nearly sent him through the roof. It was Kate, and he simply suggested he would not be home until the a.m. as he was too tired to embark on the drive that night.

After checking on Rebecca once more, Clay drifted off into a decent slumber; the emotional roller coaster drained him.

A door slamming in the corridor made him stir for the first time since last night. His phone rang on his chest.

"What the fuck were you doing in my bedroom?" Rebecca was livid and rightly so.

"That is an excellent question, one I have been pondering since I left your place, well your room actually."

"Not good enough. Wait…" the penny dropped, "where are you."

"In your living room." Silence. "I know… I know, I thought you were in some kind of trouble."

"So you just broke in?" Her head hurt so much she had to lie down.

"I can't explain myself. One thing just led to another, and that crazy woman across the hall from you said you were sick." Clay didn't dare leave the couch or attempt to hang up even though she was just down the hallway.

"She might be punishment enough for coming unannounced. Did she have any clothes on?" Rebecca sounded amused.

"Barely... Listen, I owe you more than an apology, and I have something for you, it's back at the hotel. Tell me where and when we can meet?" Again silence. "I need ten minutes of your time."

"I am going back to bed; I will call you in a few hours."

It was only eight in the morning. Clay lifted himself from the coach and made his way to his car and eventually his hotel. He dialed Kate.

No hellos or niceties. "How is your day going?"

Kate sensed his frustration. "Better than yours?"

He pulled the phone from his ear and gathered himself. "I drove a woman to drink after five years of sobriety, but that wasn't enough. I then broke into her apartment, scared the living hell out of her, and then asked for her forgiveness."

There was a definite pause before Kate responded, "Have you lost your mind... do you believe you will work better from a jail cell!"

I am so screwed, first Rebecca and now Kate.

"Clay, what exactly is going on up there?"

He gave Kate the blow-by-blow details of his evening and his stupidity. "I will apologize again to her this aft then be on my way."

"Where? In her living room? Or maybe the kitchen makes more sense? Most people gather in the kitchen." She was really pissed. "I suspect an apology isn't going to cut it, Clay. She should have you arrested, you creep."

"You're not wrong... how are you doing?" Clay was squirming trying to change the subject.

"Well my investigations have not taken me into a strange man's bedroom unannounced, so I guess I am doing just fine." Kate hung up.

***

After an aggressive run, Clay showered then lay on the bed, covered only in his bath towel, his mind drifted through a myriad of the leads throughout the years.

Alexander Bryans' car was struck head on by the van driven by the assailant just as he turned onto Brookline. For a fleeting second, they made eye contact, and as uncomfortable as it was, he was able to have a composite drawing completed to his satisfaction. Clay mass-produced the composite sketch and spent hundreds of hours posting the 'Wanted' signs throughout the city and outlying region which led to local leads; the image posted online, however, provided Clay with the most feedback.

Clay received massive hits on his website. He ferreted out what he thought were the legitimate tips, and charted the sightings geographically using pushpins on a map of the North East states.

The net result was a smattering of sightings, but no overwhelming patterns. There were no towns, villages or counties that had an inordinate number of hits. Clay called upon the faculty from the Duvall geography department to better analyze the sightings, in both a micro and macro format. However, the results remained the same: the pushpins spread from New York City west to Buffalo and south to Pittsburgh: no clustering. If the population of the area was high, there were more pushpins, if the area was rural, then the hits were minimized. His grandest hope was multiple sightings in a remote area, but that was wishful thinking.

Summer after summer, he followed the various leads traveling from small towns to large metropolises throughout the states of New England, Maine, New Hampshire, Massachusetts, Rhode Island and Upstate New York. He logged thousands of miles knocking on hundreds of doors, listening to story after story, and then following further leads. The result was always the same: no closer to the culprit.

Clay continued to daydream on his bed, then considered calling Kate, but had nothing to add to yesterday's debacle so decided against it.

He checked his phone. He had one text message from Rebecca.

'Same park bench as yesterday. XL black and a toasted bagel lightly buttered 11:00 a.m. sharp.'

Clay wondered if her text had an edge to it, or was he just embellishing a sensitive situation.

The brief awakening of blue sky had given over to a cool drizzle and fog again, which hung like a curtain against the Atlantic Ocean. This gave the park the familiar eerie ambiance from a day gone by, far from the bright clear and colorful spectacle just a few minutes before. Clay set Rebecca's coffee and bagel on the same park bench as yesterday then paced back and forth just to keep warm.

She arrived right on schedule. "You know..." She took a drag from a cigarette, causing her cheeks to suck in as she gingerly settled onto the bench. "I should have called the cops." Rebecca shifted her weight to one side leaning away from Clay just as she did yesterday. She picked up the coffee and savored the first sip looked down at the bagel and thought better of it. She stared straight ahead.

Clay studied her intently. This was their third meeting, the first was when she was a young teenager with a story behind here sullen expression, the second in her mid-twenties, a young woman showing signs of abuse, and then the present, now a little thin, her features remained striking and angular, but her skin weathered past her age. The years of substance abuse and mental strain were evident as her youth was taken away years ago.

"So?" Rebecca raised her eyebrows and glanced over ever so briefly.

Clay chuckled. "My wife does that." He weakly pointed in her direction.

"Does what?" Rebecca could not get enough of the cigarette.

"That thing with your eyebrows. She just lays into me with that look."

"Hmmm."

"Yah, must be a girl thing, but it gets me all the time. Anyway, listen, I owe you an explanation for yesterday... this morning."

"You don't have to. You heard I was sick, you were worried, blah, blah, blah." She cut him off, still angry about the break in.

Clay thought she looked remarkably fresh for the day after a binge of epic proportions. The raincoat and scarf suited her, a splash of color wrapped close to her pale complexion. Her mannerisms seemed a lot more relaxed than yesterday. "Well, I do feel completely responsible for causing your ordeal last night."

"That is a shame." She touched her forehead slightly. "I will admit that I was at 1,652 days and counting without one slip. And yeah, our little coffee date yesterday sort of pushed me over the edge."

"Yah, like I said..."

"I have a meeting later today and I will stand up and announce I am an alcoholic and I haven't had a drink today."

"Shit."

"At least I went out with a bang, not a whimper." Her eyes watered slightly.

"I am truly sorry." He paused. "I stirred this up for purely selfish reasons and I was sick to my stomach when I saw firsthand what this does to you. I just needed closure for myself, and I ripped you apart in the process." Clay waited for a response. "I was such an idiot. I am so sorry."

"That's like the fifth time you have said sorry. I believed you the first time. I thought you were on some kind of schedule, only so much time left on the case… tick tock, tick tock?" She looked over at Clay. Her hair was sticking to her pastel skin and thin lips; she fought to get a mouthful of coffee.

"It's quite nasty out, would you prefer to go…" but before he could complete his sentence she interrupted.

"I like this, remember?" Rebecca actually smiled and raised her face to the cool mist. She was sincere. "Besides I can't smoke in there." She motioned her head in the direction of Starbucks.

Clay glanced over at the patrons sitting by the fireplace drinking their flavored concoctions in a very comfortable setting. Clay and Rebecca sat in the mist-come-rain. The wind whipped up the fog, creating dense patches then almost clearing.

"Okay we can't just leave things the way they are, Rebecca."

"Of course, we can. You listened; it was good, now go. I will be fine. I don't need a knight in shining armour, especially a married one on a mission from hell."

"Well I am hardly a knight, that couldn't be farther from the truth. But yeah, I guess you could say I'm on a mission from hell. It sure feels like it some days."

She looked over at him again, her eyes intent. "Why did you never stop searching? Is your wife that messed up from the tragedy?"

Clay stared at her. She glanced over and then lowered her head and closed her eyes. "That's a fair question, I suppose." Clay stared at his feet and sat on the end of her bench. He was soaked and frozen. "You call a spade a spade, don't you?"

"Yah, I guess I've never really shown a lot of diplomacy."

"I'm glad you texted. I wanted to make you an offer."

"Oh?" Rebecca's tone suggested a little curiosity.

"I've been thinking, Rebecca, and I know this is way out there, but what if you came with me, to stay with Kate and I."

Rebecca looked over with disbelief.

"It can be for a couple of days, a week a month, a couple of hours even. Completely your call, but you get out of here for a bit. A change of scenery, clear your head."

"No, I'm good." She reached for another cigarette.

"Maybe you would be doing both of us a favor. You get an escape for a day or two or longer if you wish, and Kate and I have an opportunity to really get to know you."

Rebecca's body went ridged. Her eyebrows almost disappeared into her hairline. No one accepts an offer like that; it's just a goodwill gesture.

"I still don't know why you would do all of this. It's crazy."

"Rebecca, it is not crazy. It's what friends do, plain and simple."

They sat on the bench for a few moments.

"We're not friends, we are barely acquaintances."

"Fair enough, how about this then. I can't leave in good conscience with you in the state you are in. Is that honest enough?"

"So it's still about you, Clay."

"To a degree I suppose. I do care though, that is a truth."

"I believe you."

"What do you say, Rebecca? You will like Kate. She's easy going, kind, fun, it would be nice to have you around, and after all, you have been in our house for the last thirteen years."

Rebecca shook her head. She looked across at her apartment building, then at the church where she attended AA meetings, then towards the Boston Public Library, another ghost of hers. It had been years since she had left the neighborhood. "Okay, what the hell, I need a boost, a lift of some type. AA is great, but I have slipped and God knows I need something fresh, even if it's only for a day or two. What's the worst thing that could happen?"

"Fine, it's settled, let's go grab some stuff from your place and be on our way."

"What am I thinking? This is way more complicated than he will ever know," Rebecca mumbled. "Okay," she called out a little louder, "Let's do this, but just for a couple of days."

8

November 2, Present Day

"The crowd has erupted here as New York has tied the game at two."

"You just can't hear yourself, Jon; it's pandemonium as Boyles leads his team back on the field."

"The great Vin Scully, the sixty-year-plus veteran of baseball play by play once said, and I paraphrase, 'the orchestra arrives and its maestro steps onto the mound.' Boyles is New York's maestro on the loneliest place on earth, the pitcher's mound at Yankee Stadium."

***

"Your son wears a 12-inch Heart of the Hide Rawlings ball glove with an 'I' web when, not that long ago, he used to have a fully closed 11 ¾ Nokona, manufactured just down the road from his old home in Arlington." Wolf's voice was calm and smooth. "Who knows that shit, Allan?"

"You got that right. Maybe someone with a little too much time on his or her hands?" Allan was truly tired of the charades and the night was young.

"Time! Oh yes time. Time is something I have had the luxury of enjoying for many, many years."

"Wasting time is for losers with idle minds, drifting, playing on the Internet, playing video games, watching TV, wasting our most precious commodity."

"You're right, Allan, because we all have only so much time."

***

"This is turning into more of a rain than a light mist."

"Not only that, Jon, the temperature is starting to plummet and it's getting downright nasty."

"Yes, almost as nasty as Boyle's sinker and slider tonight. He is using this wet weather to his advantage and the Padres are really paying for it. All they are being served is lots of movement so they are swinging at balls way outside of the strike zone. The evening was set up as a pitcher's duel and the fans are feasting on it."

***

"The trouble with your son is his antics off the field." A touchy subject for sure, Wolf's voice was hollow, not calm like earlier. It was time to take the gloves off.

"Fuck you. What my son does on the other side of these lines is his business and no one else's."

Casting the bait, Wolf smiled. "That is where you are dead wrong."

Allan began scanning the lower bowl searching for an opportunity for help, maybe catching the eye of a cop or security, but to no avail. There was too much excitement in the full house and too many distractions for the men and women in uniforms. For now, he would have to bide his time but he was certainly looking for an exit strategy.

"Allan, I can tell by the look on your face that you feel like you're caught in a bad spot. Christ, if I were in your shoes, I would likely feel the same way. However, knowing what I do about you and your lifestyle, this is likely not your first sticky wicket."

"What the fuck are you talking about?"

"Well, clearly you don't want me sitting beside you."

"Clearly."

"A dilemma… agreed?"

"Yah, you could say that."

"Every day for me is a dilemma."

"Listen, pal, I don't give a flying fuck."

"I know." Wolf watched the pitcher's warm up come to a close. "No breaks, Allan."

"No breaks, son, only what you work your ass for. Create your own opportunity, like I said before."

"No fairy-tale ending from where I am sitting, Allan, not at all."

"So, you ended up in Rebel, Rhode Island, huh?" Allan could not resist the tidbit that he was fed earlier.

"Yup, lived with my grandparents. They inherited a six-year-old from their delinquent daughter."

"Spare me the sadness and despair. I suppose you were completely neglected, blah, blah, blah."

"Pretty much. Never recalled a hug, or a word of encouragement, and for the most part, remained indifferent to them."

"Oh, I got it now, son, you have been looking for a hug from me, all this time." Allan laughed coldly. "What street did you grow up on?" Allan began to test his story; after all it would not be difficult to research Rickey's hometown.

"I grew up in a wartime house on Sergeant Ave."

"Google Maps is a powerful thing."

"I am sure you know the area, a little run down. I suspect a good chunk of your clientele at the strip club comes from that area."

Allan glanced over, just another needle in the craw. "Whatever, the Internet is a useful tool."

"The House of Lords off of Pincton. Piece of shit building, in a cesspool area. Your bartender Loren, with the tattoo of a heart on his bicep runs the place for you."

"For fuck sakes enough with this shit. So, you've been to my bar and have a thing for Loren, big fucking deal." With a quick burst of energy Allen motioned to stand.

Wolf slid his right arm across his body and clasped his iron grip just above Allan's right elbow and then squeezed a pressure point that bolted Allan back to his seat. The pain was so sudden and intense that it took Allan's breath away.

"My story tonight, Allan," Wolf groaned. "Are we clear?"

Allan could barely breathe; he thought his arm was going to rip off. The pain shot up his arm and into his neck just below his ear. "Crystal." It was barely audible but enough that Wolf released his grip. "I need to use the washroom."

"Seriously? That's the best you got." Wolf glanced at Allan's right hand as he reached into his overcoat.

"No cell phones Allan." Wolf held out his hand and waited.

"Who the hell are you to tell me what I can and cannot do?"

"Just give it some time, Allan, and you will have all your curiosities answered."

Allan was more than curious. "What was your grandpa's name?" Maybe they had a business transaction that went sour. Allan was looking for something, anything to find out Wolf's true identity and call him out.

"My grandfather was a benign drunk. He was no grandpa that's for sure, no warmth, no support; he had cirrhosis of the liver and was out of my life before I turned ten."

***

"The precipitation coming down may delay this game at some point, as we are looking to start this fourth inning."

"I don't see this as a good thing for the batters. The pitchers will be granted some liberties on the mound such as blowing into their hands. This will give them a little extra action on the sliders, breakers and curve balls. It also allows the pitcher to control the tempo of the game and each batter he faces."

***

"Your son has a terrific lifetime record in inclement weather delay games: twenty-five wins, seven no decisions and only five losses. Impressive." Wolf was playing games again.

Allan Boyles turned slightly and crossed his legs away from Wolf shaking his head at the statistic not even a neurotic father could conjure up.

"Who was your grandma then?"

"Alice, does that help?"

"Who the fuck are you and what do you want with me?" Allan was about to explode. "Get to the point."

"I'm Wolf, my nickname came from friends at school. They called me Wolf, as in 'the lone wolf.' I was left to my own devices from a very early age and by a stroke of luck I turned to sports, particularly the game of baseball."

Allan twitched slightly his eyes shifting ever so little towards Wolf. Wolf saw the movement and wondered if Allan was clueing into his identity.

"How old are you?"

"Thirty-five."

"Rickey's thirty-five.

"He is indeed."

"So, did you play ball in?"

"I did. I found an old Hillerich & Bradsby ball glove and a couple of hardballs in my grandfather's shed. They were likely locked up since he was a kid." Wolf's mind drifted to the backyard on Sergeant Street. The backyard was deep and to most it looked like a neglected lawn, but to Wolf it was a sanctuary, a refuge from all that was unsafe in his world. In his eyes, the property was Busch Stadium the home of the St Louis Cardinals, his favorite team as a child. "I played a lot of ball in my backyard."

"Shit that's not ball, son."

"What? Because it wasn't organized league play with uniforms and all that shit?"

"Yah, you just played in a fantasy world."

"Well I can't argue that. It was certainly fantasy, but I sure as hell would call it ball."

"Pffft." Allan crossed his legs away from Wolf once more. "How so?"

"Every day from the first thaw until the lasting snow, I was out there. I logged thousands and thousands of hours playing the game, and the more I played, the more I honed my skills. I set up targets in the yard representing my favorite players then would stand on a makeshift pitcher's mound, boards covered in sand from an old sandbox. I had a bed sheet with a strike zone painted on it; I draped the target over a branch sixty-six feet six inches from the pitching rubber and played this glorious game we watch tonight."

"Whatever. You still live in a delusion world."

"This is no figment of my imagination; I can assure you. When I was really young my grandfather would often fall asleep with a ball game on so I would sit for hours watching the mechanics of the pitcher, their wind ups and releases, understanding strategies of the game and of course the rules."

"You have no idea what it takes to stand where my son stands today."

"That couldn't be farther from the truth."

Suddenly, Allan lurched forward and just as quickly Wolf reacted, taking his arm and draping it across his chest with a formidable thud. The elbow was so intense that Allan was winded. A bystander would never notice the subtlety of Wolf's motion as it could easily be construed as a spectator overreacting to a play on the field.

"You can't hold me like this. I am calling out for the police or security if you do not let me leave right now."

"I strongly urge you to sit still."

Allan wasn't going to listen and, moreover, did not take to threats. He lunged upward.

A ball came off the bat of a Padre and flew over their section. Wolf jumped up with Allan, yelled for the ball, pointed at it as it flew overhead and laid a devastating elbow into Allan's temple knocking him out cold. Wolf hugged Allan and helped him to his seat, keeping an arm around Allan's shoulder, bolstering his head between his forearm and his bicep.

***

"No one saw this coming, Jon."

"Boyles has men at first and third, one out, and a full count to the lanky, first basemen Valchez. You can hear a pin drop in here. How can so many be so quiet? It's the first time since the early innings that Boyles has shown any vulnerability."

"There's the pitch, a slider on the inside corner, called strike three. Boyles is one out from getting off the mound and out of a huge jam. The reverberation from this sold-out crowd rises and falls with every pitch thrown. This is definitely the fall classic, the World Series and game seven, all rolled into one magnificent evening."

***

Allan shifted in his seat; the ebb and tide of fans cheering and jeering brought him to consciousness a few moments after the blow. He reached up to the left side of his face and gently touched his temple, the pain echoed down his jaw line.

"I dare you to try that again, Allan."

"Who the hell are you?"

"That's seventy-four pitches for your boy,"—Wolf ignored the question—"and we both know your son's record after ninety-seven pitches is a dismal seven wins, fourteen losses with twenty-two no decisions. I'm sure Lacoste has a close eye on that." Wolf didn't have to look over at Allan Boyles; he could sense him squirming.

"What school did you go to?" He paused briefly. "I'm assuming you made it to grade nine?" Allan still had his cheek.

"High school for an introvert is daunting, Allan." Not exactly the answer Allan was looking for. "I skipped a lot of classes. Baseball was my only sanctuary and I would watch the others in the yard play catch and talk about their hometown heroes. America's past time was alive and well in Rebel's playground. But I was just a bystander, a wallflower if you will, just absorbing it all."

"The name of the school you prick… fuck my head is throbbing." Allan stared onto the field trying to regain focus.

"Rebel Memorial. How's the throb now?"

"Bullshit."

"I did."

"Bull fucking shit. You've just done your homework and you are here to piss me off for some Godforsaken reason."

"I can't exactly prove it to you right here, right now."

"That's because you are full of shit. You know my son went there. It doesn't take a genius to figure that out."

"I had the best and the worst years of my life at that school."

Wolf swung his thoughts back to school and found himself standing on the mound for the first time. This painfully shy introvert became the center of attention in a blink of an eye.

On a cold afternoon in February, the snow whipping around the courtyard, baseball was in the air and he signed up for the tryouts. After three attempts, Wolf finally built up the nerve to put pen to paper and signed on the dotted line.

"I had no formal training leading into the high school tryouts and played no organized ball up till then."

"Just your backyard," Allan chuckled sarcastically.

"I stepped onto my first baseball diamond in the middle of March, with a team already assembled from last season. By all accounts, the roster was set for the upcoming season, but sometimes ignorance is bliss and I showed up anyway. I remember it like it was yesterday."

"Was my son on the team?"

"Do you want to hear the story or not?"

"Stop fucking with me. Just let me watch my son in peace."

Wolf sat in silence for a few moments, and for the first time this evening he actually took notice of the game and the surroundings. Wolf concentrated on the Padres' pitcher who was digging into the mound and focussing on his catcher for the signal. Wolf's eyes relaxed into a dreamlike state. He drifted. Wolf could still smell the dust around the mound and the freshly cut grass that was woven into a checkerboard pattern, the pride of Mr. Swan, the school custodian. Wolf's steps were tentative as if walking on eggshells. No one dared to try out for this team; it was cast in stone. Essentially this was an early practice, not a try out at all. Wolf was completely unknown to the fellow players, and to call them teammates would be both a contradiction and an abomination of both the words team and mates. A teacher and assistant coach recognized Wolf from his English class; he was the tall thin boy from the back-corner desk.

"Where you played your summer ball, boy?" The teacher was making haste, clipboard in hand. He wanted to make sure this string bean wasn't going to get hurt out there.

Wolf simply replied, "Sergeant Street Center." He just nodded not having a clue what Wolf was talking about.

The boys were not very discreet, knowing how cruel kids can be. They laughed at his old runners with no tread and holes in the toes, jeans instead of track pants and cotton instead of the wickable, high functioning athletic wear. Wolf heard one of the coaches' mutter to another, "Just don't let him get hurt and we will do the first cuts in twenty minutes."

Wolf picked up a ball and walked to the empty pitcher's mound. It all seemed so familiar, built exactly the height of the one on Sergeant Street; the only difference, no bed sheet at home plate.

A young boy stood behind the plate.

"Let's see some heat, kid," came a voice from the sidelines.

Another player stepped up to the plate. Show us what you've got. The boys were smiling at one another as more gathered around. They weren't smiling after three pitches.

The Jr. coach flipped through his charts and couldn't even find the kid's name. He threw heat with movement, lots of movement. The next thing you knew, the senior boys were over and taking BP, swinging at nothing but air.

Wolf gave his head a shake, drifting back to the present. "Allan, are you paying close attention?"

Allan simply nodded. "I sure as hell hope you aren't who I think you might be." His tone was quiet and reserved.

Wolf smiled.

9

Clay crossed his arms and sat against the hood of his car. He was parked in a 'no parking' zone, so Rebecca suggested he just stand by just in case. She disappeared into the crack house fronting as an apartment building and Clay couldn't help but wonder if she would reappear.

Rebecca did return; with a small travel backpack draped over one shoulder.

"Are you totally sure about this, Clay? I mean, is your wife going to be cool with it?

"Absolutely, I think you're a good person who's been dealt a shitty hand. I am completely responsible for what happened yesterday."

"You sure? Last chance."

"We have had enough of a roller coaster ride over the last twenty-four hours, so no more broken hearts tonight and I think it is in both of our best interests if you come."

Rebecca stared at him. "Did you rehearse that?"

"No, but it came out okay didn't it?" They shared a laugh. Clay had never seen her smile. It looked completely unnatural. How sad.

Rebecca shrugged and blushed slightly as Clay held the door for her. "That's a first." She settled in and watched Clay shift into second then third. Her attention turned towards the church on Dartmouth Street; familiar faces were starting to gather.

Rebecca watched Boston's skyline get smaller in the side mirror, office towers gave way to condos, then suburbs, then industry and after that the country. She assumed a more relaxed posture, as if things seemed right for a change.

Clay noticed Rebecca's interest in the landscape. "When was the last time you got out of town?"

"We went to Martha's Vineyard for my fifteenth birthday. That was the last time." She reflected. "How long is the drive?"

"Light traffic." Clay glanced at his speedometer and set the car on cruise. "We should hit the metropolis of Gremlin around one a.m., so six hours give or take."

Rebecca didn't respond. Instead she looked over at Clay. He was handsome, smelled good, was well dressed, fit, and in control. For the first time in a long time, she felt safe, but guilty as hell.

***

Rebecca glanced into the backseat and spotted a blanket. "May I?"

"Of course. I should turn on the heat."

"No, I'll be fine." Rebecca lifted her slender frame and cocooned herself in the blanket then gently slipped off her shoes and rested her feet on the dashboard.

It was raining again. Clay set the wipers on intermittent, and in the silence all that could be heard were the wheels spraying rainfall on the highway, the wipers swishing, and the hum of the diesel engine.

They sat silent for an interchange or two. "I'm so sorry I couldn't help, Clay."

"Don't apologize, Rebecca, Jesus Christ." He didn't get the answer he was hoping for but that was no fault of hers. "Rebecca, if anyone should apologize, it's me; I just put you through all of this again. So let's move forward."

Rebecca's head was pounding; emotions sparking like a live wire in water. Dizzy and nauseous, maybe from motion sickness, but likely from the turmoil she regurgitated over the last forty-eight hours and, of course, the wagon she fell off last night. Rebecca might pour her heart into the lap of a stranger. Or was he a stranger? It was so difficult to describe the relationship between Rebecca and Clay. On one hand they were strangers, predicated on the fact that over the last thirteen years they had seen each other on only two occasions, the first shortly after the incident and then five years later when Clay was revisiting her file. In total they spent less than seventy-two hours together. Such a short encounter would suggest a passing association; however, the impact on Rebecca was profound. Clearly, they became united when this madman turned them all into victims. Initially, she was somewhat sympathetic to Clay's cause, but the magnitude of her own issues circumvented his, and the intensity of his travesty passed. When Clay showed up for the second time, five years after the occurrence, he carried even stronger resolve. Rebecca took notice and saw the man in a different light. Clay keeps reminding her that there is still healing that needs to happen after the incident: for Clay, for Kate, and for Rebecca too.

Clay's healing process was narrowed down to his intensity to solve the crime set upon Kate. It was immeasurable and no obstacle to derive the truth was insurmountable.

As the years passed and Rebecca began to pick up the pieces of her own disjointed life, she would often think of Clay and his paralyzed wife and wondered what came of their trials and tribulations. How long did he search, and did he ever find the answers or at least inner peace? Eight years later they sat on a rain-soaked park bench: Clay no closer to the truth, and Rebecca even more besieged by his obstinacy.

But despite all the emotions towards the Stoppas, their quest and the tenacity involved, one thing ran certain: they were in this together and she admired, and envied to a certain extent, the support or safety net that they provided one another. Rebecca's protective instincts grew to high alert and after living for thirteen years in a troublesome neighborhood, she became very good at it. She was streetwise, focussed and above all, incredibly intelligent.

She closed her eyes and listened to the windshield wipers push back and forth.

"Did you ever get professional help after your accident?"
"No."
"How about after being shot?"
"No."
"So me showing up really sucked."
"Yes and no."
"Okay, what's the no part?"
"Well they are kind of combined really."
"How so?"
"I was in a dark state of mind when I failed to help you, so the years of self-inflicted chastising had come full circle time and time again."
"And we have been through that, you didn't fail in either instance."
"I get that in principle, but it's not something you can just work like

a light switch."

"Yah, so visits like mine..."

"Well, the last couple of days, and with no ill intent, had reached down and ripped that protective facade that separated me from my demons and now the ghosts of my past flow freely through my mind." Rebecca paused. "It raises terror and grief, sadness and despair, at some points to unbearable levels."

"This comes from years of soul searching... have you studied this... your psychological situation?"

"I have studied it, yes, among other things."

"Did you take courses for it? At college or anything?"

Rebecca nearly laughed. "I dropped out of school at the end of high school after numerous interruptions; but I was always drawn back to the Boston Public Library. Have you ever seen inside?"

"No, I can't say I have."

"It's a sanctuary filled with columns, and arches and bookshelves that reach to the heavens; there is immaculate crown moulding and baseboards, hardwood floors, rows and rows of tables with antique green Tiffany lamps. And then there are the books, stacks upon stacks upon stacks... all that knowledge. Oh my God."

"So, I guess you attended Boston Public."

"Yah, that's funny. I refer to it as the University of Public Boston. I always wanted to get a sweatshirt made up and wear it at MIT or Harvard, sit in on a class just for the hell of it."

Rebecca went to light a cigarette, but stopped herself. Clay noticed, but said nothing. Rebecca closed her eyes again; she envisioned her support group, and how she was moving further and further from them. Maybe she was not as independent as she thought. She further distanced herself from the familiar voices wishing her a good evening as they headed back to their own private lives, each and every one of her contemporaries, with skeletons responsible for their current state of affairs making it so difficult to get through another day.

This will be one hell of a fight tonight.

Rebecca inhaled deeply then turned her head towards the side window, opened her eyes hoping the rain would distract from the cigarette cravings. She lifted her knees to her chin and stared off into the distance.

"Did you have any encouragement to continue on with a formal education?"

"No, not really."

"Parents? Grandparents?"

"No, but that was okay. It wasn't a part of my family structure. I came from labour, working class."

"Nothing wrong with that."

"Agreed." She paused. "Not a close family though."

"That's tough."

"Yah, no abuse or anything, just not a lot of good communication, and eventually none at all."

"You have little to do with your parents then?" Clay shifted in his seat

"It was gradual, starting in high school. I was a bit of a bad ass. Why buy the candy, when you can steal it, you know what I mean? So, I learned at a very young age that there was always an alternative."

"Tough without the proper guidance." Once again, Clay was trying to suggest in not so many words that Rebecca should not be so hard on herself.

"You're not wrong, but I sure wasn't looking for their advice even if it was offered. I really got mixed up in the wrong crowd."

"How so?"

"I fell for some drug-addicted guy, got into the wrong scene, knew things were bad, but couldn't stop, and then one night was raped by him and his friends."

"Oh my God."

"I never saw him again." She paused and caught a bit of a reflection of herself in the passenger window. "I was just a throw away, garbage for the curb." Rebecca noticed an interchange up ahead. "Can we pull over here? I am desperate for a smoke. I am so sorry."

Clay glanced at his gas indicator, it had barely moved from 'full'. "Perfect, I need a washroom break and maybe another coffee myself."

They pulled into a brightly lit bustling gas bar; there had to be ten bays with tanks four deep. The neon green reflecting off the rain-soaked concrete illuminated the darkness. Rebecca strolled along the storefront, her thoughts a million miles away. Clay went to the washroom for some privacy. He was looking for the first opportunity to call Kate and explain the predicament he was completely responsible for.

His abbreviated explanation to Kate was passable. He neglected to mention the baggage she was carrying and his trepidation of leaving her alone. Some details would need some massaging before pontificating. Kate had always trusted Clay's instincts; they were true, time and time again. He had this innate sense of a person, whether he or she was good or bad. So when he described what little he knew, the circumstances bringing them to the rest stop on the interstate, and his short-term plan, she accepted his judgment.

He felt guilty as hell when he hung up. Clay never held back from his wife. Maybe he would recount the rest of the details in the company of Rebecca, less likelihood of strangulation.

With coffees in hand, Clay pulled up curb side. Rebecca tossed what looked like a third butt, then shook off the sogginess and resumed her spot in the passenger seat right down to the blanket.

"You're really hard on yourself." Clay picked up the conversation.

"I need to be."

"Yah, but you've been through a lot of shit, Rebecca. Christ, you were raped and shot. Cut yourself some slack."

"I am not looking for sympathy here, Clay, you know that. I'm not a poor woebegone-type looking for attention."

"I am absolutely well aware of that. You say you have never opened up before, that in itself says a lot."

"Such as?"

"Well, how strong you are for one, and it is so sad that you have never had someone in your life that you believe might help. It saddens me to no end if that is the case. I am thrilled you are going to spend some time with us."

"Well, it sure as shit feels good to talk about it."

They were back on the road, the city lights were a distant memory and soon the interstate would split creating a darker, easier drive for Clay. The rain continued with force and he concentrated on the road.

Clay set the car on cruise then shifted slightly in the seat to get more comfortable. Rebecca turned towards the passenger window, now all was dark, so much darker than she was used to. She stared vacantly partially at her own refection, partially at the shadows passing by.

"What kind of drugs were you on?"

"Oh, you know, cocaine, ecstasy, a bit of pot and lots of alcohol. I had access to drugs, as I was a bit of a runner, a player if you will, feeding the strung-out neighborhood and taking for my own addiction." She let out a sarcastic giggle. "Now it did get interesting. I literally stole drugs from drug dealers."

"A little dangerous, don't you think?"

"Dangerous?" Rebecca chuckled slightly. "Suicidal is more like it. I would stay out at night and observe the corners; you know the drug dealer corners."

"Yah... sort of."

"They always had a stash or a stack as they called it, a sizable amount of drugs already cut and ready to distribute. When the cops came and did their rounds, all eyes were focused on them. They would often line everyone up for a bit of a shake down and I was in and out before anyone knew I existed. In a flash I made off with the evening's loot."

"Tell me that's the stupidest thing you have ever done."

It ranks up there for sure." Rebecca shook her head. "I only did it a couple of times... it was ten out of ten on the danger scale. Did I mention how naïve I was?"

Clay smiled. "A few times, yes."

"So how did you turn yourself around?" Clay adjusted to a more attentive position as he hydroplaned ever so slightly and turned off the cruise. He needed to give the driving conditions more respect.

"Well, here it comes, Clay, here's the bomb." Rebecca paused, closed her eyes wiped her nose and let out a massive sigh. "I was pregnant."

"Jesus."

"I know, right. It may have been the rape, I'm not certain, but it was certainly one of those geniuses. I had a horrific abortion, which I will never talk about, and then I was free falling, spiraling out of control, until I woke up in a jail cell with no money and no ID."

"And you picked yourself up, dusted yourself off and began to rebuild your life?"

"You have to reach the bottom first."

"You weren't?" Clay caught himself.

"I am sure you have heard that of addicts? Slowly, slowly, slowly I began to right the ship, attending meetings, got a job, at the drive-thru at the Burger King."

"Shit." Clay knew what was coming.

"Yup... then I got shot, which sent me off the deep end again, but I knew in my heart of hearts what was right, and for some reason I wanted to live and better myself. So, more meetings and back to my sanctuary at the library."

"All this by yourself... no help?" Clay swallowed hard.

"No help"

"Wow."

"Well I have a sponsor, a good guy, but he is spread so thin I try not to bother him. You are the only person who knows about the abortion."

"I am lost for words. I'm truly sorry for putting the pressure on you over the years."

"No, you helped. You were a calming influence; someone that had the tenacity of Javier... but in a good way, and the love of Mr. Darcy, all wrapped in one."

"A bit of a reader, huh, you and Kate will do just fine," Clay kept convincing himself. "Well you sure know how to ease a guilty conscience."

"One very small good thing came from the shooting?"

"Really?"

"Yah, a lump sum of cash in a settlement, which I invested in Apple and have never touched, and a small monthly allowance which allows me to maintain my humble existence without holding down a job."

They drove in silence for a short while. It was now the dead of night; the rain had put them way behind schedule. Clay slowed down for his exit. The familiar signpost read Gremlin twenty miles. "This has been quite an evening, Rebecca."

"I'd say," Rebecca's voice was so sweet and so kind.

***

"Well, this brings a tear to my eye, Kate." Before glancing at his watch, Tubs looked around at the transformation.

When the Stoppas' abode was initially renovated, Kate and Clay decided to take some of the money Clay received from the Detroit Tigers organization and build the ultimate games room. Kate always wanted this for Clay. He was so committed to her cause and she thought it could be his sanctuary, his area, and his time.

The net result was an addition, or better stated an extension to the back of the house. The stonework matched perfectly, a seamless enhancement. What was added, a thirty by forty-foot, one story extension with a low-grade roof and subtle gables. The gingerbread from the main house was toned down slightly to create continuity and a flawless extension to the main abode.

The entrance to the kitchen was through a mudroom, to the left the dining room and to the right a twelve hundred square foot games room, mesmerizing with all of the toys. The wall separating the kitchen from the games room was constructed using double-sided glass framing a hearth fireplace both practical and a cozy ambiance. The brickwork ran from floor to ceiling adding warmth and appeal to both rooms. A slate pool table was set at the far end of the sizable room, complete with portable ramps for Kate. The back wall was floor to ceiling windows, overlooking an extensive deck, hot tub, and pool. The two sidewalls were graced with rich grained mahogany wainscoting, interrupted every four feet with a beautifully handcrafted baseball bat, all 34 inches long, and all 32 ounces. That was Clay's chosen bat size throughout his career. The room was outfitted with a bar, couches, an obscenely large flat-screen TV, a juke box filled only with classic rock, and to round it out, a 1950s pinball machine, fully functional. The only baseball memorabilia in the room that meant something to Clay was a glove, set on a display with a small inscription on the base 'Thanks, Dad, for everything, Sept. 18, 1999'. Something Clay gave to his dad shortly before his untimely death.

Kate pulled back and perused the room. The pool table was covered in plywood, and was transformed from a recreational monument into a table equipped with computers and files. Set at each end of the table was a tripod with large pads of paper. Running the length of the room on the right-hand wall were three four-by-eight collapsible tables stacked with the balance of Clay's files, and underneath the tables, banker's boxes filled with more files. Dining room chairs were randomly placed in the temporary headquarters. She fired up her laptop and brought the Internet up on the large-screen TV.

Tubs stretched out his back.

"This is your doing, Kate. You're the brains, and I'm the brawn. I didn't ask; I just did as I was told." Tubs was terrified of Clay's reaction to the 'man den'.

"Don't worry, he'll believe you. There's no way you would voluntarily dismantle the shrine of Monday Night Football."

"This will be cleaned up before kick off in the fall won't it?"

Kate nodded with conviction.

"Okay. I gotta go now, I have to be somewhere."

Kate looked at her watch, "Home, I would presume?" She sounded a little curious.

"Where else at this hour?" he responded.

Kate escorted Tubs to the door, they hugged, his enormous frame curled over her petite one. Kate looked closely at Tubs as he pulled away, based on Clay's comments during their run. She could think back to Clay's question about Tubs and his appearance the other night and thought, 'Yeah, maybe Tubs is looking a little green around the gills...'. Kate sat at the front glass window and watched him pull out then closed the door. She paused... *I guess he had somewhere to go because his house is in the opposite direction.*

Tubs was not going home. He was heading to the Village of Alora, just five minutes from the town limits of Gremlin. He had some business to look after at the local casino.

Alora, Pennsylvania is a strange anomaly and a prime example of how a town can transform from quaint to greedy, the repercussions irreversible. Ten years ago, movies were filmed in the downtown Mill area, a streetscape graced with cute shops and boardwalks articulating between century old buildings leading to a grand boardwalk on the gorge.

Often the façade of downtown buildings that face away from the street are discarded, as there is only so much money to renovate, so why spend it in the rear? In the case of Mill Street, the shops end where the water begins so the finished verandas and the small cafés at the back of the buildings remain just as important as the front, creating a postcard image and a unique ambiance and charm, unlike most other downtowns. The limestone creates 'Dickensesque' warmth and conjures up images of centuries gone by.

The immediate streets surrounding Mill were eclectic and mesmerizing. Streets angled away from the main thoroughfare in extreme directions, and then ascended at remarkable rates; thus, the architectural opportunities were both challenging and bountiful. Small railway workers' homes from the turn of the century had been transformed into unique, expensive homes with additions completely in keeping with the area's heritage.

There was, however, blight allowed into the community that has tarnished the village forever, both from an eclectic standpoint and a social perspective. Alora was offered a casino, the same casino that was turned away just three miles down the road in Gremlin. The Casino Development Committee, an organization presenting itself 'For the Greater Good', was publicly humiliated by the stodgy and stubborn Historical Society of Gremlin, headed up by none other than Mrs. K Stoppa.

Rather than going home with their collective tails between their legs, the organization took the 'dog and pony' show to the neighboring community, showed them an architecturally pleasing rendering on the banks of the Grange, a hotel and fine dining facility second to none, plus a revenue stream to line the pockets of the 'Fathers that be' for the foreseeable future. It stuck.

Alora was now a quaint tourist community on the north banks of the Grange, and a condemnation of gambling, greed, glory, prostitution, organized crime, and opulence on the south. But the greatest debacle, the lights, best described as a splash of Vegas, the old and new juxtaposed in conflict forever.

***

"Thank you, Mr. Campbell, we will be right back." A leggy brunette adjusted her skirt and left the room fully aware that her ass would be the target of Tubs' attention.

The "Private Loans Department" for the Alora Kings Casino, was well furnished, comfortable and busy. The Grange room had lighting, dim and relaxing, the music generic and soft.

Tubs lit up a cigarette; smoking is not prohibited. He leaned forward and browsed at the selection of magazines set out. They were always the same, a success-driven luxury genre.

The striking woman in a navy pinstripe form-fitting business suit, re-entered the room, her skirt shifted from just above the knees to mid-thigh as she sat gingerly on the chair beside Tubs. After crossing her legs, and pulling the clipboard to her chest just as she was taught, she smiled, her teeth white and perfect. She looked fresh and alert for a Monday morning at dawn; however, her shift was coming to a close at eight, at which time the next Loans Advisement Service Representative would start her eight-hour shift. The Private Loans Department never closed, because the casino never closed. This was a 'special' department, special because it catered to a special breed of clientele. The clientele that makes its way to this wing of the gambling operation requires equity, a job with a steady income, but most importantly, bad luck and an addiction to coming back time after time after time.

"You have been approved for a twenty thousand dollar 'in house' line of credit. I'm sorry I have to explain all of this to you again, but it's my job, and one of the conditions of the loan. We here at Alora Kings cannot cut any corners, so please be patient."

Tubs knew the terms and conditions too well. He stared at the wall straight in front of him and tuned the statuesque loans officer out.

"This is not a cash loan; you cannot withdraw any part of the twenty thousand dollars from the line of credit and use it elsewhere. The credits you win in the casino will be used against this loan and any previous outstanding Alora Kings loans, until they are paid off, at which time you may turn your credits into cash." She raised her voice as if he had won something.

"This loan will be secured as a fourth mortgage on your principal residence, 112 Patrick Street, Gremlin PA. and is secured behind a first mortgage of sixty-seven thousand dollars with American Bank Trust and Capital Corporation, a second mortgage for one hundred seventy-four thousand with Alora Kings Loans Corporation, and a third mortgage of fifty-nine thousand dollars held by Alora Kings Loans Corporation. This loan of twenty thousand dollars is at a rate of twelve percent per annum and is payable monthly, not unlike the second and third mortgages. Now, we do have outstanding arrears on the second and third mortgage that will have to be looked after with this loan, so when it is all said and done, you have twelve thousand four hundred and fifty-eight dollars, twenty-eight cents worth of credit. Sign here, here and here, on these three pages and the funds will be made available immediately."

Tubs sat without emotion and signed the papers.

"Oh, one thing I forgot to mention. Because we have given you three loans over the past eighteen months, we must ask that you attend an information session on 'responsible gambling'. We ask that you make an appointment down the hall to your left within the next day or so."

Tubs nodded.

"Oh, your bar tab is cleared and you have free drinks for the next three months and you have four hotel room coupons to use at your convenience, maybe a couple of romantic getaway weekends with your wife. They are transferable to any of our thirty-eight casinos across America."

The loans officer shook his hand; a limp gesture of friendship. Her hand was cold and dry, his warm and sweaty.

Casino operators arrange rock concerts with the biggest stars from all over the world. They fly them to Godforsaken backwoods communities, pay them inordinate sums of money for a fifty-five-minute greatest hits show, feed them and entertain them, first-class service all the way, then fly them out again. Why? Because the casinos can afford it. Gambling destroys one life every ten seconds in America. It begins with bankruptcy, closely followed by a loss of their job, then divorce, followed by losing custody of their children, the drug dependency becomes a larger deal, some commit suicide, and some are murdered for unpaid debts. A few start at the bottom, and slowly work their way out of the living hell, but for most it is a slippery slope.

The gambling industry sets up counseling groups to protect the public from its own business. The gambling industry funds the help for those that are addicted and provides start-up funds for those that reach the bottom. If the gambling industry really gave a fuck about its clients like Tubs, they would shut down.

Gamblers know the odds, they know their limit, they are never forced to gamble, they pass by the 'counseling for addicts' billboards on the way to and from the casino, but they don't care, because this might be the one, the draw of the card, or the spin of the wheel that turns their luck. Wind him up, he cannot stop.

Tubs strolled through the familiar V.I.P. entrance, the one reserved for big winners and big losers. He grabbed a double shot of 'bravery' from the bar; it had a unique bite on a Monday morning after no sleep. He marched into the forty thousand square feet of lights, bells and voices, made his way past the rows upon rows of slot machines, first the nickel slots, filled with vagabonds and alcoholics, then the quarter slots, the happy couples sitting on one another's laps looking for something to do between fornications. The dollar slots, less crowded, attracted the wealthy widows and the pissed-off adulterer's partner who threw in coins like they were pennies just to get back at their cheating spouse. The last few rows of five-dollar, ten-dollar and one-hundred-dollar slot machines are left predominantly empty, but the chairs are more comfortable, and the décor mahogany, graced by the Asian high roller's wives as their husbands played baccarat in the glass rooms at the back.

Tubs scanned the roulette tables, eight in all. Three were active that morning, unusually high for a Monday, suggesting a lot of carryover from the night before. He strolled over to the booth, inserted his membership card, the teller pressed some buttons, and off he went to table number seven.

His phone was ringing and this time he chose not to ignore it. Five missed calls from his wife and he finally answered the sixth.

"Thank God, Michael, you must have had a hell of a shift. I hate to put this upon you. I have got that flu everyone seems to have and I am freezing cold and have a wicked fever. Grab some Gatorade and hurry home." Tubs' wife's voice was weak, her voice fading.

10

Kate slept well, deep and motionless.

Clay's head however, was spinning from Rebecca's horror story and he barely slept a wink.

Rebecca on the other hand, dropped into the deepest, non-drug-induced sleep in twenty years. She lay in a double bed wrapped in homemade quilts and a duvet. The large guest bedroom was straight out of a bed and breakfast magazine, filled with antiques including a dressing table and chair, a Queen Anne dresser and an old oak wardrobe. The room was cheerful and gave a sense of security and comfort, just the atmosphere that Rebecca had craved for so long.

Being a fully functioning paraplegic, Kate's routine on a weekday morning took considerably longer than someone without the challenge. As a consequence, rising at five a.m. allowed Kate the time to exercise, shower, and dress, have breakfast and be out the door approximately three hours later, give or take. She carried her challenges better than most. Kate was, however, only human, so when it rained or snowed, or the lift to the upstairs was broken, or a laneway blocked by a misplaced chair or a fallen sweater, Clay would often be the recipient of the frustration. This was one of those mornings. Clay was on his best behavior and helped Kate accomplish her morning routines and said the only correct answer when asked to pick up Julie Hook at Philadelphia International Airport at one p.m.

"Sure, no problem." He feigned a smile.

Julie had a bachelor of science degree from the University of Oregon, a master's degree from the University of Oregon in Cultural Anthropology, and a Doctorate from Rice University in Medical Anthropology. She was a professor at the University of Chicago, and a professional consultant with Alice & Co. one of the nation's largest insurance underwriters. Julie used her analytical skills to ferret out patterns of fraudulent activities, marking this part-time job as a 100K sideline.

Kate was hopeful that Julie's expertise in deciphering information might put some order to an incredible amount of material that she had gathered in record time. Using her own tragedy as the template, she was setting out to find similar patterns in the files they had compiled.

The relationship between Clay and Julie was not complicated at all. They could not stand one another. There was no specific event or issue that drove a wedge between them; they just irritated the hell out of one another. Their only common ground: Kate.

Clay spotted Julie as she passed through the gates. No friendly hellos, no niceties, and definitely no hugs.

"I thought you would be off in some obscure village following up on another sighting, maybe Sierra Leone?"

Less than five seconds and she was already pushing his buttons. "No that was last week, try to keep up."

"So, you're home for the summer looking after our Kate?"

"Our Kate doesn't need looking after, Jules. She's a paraplegic not an invalid."

She hates Jules.

"You know what I mean."

Asshole.

They walked in awkward silence to the car, and then chose a neutral topic. They chatted about the subtle nuisances of the post-secondary education on the painfully sluggish journey to Gremlin.

***

Rebecca woke up in a lovely room. It made her smile. The sheets were fresh; coolness surrounded her face, but her body was puddeny warm. Her first emotions that morning were that of happiness and content. She could not recall such a feeling. Rolling over, she noticed an envelope left under her door. She raised her head and gently touched the smooth hardwood with her bare feet and scampered to the door then back to the cuddly confines of layered duvets.

'Welcome Rebecca,

Make yourself at home. The back room is a bit of a disaster as we are taking yet another approach to finding our shooter. I realize how difficult this has been for you.

The next couple of days will be hectic around here, but I do look forward to getting to know you. As Clay mentioned, you are a welcome guest, so just bear with us over the next few days then we can get to know one another.

In the meantime, the fridge is full and there are a lot of shops downtown to explore if that is of interest. We welcome your help in the backroom, but completely understand if you want to stay clear of the insanity!

Our home is your home.

Kate

She must have read the letter ten times, with mixed emotions.

Who does this? Who is this nice? They don't even know me and 'our home is your home'? Okay, what's the catch here? Oh, the flipping shame.

The house was empty; after showering, she made her way downstairs. Rebecca fell in love with the century charm. The décor made her feel cozy and warm inside. She skulked around for a short time, but felt intrusive so she set out for a walk. Downtown sounded engaging.

She meandered west along Union past St. Joseph's Hospital, then right on Power down to the bridge that stretched over the River Grange. She stopped in the middle of the overpass and looked down. The drop was at least forty feet, and the view of the falls and the escarpment was spectacular. It was peaceful staring at the rapids and the small currents as she allowed her eyes to follow the whitewash that created swirling patterns.

I can't stay here; it just isn't right. My business is none of theirs and my problems aren't theirs. Like Clay said last night, I can't leave you alone and I need to get home. As nice as he seems, it's all about him and Kate and their case and I'm am completely okay with that. I was just an inconvenience last night, nothing more. He meant well, but I am not going to be disappointed again. I won't let myself become attached to the

Stoppas; it will only end in disaster. They can't help me anyway. I've tried to get help, but I am beyond it.

"Excuse me?" A formidable police officer lowered the passenger window to his cruiser and leaned over.

Shit.

"Yes, officer?"

He had his emergency lights on, his cruiser curbside, partially blocking oncoming traffic.

"I have been by this way a number of times over the last twenty minutes and couldn't help but notice that you haven't moved?"

Is that a fucking crime in this town?

"Am I breaking some law, officer? I was just minding my own business enjoying the view."

"No, it's not that at all. I just wanted to make sure you are okay. Are you?"

Well let's see, I'm an alcoholic, like some pills, have severe trust issues, hate cops, can't shake some major crimes committed against me over a decade ago, can't get over my own self-pity, and can't accept help from those who mean well. Oh, and probably had my first full night's sleep without fucking nightmares just last night.

Rebecca began to let her guard down. "No, I'm good, really. I'm just new here and was admiring the view; I didn't realize I was standing here so long."

"Not that long I guess, anyway... good, as long as you're okay. I apologize for disturbing you." With that, Tubs raised his window and moved along.

"Okay, so where am I? Mayberry?" Rebecca mumbled to herself.

Rebecca was so caught up in her own thoughts that she didn't realize how the temperature had dropped. The breeze was fresh and she had underdressed. She began to walk. Walking was something she excelled at. As long as she kept moving, the temperature was tolerable and so she continued across the bridge to the downtown.

There was an assorted dichotomy between the various businesses, most catered to the tourist industry: the arts and crafts shops, the Scottish regalia and the trendy cafés. However, there was still a trace of the past, as demonstrated in the J.T. Bothwright Men's Shop and the accompanying K.M. Little Woman's Boutique, both establishments stuck in the 1950s. They had high tin ceilings and ghostly stilted manikins in the display windows. Children would often mock or be frightened by the stonewall statuettes. She strolled in and out of the shops losing interest rather quickly.

Rebecca approached Gremlin's bus terminal, a grand old building. It was a miniature grand central station complete with gargoyles, pillars, woodcarvings and contemporary art. She moved towards the only teller at the station and inquired as to a time schedule to Boston. It was the milk run no doubt, but the buses did head to Massachusetts three days a week. Rebecca felt more comfortable with an exit strategy in place; she stopped short of buying a ticket but kept the printed schedule.

She strolled the north side of Main, her mood more solemn or melancholy, however passing by the B & W Diner put a smile on her face. The ambiance was more her style and as she struggled with the clumsy door. She anticipated a cup of black coffee.

A gentleman of Asian descent, wearing a full button beige top and the name Chuck embroidered in a deeper brown on the left side of his shirt, smiled and bowed slightly as she entered.

"You want special?"

"Special?" Rebecca looked for a sandwich board. It read Sweet and Sour Pork. "No thank you, just a coffee"

Chuck smiled and practically ran it to her.

She chose to sit on one of the twelve red stools facing a nondescript façade and wrapped her hands around the white porcelain cup; the warmth was comforting. She listened to the locals at the first booth discuss the crop outlooks for this season; the community had a country goodness feel to it. She grabbed a copy of the local rag and was only disturbed for coffee refills.

***

Clay set a new record time from Philly to Gremlin, inspired by the company he kept. They coasted into the driveway. Julie cleared the car just before it came to a complete stop. Clay grabbed her overnight bag from the trunk, but thought better of spilling it.

Kate's car occupied its usual spot in the drive. She had scheduled a half-day and arrived home just in time to prepare coffee.

It was always a bittersweet reunion for the two women. Julie was like a photo album to Kate, important to have around, but rarely viewed as the lustre of the past was always a bitter reminder of days gone by. The cruelty of fate was never so prevalent when Kate's competitive foe was standing over her with that look of remorse and pity. It was never Julie's intention to look at her this way and least of all upset her dearest friend; it was just a natural response each and every time. Kate and Julie always cried the second they set eyes on one another, tears of joy and heart-wrenching anger. Nothing upset Clay more than seeing his wife cry over what had been taken from her; he was blinded with rage and likely the paramount reason why he resented Julie so much.

Clay paced into the next room; it was easier that way. God, he hated that man, whoever and wherever he was.

Julie settled into the second spare bedroom upstairs, pausing as she passed the much larger guest room, but didn't question Kate's direction. She freshened up, and then pounded down the stairs, burst into the games room dressed in grey flannels and a headscarf, flicked on a computer and the flat screen, then looked around the space. "Operation 'Catch the Bastard'." Julie rarely minced words.

Tubs arrived shortly after one thirty, armed with pizza and beer. He was excited that Julie was in town for the weekend and that he would spend it in her company. Tubs couldn't care less that she was a walking analytical computer, or that she would not even notice him in the room. He just loved the look of the woman: her six-foot lanky frame, no-nonsense expression, and the fact that she was a lesbian added to the ambiance.

Clay sauntered into the kitchen, greeting Tubs and directed him with the pizza cartons. He flicked on the lights to make up for the overcast afternoon, Tubs commented that the temperature had dropped like a rock and Clay glanced out at the street in both directions curious as to where Rebecca had meandered off to.

God, I can't read about this girl tomorrow morning.

Clay walked up the front path in just his socks and stood at the end of the sidewalk with his hands in his pockets turning his head from side to side and made his way back inside catching Kate out of the corner of his eye wheeling through the kitchen. "Kate, have you met Rebecca yet?" She was on her way to the operations room to bring Julie up to speed.

"No, not yet. I left her a note though: hang out or check out our downtown."

Clay tried not to be paranoid, but a knot was building in his stomach. He went to his and Kate's small liquor cabinet and poured the remains of half-empty bottles of coconut rum, lemon vodka, and brandy down the sink. Tubs watched him with a raised eyebrow but said nothing. He picked up the six-pack he'd brought with him and protected it in his arms then reluctantly put them in the beer fridge. Clay briefly eyed the wine rack, where three bottles of the Stoppas favorite aged Malbec lay on their sides, but decided to leave them. He wasn't anyone's jailor, and besides, he'd invited Rebecca into their home; he'd just have to trust her. He knotted the bag and carried it to the recycling area.

"I'll be back shortly." Clay sauntered to the back door, but made haste once he was out of sight. He jumped in his car and pulled to the end of his drive turning west for no particular reason and worked his way downtown paying more attention to the sidewalks rather than the road. After driving down to the main drag, advancing no quicker than a fast walk he passed by the Grange Farmers Market and the Antique Mall open only on weekends. He then stopped in front of the chic coffee shops where the college students and professors alike enjoyed some social time.

"Not her style," he muttered to himself. Clay pulled up to the window of the B & W and thought he recognized her silhouette on a barstool. Parking was not an issue mid-week, as he practically pulled onto the three oversized stairs leading to the entrance adjacent to the ramp.

"Can I buy you a coffee?" Clay approached from behind. He watched Rebecca try and hide the bus information.

"I bet you say that to all the gals."

"I do."

"Does it work?" Rebecca smiled pushing the schedule under her purse.

"Only on those I know." Clay pretended not to see her poor sleuth like methods.

"Twelve cups is my limit, and I went over that about two hours ago."

Clay threw down some cash and within moments a slew of take out was handed over.

"Then let me give you a ride home."

"Boston?" Her voice quietly cracked.

"No… my home. A few days remember?"

"I'm not sure about this…"

"I can well imagine. I'm a stranger and I have lured you back here. Rebecca, do one thing for me: don't leave until you have had a chance to spend some time with Kate. And don't judge my wife by her friend. We are going at this investigation hard this weekend. I can fill you in if you are interested, but after this weekend, it's just Kate and I, so please stick around long enough to really meet her."

She nodded as they hopped in his beater.

"Were you checking up on me?" Rebecca checked the time. "Not that I can blame you."

"No, I needed a break from the guest," he lied. "You'll see what I mean when we get back."

"Did you eat?"

"Yah. Chuck wouldn't let me pay when he found out I was your guest. He thinks I'm Kate's sister."

Clay looked at her in a different light. She was certainly pretty enough. "I could see that."

They strolled into the kitchen; Clay set down dinner and turned to the games room. 'Kill the Bastard', was the new operative title on the whiteboard; 'catch' had been stroked out.

"Who are you?" No hellos, no introductions, no niceties. Julie just couldn't resist.

"Our house guest, and that's why you're relegated to the small room." Clay jumped for joy from the inside all the while answering in a protective tone, then introduced Rebecca as a friend of the family. Rebecca scanned the room then landed on Tubs. They stared one another down.

"Tubs, have you seen a ghost or something?" Clay looked over at his friend.

"No, I apologize. Rebecca, is it?" They shook hands and kept their first encounter to themselves.

Kate was much more welcoming. Dressed in an oversized Columbus blue Duvall College sweatshirt and dark navy sweatpants, her hair was pulled up in a ponytail, showing off her long slender neck she rolled over with a big smile.

"I'm sorry you have walked into this." She pointed at 'mission control'. "This will wrap up over the weekend and we can get acquainted then. It's all part of our effort to…"

"Catch or Kill the Bastard." Rebecca gestured at the screen. "Yeah, I guess we are a little punchy… already. That's not exactly politically correct."

"Sounds like a good goal to me."

"I guess we have that in common." Both women reflected on the obvious.

"I am honored to meet you, Kate; you are all Clay ever talks about."

"And you are very tolerant of my husband and his recent antics." They both smiled and turned in time to watch Clay set off to the kitchen. "Chicken." The smiles turned to spontaneous laughter.

"I don't want to hold you up so…" She looked around the room. Tubs and Julie were back on focus. "I'm just going to my room. I found a trashy novel beside the bed. I hope you don't mind if I turn in early."

"There are no such things in this house, our books are both educational and inspirational; a previous guest must have left it behind." Kate laughed, her perfect white teeth gleamed. "Hey, we'll call you down for Chinese later."

"Sounds great and thanks again, Mrs. Stoppa and it's a pleasure to finally meet you."

"It's Kate; Mrs. Stoppa was Clay's mom. Am I really that old?"

"Sorry, then Kate it is."

Rebecca made her way towards the stairs and glanced into the study. She stopped in her tracks. Never had she seen so many books in someone's home. Three walls were floor to ceiling bookshelves with a sliding ladder to reach the top shelves. They were filled with paperbacks and hardbacks, some pushed deep into the shelves others pulled out, some horizontal, others stacked.

I wonder if they would notice if I just created a little path between the fridge and this room!!

***

Kate, Clay, and Tubs gathered around the flat screen. Julie completed her own survey of the 'State of the Union' then conducted an overview of the direction she was going to take the investigation.

"Okay, I have set some limitations, borders if you will. We have our incident; we have all of the details. Now it is important to try and link other cases to ours, look for patterns and see where this takes us. We will sort by physical evidence. For example: White, Latino, Native, or Black. We will sort by type of crime, example drive-through shooting, involving theft, not involving theft, using a gun, or knife or something else. We will sort by locations, type of business, pharmacy fast food, and on and on."

Tubs scribbled in his notepad, a hazard of the trade; Kate undulated back and forth in her chair, a habit when concentrating; and Clay leaned on his chin with a look of defeat.

"We will also look at criminal profiling, for example, the behavior of the criminal. It is important to do this correctly; we don't ignore all of the physical evidence and solely base our efforts on the behavior of the offender. We will look for patterns such as the degree of risk taken. Remember: our assailant could be in jail already and if he is still out there, or caught, served time and back out there, then we need to see if there are any patterns showing his method. It is likely he is getting more refined."

"Remember that no two cases are exactly the same; we have to respect that when we are trying to link them," Tubs interjected.

"We need to find the motive, which can lead us somewhere," Julie continued.

"So, we are just going to narrow this down because we have data that links up now, and then we create a profile—and poof! I have been at this for thirteen years we don't just match things up over Chinese!" Clay was understandably cynical as he pointed with some chopsticks he had inadvertently picked up.

"Easy," Kate whispered.

"Sorry." And he was.

Tubs continued, ignoring Clay's cynicism. "Remember, criminals plan and think about their crimes before they act. It's not just something they set out to do that morning."

"Our guy planned it out," Clay added.

"Indeed."

"What's in all of these boxes?" Clay looked on the tables and then under the tables. He glanced into the emptied dining room.

Tubs and Kate nodded at one another. "Our case is over here, the Philly case which is of course an ongoing investigation, is to the left, and then we have codes corresponding to various types of crimes over here. For instance, if we need to source out a specific victimization, then we need the various state codes for the type of crime. Some states actually use the county jurisdiction codes for the city file numbers; some F.B.I. files create their own set of codes. It's all very confusing, but we can link up to most crimes if we follow the rules of the state that the occurrence took place in."

"Why was this not done thirteen years ago?" Clay spoke up.

Tubs responded. "We did not have the sharing of data like we do today, so this collection of information was completely disjointed on all levels."

"He's right." Julie jumped in.

"I will warn you," Tubs continued, "it's far from perfect. You are dealing with federal versus state jurisdiction, as well as county versus state."

"And even state versus state." Julie once again was getting a word in edgewise.

"Whatever," Clay whispered then smiled at Kate when she gave him the 'stink-eye'.

"Combine this information with an accumulation of similar crimes and the ability to sort them, we now have something to work with," Tubs finally finished.

"Let me give you an example." Tubs stood up.

"Allow me," Julie suggested.

"No, no, I got this." Tubs zoned in on Kate. "Ten years ago, or even two or three years ago, if you asked me to give you all of the drive-thru shootings involving a van, by a white guy, in the middle of the afternoon and there were no arrests, I would suggest you were on crack. The databases are now working for us."

Clay interjected. "Well how many violent crimes are we sifting through here, exactly?"

"Well... there were over four million violent crimes in our great nation last year, and over fifteen million property crimes. Shit, Massachusetts had over thirty thousand violent crimes last year alone."

"This is a needle in the haystack; I should just throw a dart and go check out another potential sighting." Clay sat back a little confused.

"No, we will narrow it down substantially, Clay." Kate was confused by his discouragement.

Clay wanted to believe 'the bastard' was out there, and Tubs was of a mind that law enforcement would ultimately win out and he was behind bars somewhere. He was interested in looking at single and multiple offenders that had been captured then study their styles, motive, and then hopefully place the criminal in some prison somewhere.

Julie stood at a chalkboard and the search officially began. "Okay, let's try these parameters. First, we are looking for a white male between twenty-five and forty, over six feet, and involved in drive-thru shootings. The second set, gang-related versus non gang-related."

"Overdressed and tattoos," Kate called out.

"Okay, fourth... worked alone, the fifth a stolen car." Julie scribbled. "Add that the vehicle was abandoned. Let's try splitting the incidents geographically, looking in the Greater Boston area, then Massachusetts and finally, the Eastern seaboard, thereby creating alternative databases."

"Chinese?"

"No, Caucasian." Clay turned.

"No." Tubs pointed at the food from the B&W. He was looking to feed his massive system and was staring into the kitchen, specifically at the island where stacked neatly were the boxes from a few hours ago.

"Shit, I forgot." Clay jumped up. They chuckled. Kate wheeled to the base of the stairs and called for Rebecca.

They set up the buffet on the corner of the pool table. Rebecca joined the group, lightly sprinkling small portions on her paper plate. She smiled politely as she inched her chair a little farther back than necessary. Glancing around the room with her large doe eyes, the conversation went faint. Papers were flung everywhere, the large-screen TV had a graph image on it, and one laptop, just to Julie's right, mimicked the big screen. A tripod with large chart paper was covered with words circled and arrows pointing in all directions splayed in green and blue markers.

Laughter then tension dominated, clearly a group that had some history.

So, this is how the professorial types come to conclusions. How exciting, how intimidating.

She was so wrapped up in the moment, she completely missed a query as all eyes were on her. "Sorry, I was daydreaming, what was the question?"

"Who do you like to read? Clay said you were an avid reader." Kate focused in on Rebecca as if no one else was in the room, a terrific trait.

"Oh, sorry, of course." Rebecca cleared her throat. "A wide range really, depending on my mood. I usually have two or three on the go at a time, maybe…"

"Oh, I can't do that," Julie interjected. "I am all over a book until it absolutely bores me then I move on. I'm not into that completion thing."

"That's all well and good, Julie, but Kate was asking Rebecca." Clay pointed with his chopsticks again.

"I keep the books in separate rooms, one by my bed, one in the living room, and one, well, by the toilet." Rebecca was quiet.

Everyone but Julie laughed.

"Yah, I'm kinda the same," Tubs interjected.

"Porn mags don't count." Kate reeled one off, and the room erupted. "What are you looking for?" Kate turned her attention to Julie as the laughter carried on. "Oh, I remember, Julie, you and your ground pepper, stay…"

Kate leaned on the table with both hands propped herself out of the chair and turned. Of course, as soon as she went to use her legs, she crumpled to the floor. Tubs came flying around the table; he brought his formidable arm across Clay's chest then reached down to Kate.

She was in considerable discomfort, as the edge of her chair pushed into her side.

"Don't try to talk," Tubs' voice was calm and controlled, unlike that of Julie and Clay who were pointing fingers in the background. "Kate. It's okay. You have winded yourself, and you have done this before I am sure. Stay calm; don't try to move just yet. I will help you up once you get your breath back... just stay calm." Tubs' voice was deep and gentle. Their eyes locked and he smiled.

"Oh, I got winded once. It was in a race; it was just awful," Julie piped up.

"Thanks, Jules." Clay's sarcasm was at the forefront.

After what seemed like an eternity, Kate and the chair were set upright. She was covered in chicken fried rice; it was in her hair, her mouth and all over her clothes. But the worst was the embarrassment. Her face was flush, and before Clay could help her with paper towels, she grabbed the plate and in a fit of rage tossed it like a Frisbee across the room. The level of tension came in like a fog off the Atlantic, thick and harsh. No one said a word or made eye contact.

For a fleeting second, she had simply forgotten she was in a chair. "I hate him, and I hate who I have become." Kate composed herself long enough to wheel out of the room. "Show's over."

That night would forever be engrained in their psyches.

The area was cleaned up in a flash, and the four sat playing with scenarios waiting for Kate to reappear.

After a suitable period of time, Clay started towards the stairs, but heard Kate attaching to the lift. She came downstairs in a dressing gown and wet hair, no makeup and no smile. "Well, that was a little embarrassing, and I apologize."

"Don't," Clay suggested.

"Never," came another voice.

Rebecca spoke up. "I went into a Starbucks; actually, it was the one we met at, Clay, shortly after the shooting. I just picked up my coffee and a car backfired on the street. I hit the deck, coffee everywhere. A lady cried out, SHE'S BEEN SHOT, and there was paranoia everywhere."

"Seriously?" Clay asked.

"Yup. I ended up giving a statement to the police, now that's embarrassing."

Everyone smiled and Kate nodded thanks. After a few moments Julie was back at the computer and Rebecca excused herself and snuck off to her book in the guest room.

They played with various scenarios and parameters all evening long, mixing and matching, looking at a variety of incidents and analyzing patterns.

Ideas moved back and forth; the number of cases shifted dramatically, from hundreds of thousands nationally, to less than two thousand in the State of Massachusetts. Add a parameter, remove a parameter, the swings were dramatic. When two a.m. rolled around, Julie felt she was making progress, Clay was ready to shoot himself, and Tubs was ready to keep going all night, his time to shine. Clay drifted into the kitchen and watched his friend from a distance. Tubs was sharing a story with Julie, as Kate listened in. He looked tired or sick or both, thinner than he had ever seen him, not that he couldn't stand to shed a few more pounds. Something was up, but he hadn't exactly had a heart to heart with his friend for quite some time.

He glanced at the stove; the clock read too late. It was time to call it an evening; so Clay opened a high cupboard, reached to the back left corner and found a baggy. He opened it up, stuck his nose in close, then walked into the games room and handed the joint to Julie.

They all smiled and headed outside. The evening's effort had officially come to a close.

11

Rebecca was the first to rise; she was, after all, deep into R.E.M. by the time the troops had settled down. Once again, her first thought was that of peace and tranquility followed by waves of guilt. Keep busy, she thought, help out. She made her way to the kitchen and stopped in her tracks. A localized storm had moved through the games room and swirled into the kitchen: pizza boxes left open, Chinese strewn everywhere and of course the proverbial ice-cream-straight-from-the-carton remains. Late night cannabis can spur a rebirth of appetite.

Cleaning this mess was a formidable task; cleaning it in a strange kitchen was daunting. First things first, she scanned the kitchen counters that spanned three walls then turned to the center island: coffee. There were two things that were consistent in her life, cleanliness and coffee, almost to the point of being compulsively obsessive. Rebecca sorted through cupboards and found a percolator with a control panel rivaling that of a fighter jet's cockpit. Once the first drops of found their way into the pot, she patted herself on the back then started the clean-up. After a solid hour of scrubbing and tidying, she managed some semblance of order. Rebecca was refueled with a couple of mugs of coffee under her belt, and then drifted into the 'situation room'.

Where to start?

She scanned the room.

I honestly think a pack of dogs would leave less of a trail.

Upon first glance all she could see was sheets of paper covered in marker, torn and shredded everywhere, garbage pails overflowing, boxes of files opened and spilled, some piled on one another.

Rebecca squinted, and then almost jumped out of her pajamas. A grunt and snort not unlike that heard from a prehistoric creature similar to a pterodactyl came from under the pool table. Tubs rolled onto his back and began snoring. He was rolled up in a blanket, a pillow elevating his feet and a knitted green tea cozy on his head.

Rebecca's phone was upstairs, otherwise...

By ten a.m. a second pot of coffee was brewed, and the two rooms looked better than they had twenty-four hours previous.

Rebecca decided that, if she was going to stay for a few days as Clay had suggested, she was going to be useful. She didn't want to leave the Stoppas feeling like she owed anyone anything.

Breakfast. Rebecca perused the kitchen with her eyes; bit her bottom lip as she had a tendency to do, then spun towards the fridge. Bacon, sausage, eggs, and toast; how hard can it be? Rebecca was not a breakfast person, a trait that usually comes to those who rise before noon, which she did not, so she was eliminated from this meal. How hard can it be, she thought to herself again, as she pulled out pans and plates and of course the food.

With the pound of bacon simmering and the sausage under the grill at 500 degrees, the kitchen took on a pleasant aroma. "Next the eggs... no the toast... I will do some toast, lots of toast and then throw on the eggs as everyone wakes up," she mumbled. Sunny side up or none at all she thought. Rebecca spun around for a coffee. This is good she thought, okay... bacon's on, sausage cooking, and toast ready to pop so now another pot of coffee. "Oh shit," she mumbled a little louder as she raced over to the stove. Oven mitts. She opened the oven to the sound of spitting grease and blackened wizened up sausage tops. "Shit," again a few octaves higher. She spun for the oven mitts. "Where the fuck are the oven mitts, way to think ahead, Rebecca," she mocked herself. "Ahhh fuck, the bacon." It was sizzling and spitting across the oven.

Rebecca settled for a series of tea towels and managed to pull out the sausage, grazing her forearm on the top of the oven, the intense heat searing through the towels into her fingertips. "Fuck that hurt." A little louder again.

And then it happened. Up until now, Rebecca vs. the Stoppa kitchen was in a dead heat but then... the toast was jammed and a spiral of smoke was rising to the ceiling, but not just any ceiling, it was the state of the art Stoppa kitchen ceiling that set off not one, not two, but seven smoke detectors scattered in bedrooms, bathrooms, the kitchen, of course, and the guys' den.

Clay leapt to his feet as the siren raced through his brain like a freight train screeching around a sharp bend. He landed on his feet and stalked the room as if making a throw to first base; Kate scrambled for her chair and lifted herself with the grace and strength of an Olympic gymnast. Julie called out, "What the fuck," and stumbled into clothes. Any clothes, the first clothes she came upon. She slept nude and grabbed what looked like a tracksuit, puce in color, straight out of the '80s with a double stripe, all that was missing were the pompoms.

Tubs bolted straight upright and hammered his head on the bottom of the pool table. "Oh fuck." He had never been hit that hard, and he fell straight back onto the ground, tea cozy and all.

"Cocksucker," Rebecca screamed. "What the fuck, how do I… FUCK ME, oh for FUCK sakes!"

Clay was the first to arrive on the scene and between the two of them they put out the breakfast BBQ, and opened all the windows and doors.

The cobwebs were lifting with each passing shot of adrenaline in Julie's head, they weren't young kids any more and with each passing year, a bender like that of the previous evening took an additional toll on the recovery time.

Kate wheeled through the kitchen clearly unimpressed, but did what any good host would, and ordered take out from chucks. "No one was hurt and the smoke will clear so let's move on."

"I beg to differ." Tubs had rolled to his side, tea cozy and all, and was running his fingers over the giant goose egg on his forehead. The green knitted helmet on his head had everyone in stitches. He reached up and pulled it off. "Oh shit, I thought this was an Eagles toque."

Rebecca continued to clean up. She wanted to disappear. Not only was the breakfast a disaster, she had clearly upset the crew with horrific first impressions. "Did the smoke alarm mask my profanity?"

"That makes more sense now," Tubs continued to rub his head, "I thought I was dreaming about being called to a domestic." Everyone laughed except Rebecca.

She tossed a tea towel on the counter rubbed her eyes and bolted down the hall and up the stairs.

Julie had already moved on, her lack of social skills rising to the top. "Well, I guess we got an earlier start than expected." She made her way to the whiteboard, throwing out scenarios and re-establishing criteria. No drugs were taken, no money was taken, a van was stolen, both pickup trucks and cars were used, no arrests, a possible inside job. We have no socio-economic background of the accused; we have no place of residence, thus no relation to the location of crime. The list went on and on and on, and the circle became larger and larger. But where was it leading? And were they getting any closer to 'the bastard'?

Kate glanced at her computer, then excused herself and wheeled to the bottom of the stairs. Sometimes the stair lift felt so unhurried, and this was definitely one of those times. After a light tap on the door, Rebecca responded and Kate entered.

"Oh Kate... umm, I am really sorry." Rebecca was seated in the rocking chair an afghan around her slender frame, she set down a paperback.

"Seriously?" and they both laughed. "Well, I did a similar thing as you did, minus the superlatives, one of the first times I spent time with Clay's mom and dad. Mine was pancakes... not quite as many fire alarms... so let's start again, and I never even had a chance to thank you for the clean-up. It must have looked brutal."

"It did." Rebecca stared at her feet.

"Well, listen, come join us if you wish, the more heads in this the better... besides, you and I had similar days."

***

By three in the afternoon, it was time for a break. Up to this point, Rebecca had slipped in and out of the room, cleaning up, refilling coffees, and then disappearing to the study where she would pick up a book, peruse it then move to an equally compelling novel.

Rebecca put out veggies and cold cuts... a safer choice. She loved the Stoppas' kitchen and with each turn, she discovered the latest and greatest of gadgetry. She got the biggest kick out of guessing the specific use of the dozens of specialty culinary tools.

She was mesmerized by the efficient design; the kitchen was huge, even an island towards the center did not close off any laneways. The spaciousness was paramount in the redesign as Kate's challenges were of course front and center in all of the renovations. Rebecca paused for a second and counted off eight floor tiles wide and then the same north-south. She chuckled to herself. In the sixty-four square feet of space filled with nothing but laneway, Rebecca could fit her complete apartment. She carried on, now daydreaming of having a kitchen like this someday, in her very own house.

From time to time, Rebecca caught Kate watching her. Each time she felt a little uneasy thinking she was stepping way over her boundaries, but each time felt a certain sense of relief when Kate nodded and smiled at her.

There was a collective stretch and sigh from the gang in the games room and they broke while lunch was being discussed.

Rebecca wanted to prepare lunch. Clay chose to stay back with Rebecca and followed her around the kitchen assisting her with 'whereabouts' questions, while the Kate and Julie went for a stroll. Tubs found a bowl of chips and a coke, uncovered a La-Z-Boy and the flat screen, and flicked to the major league baseball network.

"No love lost between you two." Rebecca pointed her utensil at the back of Julie's head, as she and Kate disappeared down the stairs.

"It's that obvious?"

"Plain as day. How'd they meet anyway?"

"You want to know?"

"Sure, I find that interesting; the coincidences and events that lead to friendships and such."

"Theirs was more of an event really. One particular event in a sport they both embraced with their entire might."

"Go on." Rebecca was busy prepping a meal; Clay was more of a sous chef, following her around and responding to her gestures.

"Julie and Kate had a very special bond, one that does not form that easily between two type-A personalities"

"Julie's more of an A-plus."

"Yah," Clay chuckled, "both girls arrived at Oregon State on cross-country running scholarships and were partners on one of the best teams in the country."

"Why is it always so important to be on the best team?"

"Well it's not I guess, but in their case, because they were on a formidable team, they received incredible scholarships."

"I see."

"Julie and Kate were under tutelage of this Swedish superstar for two seasons. Kate learned a lot from Anoka: toughness, strategy, work ethic, tenacity and grit. Julie learned as well: win at all costs, look out for number one, and leave everyone else behind."

Rebecca smiled. "You really love that girl.

"I do. After two successful seasons riding the wave of Anoka, it was time for someone else to receive the baton, and the Ducks turned to Julie." Clay rummaged for a spatula and handed it to Rebecca.

"Was that it? Kate wasn't number one?"

"No not at all, Julie earned it. Kate was a strong second."

"How many on a team?"

"Four. So how it works, the four runners line up, one behind the other on the start line. Scoring is totaling the lowest combined placements of runners one through four, so the team with the best four finishes combined won the Nation's Cup."

"So, the girls became close competing?"

"No, not exactly… it happened at one particular race in Lincoln, Nebraska, the stage for the national championship that year, and the Ducks were seeded sixth in the nation."

"How exciting."

"Kate tells it better, but I love the story. Am I boring you?"

"God, no."

"Okay, so you have two hundred and sixty well-tuned athletes lined up at the gate, with over half of the athletes capable of winning. It's a big deal, most never even get to compete at this level."

Rebecca continued to chop, dice, and create; Clay filled the sink with yet another pile of dishes to clean. "You tell this like you were there!"

"I practically was, this story has been told and retold. Kate was at her best in university, she had it all, the grades, the athleticism, the confidence to conquer all."

"Well, she may have been all those things, but from what I have seen and heard since I've arrived, she is at her best in a room with you."

"Really? I don't see it that way."

"Of course not, you live it; I'm an outside observer. Anyway, sorry, continue with the story."

"Okay, yes. At a state championship the start of a race is malicious. At the national championship the first 400 meters are an outright slaughter. The athletes push, kick, punch, trip, spike and step on each other."

"Huh, sounds like public transit." Rebecca pointed at a spatula and Clay reciprocated.

"It was such an adrenalin rush."

"Yah, and so is a black coffee and a thriller novel on a warm couch." They both laughed. "Sorry, carry on."

"Okay, so the first 400 meters are where races are won and lost. Julie was particularly malevolent and was famous for maiming her rivals. She could be ruthless when winning or losing was at stake."

"A good person to have on your side."

"True, and Kate was uncharacteristically spiteful in the opening stages of this race, doing whatever was necessary to stay on the heels of Julie."

"How fast do they run?" Rebecca wiggled her toes thinking about a warm couch and a good movie.

"The winner of this race would complete the course in less than twenty minutes, nothing short of a hard-core sprint. The majority of the race is in a forest or farmers' fields."

"So, no one sees them for a while?"

"Yah, they disappear until near the end usually."

"It must be brutal on the body."

"And nervous for the spectators. You are just waiting to see who comes out of the tree line first."

"Cool."

"Yah, so in that race they come out with less than a half mile left in the race. By that point, lactic acid burns your calves and thighs, your arms feel like they weigh fifty pounds each."

"They must have been in awesome shape."

"For sure, however, all the training is thrown out the window at this stage. Now it's all guts. It becomes a battle of wits and mental toughness."

Rebecca had stopped preparing the meal and stood leaning on a butcher's knife, its tip perched precariously on the block.

"So, they came down the final stretch, both in the top ten and Julie started to pull away from Kate, but lost her footing, twisting off the path, and somersaulted over some fallen branches. She came to an abrupt stop against the trunk of a tree, her right shin taking the brunt of the shock. Kate said she was thunderstruck and without losing a stride, she leaped off the track, grabbed Julie by her pinny, and hoisted her six-foot frame to her feet. Kate said she didn't remember her being heavy with the adrenalin and all."

"Oh my God."

"Julie was writhing in pain, screaming for Kate to let her be, but Kate would have nothing to do with it. Julie's first steps were unbearable; her right leg could maintain a minimal amount of weight. Kate lifted her arm and helped her for the first couple of steps, before Julie developed a gait better described as a fast limp getting her to the finish line."

"Oh my God."

"Kate crossed in eighth, her best race ever, a personal best and a medal for individual honors, and Julie twelfth. The combined totals for Oregon were ninety-seven points, giving them the championship."

"So best buds then?"

"Well, Julie was humbled by the experience; she had never been a team player, and certainly did not deserve that unselfish camaraderie on any given day."

"So that sealed the deal."

"Kate and Julie remained fierce competitors during their final year, but off of the course, Julie softened ever so slightly and turned to Kate for friendship."

"That's an awesome story."

"A very unlikely friendship, in my opinion, but has stood the test of time." Clay grew silent and stared off into the distance. "Julie was one of the first to visit Kate after the accident and spent as much time as her escalating career would allow. She flew in and out of Philadelphia to be in Kate's company during the extremely trying first year of rehabilitation. I will give her that much, anyway."

"Do they see much of each other today?"

"It has been over a year since the two of them had spent any time together," Clay grabbed a tea towel. "I'll tell you this, her deportment this weekend was as unobtrusive as it had been in years, and even though she has taken the lead role in the study, she is tolerable… just."

***

Union Street, Gremlin, Pennsylvania was splendid at any time of the year, but in the spring, it was stupendous and could grace the cover of any coffee table book cover. The center boulevard was lined in eastern redbud trees; the branches filled with deep pink flowers that would soon give way to a soft, round, vibrant green, delicate leaf. Tulips, azaleas, tiger-eye sumacs, flocks, Virginia blue bells, and hellebores littered the sculpted gardens along this showcase street. Combine all of this with mature willow and maple trees, and the neighborhood was a breathtaking spectacle; it was the best Mother Nature had to offer.

"What did you ever do with your trophies when you moved into the city condo? Surely it's not that big of a place." Kate pushed along.

"They are in storage; I stopped looking at them after…" She caught herself. "I pay God-knows-how-much a year to keep them in a safe place, with no intention of ever looking at them again. It's not like Cadence and I plan to have a family."

"Maybe that will change."

"What did you do with yours?"

"They are in storage as well, in the basement… with all of Clay's paraphernalia. He refused to bring his back out after the accident as well. I thought maybe with the addition off the backroom, but he wouldn't hear of it."

"He's a good man."

Kate looked at her sideways. "I should be recording this."

"Yah I retract that… Clay's okay."

"You can't stand my husband."

"We just bug the shit out of one another."

"Boy, I have to meet this Cadence."

Julie smiled. "Yes, you should. Well you should have some time soon, right? I know I always bring this up, but when you called me you assured me this is the last summer; the trail ends here. So, are you sure this is the end?"

"He promised."

"Burn the files?"

"Yup, we had it out and Clay will be good to his word."

"Well, we need to make some real progress here." Julie and Kate moved along in silence for a short time enjoying the colors, the textures and the sweet smells of the season.

Julie's curiosity got the best of her. "How do you know Rebecca?"

Kate smiled and rolled her eyes. She was wheeling in front of Julie so her facial expressions were hidden. "A random act of fate, I guess."

"I don't believe in random," Julie responded. "Random happens every day; we have random acts of goodness and kindness that cross our paths, we run into people randomly; we choose how to deal with these encounters either positively, negatively, or not at all."

"Pretty deep."

"I know right!"

"Carry on."

"I, of course, am very familiar with negative random."

"True."

"And I've learned a lot from my ordeal."

"That's for sure."

"I had to in order to hold my sanity."

"I can only imagine."

"Random is what I came away with and I had to accept the act of random. I wonder if Rebecca looks at her series of events after being shot in that manner."

"She was in the kiosk right."

"She was."

"Where was she shot?"

"Shoulder."

"Rebecca as it turns out was a key player in Clay's investigation and through a random series of events, she ended up here."

"How long is she staying?"

"Not sure. I am choosing to deal with her random appearance on my doorstep in a positive manner."

The women rounded the neighborhood, including the bridge over the falls and the downtown.

The subjects moved around nicely and since they tried to 'never dwell on the past', Kate questioned Julie about her new partner and her interests.

Julie paused for a slew of pedestrians then commented on the hustle and bustle of the downtown. Kate was proud of the town, and took Julie's compliments to heart. Without Kate's perseverance, the general ambiance of the town would have been much different. After an hour, the women were recharged and joined the others in the situation room.

Rebecca gathered them into the dining room for a late lunch. With the help of Clay, she had prepared a pasta salad with zucchini and cherry tomatoes, ham and cheese macaroni salad, pineapple rhubarb crisp and iced tea. It was displayed beautifully on the dining room table. She stood back and was quite pleased with her handiwork, and no smoke alarms. Lunch was amazing, and Rebecca insisted on cleaning up so they could get back to it. Kate loved the arrangement.

The next couple of hours were dismal. They ran in circles throwing one parameter after another trying to link their own incident and its geographic location to various sightings of the perpetrator, based on Clay's pushpin map. Maybe if there was an incident in a town that had a sighting, they could match up the composites and this might lead to something.

"Composites have their misgiving that's for sure," Julie piped up with an offhanded comment. "People just make shit up under pressure."

Clay and Rebecca shared a look; he can remember how hard this must be on Rebecca... that life has been hard on her since... who knows when, and now it is HER 'bastard' they're trying to catch too, since he's the reason her life spiraled downwards too.

The number of cases ran into the thousands, the direction of the work was losing its focus quickly and, what made matters worse, the four of them had no idea what to do next.

"Where were you guys going that afternoon?" Rebecca carried a tray of coffees into the room. She didn't look up, as she concentrated on her step avoiding a catastrophe if she stumbled.

Everyone stopped and looked over. Rebecca said so little so when she did utter a syllable everyone listened.

"A ball game." Kate was the first to respond.

Rebecca set down the tray and began handing out the cups. "What if you looked at incidents that took place on the day of a ball game?" Her voice was tentative.

"Why?" Tubs looked over.

"Why not, you've got shit here."

Clay stood up like a schoolboy. "Do it. She might be onto something."

"Rebecca, grab that group of files from last week, the Philly drive-thru." Clay pointed.

"Please," Kate added.

She complied.

"There was a game that day, correct?" Clay's voice was showy.

Rebecca nodded.

"Where was the incident?" Julie was taking the lead once again.

"Chick-fil-A," Kate responded.

"Yeah, I know it. I have been to enough games there to remember it. You can walk to it from the stadium, bring it up… please." Clay pointed at the flat screen.

Julie complied. Sure enough, using Google maps, they analyzed the neighborhood. The fast food shop was on Walnut Street, about two minutes from Citizen Bank Park, home of the Phillies.

Julie took the helm; Tubs and Kate moved to the computers. "Okay, let's break this down. Start with violent crimes on the day a major league baseball game is played, everything dates back thirteen years."

Clay of course knew that there was a MLB game every day from the beginning of April to the end of September every year, with the only exception being the three-day all-star break. They were easily able to input these dates as one of the parameters.

"Ten million plus, now we are getting somewhere," Tubs responded with a sarcastic tone.

"White males?"

"Three million plus."

"Drive-bys."

"Six hundred and fifty thousand plus."

"Drive-thru, drive-bys."

"This will take a few moments."

"Drive-thru, drive-bys that targeted pregnant women?" Clay whispered.

"No. The bullet had deflected. I wasn't the intended target." Kate turned to Clay then they both turned to Rebecca as she was staring at the floor since *she* was the intended target. Kate apologized… "I wasn't… I didn't think…"

"It's okay. We were both victims of fate that day." There was a heavy pause.

Rebecca poured coffee and as if by a matter of fact said, "How about we try drive-by at the drive-thru, must be in a city where a major league ball park is located?"

Clay looked over. Rebecca did not raise her head. He rhymed off all of the cities and their ballparks.

Again, the permutations and commutations were inserted into each of the affected cities. They waited and sipped on coffee. Clay glanced at his watch, six thirty, grabbed the phone and hit the speed dial.

"Chuck, yah it's Clay. There are five of us, so could you pull something together?" He listened. "Sure, twenty minutes is great."

The computer finally finished its search. "Four hundred and twenty-eight. We couldn't include Toronto, since there is no jurisdiction in our data banks."

"Okay, now the assailants were not caught."

"Three hundred twelve."

Julie thought for a moment. "Now the crime has no theft involved."

"Eighty-four."

"What about tattoos?" Clay added.

"No, that is an assumption. We have no proof that our bastard had a tattoo, we just know he was overdressed. Besides, everyone has a tattoo nowadays," Julie noted

"Do you have a tattoo?" Tubs was snooping.

"Does your *wife*?" Julie retorted.

"Okay, time to go get the Chinese," Clay broke in. He motioned to Rebecca. "We'll go. You guys keep trying some things here."

Clay and Rebecca drove to the B&W. He was quiet for the most part and they pulled up in front of the restaurant. "Rebecca, you were amazing back there."

"I just want to help. I really appreciate everything you guys have done for me."

"We haven't done anything yet."

"Yes, you have."

Clay held the door for Rebecca and she slipped up to the same stool she sat at on her previous visit. She had a chill and shook her shoulders, then pushed the hair behind her ears. Her expression was always difficult to read, but clearly, she was feeling pretty good about herself at that very minute.

Chuck handed over bag after bag after bag. "You must know I have Tubs over." They both laughed, and Clay handed over some cash. No dollar amounts were discussed.

The situation room was buzzing upon their return. The Chinese food was laid out on two collapsible tables. Rebecca sourced out the ground pepper.

After a couple of washroom breaks, Julie stepped up to the push-pinned map, which she and Tubs had evidently been arguing over for the last fifteen minutes.

Julie shrugged then grabbed some chopsticks and a sweet roll.

"When you do this analysis, are you looking at Greater Boston area, for example, or just the city limits?" Rebecca asked no one in particular.

"Depends on the classifications in each city. Kansas City, for instance, includes crime rates for all of its suburbs. Philadelphia only includes the city boundaries," Tubs responded.

"That's because you would overload the system," Julie remarked. "So, we should do cities only."

There was general assent throughout the room.

A few moments later. "Fifty-eight," Tubs announced.

"All right, fast food only. No pharmacies."

"Thirty-six."

"Two incidents in one day."

"Zero."

Rebecca spoke up for the second time. "Our Burger King is really close to Fenway."

"Good." Julie did a double take at the mystery woman in the corner. "Okay, let's do a ten-mile radius from the ball parks."

Kate and Tubs huddled over a computer. "Twelve."

"Twelve?"

"Yes... twelve."

And then the room went silent.

"Have we actually done something here?" Julie broke the stillness. "Everyone, grab some grub. We have work to do."

Naturally, Tubs was the first to comply. Rebecca and Kate followed suit. Clay grabbed the closest carton and began eating.

"So let me get this right." Clay pointed his chopsticks at the board. "Can we summarize what got us to twelve?"

Kate moved to the flat screen, typing as she spoke. "We've got a drive-thru shooting by a white male, less than ten miles from a ball stadium, where no robbery took place, and there was a ball game on that day, in that city.

"Does this include our incident?"

Kate flipped through the twelve. "Yes. Boston, Burger King, August 19."

Chills worked their way through the room.

"What cities are we talking about here?" Julie was asking the questions again.

"Boston, obviously. Baltimore, Arlington, Detroit, Cleveland, Oakland, St. Louis, Seattle, Kansas, Minnesota, Chicago, and last week in Philly."

"All right keep throwing out ideas here, gang." Julie looked at the flat screen.

"Who was playing besides the home team?" Rebecca ventured.

Julie raised an eyebrow. "Wow, where did you find her? Let's go... It's a leap, but why not?" She grabbed another spring roll and nodded to Tubs.

"Let's see, Boston and..."

"Texas, Nolan Ryan was pitching." Clay interjected.

"Seriously, the pitcher, Clay?" Kate shook her head.

"I know, I know. Okay, so the following: April, Baltimore played Texas as well. Clay continued flipping through the schedule archives on the MLB web site. Arlington was Texas... obviously and Toronto, the Detroit assault was a game day against Texas, Cleveland and Texas again."

Kate looked up the rest. "Texas… every game included the Texas Rangers."

A heavy silence came across the room.

"I think it means the bastard was less than an hour from this house a little over a week ago." Julie referred to the incident in Philly. Julie's voice was calm but deliberate. Everyone stared at inanimate objects not daring to make eye contact. It was just too intense.

"Obviously we have to look at each of these cases, so we need some direction." Julie broke the silence.

"What crazy link is there between major league baseball, and our shooter?" Kate wondered out loud. "Unless of course this is a wicked, cruel coincidence."

"The Texas Rangers and shootings at drive-thru restaurants?" Tubs mumbled. Perplexed and frustrated, the room fell silent again.

"This is the craziest lead since we started this thing," Clay grumbled in disbelief. He was too overwhelmed with the last hour.

Rebecca just sat quietly in the corner observing the dichotomy in the room.

"Tell you what." Tubs sat back and landed his enormous feet on the table. "I do understand how bizarre this is, however, I think we should pull the twelve case files. We have a composite of the guy, contrary to your thoughts, Julie, and maybe we can get lucky matching him with other crimes."

"Let's create a database and look for a couple of things," Tubs continued. "Firstly, let's find a facial match with a digitally aged photo. We can actually age our sketch from thirteen years ago and move it forward year by year, thus matching our best description with that of the incident in each year. Also, we can run priors on anyone we choose."

"Such as?" Julie looked over.

"Well we should look at the Rangers' organization." Tubs continued.

"The players?"

Clay jumped in. "Major league players? Nah. If we are to follow this bizarre direction… then it's a disgruntled employee, or a beleaguered Rangers' fan." Clay laughed at himself. "This is ridiculous. We'd have to look at *thousands* of people—and probably find nothing."

"Still, you never know," Tubs, pointed out. "But I'm not saying it wouldn't be a totally mundane and tedious task."

Rebecca interjected. "Mundane and tedious… right up my alley."

"Okay… so… through the premise of a fraud investigation," Tubs suggested, "I'll get in touch with the City of Arlington and the State of Texas in order to get the payroll information for the Texas Rangers association for the past thirteen years."

"So, you should compile a list and prioritize it beginning with employees of the organization that have been with them during the thirteen-year run." Julie stood over Tubs' shoulder.

"What about the fanbase that fell into the same time frame?" Kate interjected. "That sounds ominous enough don't you think?"

"Yah, provide Rebecca with their names and addresses." Julie delegated as per usual.

"Add in other inquires such as a study of incidents that might spark animosity against the team, like someone losing their job, or shitty compensation rendered."

"Minor leaguers."

"What are they?" Rebecca looked up at Clay.

"Players in the minor systems that may have paid their dues but were never given the opportunity to go up to the show."

"Okay, I will track that listing for Rebecca." Tubs fat fingers were moving overtime.

Hours and hours of hypothesizing, note taking and prioritizing. They were on the verge of watching the sunrise when everyone crashed for a few hours.

Tubs remained awake, jotting notes to himself. He was wired, no sense wasting this energy away. Sleep is overrated, he thought, and was feeling lucky.

***

Sunday morning arrived with intense cruelty. It was getaway day for Julie. They would continue their search without her for the time being and consult by email and Skype. Kate arranged a limo service for the pair, so as to spend as much time together as possible.

Tubs did sleep in his own bed then dropped by the house around noon; he looked completely stressed out, not at all like his more relaxed manner from the evening before. He briefed Rebecca on how to conduct the 'priors check'. She had volunteered for an extremely detailed yet tedious task, one she could not wait to dig into.

With no sign of Clay, Tubs said his goodbyes and left a cell number in case she had any questions. Rebecca watched the giant of a man lumber down the driveway and pause at his cruiser before getting in. Rebecca slipped over to the edge of the window, careful not to be seen as nosey. She watched him fumble with his keys, twice dropping them, then in a fit of rage, slam the door shut when he finally managed to get the vehicle unlocked. Tubs glanced around to see if anyone saw his display, but Rebecca had moved back sheltered by the shutters.

She turned back to the kitchen, her gaze landing on the wine rack for a moment too long. Kate's final words as she headed out the door had been "leave the mess". They had a housekeeper that they would call in for extra duty on Monday.

Rebecca smiled politely and completely ignored the instructions; she was full of energy and needed to keep busy. Busy was her best friend; a busy mind kept her out of mischief. Rebecca's vices were not healthy so she set to making the house right again, before settling down to do some research.

***

Clay had left the house shortly before Tubs arrived. He needed to vent out some seriously pent-up frustration. And when he felt this way, which wasn't infrequently, there was only one place he wanted to be.

Just prior to the incident, Kate and Clay purchased one hundred acres of land twelve miles north of town. The rolling landscape, a combination of hardwood forest and meadow, was intended for a simple rustic cabin to be used on weekends. When Kate announced her pregnancy, Clay envisioned a field of dreams. He wanted to build a ball diamond for his daughter where she could practice fast pitch, and hone her skills straight through to the NCAA. After the gunshot all dreams vanished. The Stoppas lost interest in the project and one hundred percent of their efforts were focussed on the house in Gremlin. For years they didn't even talk about the property; it was too painful. Eventually they decided to hold it as an investment and when the right opportunity came along, they would sell.

    Clay lugged a milk crate of used hardballs from his garage into the trunk of the VW. He made his way north and circled up County Rd. 10. The road was oiled gravel, filled with potholes, certainly the path least taken, just the quiet route Clay was looking for. A left on Side Rd. 11, two miles up a low-grade hill, then a quick right into a makeshift driveway put him on their land. He eased up to the first clearing and rolled towards a dilapidated barn that had to be an original in the community they called Lugside. Clay reached into the back seat and grabbed his Rawlings Heart of the Hide tanned leather twelve-inch closed web ball glove. Inside was a ball signed by his dad. He set that ball on the seat beside him and covered his nose with the open palm of his mitt and took a deep breath. He closed his eyes and savored the smell of the hide. After pacing sixty-six feet and six inches he dropped down a pitching rubber and dug it into the ground. His location was not by chance. He reached into the milk crate, pulled out a dirt stained nine-inch Rawlings 80 cc hardball, rubbed it up with both hands, then slid his left hand into his glove that was neatly pressed between his elbow and his side. Clay turned his attention to the side of the barn and an old faded rectangular target simulating a strike zone, painted white, but faded through the years. Inside the rectangle were four squares in each corner of the representing the perfect location for a strike, 'painting the corner' so to speak.

    Clay wound up, throwing his right knee up to his chest, raising his two hands to the sky, the ball in his right hand, but tucked in his glove. He brought the glove and ball back down to his waist, pulled the ball back and sprung forward with his hips pivoting onto his left leg and following through towards his target: the top left small square, no bigger than the hardball itself. The ball came in at an estimated 70 mph, a soft toss in his books, a good warm-up speed to limber up his bad shoulder.

    The next one thrown as effortlessly as the first but was a couple of miles per hour faster and the third reached 75 mph by his expert opinion.

"Okay, boy blue, show me what you got," Clay muttered to himself visualizing a batter.

From there he got serious, reaching down for ball after ball. "I will" *thwack* "find you. I" *thwack* "I hate what" *thwack* "you" *thwack* "have done" *thwack* "to" *thwack* "my family" *thwack* "my daughter. When I find you" *thwack* "I will not apologize" *thwack* "for my actions." *THWACK*.

Clay reached into the crate and rummaged around. There was only one ball remaining. Below his target rested the balance. "Take back your bullet and give us our daughter back!" Clay reached back and poured in a fastball that had to be approaching 100 mph, fast enough to kill someone. The ball exploded through the top right square, wood splinters burst out, and the ball disappeared into the barn.

His shoulder hurt like hell, but he felt better. At least an aching shoulder is better than the ache that somehow creeps up inside his guts…

And with that last pitch, he just fell to his knees and began to cry. Clay hated the pain and the man. Hate was far too kind a word.

If only he could just let it go.

12

June 7

Over the course of the week, Rebecca had long forgotten about her bus schedule and settled into a routine. She opened her eyes in the early afternoon each time with the same sensation: jubilation, then settled into a wave of guilt. The first vision surrounding her was tranquility, kind-heartedness, and love mixed with support; the room wrapped around her like a comforter on a cold, windy day. She felt a sense of kinship with the Stoppas. They had all been affected by the same random incident and it felt good to know that she was helping them work towards catching the man who had turned them both into victims. The guilt would soon follow and she would shake the overwhelming sensation away with a shower and then a brisk walk to the B&W, probably a fifteen-minute jaunt, grabbing herself a coffee. The morning exercise cleared her head so she could focus on the task at hand. She could never remember a time in her life in which she had a purpose and felt necessary and appreciated.

Rebecca attended an AA meeting downtown at two o'clock, one she discovered in the local rag she flipped through on the first day at the B&W. She concluded that the clientele was a lot more upscale than she was accustomed. She shook a few hands, not many, and agreed to come back the following day, assuming of course she was still in town. She made a mental note to reach out to her sponsor.

After the meeting, Rebecca grabbed a second cup of java and headed back to the Stoppas' abode. She had a little nest set up in the study consisting of a small antique table just large enough for a laptop, an old wooden filing cabinet, and a footstool piled with notes and books. The instructional tutorial on the ins-and-outs of the database from Tubs was enough to get her started and each day she would arrive back at the house shortly after two and dive into the priors' reports. Rebecca began with the Rangers ticket holders, the most daunting of lists. Fraud investigations years earlier gave Tubs a loophole and tenuous connections to access the list. When she came up with an assault or a weapons' charge, she'd jot down the name, but if it was shoplifting or theft under $5000, she's let it go. At the end of the day she would have a list of names she would pass along to Tubs.

Kate would arrive home and wheel into the study, sometimes startling Rebecca, as she was completely engrossed. For the first couple of days, Rebecca sensed that Kate felt slightly uneasy, as a virtual stranger had entered their lives, someone Kate wanted to have complete faith in, but the transition was certainly not instantaneous.

Kate generally had a pleasant facade, so Rebecca had a hard time reading her. Rebecca was more at ease in Clay's company and felt like more of an intruder in Kate's. Some afternoons they would just exchange pleasantries and others Kate would join her in the study, helping to run priors on the potential candidates in the Rangers' organization or those affiliated with the organization. On this particular afternoon, Kate rolled into the living room and pulled out her own laptop, as it was June, and her classroom was heating up for final exams, report cards and school trips. She stayed close enough so the two women could converse occasionally back and forth.

Since the accident, Kate was very committed to remaining self-sufficient and was always reluctant when given the opportunity to accept help. She was of a mind that everything had to be completed by herself or she was admitting defeat. This, however, was changing slightly over the last seventy-two hours since Rebecca came on the scene. Whether it was growing wise in middle age or just tiring more quickly, she succumbed to the constant barrage from Rebecca offering to help out. Whatever the reason, Kate allowed Rebecca to bring her books to the house from the car, to run some loads of laundry through the week, and even do the grocery shopping. Rebecca was desperate to be of any assistance big or small, and Kate was quick to realize it was a form of therapy for Rebecca.

***

Clay was sceptical at best following the weekend's discoveries; he did however think it wise to review the twelve files of the various incidents.

He had no better leads. Maybe he would discover a composite drawing from an eyewitness, or a video surveillance at one of the crime scenes. He wanted anything to prove that this bizarre set of parameters was more than just a coincidence.

Clay picked up the twelve police files downloaded to a stick from Tubs' office. His first task was to visualize the locations of the twelve incidents, so he marked them by date using florescent green push pins on his large-scale map of the States that hung in the corner of the repurposed games room. The north-eastern states were plastered with push pins and notes from years gone by. The twelve new locations stretched into California and Washington State, places with absolutely no markings over the thirteen years of investigation.

A year after their own horrific incident in Boston, twelve fast food places, in twelve separate cities, plastered across America, in a twelve-year time frame, were victimized in a similar fashion to that of their own case. Clay arranged them chronologically: Boston, Baltimore, Arlington, Detroit, Cleveland, Oakland, St. Louis, Seattle, Kansas City, Minnesota, Chicago, New York and last week in Philly. He scanned the police reports and revisited them in no particular order.

The sixth incident was in St. Louis, at Rally's Drive-thru, just two minutes from Busch Stadium, home of the Cardinals. After ordering a chicken sandwich and fries, the assailant shot the drive-thru attendant, a male, in the right shoulder, then sped off in a beaten-up Chevy truck. The assailant drove up Broadway and entered the Interstate 64, ditched the car about an hour west, lit it on fire, then presumably left in another vehicle. The incident occurred about two hours before game time, similar to that of Boston. There were no eyewitnesses that could identify the assailant. The police report was scant at best.

July of the following year, a white male in a stolen tan van accosted Allison Chardreau, the attendant at the Cowgirls Espresso, a lingerie coffee shop and drive-thru on 1st Ave., just minutes from Safeco Field in Seattle. He shot her just above the collarbone; the bullet grazed the side of her neck, a sliver from disaster. The assailant bolted out of the parking lot and tore down University Ave. to the Alaskan Way Viaduct. A vehicle that matched the one at the crime scene was found in Colorado four days later. Again, there were no concrete eyewitnesses, nothing was stolen and it was just hours before game time.

In Chicago, a McDonald's just two and half miles from US Cellular Field, and Sam's Super Burger in Oakland, three and half miles from Alameda County Coliseum, were victims to similar crimes. The Oakland incident that followed Seattle and the Chicago crime was just a year ago.

Nine years ago, in Detroit, at a Cedarland Restaurant, twelve minutes from Comerica Park, the assailant got sloppy. The attacker stopped at the second kiosk and made eye contact with Jo Anne Wilmington before attempting to kill her.

With his gun pointed out the window of a Ford F150 truck the assailant was poised to strike. However, a woman sitting directly behind the assailant in her minivan, saw the gun pointing toward the kiosk window and hammered on the gas, her front bumper crumpled into the trailer hitch of the Ford and likely saved a life. It was the only incident in which no one was shot. There were no arrests.

Clay pulled the composite photo from the file. He sat back in his chair staring at the drawing, recognizing the similarities. Clay was no closer to a motive, but he was persuaded to believe that the shooter in Detroit was the same as the one in Boston. This epiphany stopped Clay in his tracks. Any doubt he'd harbored about the new lead evaporated in an instant.

Who the hell are you? What would possess someone to go to all of this bother from one coast to the other?

The Grand Street Café in Kansas City and a McDonald's in Minnesota were crimes three and four years ago respectively. The quality of the police reports was at an all-time low. Anyone with a criminal mind reading the sloppy reports would conclude that this type of crime closes in on the bottom of the priority chain.

Victimize if you choose to, but the chances of getting caught: slim. After the close call in Detroit, the assailant improved his technique and pulled a balaclava over his face before shooting at each of the attendants. Both received glancing blows as if the intention was to miss rather than maim.

Mike's Fish and Chips in the district of Brooklyn was almost eight miles from Progressive Field in Cleveland Ohio. There were eight drive-thru locations closer to the stadium and much easier routes to the interstates 90 and 480, but as luck would have it, the assailant made this family operation his target. Mike McConnell was only twenty-seven years of age, the father of three young girls and the coach of the local YMCA basketball team. He was on the verge of expanding the restaurant because he had the reputation of having the best fish and chips on the shores of Lake Erie. Mike died of complications from gunshot wounds to the chest. There were no eyewitnesses, and no arrests. Once again, no money was taken, and the incident occurred approximately two hours before the first pitch between the Rangers and Indians.

In Baltimore at Toni's grill, the assailant passed by the single kiosk, never came to a full stop, fired two shots in the arm of Miss Cassandra Future. He then turned on his indicator, calmly made a right-hand turn, then another right onto Martin Luther King Jr. Blvd. The assailant then drove south on Interstate 295, right past Camden Yards, and home of the Orioles. The vehicle was torched in a park on the outskirts of Washington D.C. less than forty-five minutes later. Witnesses were appalled by how nonchalant the driver was. There was a quote from a passerby, 'It's as if he had done this a hundred times. He was so casual as if he was just picking up another order. No squealing tires; it was the middle of the afternoon and he just disappeared into traffic. It made the whole ordeal a much scarier situation.'

Two years after Kate's Boston tragedy, the Rangers were hosting the Toronto Blue Jays in Arlington Texas, on a sultry August evening, as the temperature had cooled to a balmy 88 degrees Fahrenheit. A man dressed in an overcoat with a balaclava hit the attendant of the Jack in the Box drive-thru on Randal Mills Rd. and exited north on highway 360, passing by the ballpark.

Two weeks ago, Philadelphia's Chick-fil-A was the location of his handiwork.

All in all, the assailant's wrecking ball crossed over 13,500 miles, touched down in twelve cities, a man was killed, fourteen were injured in varying degrees, and a the Stoppas lost their daughter. Kate was a bystander to fall at the hands of this madman. Once again… Clay's anger brimmed.

After a quick perusal of each case, Clay began to accumulate questions surrounding each of the incidents. He planned to contact the local authorities in each city to better understand the end result of each investigation. Clay was looking for a break, something unexpected that might lead to the assailant that had graduated to a killer. Surely the investigation in Cleveland was active; after all it involved a murder. He would begin with this file and the one in Detroit, if for no other reason than it was in Detroit.

Clay was struck with mixed emotions. How close was he to discovering the identity of the killer? Were these bizarre sets of parameters leading to this moment, a random set of coincidences, and was his last hurrah a wild goose chase?

13

November 2, Present Day

"Jon, whatever was said in that huddle sure got the boys fired up."

"That's for sure. Boyles didn't have his best stuff here in the top of the sixth and he was hit hard. If it wasn't for some defensive heroics on all three outs, this game could have a whole new complexion."

"I'm a little surprised Lacoste doesn't have the bull pen up and moving."

***

"That was close to the end of the line for your boy." Wolf was paying particular attention to the Yankee bullpen. "How many lives does he have?"

Allan Boyles sat silent, but not for long. "You have no idea the pressure up there. Mere mortals wouldn't even feel the ball; they would be so nervous. You probably couldn't get the ball half way to the plate."

"Where did Rickey learn to handle the stress? I thought that was your job."

"My job? I just cleared the way for him to concentrate on the task at hand, peak at the right times, and learn to excel under the pressure."

"You cleared the path all right."

"Fuck you. You know nothing about Rickey and I, only what you read in the press, which means fuck all."

"Touchy."

"Fuck off."

"Ha."

***

"The bottom of the sixth, the Yankees have a lead of one and have a player in scoring position. Jackson, the Padre's skipper has seen enough. He's going to his bullpen for his middle reliever, Gonzalez."

"The crowd is dancing in the aisles."

***

"We need to prepare for a celebration. You and I have waited a long time for this." The hooded fiend stared straight ahead.

Allan Boyles was freezing cold. The hard liquor emptied from the minibar of his hotel suite could only insulate him for so long. The cold damp evening was giving him chills right up his spine. "Somehow I don't think you are his greatest fan."

"More like someone with a vested interest."

***

"The Padres middle relief has been amazing all season and Gonzalez hasn't lost a step in this playoff run. Using only eight pitches the Yanks are gone 1-2-3. I think it is safe to say that if the starting pitching on the San Diego team wasn't the best in the league, Gonzalez would be a starter."

"He would probably be a number two starter on most clubs or at least number three."

"The Achilles heel of the Yankees this season has been their middle relief. The skipper of the Yanks would love just three more outs from Boyles and then he moves into the driver's seat with his set up man and, of course, Bodka, the Yankee's closer."

"I think you might see the closers if Boyles gets into any trouble, even at this stage."

***

"Did I mention why I was late getting to my ten-thousand-dollar seat this evening, Allan?"

No answer. Allan's eyes were scanning the security guards. On occasion he made contact with one specific male in the section off to his left, a guard standing about ten rows over and across a concrete guard way. A play on the field gathered everyone's attention. Allan leaped up and cried help waving his arms frantically toward the security.

Allan's plea blended as a frantic cheer. Wolf would take no more chances and he slowly reached into his right pocket and pulled out his switchblade that he had neatly inserted into the soul of his shoe. The four inches of hardened steel sprang open unnoticed.

"That was close enough for me." Wolf looked over at the guard who paid no attention to Allan's appeal.

With that, he put his left arm around Allan's shoulders and pressed down with magnificent force. Slowly, Wolf reached across his own torso and drove the blade into the side of Allan Boyles, twisting the razor's edge and churning from side to side with each coil, carving muscle, bone, and kidney. Internal bleeding began immediately.

"I have a gun as well. Your son is an easy target up there. So just sit still and bleed. If you move, I will kill both of you. I promise you that."

Allan Boyles sat bolt upright; the blade burned into his side like a branding iron. He lost his breath momentarily; the pain was excruciating. This stranger seated beside Boyles had created a living nightmare.

***

June 7

Clay studied ad nauseam what he considered were the two primary cases. He based his presumption on the severity of the crime and the destructive wake left behind. Neither the Cleveland nor Detroit Police Forces had a concrete lead on their respective events.

Upon the request of his best friend, Gremlin Police Force Chief Michael "Tubs" Campbell circulated the aged composite photo of the assailant to both precincts and the detectives assigned to the case. Both districts had a lot of questions as to where this info came from and why the southwest corner of the State of Pennsylvania was so interested. Tubs went into great detail as to his friend's investigation and both sides reopened some very dusty files.

All three investigative units, Detroit, Cleveland and Gremlin would communicate with one another from here on, but none were hopeful of building a case. The leads were old, the case was cold, and no forensic information was available. Closing a file successfully is incredibly gratifying; however, bringing closure to a cold case was rare indeed. When the long arm of the law gets its man and justice prevails, there is a sense of relief that all of the time and effort finally paid off. To add to this difficult situation was the undeniable fact that Cleveland and Detroit had police forces that were understaffed, overworked and extremely under financed. These cases, although tragic, were very easily overshadowed by the day-to-day atrocities of the two beleaguered cities.

All credibility would be lost if Chief Campbell suggested a link with major league baseball and the Texas Rangers so he kept that to himself. Oh, how Tubs wanted this crackpot scenario to be true and to break through with something in the Motor City or Cleveland, and pass along to his two dearest friends, the grail.

Tubs made a final phone call to Cleveland to tidy up some loose ends, one last duty before heading over to Alora. He needed to feel luck on his side tonight, and he felt he knew just the place to bring it.

***

Now into her third week at the Stoppa residence, Rebecca was calmer than she could ever remember. The waves of guilt diminished as she plunged into the tasks at hand. Maybe hard work and perseverance could make amends for the poor choices along the way. She was a woman of routines: her life in Boston was mundane and structured.

Once she managed to wade through the knee-deep bureaucratic procedure and receive a partial disability settlement from her trauma, Rebecca had enormous amounts of free time, with a small but steady income, a luxury that could be either incredibly positive or completely self-destructive. In Rebecca's case, too much idle time led to a wandering mind, and a wandering mind created anxiety and the desire to stray. Unequivocally, it was in her own best interest to set her days in a very strict manner. Gifted with intelligence, Rebecca continually assessed and reassessed herself, always careful to abate her demons when they stirred within.

If she wasn't volunteering at one of the shelters, she kept herself busy as a helper in the learned and grandiose halls of the Boston Public Library. It was there she gained her love for books and reading. She could lose herself for days in a historical fiction; her favorite period was the Tudor age and the pre-revolutionary period in Russia. She loved to be surrounded by books; often she would curl up in a cozy alcove, deep in the bowels of book stacks, not to be discovered until she appeared on the elevator leading to the exit once the lights were dimmed for the night. Once she managed to skulk away after closing, curl up in the common area only to awaken to the shriek of the morning janitor.

Rebecca's reflective smile lingered as she hugged her most recent novel while standing in the doorway of the Stoppas' study — a personal library just a few steps away.

Rain or shine, Rebecca went for her walk to the B&W, purchased a large black coffee to go, and then meandered back to the Stoppas'. There she would read her list of errands that she practically begged Kate to leave for her to look after. Rebecca's face lit up the day Clay threw her the set of keys to his jeep, the toy that was too clean and rarely driven. What a wonderful gesture, one of trust; Clay, of course, assumed that everyone drives a standard. Rebecca wasn't the smoothest of drivers; however, without a real time schedule she was able to pick her moments and the flattest routes possible in order to complete her series of everyday jobs.

Rebecca was granted access to all service shops that the Stoppas kept running accounts. A typical Tuesday began with a stop at the dry cleaners, the flower shop then the butcher shop. She loved the responsibility and the trust that had developed between the Stoppas and herself in such a short time, something that was so foreign to her.

With the errands complete and an AA meeting under her belt, she would plan out dinner, and settle into the study with a laptop burying herself in the database of potential assailants. Rebecca checked the Rangers staff, from the president to custodians, part time, full time, temporary staff, game day staff, City of Arlington employees, temporary vendors and kiosk operators. Rebecca was tenacious and would leave no stone unturned. This much she could give to her new-found friends.

The fan base analysis was daunting. The number of season ticket holders was well into the thousands. After eliminating females, African Americans, Hispanics, other minorities, the database was reduced; nevertheless, there were still too many to be investigated.

The search gave Rebecca her power so that she no longer felt like a victim. For once she felt like the hunter, not the prey. Rebecca had a reason to wake up the next day; she was getting her future back. She would rise and do it all again; it was almost perfect, even though she was kidding herself.

Each evening she would bid Kate and Clay goodnight and by two am, the computer screen burned her eyes and she would give way to a novel.

More often than not, the first down the stairs in the morning would find Rebecca curled up in a chair in a deep slumber. Clay or Kate would cover her with an afghan, without causing a stir.

Not every night's sleep ended in an idyllic morning wake up. Rebecca had a recurring dream. She could not find any common variable that caused her nightmare, as it was her nature to analyze to death the occurrences leading up to that night's sleep. It was always the same thing. She was young, high school age, and she sat in a room, but not a classroom. It was a bright and noisy room, full of colors, bright colors, but mostly red. She would be sitting in a cubicle with a pencil and a questionnaire. Rebecca could never make sense of the questions and she kept repeating the multiple-choice answers over and over. There were numbers, and scenarios that all sounded right, but the numbers would begin to race around in her head and spin faster and faster. It felt as if she was being rolled over by the various scenarios, but she had to keep trying to make sense of the numbers. The numbers completely overwhelmed her until she would panic and wake up in a cold sweat. Rebecca had one of those nights, and in the small hours of the morning she would lie awake trying to shake off the dream and slow her mind and her heart down.

***

Clay chased shadows. He visited both the Detroit and Cleveland files time and time again. It had been four weeks since 'the discovery' in the Stoppas' games room. He made a short trip to both cities, reviewed the crime scene, spoke to police and visited witnesses with the composite drawings, but to no gain. The files that were best kept at the time of incident, gave false hope that more could come from them.

Time was running out and although everyone had the best of intentions, Clay was beginning to believe, once again, that they backed the wrong horse. Major league baseball, the Texas Rangers and drive-thru shootings didn't add up. It was preposterous to link the parameters, and Clay was growing silent. Not a day passed that he didn't create an argument to extend the search, in essence, a stay of execution. However, every time he approached the hangman, she wagged her finger and said 'we have an agreement'.

Clay would bow his head; it was his wife in the chair bearing the brunt of the incident. She called the shots from this summer forward and Clay had to respect that.

The weeks were passing, time was running out. A promise is a promise is a promise.

***

June 15

No matter how difficult or busy the week, Saturday morning remained a sanctuary at the Stoppas'. The world slowed down to a very acceptable pace, a cup of java, some classic rock in the background, maybe get wrapped up in a good novel in a much-loved chair.

The Saturday mornings that Rebecca had been present, she'd insisted on making breakfast. She saw it as her 'rite of passage'. Kate and Clay were at wits' end when it came to Rebecca's insistence to help around the house. They felt guilty, but understood that the relationship was definitely a two-way street and both sides were benefiting. Kate curled up in the corner easy-chair reading an old favorite, and Clay scanned the sports section of the morning *Enquirer*, checking the scores of his newly beloved Philly's, then catching a guilty glance at the Tigers record. All the while in the background Rebecca scurried about in the kitchen, her headphones blaring and the odd out of tune blurb over top of the humming.

Rebecca gathered the balance of the *Philadelphia Enquirer* from the island counter and flipped through the sections as she began to prepare breakfast. Her love for the kitchen was genuine, but up until recently she had no one who truly appreciated her talents. She improved immensely from her first attempt in the Stoppas' kitchen.

The Stoppas were called for breakfast. Kate wheeled past the island, landing her novel on top of the 'local news' section of the paper the disheveled print now enduring some wear. The various newspaper sections sat on top of one another close to the discarded sections just a step away from the recycle bin. Rebecca glanced at the current date of the paper, and then reconsidered trashing the whole lot.

They settled in front of a beautifully arranged fruit salad, croissants, bacon, and sausage. Clay bumped into the kitchen island on his way to the table, his head wrapped in a profile of one of his favorite ball players from his childhood. Once settled at the breakfast table, they exchanged conversation as if they had been friends for years.

The newspaper placed on the island just before breakfast fell to the kitchen floor, nowhere near the three of them. Kate glanced over quite disinterested; Clay lifted his head and stared at the two girls, then at the paper and went back to his story. No harm done. Rebecca leaned back in her chair and saw the paper lying on the other side of the island. She straightened back up and picked up a crisp slice of bacon with her fingers and delicately broke off a piece into her mouth.

'Drive-thru'. It dawned on Rebecca.

Clay looked over his new reading glasses and directed his attention to Rebecca. She was leaning over her chair again this time reading the headline, albeit upside down.

'Drive-thru drive-by in the Bronx similar to Philly's'. She took a few quick steps and gathered the headline paper and had their full attention. Clay set down his glasses and leaned back in his chair. Kate stopped chewing and focussed on Rebecca's lips.

Rebecca stood at the island in her pajamas and fuzzy slippers, swaying back and forth reading out loud. "'A drive-thru drive-by in the Bronx (NY) on Wednesday had eerie similarities to the incident at the Chic-fil-a Restaurant in Philadelphia less than six weeks ago. A lone assailant pulled into a Burger King on the Grand Concourse in the Bronx, pulled up to the second kiosk, but instead of picking up his order, he turned a gun on the attendant and shot her twice, the first a glancing blow to the shoulder and the second to the right forearm. He did a U-turn in the parking lot, drove through a fence, disappeared through the Botanical Gardens, and then onto the interstate. Nothing was stolen. There is no motive, and the police have few leads.'" Rebecca found herself shaking. It was all too eerily familiar. She found herself touching the spot near her collarbone where the bullet had penetrated almost fourteen years ago. "It goes on to talk about the lack of witnesses and so on."

Clay flipped to the sports section. Since the think tank weekend, he always knew where the Rangers played and was convinced it wasn't in NY this past few days.

"The New York Mets played in San Diego on Wednesday and the New York Yankees played host to the Toronto Blue Jays, so much for the Texas Rangers." Clay moved the paper closer to his eyes just to make sure he was reading it properly… "Shit," he mumbled.

Kate glanced at the front page of the sports section that was facing her. She squinted as she focussed on the print across the table. "Flip to the front page, Clay."

Clay followed Kate's eyes and turned the newspaper around.

He read it out loud. "The new kingpin in NY lost his first outing with the Bronx Bombers. Rickey Boyles the 'legend of the mound' traded earlier this week to New York from the Texas Rangers fizzled out last night." Clay sat back and exchanged glances with both women.

"Are you thinking what I'm thinking?" Clay looked back and forth at Rebecca then Kate.

"Our link in the Ranger organization is now a New York Yankee?" Rebecca mumbled their collective thoughts.

Clay sat for a moment staring at the headline.

Rebecca poured fresh coffee. "As if this wasn't bizarre enough!" She took a sip without looking up.

"This Boyles guy couldn't possibly be the shooter though. Could he?" Kate ventured tentatively.

Clay shook his head. "It can't be Rickey Boyles running around shooting people, because for one, he has an alibi. Pro ball players arrive at the park well in advance of the game, especially if you're the starting pitcher. As I recall most of the drive-bys were very close to game time. Rebecca, can you see who was the starting pitcher at the Rangers games in our twelve cases, and the times of the incidents and the times of the games?" He continued, "Secondly: motive. Why would a multi-millionaire, Sy Young Award winning, greatest pitcher of his generation, go out and arbitrarily kill people? It makes absolutely no sense at all."

They sat in silence as Rebecca pulled up Google on the laptop. "Give me the dates; I have the Rangers MLB archive site up."

Clay read a date, Rebecca brought up the game and within a minute the box score summary appeared. "Boyles. Boyles. Boyles." Rebecca repeated the same starting pitcher's name over and over and over again as they followed up on all twelve incidents.

"He pitched in every game," Kate murmured.

"Not Boston," Clay blurted, referring to the fateful day that had changed all their lives.

"Hum." Rebecca had her head in the laptop. "Okay, I am pulling up a Boston Globe sports section from that date. Just give me a sec… sports section… It says Nolen Ryan was a late scratch that day and rookie sensation Rickey Boyles was moved up in the rotation that morning."

Clay was sick to his stomach. He paused. "Had Ryan not had the flu, I would have a daughter? Is that what you're saying?"

Rebecca was startled as Clay tipped his chair as he bolted upright and stormed out of the room.

"It's not you, Rebecca, you know that." Kate lowered her head.

"I've just never seen him like that before."

"We all have our moments."

After a few minutes he came back into the dining room. "I apologize; that was completely out of line."

Rebecca suggested she didn't give it a second thought and to move on with the situation at hand. "So, the incidents were within two hours of game time, no exceptions… so now what?"

"I need to go to Rebel, Rhode Island," Clay mumbled

Rebecca bit her lip.

"Why Rebel?" Kate queried.

"The home of Rickey Boyles."

"How do you know he was from Rebel? I don't remember reading that." Kate stared at the laptop. "Oh wait, it's baseball, you would know. A baseball junkie both on and off the field."

Rebecca's eyes widened. "How good were you?"

"Not good enough." Clay answered with as few syllables as possible.

Clay carried on. "It's about six hours on I-95… give or take. I need to pack. Will you two be okay?" He sounded like a kid going off to camp.

"You're going today?" Kate tried to come across as a little hesitant.

"I have a new-found deadline, remember?"

"We'll be fine, Dad," Kate responded tongue in cheek. She glanced around the kitchen for Rebecca, but she seemed to have disappeared. "Hey, listen, we have no idea what you are going to find up there, so just be careful poking around. Hornets' nest, you know what I mean?"

"I have no idea what I am looking for so it sounds like a fair fight." They kissed like no one was watching.

***

Clay exited the Interstate at Highway 87, three miles west of Rebel, Rhode Island, a town fifty miles south of Providence. The clock read three p.m. His hand reached over and turned down the music of Leon Russell as he crossed into the town limits.

Clay shook his head and closed his eyes in disgust as he passed the roadside placard reading 'Welcome to Rebel, Rhode Island, Home of Major League Pitcher, Rickey Boyles.' A billboard on the opposite side read 'When Jesus comes to save us, will you be ready?'

"What is your real story, Rickey Boyles?" Clay muttered to himself.

Highway 87 was the industrial route into town. Large makeshift warehouses, small manufacturing and storage facilities, rusted fence lines bordered the poorly maintained and overused four lanes. Clay rambled along trying to avoid potholes large enough to damage his undercarriage. He crossed a substantial shunting yard for a very active rail system; the landscape was a collage of varying shades of gray. He passed a big car dealership with colorful blow-ups and shining glass, completely juxtaposed against its surroundings. He then cut across street after street of substandard housing. Clay's first impression of the town: a mix of hard working, blue collar, tough, bland, industrial living, rise and fall by the factory whistle, day in and day out folks. He suspected the arts community and tourism bureau had a lot of time on their hands... either that or one hell of an agenda.

Hotel or local restaurant, where to begin?

The highway reduced by two lanes and merged onto the main street, as they amalgamated into one and the same. Now Clay faced a downtown very different from his own: a mix of very modern structures and poorly maintained older buildings. First impressions suggested they were making an effort to revive the core; however, troubled times certainly had an impact. You could almost read the economic chronology of the community solely based on the age and condition of the buildings downtown, as there was such a disparity. He pulled into the local gas station one block north of the main street. He mentioned the Boyles name to the attendant, but was met with only a cold glare, so he settled for directions to a local motel. The most direct route was the least scenic, so Clay crisscrossed though modest war time housing then entered the sixty's Mansard roof architecture and finally, towards the north end of town, 80s and 90s garage-in-front structural design. It was difficult to tell how badly the town was suffering through the current recession, but the only new construction he had come across was a cul-de-sac consisting of eight or ten homes.

The suburban commercial strip was boring: large box stores, a local grocery store, and a bowling alley, all in need of overhauls. Just beyond the forty plus store mall, was the Rebel Motel, the one recommended by the sixteen-year-old gas attendant. Clay looked across the street at the relatively new Super 7 and Holiday Inn but decided the local flavor made the most sense, so he checked into room 112, eight doors down from the motel office. Clay pulled his car up to the room door, barely allowing enough room to squeeze by. The red neon roadside sign had a high-pitched hum; Clay questioned his decision, however the noise subsided once inside. He looked around, cheaply furnished, but impeccably clean, just what he required. He threw his only suitcase on the end of the double bed,

So many shades of beige, who knew?

After freshening up, he took five steps out of his room, hopped into his VW, turned on some local AM station, and headed downtown. As he was driving down the main strip, his mobile phone began to ring. Clay glanced at the display screen: it was a New York number he recognized—a sports reporter who had been trying to get Clay's story for years. He was one of the more ethical sports journalists out there, and Clay always enjoyed his balanced takes on his subjects, but Clay had no intention of giving the guy his exclusive. He turned off the ringer, his eyes never leaving the road. He was hashing up too many old memories as it was.

Parking was not a problem. He strolled in and out of some local shops, a men's shop with dated clothing similar to his hometown, an army surplus store, and a couple of ladies' fashion boutiques. There was certainly not the merchant mix that would attract a younger crowd. It looked like the economy was in fact taking its toll on Rebel as every second or third unit had a 'for lease' sign. The older buildings, turn of the century, were three floors tall; the second floors looked to be occupied by tenants, however, the third floors had boarded windows, and in many cases, the intricate shingle work was in disrepair. The modern buildings, built with no consideration of the surrounding older architecture, were financial institutions, insurance companies, and chain store varieties filled with booze and convenience items.

Clay walked into 'The Diner, Established 1949'. The décor reminded him of the Black and White back home, but not quite as well maintained and considerably smaller. He quickly examined the two waitresses. It was quite apparent how the tables were divided between them, and Clay chose a booth that the women in her early forties would look after. With his eyes locked on his future waitress, he walked into a booth full of teenagers and collided with the table. Clay had to laugh at himself.

"Oh, if Kate could have seen that," he mumbled with a smile on his face.

Clay was mesmerized by his waitress's smile, and outward laughter as she threw her whole self into a conversation at an adjoining table. He couldn't help but smile at her enthusiasm. Clay had no idea what was being said, but he was caught up in her energy, something special that comes along only once in a while.

Sheila, or so it said on her lapel, carried a pot of coffee that looked to be an extension of her arm, and without asking, flipped his mug over and filled it precisely to allow for both cream and sugar. She set down a two-sided one-page menu, a fork; spoon and knife wrapped in a tissue, smiled, looked into Clay's eyes with her hazel, long-lashed, smiling eyes and said, "Thank you for choosing our diner." She nodded with confidence; her deep auburn hair filled with large looping curls flowed across her rosy complexion. She beamed with glorious white teeth and waved goodbye to the couple she just shared a laugh with.

Sheila returned a few moments later. Clay noticed her wince and grab her hip, as she approached his table.

"Well, it's always nice to have a new customer grace our presence." Sheila smiled and locked into Clay's eyes only. "What can I get you, dear?"

They were approximately the same age as Clay looked into her cheerful eyes. "What do you recommend?"

"The corn beef on rye, heavy on the mustard and pickles. Unless you're a vegetarian?"

"No, that sounds good." Clay smiled and handed back the menu. Once again, Sheila beamed and did not take her eyes from Clay until he broke it off.

Sheila glanced at her other tables and picked up a cue for more coffee and without breaking stride turned and completed a refill, not exuding any extra motion.

Only four or five booths were occupied. The bar stools were empty except for two teenagers sharing the same strawberry milkshake, giggling and fussing over one another. Clay picked up the local rag, *The Johansson Expository*, serving Rebel, Lincoln, Briers Creek, and surrounding areas. He leafed through the twenty pages. They were definitely having a slow news week; the front page was a summary of the Easter festivities from many weekends past, and then some international news. The sports section blanketed the local high school events, covering the upcoming football season that began in less than a month, and an analysis of all the counties' teams, both Jr. and Sr. There was a small blurb about Boyles being traded to the Yankees, but it certainly did not take priority.

Sheila delivered a healthy portion of corned beef. She winced as she filled his coffee.

"Carpal tunnel?" Clay looked at her wrist, acknowledging her painful expression.

"No, just a double shift, and I'm not a spring chicken any more."

"Your job is taxing, more so than people realize. Especially when you throw yourself into it."

Sheila filled the room with a smile, and blushed slightly. "How's your coffee?" She glanced at his thick gold wedding band.

"Great thanks. May I ask you something?"

Sheila looked around, and nodded. She locked eyes with Clay once again.

Remembering the phone call he'd received just minutes before, Clay decided to try a new angle. "I'm a reporter from the *New York Times* doing a profile on Rickey Boyles."

He watched her expression carefully and saw that her eyes had hardened considerably at the mention of the baseball star's name. He decided to trust his instincts.

"I know he's an asshole and I am covering that angle." He paused and looked up at the waitress. It didn't take a genius to see he had struck a nerve. "I have all of his numbers; I know who he is on the field, but I am really looking to find out what made this guy such a horrible human being." He could see the disdain on her face shift slightly to a bit of a smirk. It was a good call throwing that out there, Clay figured; he knew he had struck gold sitting at her table.

"I'm not sure if I can help you with that." She was apologetic, however her tone had purpose.

"I appreciate that. I was only looking for someone who might be able to help me out with his early days here in Rebel. I am only here for a day or so and I would certainly appreciate any help you can offer."

Sheila bit her tongue and looked around. "Ahhh, let me think about it." She walked away with her head down.

Clay moved the food around his plate for a bit; it was passable, but he really wasn't hungry. Tables cleared and with the exception of the kids at the counter, Clay occupied the only booth.

Sheila wiped down a table and seats like she had done a thousand times before, looked at her watch gave a large sigh then smiled at Clay who was caught staring at her.

She strolled over to his booth put her coffee pot down on the table too close to the edge… it was about to fall… but Clay tipped it, slightly singing his fingertips in the process. She smiled at him as he shook his hand in the air to cool them off. "Thanks for that, not exactly how I wanted to finish this shift." She passed along the bill and apologized again for not being of any use on his quest.

"I apologize Sheila… sorry," He glanced at her lapel. "May I call you Sheila?"

"Of course."

"I'm Clay Stoppa, by the way, hardly fair, no name tag."

"Clay, pleasure. While you are in town, please come back. I see you weren't enamored with my suggestion."

"No not at all, just healthy portions and I ate not long ago so…" He paused. "I will definitely be back tomorrow for breakfast." He couldn't help but smile.

Sheila touched his shoulder as he attempted to step by. "Just wait a second."

Clay sat again and tried to look preoccupied until she greeted some patrons as if they were the first through the doors today.

"We open tomorrow at eight a.m. Be here right as the doors open and sit in the end booth." She pointed. "Sit nowhere else and it is important that you are here at eight. An old man named Frank usually sits there. If he's agreeable to talking to you, he'll join you. He's an old friend of Rickey's dad and might give you the history or dirt of the Boyles family; maybe something in it will help. It's a start, that's all."

Clay thanked her, and then reached out to shake her hand. Out of the corner of her eye she noticed someone walking by the storefront. She accepted his hand with an unintentionally rude gesture.

"You know my daddy always said admire the athleticism, but beware of the person. That's off the record."

"Of course," Clay smiled. "Your daddy sounds like a wise man. Well, I appreciate what you have done for me today and my lips are sealed."

Clay shifted to his right and allowed room for a man who certainly cast a shadow. He must have stood six feet, eight inches and 260 pounds. It was rare that Clay came up to someone's chin. He watched the hulk walk straight over to Sheila say a few words then turn and leave.

Clay kept his eye on the two of them as he slowly ambled towards his car. Clearly Sheila was not impressed with what he had to say. His stature dwarfed the entrance to the restaurant as he exited the premises. Clay and the stranger made eye contact as he shifted into second.

Back at his hotel room, Clay filled the rest of the evening on the Internet looking at Boyles' library of bad press throughout his illustrious carrier. It seemed that as fine as his baseball career had evolved, his personal life was a train wreck. Clay knew this instinctively, but had never actually read into the details; anyone who followed the game even at the most casual level understood that Boyles' antics were not becoming of a role model.

Clay got comfortable on his motel bed, propped up some pillows, turned on ESPN for background noise and opened up a bag of granola and a soda water. He reviewed all of Boyles' early baseball history, which was available online through the weekly paper's archives website, made possible through a donation from the Boyles Charitable Fund. Clay chuckled. Prior to his major league debut, there was no denying the kid had a million-dollar arm to go along with his peanut brain. Teams won with Boyles in the rotation and it was no fluke he has dominated the majors throughout his career. He was the NCAA pitcher of the year, and fielded his position as the best in the college two years in a row. He had an unheard of twenty-eight wins and only three losses in his final two years, and the school won the grueling World Series of College Ball.

Historically, the Texas Rangers never had the pitching necessary to carry itself to post season success. They were perennial favorites to win arguably the weakest division in baseball, and always a strong hitting club, so when they drafted the NCAA Princeton sensation it was their intention to build a contender around the budding superstar.

Rickey Boyles was the complete package: drugs, alcohol, women, paternity suits, a public divorce, a playboy mentality, two 'no hitters', including a perfect game, two Cy Young awards, over two hundred and fifty wins, and the most sought after arm in the game; quite a contrast.

Rickey Boyles was a cancer on any team roster. He had no friends, he slept with his teammates' wives, and he took great pleasure creating mayhem in the dressing room: fistfights, rumors and public indignation. The more he stirred the pot, the more attention was directed towards him, and the better he played. He went 24 – 3 two years ago, a record unheard of in modern-day ball, while a team of lawyers followed in his wake, settling a divorce and two paternity suits. One sunny afternoon in Texas, he stepped on the mound sporting a fresh shiner on his left eye. The left fielder, Richard Banks, played the same game with a broken nose. He was a time bomb, both on and off the field.

14

Clay awoke at six a.m. without an alarm. His morning jog took him into town passing the illustrious Dover H.S.: home of the 1988 State Champion Baseball team. His jaunt took him past the local football stadium, the R.H. Boyles Community Complex, and the Boyles Baseball Training Facility.

Clay thought about his own hometown, and how things might have been different under other circumstances, but that was water under the bridge and he had enough on his mind. His jog was set to clear his head, not to clutter it.

After a shower and a short drive, he arrived at 'The Diner'. Clay turned off his car, rolled into an open parking spot, stepped onto the curb as the lock on the restaurant clunked, and the open sign was flipped. He followed the instructions Sheila had passed along and strolled over to the booth in the corner, then slid along the vinyl bench and pulled a copy of the *Providence Journal* from under his arm, flipped his cup over asking for coffee without opening his mouth. At ten past the hour an older gentleman walked in right on cue and shuffled over to Clay's booth.

"Well if I am to do this, two things need to happen."

"A man who gets straight to the point." Clay stood and shook Frank's hand. "Name them." Clay quickly shifted his attention from the newspaper to the old man.

"Switch seats and you pay for the breakfast."

"Done." Clay stood up, introduced himself. He winced yesterday when he blurted out his real name, but it was too late, maybe a pseudonym was more appropriate.

Not so good at this sleuth stuff.

"Where are you from?"

"New York City, I'm a baseball reporter." Clay hated lying.

"Well I can tell you lots about the family, but little about the baseball."

"Well I have all the baseball info I will ever need on this guy, it's the life off the mound that I am most interested in." A truer statement he had never made.

"So, he's a Yankee now, huh?"

"He is. Maybe Boyles has met his match in ego."

"Yah, I doubt that. No question he can pitch." Frank chewed on a toothpick. "But, his ego... Huh. No, I suspect it's bigger than the Big Apple... No doubt about that."

Clay hated the toothpick; it was all he could see, the twisting twirling, and then of course it would eventually come out, one end saggy and where would it end up?

"So why the interest in his past... now... when his career is well underway?"

"Maybe his past will better explain his present... a new angle no one has touched upon."

"Well I can give you the family background. I have lived here all of my life and no one family has had a bigger influence on this town than the Boyles family." He sat back keeping one eye on Clay, the other on the patrons as they began to fill the limited seating.

"Yah, that would be a great start." Clay moved forward ever so slightly.

"They moved to Rebel in the early seventies, so Rickey would have been four or five years old. Allan, his dad, started working at McLennan Ford as a car salesman; it's just up the road." Fred raised his eyebrows and pointed with his head. "I had never seen the likes of him, Allan that is. Personable, friendly, charmed the women, good looks, good build and the gift of the gab."

"A natural then."

"Oh yah, the bullshit flowed from his mouth like waves hitting the shore, constant and continuous."

Clay chuckled all the while shifting his focus from the old man's kind eyes to the toothpick.

"He revolutionized selling cars in this town, that's for sure. This town hadn't really advanced much since the railway became less important, but that wasn't going to discourage Allan." Fred scratched his head.

A waitress set down the wrapped cutlery, filled Clay's cup, and brought Frank a tea without saying a word.

"Within a year, the dealership doubled in sales then doubled in size, so Mike McLennan had the nicest dealership south of Providence."

"Yah, I think I saw the dealership on my way in."

"Smooth and savvy, hell, Boyles had clients traveling over a hundred miles, passing three dealerships on the way, just to buy the same damn car from him."

"That's crazy."

"Damn right it's crazy. Hell, all the other Ford dealerships had the same damn cars and from what I understand, at the same price, but he had the gift of making someone feel so special for the short sales cycle."

"So he owned the town so to speak?"

"Not quite yet, but he was becoming quite a celebrity."

"How so?"

"Well for one thing Mr. Ford himself shook Allan's hand at some high achieving banquet bullshit… no matter… Allan was shrewd."

"In what sense?"

"Threw a portion of his commissions back into the business and after a short period of time he purchased a piece of the pie. He was slowly taking over Mike's business, and I'm not sure if Mike minded so much. He was getting close to retirement and maybe saw this as an opportunity to close in on some nice coin on his way out the door."

"So, that's how he made his fortune?"

"Sort of… Boyles was a marketing genius, something we had never seen. He opened a used car lot in association with the new one on the same property. He took the customers car in on trade, fixed up the trade in at their new state of the art service shop and sold it next door. He had them coming and going."

"Hmm." Clay needed to move this along a bit.

"Then came the advertising. Christ, the whole town was sponsored by McLennan Ford, radio and TV saturated by the guy… no one could believe this guy's energy and enthusiasm. Next thing you knew, McLennan was bought out. It was the last we saw of old Mike, and he moved to Florida somewhere."

Frank stopped short as the server approached to check on the hot beverages. He didn't begin again until she was on the other side of the booth.

"The next thing you know, the signs are changed, and Boyles' mug is everywhere and then came his lucky break. Along with the dealership, came one hundred acres of prime real estate... well as prime as it gets here. Of course, Boyles created the premise with his 'center of the universe mentality' that this was the future of retail development and a big mall developer purchased about half of it from him, half cash and the balance he held in paper."

"That was the good luck?"

"Well, I'm getting to the good luck."

The waitress arrived with the 'two of everything breakfast' mounds of food on each of the plates. Clay didn't recall ordering, Frank removed his toothpick and it disappeared below the table somewhere.

Thank God.

The restaurant was filling up and the decibel level was increasing. The Diner had a strong breakfast crowd, Clay noticed.

"Well, the developer went tits up and Allan got the property back, plus kept the millions in down payment."

"Good luck."

"Yeah and then some." Frank looked a little annoyed. Clay nodded.

"He sold it again, and the same thing happened. So, when the third guy came along, he had already made his fortune. When it was all said and done, the dealership and land that cost him one million dollars netted him twelve million dollars plus he kept the dealership and the back fifty acres."

"How do you know all of this?"

Frank paused and looked down at his breakfast. "I was Allan's friend in the beginning."

"The beginning... that sound a little ominous."

"I was a lot older than him, but we both loved golf, and since I owned the only golf course in town at the time, we would share lots of stories, while we walked the course." Frank ate for a few moments then looked up.

"Do you two still play?"

"Some people make money and never change, and others," he

reflected. "It's the age-old question: does anyone get better with age?" Frank's eyes glazed over slightly.

"I'll take that as a no then."

"Right before my very eyes, Allan became the biggest asshole this town has ever seen." Frank certainly called a spade a spade.

"Okay then." Clay's interest increased.

"He turned his back on the town that embraced him." Frank paused to enjoy his eggs.

"Let me guess, he started to buy up the town."

"A slum landlord with power... power and greed."

"That's not a good combination."

"That's for sure. Boyles no longer sold cars; the dealership had a life of its own, so his time was spent collecting rent using his dimwit leftovers from the NFL wannabe club."

Clay thought briefly about the man that cast his shadow on him in the entranceway yesterday. "I think I saw one yesterday."

"He has a slew of them. He has his own entourage. The results were grand, not only did the locals revere him, they now they feared him."

It's good to be King of your own little town.

"This sounds a lot like a mafia twist." Clay spoke quietly.

"It was exactly like mafia." Frank lowered his voice as well. "Right down to the strip club: Misty's." Frank spat with disgust.

"How old is Rickey by this point?"

"Rickey was a little cocksucker."

That was not actually my question?

"He was a spoiled, protected little shit who could do and say anything to anyone. He also happened to be an extraordinary athlete and Allan loved a winner and his son did just that. Winning was Boyles' second favorite thing to do, intimidation was his favorite."

"Rickey was the second coming," Frank continued. "Allan was blessed with a son who could throw a hardball with pinpoint accuracy at the age of six. Have you seen the baseball academy just down the road?"

Clay nodded.

"Well he built that for his son, and had all of these ex-pros come into town and tutor him."

"So, let me see if I have this right. We have a ruthless businessman, with Mafioso tendencies, who is blessed with the golden child with the million-dollar arm, which he harnesses into a major league pitcher?"

"Yes."

"Has anyone ever written this story?"

"Not that I'm aware of."

"Did Rickey play his entire ball here in Rebel?" Clay already knew the answer from his own research.

"As far as I know, yes."

That was incorrect, but no matter. Clay excused himself to use the bathroom. He glanced around the restaurant looking for Sheila, but instead recognized the gorilla that had words with her yesterday. He was sitting at a booth in the far corner and made no effort to hide the fact that he was staring at Clay.

Clay could only have been two minutes in the restroom. When he came out, both Frank and stranger had left.

Clay threw down a twenty and raced out the door. He recognized no one. After asking his waitress a few questions and those at the neighboring table, Clay had no clues.

He drove around the block a couple of times then dropped back into the restaurant and asked again of Frank's whereabouts. The man was a little quirky, but did not seem the type to just get up and leave Clay thought. Frank apparently did not put up a fuss as no attention was drawn to him, as everyone just shrugged no.

Clay's only connection to Frank was through Sheila and no one would fess up to her whereabouts on a Sunday, even when he suggested it was urgent. Clay was an outsider, a stranger, and he would be treated as one.

He was also well aware of the fact that he was treading on a very touchy subject; Kate's hornets' nest came to mind.

Clay sat behind his steering wheel, his VW parked on the main street as he let his mind wander. He was more than curious as to the events over the past twenty-four hours; however, few questions were answered. A cruel and sometimes unethical businessperson and father of an asshole future 'Hall of Famer' may be unpopular and cause a great deal of resentment in a small town, but it by no means ties his own tragedy to Boyles' life of disdain. No connection whatsoever.

Clay was aware, however, that he had drawn instant attention somehow and was curious as to why, the hulk watching over him, Sheila's concern to remain 'off the record' after doing nothing more than expressing her opinion, one that would be shared by most in this dismal little town. Had he known that so much attention would be drawn to him in the first place then maybe he would have taken more time to create a better cover? "Who am I kidding?" he muttered to himself, "zero cover." Time would tell if this was an issue. Clay popped back into the restaurant one last time and decided to come back on a shift change; maybe Sheila would be in by then.

He drove past the car dealership and the baseball academy, viewing them from a completely different perspective. He passed Misty's Bar and Grill, and suspected the thug or thugs keeping an eye on Boyles' little empire gathered there for lunch. "A scene from the *Sopranos*," he mumbled.

His next destination was Dover H.S. A long shot on the weekend, but with any luck he might get in. He was relieved to see cars in the parking lot; maybe some keen teachers or administration preparing for the upcoming fall semester. Knocking on the main doors produced nothing but sore knuckles, so he moved to the office windows. Clay startled a woman who was engaged with the photocopier paper tray; she looked cross then motioned to the main doors.

A very large and imposing African American woman poked her nose out and with an equally great voice advised that the class lists will not be up for two more weeks, and any out of area registration had to be done by appointment only. The door was shut in an instant.

Clay knocked again then raised his voice. "I'm looking for someone, completely unrelated to the upcoming semester, maybe you can help me, and it will only take a minute."

Clay poured on as much charm as he could muster. It was completely out of character and it showed, but it worked. She had piercing eyes and a large smile and allowed Clay into the lobby that connected the school's office, staff room, gymnasium, cafeteria and washrooms. There he waited for the school Principal McMorlly. He was under specific instructions to 'stay put' or his ass would be back in his vehicle before he could say Piggly Wiggly. She waddled off to the administration offices.

The school was completely stereotypical of the sixties' construction: large polished granite floors, heavy wood walls with shag carpets framed as a form of decorative flavor, the ceiling housed dropped fluorescent lighting. He was drawn over to the trophy cases across from the office. The glass structure ran the length of the wall, over forty feet in all. Clay adjusted his leather bomber jacket then, strolled in front of the display hands in pockets. It seemed to be set up chronologically within each sport, beginning with, what else but football, and then cross-country running, volleyball, and basketball. He admired photos of badminton stars, javelin record holders and steeplechasers. He then stood in front of the baseball section and the shrine. The last four feet of wall space was dedicated to Rickey Boyles, boy wonder.

Clay strolled over and peeked into the gymnasium. Clearly athletics was of paramount importance at Dover High. The sports center was state of the art, a triple gymnasium, complete with three basketball and volleyball courts and at least six badminton courts along with bleachers, and an electronic central scoreboard. Off to the left was a fitness facility and what looked like a dance studio. Clay walked back out to the main hall and noticed a plaque.

The Dover Gymnasium
Constructed through the
generous donation
from
The Boyles Foundation

Through the glass reflection of the trophy wall, Clay watched Principal McMorlly approach in his blazer and tie. A little overdressed for a weekend, but no matter, Clay thought.

"Thank you for seeing me on such short notice. I was just admiring that the Boyles family gives back to its community. I'm with…" Clay was interrupted.

"I've been expecting you. You're with the *Times* in New York."

Clay was caught off guard. "Who suggested I was in town?"

"Oh, it's a small community."

"So I have gathered," Clay wasn't smiling. "I'm just looking to finish off some research…"

"You didn't get enough from Frank?" McMorlly cut him off.

"Clearly this town has its distinctive line when it comes to the Boyles family, and I see where yours lies." Clay's eyes indicated the plaque. "Sorry to waste your time."

Clay turned to towards the doors and began to walk.

"I've got nothing to hide here, and I don't appreciate the insinuation."

Clay just gave a backhanded wave and carried on towards the exit.

"Mr. Stoppa, we have nothing here at Dover that would interest you. All the school records and such, we don't keep the stats here, just the hardware." He motioned to the trophy case. "You might want to have a chat with his old High School Coach, Peter Riggins… nothing for you here."

Clay immediately recognized the name but could not place it. He stopped and turned around. "Where can I find the coach?"

"He retired years ago and has settled just up the road in Malcolm, a crossroads really, just a few miles down the road. You can't miss it; there's a big fountain out front. He's an avid gardener, so you'll probably catch him outside."

"I'm sure he will be expecting me."

The two men waved and gave polite smiles.

***

Chuck watched Rebecca cross in front of his storefront, one large pane at a time. He reached under the counter and grabbed a sign just as she entered. She was distant, deep in thought as she hopped up the two concrete steps to the restaurant level.

Rebecca smiled at Chuck as she approached the counter to grab her coffee to go.

"Rebecca, would you be so kind as to put this in the window." Chuck smiled and passed her a faded 'Help Wanted' sign, one that looked as old as the business itself.

"Sure," she replied as she read the sign. "When do you need help

Chuck?"

"Lunch crowd mostly, so ten to two or three."

"Do you need experience?"

"No, we will train."

"How do I apply?"

"Oh." He paused. "You just did."

"Oh, okay great. So when do I interview?"

"You just did."

"Terrific, how did I do?" Rebecca raised her eyebrows and lifted onto her tiptoes.

"You got the job. When can you start?"

"Today, yes today, no wait, I have a doctor's appointment. Is tomorrow okay?

"Tomorrow it is." Chuck reached out his hand and Rebecca shook it enthusiastically with a giant smile. She grabbed her coffee and set down a dollar and change.

Chuck pushed it back. "Employees do not pay for their food or coffee, one of the perks."

They both laughed. "See you tomorrow then."

"Tomorrow," he agreed.

Rebecca now had a spring in her step, ready to start standing on her own two feet and working towards the future instead of being anchored to the past. She passed through the picturesque downtown, admiring the summer baskets that spilled color over the sidewalks. She passed by the chic clothing shops and a couple of pubs before reaching the professional building, McLeod and Associates. Kate referred Rebecca to her own doctor, an opportunity Rebecca could not pass down.

Dr. McLeod, a general practitioner, had been the family doctor in Gremlin as long as anyone could remember, took over an existing practice, so in essence had very strong ties to the community for decades. McLeod was to deliver Kate and Clay's daughter, but instead became Kate's physician for rehabilitation, not only physically, but also mentally. McLeod was not a psychologist nor did he pretend to be, however he had a keen sense of mental illness, as a close friend of his own, and a fellow colleague, took his own life. Since that horrific event, he had steered his practice towards those in need of mental health care.

Kate was convinced Rebecca would be in terrific hands if they formed a professional union.

Rebecca sat in the waiting room, a bright cheerful environment, and one that was important to Dr. McLeod. She took a few moments to reflect. This town was becoming more and more a part of her life... in fact, she had not given Boston and her life of the past ten plus years much of a thought recently. Over the past decade she did not have a job, a doctor, a group that might best be described as peers, a purpose, and she sure did not have anyone who cared for her. Maybe she was done with Boston... but for now, one day at a time.

A man best described as a warm and gentle grandfather greeted Rebecca in the reception area. Dr. McLeod's thinning silver hair fell over his dark eyebrows. His large yellowing teeth glistened with his outrageously welcoming smile and warm gentle handshake; his enormous paws enveloped Rebecca's long thin hand.

"Kate speaks so highly of you, Rebecca, so I just had to meet you for myself."

Rebecca felt even better than she did ten minutes ago. They sat and chatted for a few moments. McLeod put her completely at ease. "Well, Rebecca, I have a patient list longer than my arm, but that will not stop me from bringing you on board if you are comfortable with that."

"That would be terrific... yes."

"Good then. I will require a physical... blood work etcetera, which you can set up at Groves, just down the street from Kate and Clay's place. I will write you out a script if you can do that for me."

"That will be no problem."

"Oh, one more thing, Rebecca..." Dr. McLeod looked over top of his glasses.

"Sure, what's that?"

"I work with both the mind and the body. I'm not a psychiatrist, however, the mind is a most powerful mechanism that I never underestimate, so I need you to give me something about your current state. Something I can work with; something I can be thinking about before our next appointment."

Rebecca stared at him like she had seen a ghost. "Okay, well..." She recovered slightly then coughed nervously. "I have a recurring nightmare... I suspect that's pretty typical, huh?"

"Can you describe it?"

Rebecca did, after all, the memory was very fresh.

"Does it always awaken you at the same point?"

"No... I... I have had it carry on into a car." Rebecca was visibly shaken. "Can we pick up next time?"

"Yes, of course, plenty of time for this. One step at a time."

"Thank you, Doctor." And with that she slipped out of the room.

"Rebecca!" McLeod called out.

She reappeared at the door only ducking her head through the opening. "Let's see each other every other week, shall we?" His reassuring smile was a pleasant façade, which did not fool Rebecca.

"Sure thing."

15

June 16

The Village of Malcolm was well described as a crossroad, a beautiful one at that, located just minutes up the road from Rebel. A stark contrast from the industrial ambiance of Rebel, Malcolm was peaceful and affluent, consisting of a rustic general store, a coffee shop, and an antique dealership, all under one roof. Then, a little farther down the hill, eight Cape Cod style houses were set on formidable properties. The overall setting like a scene from a storybook. It wasn't hard to pick out Coach Riggins's abode; his seemed to be the most impressive of all, marked by a large sailboat sitting on a trailer in the driveway. The house was ocean blue clapboard, with the wraparound porch boasting every hosta imaginable all in full bloom, enshrining arbores and pathways, fountains and hedges. He must be one heck of a coach, Clay thought. Clay coached at Duval for his love of the game—and certainly not for its salary, which was modest to say the least.

Clay sat in his car, pulled out his smart phone then searched Riggins's in order to jog his memory.

Of course, baseball's Division Two coaching guru, how could I have missed that one?

Clay put his phone in his pocket then stepped out of his car, strolled across the street to what had to be Riggins's abode. A tall thin man was shoveling some peat into a wheelbarrow at the back of the property. Clay caught his attention with a wave and was motioned into the backyard.

"You're more than welcome to walk the property; people do it all the time. I don't mind."

Who the hell walks these stupid little pathways, they lead nowhere?

"Well, I was actually here to see you."

"Oh, you're the reporter. Clay Stoppa."

Clay shook his head. "I should have expected nothing less," he mumbled to himself.

"Funny though, I think I know your name from somewhere else."

I'm up for the D2 Peter Riggins Coach of the Year Award this fall. Just putting two and two together now.

"You have probably just read my freelance work," Clay lied.

"Maybe." He looked off into space hoping his memory would be jogged. "No matter… so you are looking for some dirt on Boyles?"

Yes.

"Whatever you can help me with would be greatly appreciated. Word travels faster than my Jetta."

"Small town."

"Right." Clay paused.

I've been made, no doubt. I wonder what this means for old Frank.

"I just have to say, that I am honored to meet you," Clay told the older gentleman. "Your coaching at SUNY Cortland is legendary. What was it, three players jumped from your teams straight to the majors?"

"Yes, three. You did your homework."

Clay didn't want the conversation to turn to division schools just in case it tweaked something. "I am a true fan of the game and I have always followed the college ball. Is there anything you can tell me about Boyles from his years in Rebel?" Clay shifted the conversation along.

"We both arrived at the same time. I was coaching in Providence and having some success. Follow me." They walked up to the porch and sat in deep wicker chairs. His wife, a tiny woman with swarthy skin, clearly the outdoors type, brought out lemonade. Clay stood up in her presence and thanked her for the hospitality.

"I just met the only New Yorker with manners," she quipped as she went back to the kitchen.

"So what made you choose Rebel?" asked Clay.

"I was lured here by money. Rebel offered me twice what I was making in Providence. As it turns out, half of my income came from Allan Boyles… you know his background by now, and that is who I was to take orders from."

"Frustrating as a coach for sure," Clay added.

"Yah, as it turns out he liked to give out the orders. Had I not been so naïve…" He pondered the circumstances. "Anyhow… I arrived in town and Rickey was a junior."

"Where was he before that?"

"Some private school up in Providence, Minkle if I recall… not far from my school. I knew who he was…"

"You played against him up there?"

"Yah, we played against him up there, some exhibition stuff as we were in different school boards. Rumor has it that he wasn't big on rules, or at least abiding by them."

"So, you knew you were walking into a hornets' nest." Clay borrowed the term.

"Yah, the rumors flew in Providence."

"Such as?" Clay prompted.

"Allan's money only reached so far so they had to part ways. The kid was caught drinking and doing drugs. Boyles Sr. was given the ultimatum, get your boy out of dodge, or have the book thrown at him."

"Why would you walk into this?"

Riggins took a sip of the tart refreshment. "As it turns out, the ball team here at Rebel was spectacular. Boyles knew it and with just a little tweaking, it could be something special." He paused and whispered. "And the money…"

"Sold out?"

"To a degree. Sad really, as the previous coach was doing a fine job. However, Boyles and he didn't see eye to eye."

"All about Boyles, huh?"

"Oh yah, Boyles made a deal with the principal at the time and I showed up on the scene, oblivious to all of the shenanigans."

"Really?"

"Well, maybe not *all*. Truly, all I could see was double the income and a team with a strong record over the past couple of years… my time to shine and make this my step to the college level."

"So, you…?" Clay prompted.

"Well I walked into a lion's den. I had signed an iron clad contract for two seasons, and even though we won it all in my second year, Boyle's final year, these were the darkest days of my coaching career."

"But you retired here?"

"We bought before I got the college gig and my wife wasn't big on the city life, so here we are."

Highest paid high school teacher in history, right here.
"Nice spot."
"Yah, we like it. I'll give you a tour of the garden later."
Oh boy.
"Terrific. So how good was Rickey?"
The ice rattled in the tall glass as Riggins took another sip. "The kid was untouchable, you couldn't hit off of him and you couldn't coach him. He was better than most, popular with the girls, couldn't give a shit about his teammates, and had a pile of cash to throw around."
"Some things don't change." They both smiled.
"Did he get into any serious trouble off the mound?"
"No, not that I know of, having said that I didn't pay a lot of attention to him off the field. I'd had more than my share of his arrogance on the ball diamond."
"And his dad?"
"His father smothered him. If he wasn't such a cocky little bastard, I would probably have felt sorry for him."
"Huh."
"You know his dad, the lousy fuck, came to every practice. He would sit in his town car usually leaving it idling with the air conditioning on and just watch. I offered my players fifty bucks if they could foul one onto his windscreen... some came close."
Clay smiled. "Needed more inside pitches."
"Ha."
"What was your record here at Rebel?"
"Thirty-one and one over two seasons, twenty-four and four in tournaments including the State championship."
"Spoken like a true coach." Clay paused and looked over at the coach. He was staring into his garden. Clay reflected on the team record. That type of success could not rest on just one solid arm on the mound. It sure didn't add up and he had a hunch. "Did you keep any game sheets?" Clay's voice was a little anxious, a bit of a knot in his stomach.
"Son, this is baseball, all we do in baseball is count ... you know that. Come with me."
Clay followed Riggins into his basement; the rec room was modern, over-lit, the light bouncing mercilessly off the white walls interrupted

only with baseball paraphernalia. Riggins opened a drawer below one of the many trophy cases and pulled out a series of scorebooks. He was sorting them looking for the two seasons in question.

"You said the team was thirty-one wins and one loss over the two seasons."

"That's correct." He continued to sort.

"What kind of a schedule did you have?" Clay was leading up to something.

"We played home on Tuesdays and away Thursdays, tournaments ran on the weekends."

"So what kind of a rotation?" Clay was trying to understand the pitching set up. He had to have a terrific rotation; Rickey could only be responsible for half the wins at most.

"I ran with only two starters, both seasons."

"Two starting pitchers all season?" Clay was practically yelling.

"Yah, Boyles and Franklin."

"Who was Franklin?" Clay moved to the edge of his seat.

"He was my number one actually."

"Excuse me?"

"Yah, he was the glue." The coach continued to search, his voice expressionless.

"The glue? Why am I only hearing his name now? Better than Boyles?"

"Different… a lefty for starters, and methodical, had to work the count, study the batters. Not overpowering, but smart. So smart." Frank looked up.

"Tell me more."

"I never coached such a bright baseball mind before or after. He threw the only 'no hitter' I ever coached, a real gem of a game. Oh, here they are." He pulled out a series of Dover H.S. scorebooks. "I scored every game from the dugout myself. Always have."

Clay flipped open the scorebook for the final season. It had all twenty-four games. Clay read it like a book, gibberish to most, all the lines and numbers, but to Clay the pages flowed like he was actually watching the game unfold, following all of the outs, the hits, the pitching changes, so for a trained eye, one could follow the game as if listening to it on the radio. The 'Pitcher of Record' was indicated on the bottom right-hand side of each page, Franklin, Boyles, Franklin, Boyles, Franklin and so on.

"Here's our State championship logbook." He handed it to Clay without looking up; Riggins was now preoccupied with other treasures.

Game one, Boyles, game two, Boyles, game three, Boyles and Game four Boyles.

"You didn't start Franklin in the state tournament?"

"No, he was injured."

"How could you go with just one starter?" There are strict pitch count rules protecting the arms of the young players. "Without at least two days' rest, Boyles could not start."

"Game One was the Wednesday evening and our draw had game two early Saturday. We were to play Game Three Sunday afternoon, but we were rained out. Well not exactly rained out, we had a flood on our diamonds."

"Which diamond, the one here in town?"

"Yes."

"That's one of the higher elevations in Rebel. I approached it from different directions and it is definitely one for the higher elevations here."

"Yah, someone left the sprinkler system on all night."

Convenient.

"So, we had a reprieve to Monday and the finals were set for Thursday."

"So, lots of time for Boyles to be seen at his best," Clay deduced. "So, I guess you met the maximum pitches thrown by an individual pitcher."

Riggins simply nodded.

"What was Franklin's injury?"

"His pitching arm."

Clay felt a twinge in his own shoulder—a common side effect of the game he loved. "Was it serious?"

"It ended a promising career." Riggins did not flinch, he responded cold and withdrawn; still preoccupied with some photos he came across.

"Poor kid. He must have been heartbroken," Clay spoke the words with meaning.

"I never saw him again after his injury," Riggins informed casually.

The words shook Clay to the core. It must have shown on his face.

"Don't get me wrong—I still feel bad about that. It was the night before game one and I had set Franklin as my opening day starter. Boyles' dad wasn't too impressed; in fact, he called me out and threatened me if I didn't put his son into game one. I drew the line and that's when I found out who was bankrolling half of my salary."

Clay looked around at the well-appointed basement. *Yeah, I can believe that.*

"He was screaming bloody murder and was going to the principal, and the school board. Turns out, all his threats towards me were for nothing, because the next morning one of my assistant coaches shows up at my doorstep and tells me that Trevor Franklin's pitching arm was toast."

Clay paused. "Where is he now?"

"No idea," Riggins said disinterestedly. "Like I said, I never saw him again. I always meant to check in on him, but..." Riggins shrugged. "You know how it goes."

How could you never see him again?

Clay thought about how attached he was to his players each and every season. "Nope, not really," Clay said honestly.

I don't want to win an award with your name on it.

Riggins stared him down. He'd been put on the defensive. "The week before States I was offered my college job, the one at SUNY, you spoke of it earlier."

"So?"

"And I was being flown back and forth between here and Cortland. The only time I was in Rebel was for our actual games and then back to meetings."

"Heart-wrenching." Clay knew he wasn't listening.

"Hell, I barely made it to the pregame speech. We won the championship and I was gone, that evening. I only came back for the ring night the next season."

Clay decided to back off a bit. He was here to learn about Boyles, not critique the ethics of the head coach. "What kind of commitment was expected of the players to be a part of your team?"

"We practiced or played four nights a week, the boys had to maintain a 3.0 grade average and our weekends were pretty busy with tournaments… between ball and schoolwork not much time for anything else." Riggins turned back to a box of baseball paraphernalia.

"Here's a picture of the kids after the ring ceremonies. There is Boyles." He pointed at a kid with a cocky look on his face in the front row.

Clay narrowed his eyes and glared at Boyles' arrogant stance. "Where is Franklin?" he asked absentmindedly.

Riggins put on his glasses. "I don't see him there. He must have been kept away by his injury."

"You look pleased with your boys," Clay noted, referring to a younger Coach Riggins' broad grin. Injured player or not, he looked genuinely pleased with himself.

Riggins grunted. "Like I said, I was on my way to a college, a dream job, and I was just four games away from never having to look at Boyles Sr. and his entourage again."

Clay thanked him for his time, closed his note pad, jogged to his vehicle, and did an aggressive U-turn racing the clock. 'The Diner' closed at five p.m. on Sundays; Clay was hoping to catch an employee and press for the whereabouts of Sheila as he raced into town.

***

The knock was at the back door. Frank turned the corner into the kitchen and recognized one of Boyles' giants, Max.

"You looking for a banana," he grumbled to himself as he turned the latch. "To what do I owe the pleasure twice in one day? Unlike you, I hear things once and understand them."

With ferocious conviction, Max kicked the bottom of the door causing Frank to collide with a corner cabinet and stumble towards the floor. Again, with no effort, the perpetrator pulled Frank to the middle of the room, put a hand on the back of his head, leaned him over, and drove his fist into his stomach with such force that he lifted poor Frank off the ground.

Frank momentarily stopped breathing. Max lifted him again with a heartless punch to the rib cage and allowed him to crumple to the floor, recoiled and whimpering like a wounded dog.

Max's steps were large and heavy with conviction. He ducked into the living room and then the dining room. No signs of Sheila. He ran up the stairs three at a time reached the top and heard the shower turn off.

"Dad?"

No response.

"Dad, what was all of the banging did you drop something?" With no response, Sheila toweled herself off quickly.

The door to the bathroom exploded open with such force that the mirror cracked. Sheila screamed and cowered, confused by the force.

Max stood in the doorway. Sheila screamed and pulled back the shower curtain covering herself the best she could. He put his finger up to his mouth suggesting she be quiet. When she didn't take his suggestion, he drove a fist into her nose to douse her shrill cries. Blood exploded in all directions.

He raked over her body with his eyes. "You know I have always wanted to fuck you. The way you bend over in that diner of yours pouring all of that coffee."

"No, please no, I'm begging you."

He jerked the towel from her body leaving her completely exposed. Sheila's body was in plain view. "I knew you were hot under that uniform."

"No, please, I beg you." She cupped her hands over her breasts in a vain attempt to cover up and crossed one leg over the other, again trying anything to feel less exposed.

He glanced at his watch. "Well, you're in luck because I'm on a bit of a wrecking crew schedule today. Don't talk to that Clay fuck. Have you told him anything?" His pointing gesture pushed her back to the corner.

"No, nothing, I thought he was a reporter, but when I... I won't say a thing."

"Well, just to make sure, I'm going to give you something else to think about for a while."

His fist shot down on her face like a lightning bolt. She cried terror and scrambled in painful delusion. He put her in a head lock looked at her ass and legs in the mirror, smiled at himself then drove his fist as hard as he could into her ribs again and again and again, each time her blood-curdling shrieks cried the horrific pain.

Finally, he stopped, stuck his fingers inside of her and rubbed them under his nose. Sheila fell against the tub, sobbing, her blood smeared all over the bathroom.

***

Quite a day, Rebecca reflected on her new job, the first in a long while, the doctor's appointment and an opportunity for professional help rather than the self-taught prognosis from the Boston Public Library. However, her confession with the doctor dominated her train of thought. The dream and her overwhelming rush of guilt ringing in her mind repeatedly, Rebecca knew she was in a profound hole.

After completing some errands for the Stoppas, she dropped off some info at McLeod's office reception and then a short skip to the Central United Church at the corner of Main and Power. She slipped into the side entrance, a 1970s blight attached to the glorious turn of the century limestone structure. Choosing to sit in the last row closest to the exit, Rebecca tuned out the AA meeting and contemplated her dilemma.

The meeting was brought to order and after a few formalities, the twelve or so in attendance turned their attention to Rebecca.

"Oh, shit. Did I miss something?"

There were a few chuckles "Yes, Rebecca, we were wondering if you wanted to share today."

"Oh, wow, missed that, sorry… um no, not yet, but soon I believe." She stood and walked over to the coffee and smirked. The canister looked identical to that of the old church basement in Boston, and the coffee, just as black… syrupy sludge that she had become accustomed to. How did it come this far, she thought, and had anything really changed? She still attended meetings, maybe this group a little upscale, but the premise remained the same, she was in constant need of help, and the meetings were a crutch. Rebecca leaned on her arms and sighed, the truth was, she could not allow herself to reach the root of her problem therefore every step forward towards recovery invariably resulted in a step or two in the other direction. Ironically, Rebecca knew the root of her evil, but would not face the truth. It was easier living in a world of less rather than face her demons head on and let the chips fall as they may.

***

Clay pulled up curbside and recognized the waitress from his morning visit flipping the closed sign. With the emergency brake barely engaged, he swiftly exited the car and ran to the locked front door his movements as smooth as silk. The waitress shook her head and pointed to her watch. Clay gestured that he had a question and wasn't looking for a meal. Reluctantly she came back to the door.

"I'm looking for either Sheila or Frank. I don't know either last name, but it is imperative that I speak to one or the other. Did Sheila work today?"

The young girl in her yellow uniform looked him over then blew a large pink bubble holding the door just wide enough for a nose to peak through.

"You're that guy who claims to be a reporter asking all the questions and getting everyone in trouble."

That's a lot of information.

"What do you mean?"

"The two Max's were by and you don't want to mess with them. They were something pissed and looking for you."

There are actually two of them looking for me? Lovely.

"Okay, so maybe I'm looking for them." Clay knew she was referring to the no-neck monsters. "I need to speak to Sheila. It's important. Where can I find her?"

"She didn't drop by today, besides you're like the plague around here."

"Christ, help me out here."

"She's always here, she owns the place."

"Okay, I have to speak with her. One of the Max's left with Frank and I'm now very concerned."

"Max left with Sheila's dad?"

"Frank is her dad?" Clay glanced at his watch. "Look, I'll figure this out another way. I'm sure they are part of your Chamber of Commerce. I'll just Google them so just save me some time here."

"Sheila and her dad, they live together on Mulberry. A little blue house, but I didn't tell you that. It's just around the corner two blocks; turn right about half a mile away. Do you think something's wrong?"

"I'm not sure. I hope not."

By now the cook had joined them at the door; he gave the young waitress a friendly bump from behind that she seemed to like. They both looked across the street as if expecting someone to appear.

The young waitress's directions were perfect as Clay wheeled into the freshly blacktopped driveway of a little blue house, once again jumping out of his car as it rolled to a stop, and walking hurriedly across a concrete block pathway similar to those used in newly developed subdivision housing. He focused his attention towards a windowless front door of the only older house in a subdivision of new builds. He opened the screen and knocked. No answer. He tried again, glancing over at the two cars in the driveway.

Clay marched into the fenced back yard, realizing the gate must be on the other side of the house. Using one hand, he sprung his legs over as if he was coming on the ice on a line change in a hockey game, and then up the three stairs onto a tiny deck. The sliding door was open and the screen door ajar. Clay entered the kitchen cautiously then saw Frank's legs just beyond the island. Clay rushed to his side, reached down, and checked his pulse, pulled out his phone and called 911.

"Emergency assistance."

"Yah, this is Clay Stoppa, I am at…" Clay bolted down the short hall and opened the front door to retrieve their address. "133 Mulberry."

"Ambulance and police have been dispatched. What has happened, Mr. Stoppa?"

"Um… okay…" Clay glance at Frank. "There has been an assault, a break and enter I suspect." Racing down the hall, called out Sheila's name, he heard a whimper from upstairs. He bolted up the twelve stairs in three steps.

"Send two ambulances." Clay remained on the phone with the emergency dispatch. He reached the top of the stairs and glared down a short hallway. There was blood on the door jam, and drips of blood leading towards the bathroom at the end of the hall. The door was ajar and a smear of red marked the door handle and the doorframe. In the short time since the brutal assault, Sheila managed to crawl into the bedroom, but couldn't raise herself to reach the phone... she'd collapsed on the floor, face down.

"Jesus Christ." Clay headed towards the bathroom, but the moaning came from the bedroom on the left. He pushed open the door slowly.

"Are you still on the line?"

"Yes, Mr. Stoppa."

"I gotta go. Just get the ambulance ASAP."

Blood surrounded her broken body, a smear of deep red fluttering out from under her. She looked almost like a fallen angel lying there, her broken wings painted in blood. Clay had a flashback of Kate lying on the sidewalk on Boylston. He felt like the wind had been completely knocked out of him.

"Sheila," he whispered as calmly as his nerves would allow.

Her deep curls of brunette hair covered her face. He could see blood everywhere she rolled on her side exposing ribs scarlet red with deep brown bruising.

He grabbed a robe and covered her. She leaned into his side and cried. Blood bubbled out from her broken nose with each sob. "Dad?"

"Yah... I am going downstairs to check on him. He's had a fall but will be okay." Clay had no idea. Enough said as he placed pillows and sheets around her, careful not to ask her to move any more than she had to. He stared once more at the pattern of blood on the ground and it conjured up horrible memories and blinding rage.

"He will be fine," Clay reassured once more as Sheila's terrified expression suggested her doubt. "I will be right back." Clay bound down the stairs with the few pillows he gathered from what he presumed was Frank's room. He pulled a blanket from the top of a settee without breaking stride and reached Frank on the kitchen floor. Unlike Sheila, there were no visible signs of blood, but the fetal position that he laid in and the considerable amount of pain he was in suggested some significant internal damage. There was no denying the fact that Frank was in trouble. Clay listened for the siren outside, the two or three minutes felt like an eternity.

Frank groaned as he stirred and attempted to acknowledge Clay's presence. "Frank, lie still." Clay managed to get a pillow under his clammy head and covered him the best he could with an afghan, tucking it under where possible. "Lie still. The ambulance is on its way. I will grab you another blanket." With that Clay sprung to his feet popped his head around the corner and grabbed yet another homemade colorful blanket and laid it carefully on him. "I will be right back."

"Sheila?" he managed.

"Yes, she is comfortable upstairs, just waiting for an attendant."

Clay charged up the stairs and found Sheila exactly how he left her. She looked up at Clay as he slinked to the ground to be close to her. "Don't move. They won't be long. Your dad is lying in the kitchen in considerable pain, but is completely lucid." Clay looked around at the struggle. "Why would someone do this?"

Sheila's large and colorful eyes, a little less terrified than before, looked up through her brunette locks to Clay, reaching for reassurance.

"I am not good at this." Clay looked around. "I am thinking the best thing right now is to lie still. Are you in a lot of pain?"

"Not so much when I lie still."

"Then that's best then." Clay grabbed a damp cloth and wiped the blood that was caked on her neck and shoulder. Her nose had congealed but he didn't want to get too close. Clay was gentle and Sheila closed her eyes. The air went eerily calm.

Finally, the sirens could be heard.

The attendants came straight into the kitchen; both immediately attended to Frank. Clay flew down the stairs.

"Someone upstairs?" A paramedic started towards Clay.

He signaled for the male attendant to stop. "Can she go?"

He signaled to the female of the pair.

Clay led the female paramedic to the bedroom and she began to attend to her.

"Do you know who did this to you, Sheila?" Clay remained close.

She shook her head no, but he could see the fear clouding her eyes.

"Were you raped?"

Again, she shook her head.

The police arrived shortly afterward and both victims were sent by ambulance to the hospital. They questioned Clay and asked that he not leave town. He nodded and then suggested he would be going over to the hospital shortly, but had to take care of something first. He too did not suggest the assailants' identity.

Clay left the driveway slowly but once he was out of view, he put his foot down, shifted into second, then revved into third.

Clay was unspeakably hostile, his mind burning with revenge. He couldn't get the image of Sheila's bloodstained carpet out of his mind. He jerked, pulled, revved and pushed his car down the side streets zigzagging straight to the strip joint with every intention of ripping the heads of off the two Max characters; he glanced at the baseball bat rattling around in his back seat. He turned the corner towards Misty's, coincidently fast approaching his own hotel on the right. His eyes perused the motel parking lot. A giant of a man was closing the door to Clay's room. It had to be him. Obviously, he was under some form of surveillance from his first stop at the restaurant. Clay impulsively cranked a hard right partially hitting the curb drawing attention from the perpetrator as he closed in on him. Max froze at first sight then smirked at his good fortune.

The man was a behemoth, at least six inches taller than Clay, and outweighed him by at least one hundred pounds. Clay's size, strength and fighting experience would suggest catastrophic results for him, but his rage and his familiarity with a wooden bat might suggest different results.

Clay leaped from his VW. Clay was within ten feet of his opponent and stared up into his prehistoric features. Max's huge forehead and heavy eyebrows rose as he glanced at the bat in the hands of the slender adversary. Max's posturing was that of a very confidant man.

Clay eyed his enemy's right hand as he was pulling a pistol from his belt and with the flick of a wrist; the 33-inch 30 oz. Louisville Slugger knocked the gun out of his hand with uncanny accuracy and it slid twenty feet down the parking lot. Before the gorilla could respond, Clay leaned a line drive into his rib cage sending him stumbling to the middle of the parking lot.

Clay was somewhat concerned that his adversary was still on his feet, as he had laid into him with incredible force. Maybe getting out of the car was a stupid idea.

Max stumbled to the right, large steps at first to maintain his balance then shorter more surefooted movements. He grunted as he touched his rib cage then turned with vicious terror in his expression. Clearly he underestimated his opponent, and clearly he would not make the same mistake twice. Max lunged with rage in his eyes; he was set to tear Clay to shreds.

"You cowardly fuck." Clay nailed him again in the ribs before the recipient could touch him. Clay moved ever so slightly to his left, enough to miss Max's attack, but remained close enough to remain on the offensive. Clay too underestimated the force and strength of such a hulk of a man.

"How could you do that to a woman?" Clay had himself in a rage. He could no longer be sure which injustice he was avenging.

He deftly slid behind Max and waited for him to turn. At the risk of killing him, Clay sent a swing at his head as if it was a fastball coming in hard over the plate. CRACK. The primates' jaw dislocated, teeth flew onto the tarmac, and he dropped like a lead weight to the ground, howling in pain.

Once he was convinced the Max wasn't recovering without assistance, Clay ran into his hotel room grabbed his suitcase tossed it in the back seat then spun out of the parking lot. In the rear-view mirror, a man laid in the middle of the tarmac in horrid pain. For a fleeting second, he considered dialing 911, but that quickly passed.

I hope the whole town walks by you and no one lifts a finger.

Clay had one stop before the hospital. He remembered seeing it on the highway into town: Rose's Bar and Grill, 'the best steakhouse on the eastern seaboard.' His car drifted into a parking space. Clay headed straight to a barstool close to the exit. The long walnut masterpiece gleamed in the late day sun and Clay squinted at the reflection.

"What will it be?" An uninterested bartender looked over.

"Single malt scotch, make it a double."

He set up a hefty-bottomed tumbler and poured a generous portion. Clay noticed his bigheartedness and acknowledged with a simple nod.

"Don't go." Clay tipped the liquid gold back. "One more please."

The bartender obeyed, and just as quickly it disappeared. Clay dropped a twenty on the bar and left.

He sat at the wheel for a moment trying to comprehend the last hours. The only scraps he had ever been in were on the playing field, and baseball players, as tough as they think they are, can't fight very well. His nerves had settled some; however, without a strong grip on the wheel and the stick shift, his trembling would be very noticeable. The pop of the clutch resulted in a loud squeal and off to the hospital he went.

Boy, have I struck a nerve in this hellhole.

***

An intimidating man, simply by his immense presence, held the exit door at the B&W restaurant for Rebecca. They smiled politely at one another. She was heading back to the house with takeout; Kate had a subcommittee meeting with council at the house and Rebecca wanted to surprise her with dinner.

The giant answered his cell phone as he sauntered to the rental car. "Max here."

"We have an issue back here; apparently our friend didn't take too kindly to our handywork on Sheila and Frank so Max was roughed up a little."

"How much is a little?"

"He won't be leaving the hospital for a long while, and his new favorite food is soup."

"So what does that mean down here?"

"You have a green light."

Max closed his phone slammed the car door and peeled away from the curb. Back at Gremlin's local hotel he asked for a five a.m. wake up.

***

The hospital was surprisingly large in relation to the ten thousand or so that lived in Rebel, obviously a county facility. Clay walked over to triage and scanned the nursing charts, Sheila and Frank Delaney. Clay recognized one of the cops from the crime scene then nodded as he walked by.

Nurses with charts, machines beeping and blinking, it was bedlam on a Sunday night. Clay scanned the emergency department, and spotted Sheila lying in a gurney, her father in the same curtained area.

He walked towards the two and then was in earshot. "I can't believe what I have done." Clay covered his mouth; the bruising on her face was swelling up like a melon.

Sheila waved his pitying look away. "I'll be fine. Really."

"How is your dad doing?"

"He is stable, he'll make it. Dad had chest pains, but they seem to have that under control."

"What about you?"

"They just took some x-rays, and clotted my nose. A broken nose is so becoming of a woman. I'm guessing a few breaks or cracks in the ribs."

"If it makes you feel any better, the other guy got what was coming to him."

"You beat up Max?" Sheila sounded surprised.

"Let's just say he's probably undergoing a very painful surgery right now."

Sheila's surprised expression turned into a small smile.

"You are remarkably calm."

"I am just glad my dad is okay. And the drugs, I'm feeling no pain."

"I still can't believe I did this."

"It was just a matter of time."

Sheila's response surprised Clay. "What do you mean?"

Sheila paused before speaking. "Who are you Clayton?" Sheila made eye contact then drifted her attention back to her father again. "You ride into town, ask questions, lie about your identity and cause a shit storm. It's like you have a secret, but rather than tell us your secret you rip into the bowels of our town and get a lot of people hurt." Her eyes watered.

"If you are up to it, I'll answer your question. I certainly owe you that and then some." He stared at all of the monitors. "I'll tell you who I am and what brings me to Rebel. If any of it makes any sense at all, and you don't think I am batshit crazy, then maybe you won't be quite as upset at me."

"Okay, Clayton Stoppa, why are you here causing all of this grief and disruption?" The medication was beginning to settle in and the pain was at least tolerable.

"Well, here goes."

"Yup."

"Are you up to it?"

"I highly doubt I could sleep anyway, so on with you."

Clay went back thirteen years, the incident, the investigation, and the trail of leads, year after year of disappointments, false hopes and no results and the blind faith to keep on going. A passing nurse interrupted him on occasion, but for the most part he regurgitated a very convoluted investigation in a very short period of time.

"That is truly remarkable; your drive. I think I would go insane."

"I think it has kept me sane."

"Of course, then what happened, what led you here?"

Clay stared down at his feet. "Then we caught a break. At least we thought we did. A drive-thru with similar consequences occurred in Philly. This led to a bizarre hypothesis that involved major league baseball, drive-thru shootings and the Texas Rangers, but that was going nowhere until last Wednesday in New York City. A drive-thru shooting similar to the twelve we were investigating, but only this one did not involve the Rangers. It threw us for a loop until my wife, and friend Rebecca, linked the trade of Rickey Boyles to the crimes. I came up here to snoop around and see if there was any merit in our direction. I even met with Riggins, the coach."

Sheila raised her eyebrows. "Haven't heard that name in a while. Did he tell you how Rickey's dad paid his salary?" There was bitterness in Sheila's voice.

Clay nodded. "If it wasn't for his dad, and for his lucky break just before the State championships, who knows if Boyles even would have made it to the majors."

Sheila's eyes narrowed. "What do you mean lucky break?" Her voice was suddenly dull.

"Riggins told me that his other pitcher got injured just before the State championships, so all the scouts' attention was on Rickey, even though the other guy probably deserved it more. Trevor Franklin."

"Trevor Franklin," Sheila whispered. "Jesus fucking Christ." She closed her eyes; the physical pain was dulled by the mental anguish.

"You okay?" Clay asked, rising to his feet in concern. "Do you need me to get a nurse?"

Sheila shook her head no. "It's just that name... Trevor Franklin..." She closed her eyes again as if trying to push a rush of thoughts out of her mind.

A few moments passed, and her bruised face relaxed. "What I don't understand is why everyone that I talk to gets threatened or worse," Clay's voice was bewildered.

"Because, by a stroke of luck, you spoke to one of the only people in this town that could hurt the Boyles tandem."

"You or your dad?"

Sheila bowed her head and pointed at herself.

"Surely others have interviewed locals about the wonder child over the years?"

"Not so many, actually; he keeps his life in the headlines so no one really needed to come here. Rickey's trail was thick enough in Arlington with all the antics."

"I can buy that, sure. But still, why all the suspicion when I arrived?"

Sheila thought for a moment before answering. "Because you're wading into a hornets' nest... one that hasn't been poked at for many years."

Clay thought of his parting words yesterday. "You mean how Allan Boyles basically paid to get his kid into the majors? Surely that's not a secret. Stuff like that happens all the time."

Sheila shook her head. "No, not that part. The other part... the part about Rickey getting to be Riggins' only pitcher just before States."

"I won't deny it—that sure was a lucky break for Boyles. But kids get injured all the time."

Sheila huffed. "Not like that, they don't."

Clay's eyes narrowed. "What do you mean?"

"Clearly Riggins didn't tell you *how* Trevor Franklin got injured?"

Clay thought back. "No, just that it was his pitching arm was toast. I figured he'd hurt himself training or something."

Sheila shook her head adamantly. "Trevor suffered a horrible accident the night before the State championships. *That's* why Rickey got to be the number one pitcher."

Clay was perplexed. "What kind of accident?"

"The kind that no one wants to talk about." She looked over at her father. "The kind that people don't like other people asking questions about," she added pointedly.

"And you think there might be some sort of connection?"

Now Sheila was nodding. "Well maybe, I guess there is some symmetry, some chance, I don't know for sure. God it's all so… so… God, I always wondered if this would ever come full circle."

Clay could see that Sheila was getting agitated. "Are you sure you are up to this? Maybe you should rest."

Sheila shook her head adamantly. "I'm not allowed to sleep. They're monitoring me for a concussion. Besides, it's about time I told someone. In fact, it's been burning a hole in me for years. I'm tired of suffering on account of that bully's sins." She gestured to her present condition.

Clay was struggling to follow. *Which bully? Rickey Boyles? His father?* He leaned in, urging her wordlessly to continue.

Sheila let out a huge sigh and stared off into the distance for what seemed like an eternity. Clay sat patiently, the beeps and clicks, the buzzers, and oxygen flowing, now fading to the background.

Sheila's eyes glazed over as she drifted back to a specific time and place, away from this one. "Trevor never had a girlfriend; he never was caught even looking at a girl, however, he did fancy a senior named Abby Lee Haason. She was colorful, a little thin, popular, not a top student, but would get by. We were close… Abby Lee and me… for a while at least." Sheila was in a zone. "Abby Lee didn't pay much attention to Trevor. I told her about his crush on her, but she ignored him for the most part."

"What's Abby Lee have to do with any of this?"

Sheila looked over at Clay, her eyes watered up. "She was a big part of that evening."

"Oh, sorry, okay, carry on."

"She worked part time at the Lic-A-Chic, a local chicken joint, off of Howard. She would often tell me that Trevor would take his grandfather's old Chevy through the drive-thru, sometimes gathering enough nerve to pass by more than once in the same evening."

"Wow, the drive-thru strikes a nerve, let me tell you."

"No doubt."

"Carry on... sorry."

"I likely knew him as well as anyone." She thought for a moment.

"Trevor, you mean?"

"Yes, Trevor." Sheila shook her head. She considered her next statement. "Trevor was misguided by his ignorance of life's positive experiences."

"In other words."

"He mistook Abby Lee's kindness for something beyond client customer relationships."

"He was a little naïve?"

"He was a lot naïve and like most, his first crush was a lasting one, and with Abby Lee now it wasn't enough to admire from a distance."

"Did you ever date him?"

"No, it wasn't like that, I just looked out for him."

Clay smiled. "That's nice."

"I never intended to go further in school so I never wanted to get too attached to guys like Trevor."

"What do you mean?"

"He was smart, kinda cute in a rugged way, a great ball player; he was destined for college and maybe great things."

"That is very unselfish. So, you saw him play ball?"

"Oh, I loved my ball and I watched a lot of it, and Trevor was the best. He was the best player Dover has ever seen." Sheila shook her head.

"Better than Rickey?"

"Are you kidding me? Boyles couldn't hold a candle to him."

"Remarkable, two great arms at the same time in the same school."

"Anyway, Boyles Sr. blusters into town and brings 'wonder boy' back into the mix."

"Where was he?"

"He was off at some Ivy prep school I think."

"Right, of course. He had discipline problems or something?"

"Yah, I suspect it was pretty expensive to keep boosting his grade average even for the likes of Allan Boyles."

"So when did Rickey reappear?"

"He was here in little league, left and came back in his junior year."

"So two years at Dover then." Clay was thinking back to Riggins' scorebooks. "So, the kid is back, and Trevor is expected to play second fiddle to him? Did that cause a rift?"

Sheila bit her bottom lip and shook her head no. "Trevor wasn't the type to cause problems; in fact, he would go out of his way to avoid them. But the harder he tried to stay clear of confrontation, the more it came up."

"Such as?"

"His natural athleticism, he was just so at home on the mound, and he was smart too. He out-thought his opponents, such a treat to watch." Sheila managed a smile.

"So what confrontations, exactly?"

"Allan Boyles… Boyles Sr. You should have seen the expression on his face when Trevor pitched. He was seething. His whole body was tense. He would go rigid, clench his fist, and hide away in his parked car just down the third base line."

"Did he bully Trevor?" Clay wouldn't put it past him from what he had gathered.

"Well… bullying, no. But it eventually came to a head."

"When?"

"Well I guess the Audit Tourney, the one that all the NCAA scouts come to."

"Yah, I'm familiar with it." Clay was extremely familiar with it.

"Rickey pitched the first game and was pulled in the eighth; they were losing, but came back and won, so he got a no decision. However, Trevor pitched a one hitter the next morning, so poetic."

"Spoken like a true fan." Clay smiled then leaning forward in his chair anxious to hear more. "So did the two boys have it out or something?"

"Rickey and Franklin had little to do with one another: they never hung out together, they never liked the same girls, Trevor wasn't a partier, and he was pretty boring by most accounts. He kept his grades up; he worked hard on his baseball and kept to himself mostly."

"So, what happened then?"

"Then the final recruiting started."

"Ahh yes, the recruiting."

"All the top colleges zoning in on little old Rebel."

"Yah, I could see that, all the hotels and your dad's restaurant brimming with business."

"All so dreadfully exciting and wickedly stressful for all those involved all at the same time. It was all Trevor could talk about"

"Likely brought out everyone's true colors, I suspect?"

"You have no idea." Sheila shook her head.

"Carry on."

"It was all going to be okay. Trevor made up his mind he was off to a school in Rhode Island; it was close, relatively small and a decent team."

"And Rickey?"

"Boyles Sr. had his sights on an Ivy school for his boy."

"And that's what happened, he ended up at Princeton."

"He did, but his record at prep school didn't hold him in good stead. His marks were suspect and he just didn't have the Ivy swagger."

"He had an arm though."

"Yah and that was the problem."

"I don't understand."

"That's all he had. Boyles Sr. needed to make a monster splash for his boy in his final season and the stage was set at the State Finals Tournament."

"Win the four games, make sure your son is the hero and get that full ride to Ivy land." Clay finished her statement as he passed Sheila some water. She pushed back a couple of huge auburn ringlets, took a sip, paused, and looked over at her dad. He remained peaceful.

"So, we are approaching the state finals and Trevor is pitching up a storm. Then, in the last game of the season, he does it: a no hitter."

"They're incredibly rare. A sight to behold."

"I was right there. I can still see it as clear as day: the fans, the coaches, the players, and the sweetest part of all; Allan Boyles sitting in his Cadillac, engine running watching the whole thing."

"So, all of the ducks were in a row and they were favored to become State Champions. The one, two punch of Trevor Franklin and Rickey Boyles." Clay summed it up.

"A cataclysmic season; the town was so onside. I remember we had this huge banner made up and it hung outside the restaurant."

"That's awesome."

"The guys on that team were like rock stars. I loved it! The town had never been drawn together so strong. Triumph after triumph"

"So, Trevor was to pitch game one obviously."

"Yup."

"He didn't pitch though; I saw the score sheets today." Clay was leading her.

Sheila's expression changed, her voice dropped. "That was the longest night of my life, even longer than tonight." She looked over at her father, who was still in a drug-induced slumber. "It was the night before the big game. The last time I saw Trevor was that night."

"Seriously?" Clay had a chill. "Was Trevor…?"

"Trevor saw me walking somewhere, I am not sure where exactly… it doesn't really matter, and he pulled over and gave me a lift. He was in his grandpa's late model Chevy sitting behind the wheel. He had just come off the big season, and his look in the rear-view mirror was the best I had ever seen. His confidence was never higher than at that very moment."

"What the hell happened?"

Sheila's expression grew dark, her voice hollow. "Boyles Sr. is an appalling man."

Clay felt his eyebrows rise. "You mean Trevor's accident? You think Rickey's dad had something to do with that?" he asked incredulously.

But Sheila was lost in her own thoughts. "It is such a shame they won that year." She sipped her water from the white Styrofoam cup.

"What happened that night?" Clay swallowed hard.

"So I got a call around midnight. I remember it like it was yesterday. It was a Wednesday night; I had fallen asleep on my trampoline in the back yard."

"Who called?"

"Abby Lee, it was Abby Lee. She was in hysterics. She was paranoid, acting all weird and shit, so I picked her up just around the corner from her house. She was hiding in the bushes and ran out to my car. She asked to go somewhere quiet and safe so we could talk, so I drove out of town about five miles south of here to Lake Shannon. Abby Lee was shaking the whole way out there. She kept looking over her shoulder, but every time I said something she said 'not now, just keep driving.'"

"She sounded scared out of her mind."

"She was acting like a mad woman, so paranoid. She had a bottle on her." Sheila bit her upper lip and turned her attention to the florescent ceiling lights.

"Nurse?" Clay pointed at Sheila who motioned for a refill of ice water. Her side was beginning to ache again and she asked for more painkillers. The nurses sent for the doctor.

"Abby Lee told me what happened that night."

"To Trevor?"

Sheila nodded. "So... at around ten p.m. the night before the big game Trevor pulled up to the drive-thru completely on queue."

"Wait," Clay interjected. "Franklin had his accident at a *drive-thru?*" Too many thoughts were going through his mind to process. He felt bile rising in his throat.

Sheila nodded. "Yeah, at the drive-thru." She took a deep breath before she continued with her story. "Only Abby Lee and Vern were working. The other two employees were sent home about an hour earlier. There was a master plan and Abby alone was at the center of it."

"Trevor pulled around to the intercom and ordered. She stood at the drive-thru waiting, while Boyles Sr. stood out of sight, just to make sure this went down correctly. Abby Lee was incredibly desperate, so desperate for the money and she was doing something without asking enough questions and that was just like her. She had plenty of time to skip out from that shift on that evening, I'm sure of it."

The doctor came by and checked a few of Frank's vitals. She then asked Sheila a few questions, scribbled something on a chart and was off.

"So, Abby takes Trevor's order and when the glass door rose up and he reached for his soda pop, but she pulled it back to her chest. He reached in further and she moved slightly further back and then BANG." Sheila hammered on the tray. Clay almost fell out of his chair. The noise rattled a few patients into various states of consciousness.

"Sorry." Sheila took another sip of water. The nurse came by with some pills in a cup and some fresh water.

"There was an explosion and the window shot down like a guillotine; the glass had been altered and the bottom of the drive-thru window was filed razor sharp. Glass sheared muscle and tendons in his left forearm. The glass pane lodged into his skin and snapped his forearm in half. Abby Lee heard the bone crack. He screamed and tried pulling his arm back but the flesh and tendons ripped away from his elbow. Boyles had set a plastic explosive in the release mechanism of the take out window and removed the metal plating on the bottom so the glass would act like a razor." Sheila's voice became monotone as she was now repeating herself.

"Jesus Christ," Clay mumbled.

"Apparently explosives were not his expertise, because he blew the place apart."

"Oh my God."

"Trevor's left arm took the brunt of the detonation; his searing flesh burned and reeked in the kitchen. Abby Lee was sick just from the smell alone. She said she could see that he was in indescribable pain. Trevor's face was contorted and the shrieks could be heard a mile away."

"Abby must have been in shock when you got her. How could a normal kid be coerced into something so horrific?"

"Money, a *lot* of money. She says that Boyles suggested he was only looking to shake the kid up, bruise him up a bit, and make him take the second or third game."

"What a fucking train wreck." Clay ran his hands through his hair.

"She said Trevor stared out the window at his arm as if it wasn't real, as if it wasn't his own. His arm was branded to the window."

"Then what."

"Something happened and his car jerked forward. The momentum of the car pulled his body out of the driver side window, while flesh and muscle peeled from his forearm. By now, Abby is trying to do something, anything, she was screaming like a mad woman. Vern, her boss, is running for the fire extinguisher. Trevor's arm was smoldering and his shoulder severely bent out of shape."

"He was tortured. Jesus Christ." Clay bowed his head and ran his hands over his face. "You're telling me the three of them got away with this?"

"The fire chief, the police chief and the ambulance chief were the only ones at the scene of the crime. It was all covered up."

"All three were on his payroll?"

"The next summer all three of them had new cars, were swimming in their new pools, and playing golf at Allan's club for free."

"You're telling me *no one* asked any questions? Not his grandmother, not Coach Riggins... nobody?"

"His grandmother took the police's word for it, I guess. And Riggins?" Sheila eyes narrowed and her brows set. "Riggins was happy to look the other way. He'll look any way he's told to, for the right price."

Unbelievable, thought Clay. The shootings at our drive-thru on Boylston might very well have been intentional. The events of sixteen or seventeen years ago, a cruel and horrific deed may have had repercussions across the country.

After all these years, the shooter of Kate and Rebecca and the death of my daughter originated here in Rebel, Rhode Island. Clay was quickly convincing himself.

"Is this him? Is this Trevor Franklin?" Clay pulled his folded composite from his wallet the creases fragile and worn. The same composite photo from thirteen years ago that Clay posted on walls and telephone poles and bulletin boards.

She just nodded and began to cry.

Clay stared at the photo in a different light. For so many years he was simply the bastard, the man who took away their family and put his wife in a chair, forever. Clay sat and stared at the photo trying to let it sink in. He now had a name. Thirteen years of hunting, and the man had a name.

"Where is Abby Lee?"

"She chose the low road, packed up, took an undisclosed amount of cash and moved to Boston, and that was the last I heard of her."

"And Trevor?" Clay swallowed hard.

"He spent months in a hospital, skin grafts and reconstructive surgery. He refused to let me up to see him so I respected his privacy." She paused. "I regret that very much. They say he had ten to fifteen percent mobility in his shoulder and less in his hand, but it could have been better had he kept trying. He became increasingly violent and once attacked his grandmother. She had him committed to a psychiatric ward. I know he got out eventually, but I lost track."

"The local ward."

"Yes, Mulliganskull."

Clay made a mental note for the morning. "His parents?"

"Both dead, at least that's what he told me once; I'm not entirely sure. I didn't pry. I know this though, Trevor's parents were junkies from the outset, they found young Trevor as a nuisance and shipped him off to her parents."

"You have no idea what happened to him?"

"No." She thought for a moment. "He did sell the family home."

"Where did he go?"

"No idea... so there you have it, Clay, Rebel's deep dark secret. And its Rickey Boyles' father at the heart of it." Sheila looked over for the first time since she began. "So now what?"

"Not sure, this is quite a revelation." Clay was just starting to absorb everything. "I have a cop friend at home. I'll see what he can turn up. In the meantime, I'll go to the psych ward I guess, and maybe the real estate office. What about Boyles Sr.? Does he still live here?"

"He doesn't spend much time here any more. Onwards and upwards, I guess." Sheila laughed bitterly. "He has liquidated a lot, all but the strip club. That's where his goon pals spend most of their time... when they're not beating the hell out of old men, that is." Sheila looked over at her father. Her eyes welled with tears once again.

Clay's jaw clenched. "So where can I find him?"

"He keeps a place here and in Texas. I suspect he is in New York City with his kid. After all, Rickey's success is all he ever cared about, anyways. And Lord help anyone who got in the way."

A nurse came to Sheila and her father. "We have a semi-private for both of you." With that, tubes were adjusted and monitors temporarily turned off as the gurney was setting up for transfer.

Sheila turned to Clay and wished him good luck, basically giving him permission to move on. He waved as they were moved towards the elevator doors.

Clay shook his head at the train wreck he left in his wake and then staggered to the foyer, it was four a.m., twenty-four hours without sleep. The coffee and lack of food made him very light headed. He slapped his own face lightly trying to get his wits about him.

Intensive care.

He raced up the stairs with the sudden burst of adrenalin curious about the whereabouts of his friend Max. Maybe he just came out of surgery, reconstructive likely. The floor nurse pointed to the head nurse across the hall.

She was a tall thin woman, standing eye to eye with Clay. Her expression was painful when she eyed him heading towards her; she put one hand on her hip a clipboard resting in the palm of the other. She tapped it lightly against her thigh. The bowl of nails she ate for breakfast gave her such a pleasant demeanor.

Clay waited a few seconds "Okay, you have a recent admittance a jaw injury, hulk of a guy, I need to see him."

Her eyes cast down the hallway then towards the nursing station, everyone was wrapped in something. "Are you family?"

"No, I put him in here and I just want to remind him of something, Nurse Frulack." Clay read her I.D lapel.

Nurse Frulack was quite taken by the response. "I should be calling the police."

"No, you should be throwing me a parade. Now, where is he?" Clay looked right into her eyes.

She looked him over. He could sense her sizing him up. The scales must have tipped in his favor.

"Max Bentley has kept our intensive care busy through the years, but never as a patient… until today… Room 307, but hurry, I'm off duty in ten minutes." She pointed down the hall.

Guilt and euphoria ripped through Clay's mind. He felt horrible about the state of affairs for both Sheila and Frank, yet he was ecstatic that in about two hours he could call Kate and give her the news. They had finally identified her shooter. The bastard and, surprisingly, a future hall of famer's dad would be held to account for the lives he had ruined. Thinking of his unborn child, Clay felt a lump in his throat and gulped it down.

For the lives he had taken.

It was truly a team effort full of tenacity, hard work, intelligence, devotion, and a stroke of good luck; the culmination of thirteen years of effort now hinged on finding Trevor Franklin's whereabouts.

Clay burst into room 307, a double occupancy room with only one tenant. 'Max Bentley,' it read on the chart at the foot of the bed. He lay motionless; a tube ran up his nose, another down his throat. His head was enormous with a bandage that wrapped around his forehead and chin. It looked like a turban gone wrong. His feet hung over the end of the gurney.

Clay felt no remorse. He strolled around the room closing the blinds, grabbed a chair and lodged it under the door handle, then reached for a second chair on wheels, spun it around, straddled it, pulled up to the bed and bumped it hard, causing Max to open his eyes and look toward the ceiling. Clay reached out and slapped him. He felt an enormous sense of satisfaction as his palm collided with the pulpy flesh. Max squealed, his eyes burst wide open, shocked no doubt from the sudden attacked followed by agony. His natural instincts, always aggressive and hostile tossed him up in the bed, but he backed off quickly when the pain was too intense. Max's eyes glanced towards the buzzer for the nurses' station.

"Yah, go ahead, press it." Clay pointed with his eyes towards the same buzzer. "Here I'll do it for you." In an intentionally clumsy manner, he reached over the ox and clicked it over and over again.

Clay waited fifteen seconds just staring old Max down. "No one is coming. We all hate you. I have posted a sign on the door," Clay ad-libbed metaphorically. "'I am a rapist, and a bully, but I am also a patient, please govern yourself accordingly'. Here's hoping things go well for you here."

Clay leaned over him, almost nose to nose and looked at his handiwork. Max followed him with his eyes; his range of motion was poor, probably due to the three broken ribs.

"I know you can't talk because your jaw is wired shut, so you will just hear me out." Clay examined the bandages. "You know, a baseball bat is a lot more resilient than a human skull. You are warped and twisted all over the place now and you do have a similar stitch pattern to that of a 33-inch hand crafted chunk of lumber." Clay got right in his face. "I played ball, and that bat I used was my back up, so don't make me use my 'go to' stick next time."

Max's eyes were watering, and his heart rate accelerating, terror had him completely wound up.

Clay raised his index finger and wagged it in his face. "Find a new favorite restaurant. If you so much as look at either Frank or Sheila, I will drive up the coast and finish off what I have started. Am I crystal clear?"

Max looked away.

Clay viciously squeezed Max's jaw, it felt good to inflict revenge and he squealed like a pig. "You processing what I said or just really, really stupid."

Clay finally released.

Max quivered and then nodded slightly.

"I am not fucking around here, Max, and this goes for the other Max and your brain trust back at the peelers club. Are we clear?"

Max didn't move. Clay slapped him viciously, causing him to writhe in pain his back arching.

"Are you taking me seriously, Max?"

Clay grabbed his jaw again and squeezed mercilessly, Max's broken jaw cracked slightly, and he howled like a wolf. He grunted and moaned, then straightened himself up the best he could and nodded emphatically.

"Good, then we have an understanding." Clay pulled the chair back and strolled out of the room, Max followed his every step intensely.

"Remember the sign on the door; don't expect the staff here to be very affable. That means nice."

16

Max II rose at two thirty a.m. put on some gym clothes, did some calisthenics, went down to the lobby, and cancelled the wake-up call, went for a light jog, then back to his room. He showered and dressed in a dark suit, blue shirt, tie and cufflinks, hopped in his car, pulled into a twenty-four-hour convenience, ordered an extra-large coffee then parked across the street from 475 Union Street West, the home of Kate and Clay Stoppa. There he waited.

***

Clay nodded at Nurse Frulack and made his way outside, turned his phone on and checked for messages. Two showed up… both from Kate. The first was to wish him a good night's sleep and the second, to call after her push. She had a professional development day Monday and had planned to set out early, at around six, and do their familiar loop. He looked at the time; it was almost five thirty, so he dialed her cell and predictably got no answer. She probably had the thing on vibrate and wasn't out of bed.

He called Tubs' cell but as always, straight to his answering machine. Clay's third call was to the Gremlin Police Department, on the off-chance Tubs was in early. No such luck; Tubs was apparently not working that night. Clay left a message with the night officer for him to call, suggesting it was urgent. Clay looked at his watch and noted the early hour. He dialed Tubs' home number.

"Sally? It's Clay. Sorry for calling so early, but I need to speak to Tubs."

Clay tried to listen patiently as Sally assured him she had been awake for a while; she was getting ready to take Harper to her mother's for the weekend.

"Michael isn't at home; he's been on the night shift all evening."

Huh?

Either the officer who'd answered his call at the station had been misinformed, or there was something that Tubs wasn't telling his wife. Clay pushed the thought out of his mind; he had too much to think about at the moment.

"Well, can you leave a note for him to call me on my cell as soon as he gets in? It's... it's really important." Clay's voice cracked as he hung up.

As Clay strolled back to his car in the early morning sun, his eyes burned from a lack of sleep, his hands a little shaky for the same reason.

New experiences, most of them bad, but a revelation to share with everyone back home. He planned out the day. It should start with a couple of hours sleep, then head up to the psychiatric ward and see if Trevor Franklin remained an outpatient here in Rebel, or if his file had been transferred somewhere else.

It was just before dawn; Clay's adrenalin was in full swing, so sleep was out of the question... off to the psychiatric hospital then home.

What happens when I find this guy? My God it feels like a lifetime. What do I say to this guy? Clearly, we aren't the only victims as he has run a string of these drive-bys. What if he just blows me off? I think I would absolutely lose it on him. I get what happened to him was horrific, I can't imagine, but my wife and child...

Clay swallowed hard. Allan Boyles, what a piece of work. Indirectly, he is as much to blame.

I will deal with him too.

If Franklin had already been discharged from the institution, which seemed likely, Clay decided that he would make his way to the real estate office to see if they had a forwarding address. Tubs could throw out a nationwide manhunt for the guy, go federal, state and county with his search, and maybe convince the F.B.I. to get involved. Clay's mind was racing.

Clay arrived at Mulliganskull less than an hour's drive west. It was just after six a.m. After grabbing a stale coffee at the only gas station for miles, Clay pulled into the visitor parking and stared at the limestone structure. He pulled out his phone and searched 'Abbey Lee Haason, Rebel, Rhode Island'. He got a hit, but not what he was expecting. The local *Spectator*'s headlines read 'Tragic End to Inaugural Drive'. A car driven by a young teen in her sixteenth year ran a red light and the passenger side was t-boned by a pickup truck. The passenger, Abby Lee's mother, was killed instantly, the driver, Abby Lee, was driving from the licenses registration office where she had just completed her written examination for her driver's license. They were two blocks from home.

"Holy shit," Clay mumbled to himself, "no wonder she got out of dodge!"

The architectural layout of Mulliganskull Psychiatric Hospital, located in Amish Country about one hour due west of Rebel, was in the shape of a hand. The imposing structure cast a shadow of fear on all that set eyes on it. The structure implied dominance over such passive surroundings. The contrast of rolling hills and prosperous farmsteads with the repugnance of a building set on a hill, as if to say 'I am here to scare the living hell out of you'.

The knuckles of the hand represented the administrative layers, entrances and exits, the cafeteria, recreational facilities, meeting rooms and so on. The fingers represented various wards.

Ward A, the thumb, was for the criminally insane, those who were a threat to themselves and others. The patients in this hallway were locked up in the individual units, separated completely from one another. In most cases they were convicted murderers and in some cases multiple offenders deemed untreatable. They had no direct interaction with any other inmate, for the safety of everyone involved.

The first finger, Ward B, housed long-term condemnations of the criminally insane. They were of little harm to themselves, but would likely destroy one another if given the opportunity. Deemed incurable and long-term inmates, they had limited and highly guarded social interaction.

Ward C also known as the second finger or simply 'the bird' also housed individual cells for each inmate, but the crimes were less violent and the chance of being integrated back into society, much more likely.

Ward D was a transition ward; inmates could go either way, if disruptive, then to the bird, but with improvement, then to Ward E, the index ward, a step closer to life outside of the institution. Patients of this ward were generally short-term stays, a timeline of less than two years. Generally, no violent crimes were committed; typically, the misdemeanors included incidents such as break and entries, public disturbances, white-collar psychopaths jailed for embezzlement or fraud. They would make this their home after a while.

The fingers never crossed.

Patients could move internally from one ward to the next, but the actual patient body of Ward B would never interact with those in another ward; in other words, any public or social settings such as meals, recreation or rehabilitation would never mix.

Clay entered the administrative area and walked over to a sleepy security guard. "If I was looking for info on a patient or likely an ex-patient how would I go about it?"

The overweight security laughed. "You would likely fill out a series of forms, set up a meeting three months down the road and have that postponed."

"I like the truth." Clay managed a smile. "And what if I just wanted to know if a patient is here?"

"Admin opens in a couple of hours; there is a coffee shop just down the road."

"Thanks." Clay turned on his heels and walked back towards the imposing main door. He paused for a janitor and found himself boxed in by freshly mopped floors, the marble sparkling in the glistening wet film.

"I am going to make a mess of this?"

"Not a worry. Thanks for taking notice." A well-built man of small stature with a friendly smile looked up at Clay.

"I feel bad, it's pristine."

The man in the smartly pressed uniform smiled and glanced over his work.

"You're a Philly's fan I see."

Clay motioned at his cap. "Yes."

"A tough team to be a fan of."

"You too?"

"Unfortunately, yes." They shared a laugh.

"I moved up here from Philly twenty years ago. They pay more when you clean in a potentially dangerous environment so I couldn't pass it up."

"Wow twenty years, I guess you've seen them come and go." Clay's voice traveled in the vastness of the hallway. In the distance, they could hear indiscernible chatter.

"Seen 'em and heard 'em. The patients talk to me more than the doctors... more trust and a lack of intimidation likely."

"Yah, that would make perfect sense."

"What brings you to this Godforsaken place at this Godforsaken hour?"

"A patient... more likely a former patient."

"Yah, there have been many pass through."

"On the off-chance you wouldn't know a Trevor Franklin? I know it's a long shot."

"No, that name doesn't ring a bell." The janitor leaned on his mop handle. "Family?"

"No, he was a kid, a ball player who had an accident and ended up here."

"Lefty!"

"What?"

"I called him lefty, his arm was mangled and he was a lefty."

"Yah, that's him." Clay was astounded.

"I don't remember them all but, he... he was special. Mulliganskull was a cakewalk for him."

"What do you mean?"

"Pure genius. After about four months in the infirmary tending to his mangled arm, Lefty was moved into Ward C where he began his painstaking journey to get his ass out of here."

"Why do you know this?" Clay leaned against the wall; the janitor whose navy jumpsuit had Jerry embroidered in script on his left chest continued leaning on his mop. He paid no attention to the echoes from distant hallways. The noise was very unsettling to Clay, haunting in a sense

"He was young and scared; I was old and not scared so we would chat. He was set to be here a while, but... man he was a quick study."

"I'm Clay. May I call you Jerry?" Clay introduced himself with a handshake.

"Of course, Clay."

"So what do you mean quick study?"

"He was on the fast track to a positive relationship with the doctors responsible for his future."

"How do you know that?"

"He trusted me and he practiced on me. He would attend his group sessions, taking it all in, gauging what were considered to be positive and practice his next move on me. He was crafty, and within months was moved to the fourth finger."

"You knew him well?"

"I wouldn't say that. No one really knew that kid. He was cold, cold as ice, an unhampered liberty to do just as he pleased."

"A lack of conscience?"

"Yah, I see them all the time. You learn quickly which ones you can talk to and which ones you don't even dare make eye contact with."

"I'll bet." Clay turned to the voices then looked around at the vast open-air entrance and then trained in on the iron doors.

"He once said, he would leave this 'Alcatraz', but on his own terms, and it would take some time, but time he had."

"This is an eerie place."

"It is. Time stands still at Mulliganskull; Christmases, Easters, birthdays, and other special events mean nothing. Monday morning, or a Friday night, it's all the same for the inmates."

"So, he's gone then."

"Years and years ago. Two years of residence at the fourth finger, and an exemplary record, put that boy on weekly parole, the final straw was an Academy Award-winning performance for the parole board. As it turns out a psychopath is twice as likely to be granted parole; they are so hard to read." Jerry squinted and smiled. "The intelligent ones, like Franklin, have a leg-up on the powers that be, no inhibitions and the ability to manipulate the convoluted psyche of a normal person." He winked at Clay. "Done my research over the years, figured if I was going to be surrounded by them and the only thing between them and me is a broom, then I better have a good idea of what I am dealing with." They both smiled. "During Franklin's tenure here at Mulliganskull his grandmother died and this presented an opportunity for the young man.

Again, he performed an Oscar-worthy performance, using her death as an opportunity to show remorse for his violent behavior and a chance to repent his sins. His presentation was the icing on the cake and just two weeks shy of the fifth anniversary of his accident, Franklin was given a conditional release from here."

"I guess you never heard from him again?"

"No, he was long gone."

"You have been most helpful. Thank you for your time."

"Pleasure, I just hope you figure everything out."

"Me too."

Clay left dew prints in the grass as he cut across the vast lawn towards his car. A shiver ran up his back as he picked up the pace to distance himself from that hellhole.

***

In the months prior to his release, during weekly passes, Franklin was not sitting idly by on a park bench somewhere. He had set the groundwork in place to re-enter society on his terms, it was up to Clay to seek out the remnants of his trail from some thirteen years ago.

Tubs provided Clay information on the law firm that Franklin had been assigned by the state to represent him. Clay took a leap of faith and thought, 'Why would Franklin seek out new counsel when all he really needed was someone to probate his grandma's will?' Clay rolled up to Argue & Writs Barristers and Solicitors. He smiled at the irony of the name.

What a long shot, he thought as his car came to a rolling stop; it was eight a.m. on a Saturday so the best he could hope for was a contact name before heading back on the road. He hated the thought of another couple of days in this town.

Clay strolled up to the door and read lawyers' names, four in all then turned to take a photo of the window. Now to search out the real estate office in town, how would he ever find a house sale from thirteen years ago he wondered? Clay stared up and down the dismal downtown and glanced over at the City Hall building. Maybe Monday he would go to the land registry office and do some title searching, he did have

Franklin's last known address. He turned back to his car and accidently cut off a woman fumbling with her keys as she locked the law offices.

"Excuse me; are you a lawyer with this firm?"

"No, a legal secretary, the lawyers are teeing off right about now."

"Of course." Clay chuckled. "What was I thinking?"

"Do you need an appointment? I can give you a card, Janet is the newest partner and the least busy, she could probably fit you in this week."

"I was actually looking for Mr. Hones."

"Oh." Her face dropped, and she turned towards his name on the window. "He died last summer… cancer… awful."

"I am terribly sorry, maybe I will call her."

"What was it you wanted from him?" Clay followed the women to a red car and opened the passenger door for her so she could unload the box of files. "Thank you, a gentleman; I was his personal secretary for twenty-eight years."

"Wow… well he had a client, Trevor Franklin." Clay stopped, as the expression on her face was that of disbelief. "Sorry, did I strike a nerve, I…" he paused not looking to offend.

"A name only spoken in whispers in these parts."

"Can I buy you breakfast or a coffee, maybe you can help me out?"

She stared at the files in the front seat. "Why not."

"Clay Stoppa." he held out his hand.

"Dorothy Therobout." The hand of a sixty-plus-year-old woman took Clay's and squeezed his ever so slightly.

Clay noticed the tattoo on her wrist as she pulled back. "We'll just go across the street to Dunkin's." She pointed with her head as they crossed the road. "The last name I expected to hear in this town was Franklin's; who are you, Clay Stoppa, and what in the world are you looking for?"

"I really didn't come here to explore his story, but it came up when I was looking into Rickey Boyles."

Dorothy shook her head in disgust, a common occurrence when his name was uttered. Clay held the door for Dorothy and waited for her to slide into the booth first. "Not a nice family. And what brings you here?"

Clay gave an extremely abbreviated version of his own story, no sense fabricating his ties with a newspaper any longer. He shook his head at his stupidity.

"Well that's a long shot for sure… but the Boyles family are nasty, and I guess anything is possible. So, you found out about Trevor Franklin how?"

"Going through his high school pitching records and a meeting with his old coach, Riggins, and well things didn't add up."

"Trevor disappeared you know, a lost soul with no guidance, Lord knows where he ended up."

"You… your firm represented him?"

"Sort of… his release from the psych ward was not finalized and we were working through the logistics. He had day passes and some weekend passes and the boy never stopped. He must have studied some law in the ward because he came to us so prepared."

"What do you mean?" Clay popped up and grabbed two coffees and a glazed dutchy for Dorothy.

"After his grandmother died, he had the house listed and sold in days, furniture and all. She had a small inheritance of cash, which he laundered into hard cash as well."

"How do you know this?"

"Two pawn shops here in town and everyone knows everyone. He had gold watches flying back and forth, one of the pawn dealers was a client of ours, and he wanted to make sure things remained above board."

"How well did you get to know him?"

Dorothy's eyes welled up slightly. "My biggest weakness is my… my…"

"Kindness?" Clay pointed with his eyes at her tattoo.

Dorothy flipped her wrist exposing the delicate calligraphy. "Yes, I suppose you're right." She paused. "He and I chatted some, I suppose I may have reminded him of his grandmother. He was… oh boy… how should I say it… complicated." She paused, wrapped both hands around her coffee, and looked outside. "Trevor was spooky and kind at the same time. He showed virtually no expression or emotion… but he did and said some kind things to me."

"For example?"

"Well… the last I saw him he asked me to come out to his car for a moment, he had this old beater, a grey Chevy something his grandma left him. He parked in the back, it was late in the afternoon on a Friday, and no one was around, but I trusted him. I remember looking into the back seat and he was loaded to travel. I knew he was up to something, but he was given such a raw deal I thought… good for you, get the hell out of here, no one has done you any favors. So, Trevor picked up a USA McNally road map and unfolded it across the hood of his car and then he pointed at the State of New Mexico, and I said, is that where you are going, Trevor, New Mexico? He slowly shook his head from side to side, lifted his finger, and set it on the most desolate spot on the map. It was this giant space of nothing where no highways intersected north and south. *That's where I am going.*"

"So where was it?" Clay sat forward and motioned for two more coffees.

"Trevor pulled out a larger scale version of the State of New Mexico and showed me a blank section of land about the size of his thumbprint with only one desolate road and a pinprick by the name of Ramon, New Mexico. 'That's where I am going,' he said, 'a dust bowl two hours south west of Albuquerque.'"

"So he told you? He obviously wanted someone to know."

"Well that's the interesting thing. He asked me to never say a word, and I asked him why he wanted me to know. He turned to me and looked me straight in the eyes and said, 'If I don't tell someone, I will completely disappear.'"

"He folded up the maps and grabbed some stuff from the back seat and threw it in the trunk."

"What else… you are hesitating." Clay pressed ever so slightly.

"I caught a glimpse of some cold hard cash, wrapped in plastic and bagged in large canvas with heavy metal zippers. Franklin put Rebel in his rear-view mirror two hours after his release from the ward. He never met with his parole officer. No one from his past saw or heard from him ever again."

Clay finished off his second cup and stared over at Dorothy.

"Here's my card… for what it's worth." Dorothy rummaged through her purse. "Maybe something will come up and you may have more questions."

"Thank you, you have been very generous with your time this morning. May I ask one more thing?"

"Sure."

"Did you have much to do with Rickey or more likely, his father?"

"No, nothing really, only rumors and propaganda. Boyles Sr. used a high-flying firm in Providence for his legalities, and, of course, Rickey was just a kid when he moved away from this disaster." Dorothy threw her arms in the air motioning at Rebel in general. She motioned to slide out from the booth and Clay jumped up and squared up with the fellow behind the counter.

Clay angled towards Dorothy's car; however, she waved Clay to continue on to his car, and with an equally gentle handshake, Clay turned towards his car. He threw both hands in his pockets after throwing on his thin-framed sunglasses to cut down on the morning glare. He walked very slowly staring at the sidewalk below him. Clay was deep in thought. Trevor was a tragic figure, no doubt, and he certainly had reason to despise the Boyles family, however, Clay did not feel any remorse for the shooter.

He stopped and spun around thinking he had passed his car and was ready to hit the alarm button when he spotted 'old faithful.'

As he approached, his eyes narrowed in on an envelope on the window. He glanced at the other cars parked on the street and in the parking lot close by, but his was the only one with the accessory. With a look of concern, he pulled the plain manila envelope from under his windshield wiper. He aggressively ripped it open and read it hastily.

"Jesus Christ. Fuck me." Clay broke out in a cold sweat and reached for his cell phone.

17

June 17

Kate forced her phone in the side pouch of the chair; the ringtone was inadvertently left on vibrate. The morning was fresh, and the sun was on the rise—the forecast called for a glorious late-August day. Kate quietly worked her way outside, careful not to disturb Rebecca, who had stayed up late to clean up after hosting a committee meeting.

A six-a.m. push was extremely early; it was closer to six thirty before the dedicated Kate Stoppa was outside. Too often, Kate skipped an exercise class or one of her eight-mile circuits. As Rebecca's comfort level increased, she became more and more insistent that Kate not miss a workout, but even that nudge wasn't always enough.

She set her iPod to Bon Jovi; he was sexy and upbeat and she was really missing Clay. Her first few pushes along Union Street were sluggish; her right shoulder ached, probably from the way she slept. Union to Tower was a slight upgrade, just enough to force stronger strokes, thus getting the blood flowing a little sooner. South on Tower was a little tricky: a downhill grade that forced Kate to use her brakes. The batting gloves were slipping slightly, and she made a mental note to let Clay know a new pair was in order. The downhill ride was the lesser of two evils; the uphill portion at the end of a circuit was grueling on her arms.

The driver of the black sedan passed by Kate unnoticed, turning right onto Main Street and went around the block. He then pulled in behind Kate, but remained as far back as his eyesight would allow; no one else broke the silence that morning, all was quiet in Gremlin.

Once she wheeled over the bridge, two substantial inclines were the next trial, the first noticeably short and steep—an odd setting for the old fire hall. Chief Ferguson tooted his horn and waited to turn left. Kate managed a smile and a short nod, careful not to lose her stride. The second incline came shortly after the first—she had just enough time to build some speed and dig into the steepest grade she would face. Upon reaching the top of the hill, her arms always felt like rubber, and it would be a good half a mile before she had her breath and some strength back. From this point forward, the topography undulated gently, so it was clear sailing for the balance of the circuit until she re-entered Gremlin.

The time was closing in on seven a.m. Her phone began to vibrate, but she was completely unaware of any distractions except her music, a little louder than it should be. She began to enjoy the rush of adrenaline flowing through her body. She loved that feeling—that feeling like she was flying on wheels. It felt as if nothing could stop her.

***

The driver of the black sedan pulled over at the town limits, the industrial road was a short jog to the right. He got out of his vehicle relieved himself just steps from the car, and then did some stretching; he was stiff from sitting for so many hours. He stared over the hood of his car and watched Kate wheeling off in the distance. The sun was completely above the horizon now; Kate's silhouette disappeared behind a row of two-hundred-year-old maple trees in full bloom. The wheat was ready for its second cut and the golden amber swayed in the light breeze. Max flicked his cigarette onto the oil-soaked road.

Kate's pace was powerful; she had strength once again in her arms and was entering a controlled rhythm. She glanced at her trip meter and checked her pulse: all functions stable.

Once she was completely out of sight, Max got back into his rental sedan, pulled the handgun from the glove box, and stuffed it under his belt. He put on driving gloves, checked his look in the rear-view mirror, and pulled back onto the county road. He didn't see one vehicle on the road besides his own.

***

"Yes, T. F. Green International Airport general info."
"T.F. Green, how may we assist today?" The customer service representative's pleasant response annoyed Clay.

"Any flight Delta, Continental, Southwest, US Airways to Philadelphia, this is an emergency." Clay was racing towards the interstate.

"US Airways flight at 2:53 this afternoon."

"That's it?" Clay's voice was the sound of desperation.

"I'm afraid so, we can look for connecting flights, would that help."

"No." *I have to make a decision now. Fuck.* Clay slammed his phone onto the dashboard and entered onto the southbound ramp, curling onto the highway at a blistering pace, his VW barely hugging the road. The note lay open on the passenger seat.

'You were asked to leave, but I guess you needed a better reason to go home to Gremlin. Your precious Kate is in trouble.'

His next call was to the Gremlin Police Department. "Who is this?"

"Constable Jake Miles, who is this?"

"It's Clay."

"Oh, Mr. Stoppa, the captain isn't in yet."

"Yah I know, do me a favor and go past the house, my house, will you?

"For sure, Union, right?"

"Yes. Go make sure Kate is okay. She may be out for a push."

"Is there a specific route?"

"Yes." Clay filled the young Constable with directions.

Where the hell was Tubs?

"We have a house guest as well, Rebecca."

"Okay, I will find her as well, what is this about?"

Constable Miles was grabbing his belt and walking towards the door. Reception wasn't open until seven a.m.; the small police department would be empty.

"I have reason to believe my wife is in danger, could you get over there and call me on my cell, 919-555-2414."

"Will do, Mr. Stoppa."

Clay hung up and pushed his speed to eighty-five miles per hour. He tried calling Tubs on his cell and at home but got no answer. He was helpless for the next four hours.

***

Kate was in the zone as she approached the liquor store in the adjoining town of Alora. Max pulled his black sedan to within yards of Kate. She was oblivious to the perpetrator; her iPod continued to pound out a live track of Bon Jovi.

The liquor store was on the same riverbank that graced Gremlin. It was a stand-alone building, a three-story limestone with small rectangular windows on each floor—formerly a cutting mill—tucked down a hill; an absolutely beautifully renovated shop. Kate loved this turn around because of the huge and newly paved parking lot. She always coasted into the lot, it was a long gently rolling entrance only wide enough for two vehicles to pass, and then it opened up into a lot that would hold upwards of thirty vehicles quite comfortably. She smiled after a quick glance at her watch, it was just past thirty minutes; it was a very good split.

Max pulled up and parked at the top end of the driveway blocking the entrance. He got out of his vehicle, itching his tattooed neck with his car key, then glanced quickly at his surroundings and was satisfied only he and Kate graced the surreal setting. Max ran up behind Kate then took control of the wheelchair, flipping her right earphone away. Confusion quickly became terror, and Kate reached for her brake.

"What the hell?" Kate glanced over her shoulder at the stranger who had taken control of her chair.

"Kate, keep your hands where I can see them." He had a firm grip on the short handles of her chair and thundered ahead his powerful legs picking up speed.

"What the hell are you doing? Who are you?"

"Your husband is not a good listener and is prying into our past. It's none of his business." Max was beginning to pant.

"Past? What past? What are you talking about?"

The building was coming up quickly; Kate sat perfectly still, her eyes darted back and forth. She contemplated how to protect herself from the inevitable crash. "Let go of my chair."

She looked over her shoulder once again staring up at an enormous man's chin.

"I am here to send a message that we aren't fucking around, and that 'tune up' on my partner, will not go without retribution."

What partner, what tune up, what retribution? What the fuck has he done in Rebel?

With that, the stranger increased his tempo and broke into a sprint, his muscular upper torso pushing Kate towards the building with all of his might.

"Stop, for God's sake, okay, you have scared the shit out of me, what do you want from me?"

***

"Mr. Stoppa." The officer got Clay on the line. "She's not here; Rebecca said she went for a push. I am tracing the route now."

"Shit. Okay, get going… now."

***

"For fuck sakes I'm in a chair here, what are you doing, you animal?"

Faster and faster he ran the chair towards the building. The three-story structure now cast a shadow on Kate. She began to scream as they drew closer and closer. Max could not run any faster; Kate had never moved this quickly in her chair the wheel bearings hummed louder and louder.

Pavement was quickly coming to an end. He released the chair just as the parking lot turned to grass. Kate reacted quickly to her first opportunity to establish control of her chair and jammed on the brakes but pavement gave way to a grassy slope causing her to spin and turn sideways. The right wheel jammed into a rut, grass and dirt flying into the air, her momentum flipped the chair, the first rotation was completely in the air and the chair landed right side up. Kate tried to release the strap around her waist and throw herself clear however she ran out of time. The chair spiraled out of control, and Kate's foot came loose from the harness. Because she had no control of the appendage, it caught the jagged stone corner of the building, ripping her knee apart sending her kneecap sideways, and then tearing a gash the length of her shin.

Kate was having spasms of terror quickly followed by seconds of clear thought as she scoped her surroundings looking for an opportunity to right herself and ultimately save her life.

Now the chair was spinning three feet in the air like a top parallel with the ground. She threw her arms out to brace for the next clash with the earth, but the series of large landscape boulders just prior to the top of the ravine came up too quickly. Kate gritted her teeth and braced herself piling into a rock shoulder first, snapping her collarbone so severely the bone tore right through her skin.

She let out a blood curling shriek and sat petrified, helpless, and in insurmountable pain, waiting for the next jolt.

Kate picked up momentum down the steep slope, rolling and bouncing towards a fence that separated the liquor store property from the scenic look out, over the gorge and a sixty-foot drop to the rapids below. Kate's pulverized shoulder pounded against the ground time and time again; it was all she could do to keep her head tucked as low as possible, the thrashing unyielding.

The pain was unbearable as the chair tumbled and jarred her body. The chair began to bounce like a beach ball flipping over itself until it cleared the six-foot high chain link fence that separated the grounds from the gorge. Kate sailed over the last precaution before the sixty-foot plunge to the shallow swift moving water below. She screamed terror not believing what she could see.

Kate felt the speed of the drop and knew it was over. She dropped like a cannon ball arching towards her abyss. The only thing between Kate and sure death were a string of maple trees lining the steep banks defying gravity as they grew tall and straight towards the sky ignoring the sixty-degree pitch that they laid root on.

Kate began her descent, still conscious and writhing in pain. She was strapped to a chair witnessing her final fate, scared of death, scared of its finality and wishing for her life back. She wished to snuggle up with Clay, she wished for a better hand to be dealt, so much was passing through her mind in just seconds.

A branch pierced what was left of her right shoulder, skewering her like a shish kebab, instantly stopping her free fall. She was pinned face up unconscious and bleeding out. Skewered to a branch that waved in the fresh summer breeze, Kate laid precariously close to fatal disaster.

Constable Jake Miles gave the right of way to the rented black sedan, as it turned left unto the county road back towards Gremlin. Miles wheeled into the top of the liquor store parking lot and saw nothing then turned back towards the station.

***

"You didn't see her anywhere? Okay, drive the route again, you must have missed her, she never deviates from the route… am I clear? And tell Mike he must call me as soon as he arrives this morning." Clay hung up and called the house. Finally, an answer.

"Rebecca, did you see Kate leave this morning?"

"No, what's wrong? An officer came by looking for her, but he wouldn't tell me why. Oh my God, is Kate okay?"

"It's a long story, but I believe Kate is in danger, so you need to find her and bring her to the police station and just stay with her. I'm still another four hours give or take. There may be a giant of a man looking for her."

Rebecca flashed back to the B&W. "I think I saw him last night; a huge guy with a tattoo on his neck. He held the door for me at the Black and White."

"Jesus Christ, call Miles back and give him a description. Where the fuck is Tubs? Rebecca, take the jeep and look for her, you know where we normally go. But be careful yourself."

"On it. Fuck."

Clay rang both Tubs and his wife, but to no avail.

Clay was completely out of character, panicking, he never panicked; he was racing down the highway, thinking the worst for Kate and entirely not in control of the situation he caused.

***

Tubs studied the last twenty rolls of the wheel, as if it would make a difference on a completely random outcome. He called for twelve chips.

"What would you like the value to be?" a leggy blonde asked as if she cared.

"One thousand dollars per chip."

With no emotion the dealer set a white chip on the '$1000.00' counter and spun the wheel.

Tubs played with his wedding band then reached onto the board; his thumb and index finger flipped the chips one under the other. Number five, number thirty-one, his wedding date, number seven, number twenty-six, Harper's birth date, number eleven number eight, his wife's birth date, number twelve, number seventeen, Clay's birth date, and finally black and even.

"No more bets." The dealer waved her hand across the table. The ball slowed down, and began bouncing around. It settled on red, thirteen. Using a large rake, the blonde ran the metal along the green velour pulling all of the chips to her station. There was no winner on that spin.

Tubs showed no emotion as he strolled away from the table one last time. Three hundred and eighty-four days ago he and Sally had no mortgage and a small savings account set aside for their son's university education nine years down the road. 'Red thirteen' capped a losing streak that began a year and a half ago and his current economic position, credited to the maximum with no equity in the family home, over forty thousand dollars on credit cards and a ten-thousand-dollar promissory note to a private lender. It was all hidden from his wife; she knew nothing. He wasn't sure how Sally would pay for Harper's five hundred and twenty-five-dollar hockey pre-registration on Wednesday.

Tubs strolled to the VIP Casino parking lot, unlocked the car and before sitting behind the wheel he pulled out his government issued automatic handgun, reached into his jacket pocket and found a clip with two bullets.

The morning was glorious, not a cloud in the sky.

Tubs made a left out of the parking lot, crossed the River Grange and headed right towards Gremlin approaching the sign pointing right to 'Brooks Look Out'. It was there he proposed to Sally, his wife of nineteen years. He thought of what she was likely doing right at that moment; probably packing Harper's bags in preparation for her trip to her mother's. Tubs was glad she would be out of town. It would be easier that way.

Tubs pulled up sharp and stayed back from the intersection allowing Constable Miles and a black sedan to clear the crossroads. Once the two vehicles were out of sight, he decided the lookout would be a fitting location. He crept down the liquor store parking lot decline, the same one used for 'Brooks Look Out' and pulled out his gun stepped out of his car and watched for other vehicles. There was no one around. He traced his steps of twenty years ago. It was dusk on a Friday night, and Sally wore a bright yellow dress with white trim and bobby socks. They had just left a fifties theme sock hop at the local community hall. Tubs was sick to his stomach shaking at the thought of a wedding proposal to his high school sweetheart. He had just been hired as a police officer and the time was right to settle down with his only love.

Tubs entered the undersized path to the look out, checked the clip one more time, then stuck the barrel of the pistol in his mouth, tilted it upward putting pressure on the roof of his mouth then turned towards the river.

His eyes adjusted to the tree limbs above.

He pulled the gun from his mouth. There was no logic to the sight in front of him. The first thing he recognized was Kate's wheel chair. Tubs stood stunned for a few seconds trying to comprehend what he was staring at. From what he could discern, Kate was lying in her wheelchair facing upwards suspended by a branch that had pierced both Kate and the chair.

"Kate." He screamed over and over but with no response. He had no home for his handgun so he stuck it down the side of his slacks then pulled out his phone and called the direct line to the hospital's main reception.

"Patch me through to emerge." He raced around the lookout to get a better vantage point. "Who's the doctor on call?"

"Langstaff."

"Put me through, it's Police Chief Campbell."

"I think he is with someone."

"If you don't want"—he caught himself—"I would get him on the line RIGHT FUCKING NOW."

"Langstaff."

"Bill, its Mike Campbell."

"What's all this, Mike?" They had little to do with one another socially, but through the years had their fair share of emergencies to work through as a team.

"I need you at the liquor store in Alora. Kate Stoppa has been in a serious accident and can't be moved."

"Car accident?"

Tubs looked around, he glanced up the parking lot at the lane way. *What kind of speed was she going and how do you get this far out of control? This makes no sense at all.*

"No, I doubt that." He quickly accessed the situation. "Get over here ASAP. I wouldn't ask if I thought we had an alternative."

"I'll take your word on this."

Tubs proceeded to call every emergency number in the county: fire, EMS, and his own department to send every available person. Exhausting every avenue of help he knew, he stood at the point closest to Kate. She was skewered to the maple branch about fifty feet from the ground: ten feet below the lookout point and approximately twelve feet horizontally from where he stood. He called out her name time and time again but received no response. Kate was in a sitting position, best described as the angle a roller coaster seat is set, just before reaching maximum height before the first dissension. The branch in question was only two inches in diameter unable to sustain the weight of either Kate or her chair. Her saving grace was the significant branch below the chair. The branch's lateral growth spanned out in the shape of a hand; the wheels of Kate's chair rested on the series of branches intertwined from the neighboring tree.

Constable Miles was the first to arrive. "Oh my God, is that Kate Stoppa? Mr. Stoppa has been flipping out looking for her. And for you."

Tubs said nothing. He had the overwhelming feeling that he'd failed his best friend.

"Is she alive?"

"She sure as hell better be."

"How the hell are we going to get to her?"

To Tubs' ears, the question sounded like an accusation. He had to do something. "Boom trucks," he muttered, determined that he wouldn't fail his friend again. The next call he made was to Bill Johnston, one of the 'good old boys' in town and owner of the largest construction company in the county.

Bill Johnston answered on the second ring.

"Bill? Its Mike Campbell, Kate Stoppa's had a horrible accident; I can't even tell you if she is alive, but I need your help. I need you and a couple of boom trucks at the liquor store in Alora. Sounds crazy, but trust me on this."

"Consider it done. I'll call Donna at the electric company, she can help us too." Bill didn't ask for details; he was a man of results.

Just then, an ambulance sped over the hill and came to an abrupt stop just in front of Tubs. The two paramedics began to survey the scene, mouths open.

Tubs thought of calling Clay's cell phone, but he didn't know what he could possibly say. He decided to wait to hear what the doctor said first, and then chastised himself for being a coward.

A few minutes later, a fire truck arrived, sirens blazing, with Johnston's boom truck close behind.

Rebecca drove into the chaos of emergency lights blazing, as she was following Kate's route in hopes of locating her. She began to panic as she pulled into the liquor store driveway and recognized the familiar face of Tubs, but this time he had his game face on and he was all business.

Where the hell is Langstaff?

Tubs spun around and then his shoulders shrank a little.

Where was I when I was needed?

Tubs took the helm, steering trucks to the brink of the cliff, organizing the booms and sending fire and electrical workers to the base of the trees.

"No one moves until I give the word." The Police Chief held the electric blow horn.

***

November 2, Present Day

"I think this will be the end of the line for Boyles; he has walked the first batter in the seventh. They are clinging to a one-run lead and there is a convention on the mound."

"It's hard to believe Boyles could raise a smile out of his manager at this juncture, but he has. The winner of this game wins the World Series; it's as simple as that, and these two are carrying on like they haven't a care in the world."

"Wow, isn't that something? Boyles keeps the ball and will face the next batter."

"Boyles reaches into his experience vault and leaves not one, but two of the Padres caught looking at strike three. This isn't the time to get cute in the batter's box."

"Boyles has slowed this game right down; he is tired and is now turning to his veteran savvy, trying to get into the heads of the Padres batters. He has two down and has just walked his third batter of the night. He now faces his nemesis from years gone by, Jack Hawkins, a utility player that has been brought into the spotlight here in the seventh."

***

Wolf pressed his glove against Allan's wound. Boyles almost passed out from the pain. "You have had a grand impact on me and my family. A man of your character must have some form of a conscience, so I ask you, what event in your life, as you reflect in your final hours, give you chills, and maybe twinges of guilt?"

"Fuck you." Allan Boyles sat still; his stomach was nauseous.

"Nothing comes to mind? Okay, take a guess at who I am. For each wrong guess I will ram this knife into your side and twist it."

Boyles swallowed hard.

"I'll give you a few moments."

"I know exactly who you are."

"Oh, do tell."

"You are a fucking lunatic who wants fame."

"Okay, at the count of three my name better come out of your mouth… the one person you went to terrible lengths to ruin, the one person you took just a little too far; otherwise, I collapse your right lung. One, two…"

***

Clay swerved a little, startling himself.

Okay, man up Clay. You caused this, you fix it. What's going on back home?

With that he piled past a convoy of trucks like they stood still.

***

Tubs huddled with Doris Hartley, the head of electric, Bill Johnson and Ted Ferguson, the fire chiefs for both towns. They didn't have a lot of time. Kate was not responding to their voices. Maybe they had all the time in the world.

The light breeze was enough to sway the branches, and with each creak they collectively held their breath. After some harsh words for one another and a lot of finger pointing, the plan was in place. The impromptu emergency task force had four strong-willed personalities locking horns, but for all the right reasons.

Tubs pulled them apart and sent everyone on task.

Six pull ropes ignited, six chainsaws the engines humming then peaking and straining on the hardwood branches, wood chips flying everywhere. The crew below cleared a steady stream of brush in and around Kate's tree and the adjoining trees thus creating a clear-cut large enough for the four buckets to close in.

Tubs was screaming out orders, his face contorted and flushed red, nothing happening fast enough. Doctor Langstaff arrived; the last on the scene, Tubs practically carried the man to the first boom and sent him to Kate. Everyone stopped. The chainsaw tempo dropped to idle; all emergency workers just stared at the first boom as it crept at a painfully slow crawl towards Kate. The boom operator pulled up as close as he dared, the doctor reached over and touched her wrist. He signaled for silence and the chainsaws were turned off; you could hear a pin drop. The doctor cocked his head to concentrate; his hand remained on Kate's wrist.

"I have a pulse." Cheers erupted. "It's very weak. We have to get her out of here."

By now, firefighters had suspended ladders sixty feet in the air and rested them on the branches closest to Kate. They crawled across like spiders on a web closing in on the wheelchair then began to examine how to ultimately release Kate.

"I can only get her so stable up here; we need to find a way to get her to the ground. Call for an air ambulance to Philadelphia General and ask for Dr. Harrison Jacobs to meet me in surgery. He's the best I know." Doctor Langstaff directed his order to Tubs.

"I need her blood type sent over to Philly."

They set up two intravenous lines, one a saline drip, the other O negative blood.

"Get as many branches clear... have we figured out how to move her yet?" Tubs called over to Donna in the hydro boom.

By now the other two buckets were in motion, Tubs and a paramedic in one and the fire chief and a hydro worker in the other.

Tubs made a phone call as he pulled his bucket back.

***

Clay picked up. His frustration flared and he couldn't control his anger. "Where the fuck have you been? I think Kate's in trouble and Rebecca and Miles can't find her."

"Are you driving?"

"Tubs don't fuck with me."

"Maybe you should pull over, Clay."

Clay gritted his teeth and pushed the accelerator down further. "What is it, Tubs? Just tell me."

"Okay, I have found here. She is alive."

"Alive?" Clay's voice cracked. "What does that mean, alive?"

"It's bad Clay; it looks like she... like she lost control of her chair and descended off the gorge behind the liquor store. She's currently pinned to a tree trunk."

Clay was trying to formulate in his mind a mental picture. He calmed himself took some deep breaths before speaking. "Okay, I can't quite understand what you're saying here. She hit the trunk of a tree?"

"No... not exactly, the only thing holding her from a sixty-foot drop is a bunch of branches." Tubs just could not tell him about the branch going through her. Clay tried to speak, but couldn't formulate any words.

"She is unconscious. We have boom trucks, hydro and Jack Johnston, fire, and ambulance as well. I've got Dr. Langstaff in one of the booms and he is dressing some of her wounds and starting some IV drips as we speak."

"She is in a tree? How, why?" Clays eyes welled up, a dangerous situation at his speed.

Tubs sensed his state. "We have air ambulance on their way; she will be at Philly General, so go straight there."

"Air ambulance, you've got to be fucking kidding me." He repeated Tubs statement. Clay could not believe his ears.

"Okay, don't lose her, Tubs." Clay's eyes were streaming, his stomach in knots.

"I really got to go here, buddy."

"Go." I am going to fucking kill the bastard who did this. Okay, be strong, you are no good to anyone in this state. He thought about the note and imagined the terror in his wife's eyes. I'll kill him, I'll find him, and I will rip his throat out with my bare hands; I am going to fucking kill him.

***

Tubs pulled his bucket back slightly to reassess. He looked into the parking lot and saw Rebecca among the group. Their eyes locked briefly and Tubs went to his blow horn. "Okay, people, we have a job to do here, so let's be strong and as a team get this done."

"The air ambulance will be here in thirty-five minutes." Miles called up.

"Okay Doc, what do we know?" Tubs called out.

"This branch here"—he pointed at the one that shot through her shoulder like an arrow—"It cannot move. That's as far as I have got." With the assistance of a paramedic, Langstaff was putting in sutures and continuing to block off the bleeding.

Tubs called Fire Chief Ferguson and Donna, the head of hydro, over to him. Their buckets converged just a few feet from Kate and the doctor. They pointed and discussed options for about two minutes then reviewed it again.

"Okay, doc, we are ready."

"What am I doing?"

"Staying as close as you can to Kate and let us know when we can get in there."

The doctor finished up and nodded for the team to move in.

Two firemen stood on branches below Kate, one directly under her chair the other off to the side holding a chain saw. A boom was positioned above Kate with Chief Ted and a line cutter. Donna and Tubs got in tight to Kate and the doctor and paramedic were pushed out slightly and no longer able to reach her.

"On the count of three, Joey, you will steady the branch that goes through Kate, Donna and I will do the same up here. Ted, you and Jordan below will cut the branch, in our case just above our hands and in your case"—he pointed at the firemen below—"just below the hands. Once the branch is cut, some of the weight is going to rest on you, Sam."

Sam adjusted himself under Kate's chair; his safety harnesses checked and double-checked. He pressed his own back against the back of her chair. When the branch is eventually cut, he would be in a position to take all of the weight. "I've got this," Sam called out.

Tubs adjusted his bucket so he and Donna could hold a handle of the chair in one hand and the branch in the other. The boys with the chain saws waited, the motors idling softly.

"She can't lose any more blood; I can't stress this enough." The doctor leaned over his bucket.

All systems go. They waited for Tubs' command. He waited for the breeze to give way, staring at the leaves quivering above Kate's head.

Maybe I did shoot myself and I'm in hell; Kate is actually at home in bed.

"Slice the branch gently, allow the chainsaw to do the work, put no pressure whatsoever on the branch. Those of us holding the branch do so with a steady hand. We are not removing the branch from her shoulder; we are not removing Kate from the chair." He checked the breeze again.

"ON THREE. ONE, TWO, THREE."

The branch was cut in less than a second and the rescue team held the limb steady. The weight of the chair moved onto the firefighter below, he was surefooted and steady; Tubs and the others held the chair with their free hand and adjusted the buckets under the corner of her chair.

"She is bleeding; the fresh gauze is going red." Tubs' voice was fretful.

The doctor moved in as close as he could. "Shit. We've got to get her to land. Now!"

Rebecca stood off in the distance, holding her hand to her mouth bouncing up and down in anticipation.

With one hand on the branch and one hand on the chair, Ted and Tubs locked eyes. With one hand on the chair and one hand on the controls, the line workers, Alex and Donna, locked eyes.

"Steady." Donna called out as the weight was lifted from the firefighter below, and now the chair was suspended fifty plus feet above the ground.

The buckets moved in sequence, the jostling kept to a minimum. In the distance the chopper could be heard. Slow and steady they crossed the air, working in unison, upwards towards their ultimate destination. A gurney was set on land with firefighters and other paramedics anxious to help out. After what seemed like an eternity, they reached the lookout and Kate was passed over to the land crew.

"We are transporting her chair and all. We will deal with the branch and harness at the hospital." Doctor Langstaff was more than definite.

The rumbling of the air ambulance brought on another cheer. Tubs wiped sweat from his brow as a rush of emotion swept over him. He paced back and forth and waved to Rebecca off alone in the distance. Around him, workers hugged and shook hands; the team came together with a common cause leaving success as the only option.

Langstaff, the fire chief, and a paramedic would board with Kate. Tubs watched in silence as the helicopter readied for takeoff. Langstaff came over and praised him for orchestrating the situation. "Without you, Campbell, she would never have had a chance. Good work." Tubs knew that was rare praise from the doctor. They shook hands in an unspoken truce. Everything was so surreal.

Tubs walked over to a patrol car and leaned on the hood, resting his hands on his knees. Emotions were running high and getting the better of him. Sally should have been a widow an hour ago, Tubs dead by his own hand; instead, he was marked a hero. The rescue team was beginning to pack up, mostly in silence hoping for the best. Tubs looked around and saw Rebecca sitting on a grassy knoll sobbing into a towel that was left behind.

"Rebecca." Tubs waved. "Come on. We've got to get to Philly."

Rebecca nodded and gathered herself the best she could and scampered down a slope to his car, then opened the passenger door only to see his pistol. Tubs grabbed it and threw open the glove box. "Sorry about that."

Rebecca was street savvy and sensed there was more to it than a misplaced gun. It was awfully careless for a cop. "No worries." They hopped in the car and prepared to set off for Philadelphia's General Hospital. Tubs hands were noticeably trembling, so he used the steering wheel to suppress the shaking. Rebecca watched from the corner of her eye.

"It's no use. Will you drive?" Tubs rolled out of the car and walked around the corner of the liquor store, then vomited into a garbage bin. He took a moment to stroll back and forth then climbed in the passenger seat. He signaled to Rebecca, who engaged the engine and headed for the interstate.

Rebecca sure picked a poor week to give up smoking. They both lit up as she bolted down the highway. Tubs closed his eyes. A phone call startled Tubs from his light sleep; it was Clay calling Rebecca's phone. They put him on speaker. Rebecca filled him in on the air ambulance and its ETA, careful not to discuss the severity of her wounds and how they came about.

"Tubs, you there?"

"I am." He kept his eyes closed.

"I have a suspect for you. He goes by the name of Max; he lives in or around Rebel, Rhode Island and may be boarding a plane or train to Providence. Also, check the car rental agencies in Rhode Island and greater Philly."

Tubs thought back to Miles and the black sedan just as he entered the liquor store. "I'll make a call right now and get the state troopers to do an alert on a lead I may have."

"Listen, Tubs."

"Yah."

"Thank you."

"We saved each other today, Clay," Tubs muttered under his breath, too quietly for Clay to hear. Rebecca looked over at him, but said nothing.

"Listen, Clay, you slow down and drive safe. Kate needs you alive."

"Okay." Clay obliged and reduced his speed by one mile an hour.

***

Giuseppe Ante nodded in approval as he walked around his sedan, took an envelope and stuffed it in his lapel pocket, looked both ways, then snapped his fingers. The Philadelphia mobster agreed to loan the car to his old friend from Rebel, no questions asked. The rendezvous was at a nondescript hotel on the airport strip.

A driver pulled Max's car curbside, jumped out, and held the door for him. Max hopped in and allowed the valet to load his overnight bag from the sedan.

Within five minutes he was heading north to Rebel, Rhode Island, no one the wiser.

***

Four hours after Tubs found Kate and three hours after she arrived in Philadelphia, she remained in surgery. Rebecca paced back and forth, one eye on the clock, the other on the hallway waiting for Clay. Tubs nodded off, as he was physically and emotionally spent. He attempted suicide, went bankrupt, and became a hero; it wasn't even noon.

Two hours later Clay arrived. He and Rebecca hugged. She pointed at Tubs, but suggested to let him sleep.

"When did you sleep?" Rebecca looked into Clay's raccoon eyes.

"It's been a while." Clay rested his head against the painted cinder brick behind the waiting room chairs. This scene was oh too familiar. His mind went adrift.

Kate laughed a lot more before the accident. After she was confined to the chair, Clay would watch her daydreaming while doing mundane chores, her face reflective and terribly sad. He rarely talked about their lost child and never talked about her body and how her lower half had deteriorated so.

The good times were still better than the bad. They would snuggle under a blanket during a snowy Sunday afternoon and eat popcorn watching all of their favorite movies. They would pick themes and rent a dozen movies, flipping through the boring parts, throwing popcorn at the screen and cheering when the hero saved the day.

They competed in the Philadelphia marathon a number of times, together. They always made a long weekend of it, renting a penthouse suite and spoiling each other with room service and hot tubs. They loved each other dearly; maybe the accident drew them closer in one sense. But when it was all said and done, Clay continued to struggle with the debilitating results of that fateful day.

Clay was sitting now, his head resting on his hands in a prayer like position. He waited with his eyes closed as his thoughts drifted off once again, this time, to a completely non-productive train of thought… the 'what if' scenarios, the scenarios that had no rational basis, but continued to dominate and torture his mind. You want to bang your head against a cement wall because nothing good can come from such conjecture. So instead of shaking it off, you paint new scenarios, like walking the beach together or playing in the tall grass, or building their cottage ten miles out of town, or just pushing their daughter on a swing. That thought immediately stained his despair with anger.

"He has a name." Clay broke the silence.

Tubs pulled his head from the wall and uncrossed his folded arms from his formidable mid-section. He opened one eye and turned it towards Clay. "Who has a name?"

"Our shooter. The man who shot Rebecca and Kate." Rebecca stared at her feet.

"Trevor Franklin." Clay was calm.

"Trevor Franklin?" Tubs repeated. "Do we know this guy?"

"No, as it turns out he was a victim himself."

Rebecca covered her mouth, looked at Clay, then brought her hand down quickly.

"Trevor was a ball player on the same team as Rickey Boyles in high school. It was Rickey's dad who couldn't stand the competition and he maimed Franklin for life. At a drive-thru no less."

"A horrible secret." Rebecca turned away from the two men.

"Mr. Stoppa." Clay jumped to his feet and Rebecca followed suit. Tubs jolted to attention and stood beside his best friend. Dr. Langstaff and a Philadelphia General surgeon were walking towards them.

Doctor Langstaff allowed his co-worker to do all of the talking.

"All in all, we are cautiously optimistic. She is a hell of a fighter."

The doctor was a small, physically fit man standing in his scrubs; sweat marks on his chest and under his arms. "I am cautious because she lost so much blood. Her body has endured incredible trauma, so we now have to see how she reacts."

"Can we see her?" Clay glanced over his shoulder.

"Soon, yes."

"She was pretty banged up." Tubs was hinting.

"Yes, we removed the branch, put numerous pins in her arm and shoulder, we did some preliminary plastic surgery, but that can be an ongoing procedure."

"And her leg?" Tubs continued to probe.

"She shattered her leg, and we have repaired it. Her collarbone was reconfigured and she will always have a bump on the right side now."

"Her shoulder. She needs her shoulder for her wheelchair. Can we see her?" Clay asked again.

"Of course, yes, however Kate is being kept in a state of drug-induced unconsciousness. We need her body to bounce back from such severe stress and this is out of our control."

"Why unconscious?"

"The less stress on her right now the better."

"How long is she going to be drug-induced?"

"She will be in intensive care for quite some time and will have a full-time nurse in her room for the first forty-eight hours at least. We want to monitor her progress as she comes out of the anaesthesia."

"Then what?"

"We will reduce the painkillers over the next forty-eight hours; however very slowly as she does not need any more strain on her heart.

It's a good thing she is in such fantastic cardiovascular health, otherwise she would have arrested."

"You can go see her, but we ask that you allow us to do our work over the next couple of days. It would be in everyone's best interest if you get some rest while she rests."

Clay thanked both men and turned to the nurse insisting that all three be allowed to see Kate. The nursed warned that she will not look good and is covered in monitors and tubes.

As it turned out, no matter what the nurse said, it could never prepare Clay for that moment he set eyes on his wife.

With Rebecca and Tubs following tentatively behind, Clay walked into Kate's room, and fell backwards. She looked exactly like a person strapped to a chair rolling and bouncing and finally skewered into a tree should look like... and then some. She looked like hell. She actually looked worse than that. Her skin color was sickly white; she had bandages on top of bandages up her right side, a tube shoved up one nostril and one down her throat. She had three IV bags funneling into one line that was taped to her forehead. Three computer monitors mounted above her bed flashed green and red lines, bouncing across the screen beeping and chiming. She had a catheter and a tube running down her neck disappearing into her green gown.

Clay pushed his hair back and paced. He was flashing back to the last time he was at his wife's bedside in an emergency room. The similar smells and sounds all too overwhelming, Clay's despair flared into anger. Clay's rage was now channeled in two directions, first Franklin, the shooter, and then Boyles Sr., the catalyst of this situation.

Rebecca stood with her hand covering her mouth, crying silently; Tubs went straight to the bathroom and was sick once more.

Clay was the first to approach Kate. He pulled up a chair beside her bed, reached under the tightly drawn bed linen and found a couple of fingers he could hold. He looked into her closed eyes and he laid his head on the bed then cried like a baby. Rebecca and Tubs quietly exited the room silent and weepy eyed.

"Oh God, what have I done to you, Kate? I am so sorry. Had I known it would end this way I would never have done this. I love you so much." He blustered and cried. "Take us back, Kate, take us back. I am completely, unequivocally responsible for this." He focused on her closed eyes once again.

He pulled her hand to his mouth and kissed her fingers. His face went bright red until he exploded with tears once more. He wept until he could no longer.

***

Tubs brought coffee to Rebecca and Clay who had collapsed on a bench just down the hall from Kate.

Rebecca broke the silence. "So, what is the record for going with no sleep?" She had one eye on each of them.

"I have to go home tonight, guys. I need to hug my son and sit down with Sally."

"Do that, Tubs," Clay urged quietly. "Hug them both for me. Anything happening with Max?"

"Nothing at the airports or car rentals that we have picked up. I haven't got anything back from the trains, either. But I'm hopeful I'll be able to make more progress back at the station."

Clay had moments of blinding rage, followed by dismay and hopelessness. He was losing the battle of wits. "We should stay the night and regroup in the morning." Clay turned to Rebecca.

"When's the last time you slept, Clay?" Rebecca asked again. Her voice was taking on a maternal tone.

"About forty-eight hours ago," Clay admitted.

"You're going to the hotel across the street," Rebecca informed him. "No excuses. You need sleep."

Clay finally relented.

"Are you sure you're going to be good to drive, Tubs?" Rebecca asked, remembering the scene in the car only hours ago.

Tubs nodded. "Yep. It'll be a good chance to clear my head. I've got a lot of thinking to do."

Rebecca nodded almost imperceptibly.

They departed with hugs. Rebecca and Clay headed across the way to the hotel after checking in on Kate one last time. Clay collapsed onto his bed and started to cry again. He shed tears until his body shut down as if to say enough. He didn't stir for the next six hours.

***

November 2, Present Day

"You could not have scripted this game any better"
"It's like the perfect storm, weather, gamesmanship, intrigue."

***

"I mean it, give me a name, Allan." Wolf continued his threat.

Boyles moved his hand ever so slowly and touched Wolf's hand. "Trevor Franklin, you are Trevor Franklin." Allan Boyles was in a living nightmare.

"Some names you never forget, right, Allan? Seventeen years later we come full circle." Franklin removed the glove from his left hand and rolled up his sleeve. The scarring was raw, his skin like beef jerky. The reconstructive surgery looked primitive; he had layers of skin grafts flopped over in different directions, a collage of mutated cells. The tendons and muscle tissue on his forearm were indented to the bone. A million-dollar shoulder and a mutilated arm; it still looked painful, all those years later.

Trevor pulled back his hood for the first time and the men turned towards one another. Their eyes met, Trevor's cold and calm, and Allan's desperate and crying for a break or forgiveness or something.

"You're pathetic, Allan."

"I am."

"Where were you when I lay in that hospital bed going out of my mind?"

"I went too far."

"Ya think?"

"I know."

"With a blink of an eye, you took it all away from me, all the hope and opportunity, gone." Trevor put his hood back up. "Did the alcohol deaden the nerves?"

"Somewhat."

"The cover up must have been your finest hour."

"Money."

"You learned years ago that people will turn their backs on morality when the almighty dollar is waved; after all, you built your empire on that principle."

"That is true." Allan sounded defeated.

"I didn't pass out… did you know that?"

Allan just shook his head.

"Of course not. It would be just shy of five years before I would leave a medical institution."

"Mulliganskull."

"Yes." Franklin paused and reflected. "Imagine—if you can—having cancer of the conscience." Trevor paused and the two of them exchanged glances.

"I don't understand."

"You completely lose your conscience and over time you have nothing at all, no feeling of guilt or remorse no matter what you do."

"You?"

"Yes, no limiting sense of concern for anyone, no sense of shame no matter what action I take."

"No, I can't imagine." Allan was shivering.

"It is unfathomable for most… but not me."

"What are you saying here?"

"When events in your life pile up like a series of building blocks, like they did in mine, then maybe a straw does break the camel's back. If that straw is a horrifying mishap?"

"The drive-thru." Allan was clearly in another place and time.

"Yah, it turns your already teetering world… upside down, then… you end up like me…"

"A psychopath." Allan bowed his head slightly.

Franklin turned to Allan and smiled then let out a hollow, creepy laugh. He could see the life draining from the man's eyes.

Franklin sat back in his stadium seat and allowed his shoulders to drop. He could not recall the last time he relaxed. It certainly wasn't in the last forty-eight hours. It certainly wasn't upon his arrival in New

York City and likely not after the trade was announced. Franklin was on hyper alert for at least a month, and with his own name coming from the lips of Allan Boyles, he allowed himself a moment or two of relaxation. The torment of seventeen years culminating tonight, in Yankee Stadium, Game Seven of the World Series, was enough to set stir some emotion from the emotionless Franklin.

The two men sat in silence for a few moments taking in the events of the past few hours.

Franklin's eyes turned to Rickey Boyles on the mound.

That could have been me. That should have been me.

His thoughts drifted into his past. The first time he'd ever found love and encouragement in his life had been on the baseball diamond. It was to be his savoir; his education was riding on it and hopefully someday being paid to play the game. He trusted two things: his instincts and Abby Lee. Both failed him that fateful night and when he came to his senses three days later, his world had changed forever.

Gradually the fog lifted and questions were answered. *How bad is it? Really bad. How long will it hurt like this? A long time. When do I get these bandages off? Not in the foreseeable future. When can I pitch again? Are you a lefty? Yes. Never.*

His grandmother's knitting sat on the end table when she left each evening. She sat by his side in the hospital each day, however they had very little to say to one another. Sunday afternoon, after church she walked back to the hospital and to his room then took up the chair and lifted her knitting.

Franklin would pick up the local rag and read about Rickey's draft, and his Ivy League School opportunities. 'Local Boy does Good'.

"I prayed for your quick recovery so you can get back out on the field and do the things you do. I'm sure when that cast comes off you will have nothing to worry about." His grandmother would say, without stopping her needles.

She was absolutely right about one thing. He no longer worried. In fact, when Trevor reached over and snatched the knitting needles from her hands then pierced her abdomen and then ripped the bandage off his arm and stuffed it in her mouth, he wasn't worried at all. He simply walked out the door and down the hall, took the elevator, stepped outside, hailed a taxi and went to his house. After collecting some clothes and loading the Chevy he was gone.

A nurse walked into Franklin's room and began screaming. Staff ran to the room sickened by what they discovered. Franklin's rotting bandage was stuffed in his grandmother's mouth so she could not scream; he tied her arms to the bed and left a note.

'Don't worry, Grandma, it's only a flesh wound, you will be knitting away again before you know it.'

Police were called and the room was sealed. Franklin's grandma was rushed into surgery to remove the needles.

Franklin did not travel far. He sat in an idling car parked in the far corner of the parking lot of the Lic-A-Chic and watched the patrons enter and exit. He could see the blackened brick above the drive-thru window. The entranced was taped off for the renovations. Through a series of glass windows, he watched for Abby Lee. She always worked noon to close Sundays because the shift paid time and a half. He waited and waited; she was the easiest to recognize even from his vantage point, five foot five inches, a little too thin and always in the shortest of short skirts. Twenty minutes passed; if she had just started her break, she should be back on the floor any time.

The painkillers were wearing thin. Franklin examined his charred arm and disfigured bone structure. He picked up the knife he gathered from his grandmother's kitchen utensils and ran his thumbnail back and forth across the razor-sharp edge skimming just a little residue each time.

She will suffer like I suffer. No, painkillers. She must suffer like I do. Then I will deal with the others. And I'll save Allan Boyles for last.

Franklin may as well have left a trail of breadcrumbs to his clandestine location, as both state police and the local authorities sped into the Lic-A-Chic parking lot. The first car came head on with Franklin's and stopped inches away. The second car pinned his driver's side door and a third, the passenger side door. Franklin sat unimpressed and watched six men surround his vehicle all guns pointed at his head. The officers stood behind car doors and waited for any aggressive motion. One officer screamed for Franklin to raise his arms, but he sat still, daring the trigger to be pulled. The standoff lasted quite some time, had Franklin sneezed it would have been the end of him. His eerie coolness unnerved even the hardest of police officers. No fear, no remorse, just clear thought. Even the raw flesh of his forearm and the agony that emanated from it could not distract young Franklin.

Franklin broke the silence. "I will never make this mistake again." And with that he raised his hands above his steering wheel. He was escorted to a late arriving ambulance.

***

"Well I guess the big question again, is whether or not, to leave Boyles in?"

"I suspect he'll pitch into the eighth, but the first runner he allows on base, will be his last."

18

June 18

Clay awoke with a start, sat bolt upright and shook his head.

What time is it?

The clock read 4:07 but he wasn't clear whether it was a.m. or p.m. He remained in a state of shock. After a moment, Clay's world came crashing down when the fog dissipated; he wanted to be transported instantaneously to Kate's bedside. What if he slept through a call? A quick glance at his cell and the hotel phone calmed him for the short term. He jumped out of his clothes from yesterday and into the shower in a state of panic, considered shaving, and then threw on some fresh clothes. He was surprised to see his suitcase on the mini bar across the room.

He chose the stairs and skipped down the three flights taking four stairs at a time, then sprinted across the street. As Clay rode the elevator up to the ICU, he perused his phone. One message from Tubs, saying he had nothing to report. Turning left he approached Kate's room his heart was in his throat. Two deep breaths at her doorstep then the door was pushed open. His stomach acid left an aftertaste in his mouth.

The nurse looked over her spectacles. "No change." She was scribbling on a chart after looking at all three monitors.

"Is that a good thing?"

"It's not a bad thing." She continued to scribble.

"Do you think she'll wake up soon?" Clay almost whispered.

"We're expecting very little change for the time being. In fact, we want to keep her exactly as she is now, at least for the next twenty-four hours. Day three is when we're hoping to see some change."

"Day three? You mean, tomorrow?"

The nurse nodded curtly. "Yep. That's when they'll start reducing the morphine, and hopefully her body will start coming out of it."

Clay was no longer dizzy from exhaustion, but his flashes of rage and sadness continue to bounce around in his head.

"May we have a moment?" Clay swallowed hard.

The nurse looked up. "No."

"No? Don't you have to use the bathroom or take a break or something?"

She looked at her watch. "Give me five minutes and then you may have five minutes."

"Thank you." Clay's eyes filled with tears as he examined his wife.

He slipped into Kate's washroom and took a moment in front of the mirror; his mind was already made up. Situations arise and we either succumb to defeat or we rise with vengeance. Clay Stoppa certainly didn't get the results he was looking for over the last few days, but he was preparing himself mentally for today. Sometimes an eye for an eye would be the only form of retribution that seemed appropriate. He was never so angry in his life. Angry enough to kill? He closed his eyes and envisioned Kate in the next room.

No one gets away with doing this.

Clay was no longer looking at the big picture, the years of investigating; the discovery of Franklin and Boyles Sr. He was focused on one thing, that being the present and the villain that was right in his face: Max.

"What a fucking coward, wait till I get finished with you," he muttered to himself in the mirror.

Clay re-entered the room, and the nurse gave them some privacy. He found Kate's hand under the blanket.

"Kate you will pull through this, you have too. We have too many adventures in store." He swallowed hard, then continued. "I love you and I don't know what I would do without you. We are supposed to grow old together. We never saw it any other way."

He composed himself. "Why are we always at odds?" It was as if he was reading her mind.

"You would tell me to let it go, the police will look after it, but we both know that's not how it works. It didn't work that way last time, and it probably won't work that way this time, either. So, at the risk of really pissing you off again, I am going to right a few things today Kate and will see you this afternoon. It's only four thirty in the morning and I will be back in twelve hours, I promise."

The nurse re-entered.

"When is the doctor coming by?"

"A couple of hours from now, I suppose."

"And there's no chance she might come out of it today?"

The nurse shook her head firmly. "Like I said, there'll probably be very little change until tomorrow."

Just as Clay pulled out his phone with the intention of updating Rebecca, she tapped lightly on the substantial door and walked in with two coffees handing one to Clay, all the while starring at Kate. No words were exchanged. Rebecca pulled up a chair and sat on the other side of Kate pulled back her pillow slightly and began to play with her hair.

It was plain to see her eyes were red from crying.

Clay broke the silence. "Rebecca... she's going to make it. I have never met anyone with more resolve."

Rebecca looked over and nodded as she wiped the tears from her face. "How could someone do this?"

"I was just asking Kate the same question." Clay held Kate's hand. "Will you go to a mall at some point today and get us both some clothes? We may be in town for a bit. I have to take care of some things and will be back by three... four tops."

Rebecca nodded. She was holding her coffee cup with both hands, one firmly gripping the other.

Clay looked at her carefully. "How are you holding up, Rebecca?" He didn't want to ask the question directly, but he was sure she'd know what he was driving at. If his hotel room had a mini bar, hers would too.

"I'm all right, I guess," she mumbled. "I haven't... I'm good. I don't know how you're surviving so well, though. It's so hard, seeing her like this..." Rebecca trailed off, her eyes shifting to Kate's unresponsive hand, which she grasped in hers. "It's easy to just want to forget... to forget that people can do such horrible things to each other... Sometimes it just feels like I'm lost in the wilderness and I'll never find my way out. I can't believe my hole just got deeper," she whispered.

Clay felt a lump forming in his throat. "I know exactly what you mean, Rebecca."

"You couldn't." Rebecca mouthed the words.

"But listen to me. Kate needs you here," Clay told her firmly. "*I* need you here. We need your strength right now. Please."

After a moment, Rebecca nodded. "Yeah, okay. Okay. No drinking, I promise. But cigarettes are fair game. At least for this week."

Clay somehow managed a smile.

"Do you need to get back to Gremlin, Rebecca? To go to work?"

Rebecca shook her head and said, "Nope. I called Chuck and he says to take as much time as I need. He sends his love. Any word from Tubs?" she asked.

Clay shook his head. "He texted to say that they've put out an all-state alert, but so far, nothing." The thought of it wrenched Clay's guts, galvanizing him for what he knew he had to do that day. "Okay. I have to go."

"Clay, whatever you're doing, make sure you do it right." He thanked her for not trying to stop him.

Clay tried to clear his head during the arduous drive to the airport. He calculated, the flight to Providence, thirty minutes, car rental, twenty minutes and a forty-minute drive to Rebel, and then the reverse, Clay figured he had a maximum of four hours in town.

He quickly passed through the checkpoints for flight 312 to Providence. He purchased a walk on with no luggage and went straight to his assigned seat. The flight was no more than ascending to twenty thousand feet, followed immediately by a dissension to Providence, thirty-three minutes in all. He laid back his chair waving off any snacks or beverages, one last opportunity to clear his head and prepare for the day. There was no sense in thinking any further than today, this morning to be more specific.

Clay closed his eyes. Some days are better than others; we learned that at a very early age. Some days we do what is necessary and some days we stretch ourselves and do something that transforms us for better or for worse. This was one of those days.

Clay rented a bland four-door and bolted towards his hellhole, Rebel. The closer Clay got to the scrappy settlement the angrier he got. Stop one: Clay pulled over, out of plain sight from the rental agency, opened the trunk, loosened off the tire iron, and tossed it in the back seat.

He glanced at his watch then raced to Rebel High School. Clay was all business, no good mornings, no smiling and certainly no apologies for interrupting. He walked past some administrators straight into the main office and found the secretary from a few days ago.

"What the hell are you still doing here? Someone said you caused a ruckus and fled town."

"I don't flee from anything, I need your help with something."

"They also say you're not who you say you are."

"I'm Clay Stoppa and I am here to do some housekeeping. Now, may I see one of your yearbooks?" He pointed at the series of books shelved behind her formidable frame.

"You most certainly may not." The secretary crossed her big black arms across her big chest.

"I'm looking for Max Bentley's kid," Clay bluffed, hoping his risk would pay off.

"Why? What has he done now?"

Thank God he has a kid.

Clay shrugged. "Nothing. I'd just need to play poker with his dad. He's in the hospital, as I'm sure you've heard by now."

The woman narrowed her eyes. "And you just wanted to remind him of all the good things in life?" Clay took note of a hint of retribution in her voice. It seemed that Max Bentley's reputation had a far reach.

"Something like that."

She grabbed a yearbook and dog-eared a page. "Do I have to see you again?"

"I think Rebel falls somewhere in between Beirut and Mogadishu for places I want to revisit."

She handed over the book to Clay. "You wouldn't actually…?"

Clay raised his eyebrows, enough said. They bid each other adieu. He peeled out of her office following in the same tracks he had so few days ago, to the crossroads where Coach Riggins's stately house was located. Clay pulled into his driveway and slammed the gear into park then bound up the front steps and pounded on the door. No answer. He looked back over the front yard and noticed that the sailboat was gone from the driveway. Coach Riggins was probably sipping a gin and tonic in Greenwich Bay by now.

Gutless bastard. Clay thought as he trampled over a particularly well-tended patch of lilies.

It's not worth it, anyways.

He threw the rental into reverse and headed straight to the hospital and room 307. He sourced out the same head nurse as before, another stroke of good luck. Five minutes, he gestured.

"I can't let you go in there, its unethical." She stepped in front of him.

"Let me explain unethical." He walked with her down the hallway. "First of all, I am sure by now you know what this guy has done to Sheila and Frank, which is why I did this to him."

She nodded.

"My wife lies in critical condition in Philadelphia because of his sidekick. I need to find Max's cohort. I am hanging on by a thread. I have a flight back to Philly in less than two hours and I still have to beat the pulp out of a second guy twice my size. May I have my five minutes?"

"I heard none of this."

Clay entered the room, grabbed a chair, shoved it under the door and closed the blinds again. As he approached the beast, he pulled duct tape from his jacket and peeled it open with his teeth. He grabbed the right wrist of the buffoon and bound it to the bed rail. Max roused, but before he could defend himself his other hand was taped. Clay then put duct tape over his wired mouth and nose then punctured two nostril holes with a pencil. After taping his ankles, it looked like a fair fight.

Clay took the base of a water basin and pressed it firmly against Max's chin. Under the tape he shrieked in agony, his eyes wide with terror. Clay thought the direct approach best. He pressed the basin into his chin a couple more times before asking the question.

"Where's your friend?" He pressed again, now the gurney was gyrating across the floor, Max's body arching, his eyes suggested he wanted to kill Clay, but on the other hand he looked terrified of the madman on a mission.

"You can't scare someone like me. I no longer have anything to lose." Clay's voice was calm and clear.

"What is your friend's name and where can I find him this very moment?" Clay rolled the basin in his hands.

"When I hit you, I am sending your jaw through that window over there." Clay grabbed a scrap of paper and pencil left on the sideboard. "Write the answer. Where can I find him?" Clay released the tape on his right wrist after binding him above the elbow.

He began printing 'F-U-C-'

"Yah, I get it, you would probably spell it wrong." Clay leaned against the wall. "You know hate is a strong word where I come from, and I fucking hate you."

Clay got in his face. "You know why you can't scare me?" He flicked his jaw and made him twitch. "Because my wife is within an inch of dying and that has me terrified. I have nothing left to scare."

Clay pulled out the yearbook he picked up a few moments earlier and flipped to Mrs. Carol's grade four class photos. Max went ballistic kicking and screaming.

Clay got into his face. "I will stop at nothing. You're my first stop so make up your mind." Clay took the basin and swung it violently landing directly on both shins, egg sized bruising immediately appeared.

Max screamed for mercy. Clay clamped his bruised and broken jaw again. "This isn't bothering me in the slightest." Max shook his head no and pointed at the scrap of paper.

He finished printing. Clay moved to within an inch of the creature, their noses almost touching. Clay could feel the terror in his irregular breaths.

"If he is not there, I will be back." Clay's voice was calm. "I estimate you will be out of traction in six weeks, so I'll be back in five, you can guarantee that." With that he ripped off the duct tape.

He nodded at the nurse and took the stairs to the main floor.

Using a GPS, he drove to the gritty side of town, traversing what seemed like endless railroad crossings at each intersection and ugly buildings with makeshift additions, constructed of the cheapest materials available on that given day. A brick façade with an Elizabethan architecture would give way to a lean-to addition covered in Insulbrick, also marked in lime green aluminum siding. Between the buildings, vacant unkempt lots were fenced and filled with scrap metal, tin and rusting car parts and an abundance of litter in knee-length weedy grass.

Clay pulled up to a string of five buildings; all dirty brick facades and neon signs. He spun his car to the opposite side of the street directly across from Al's Pool Hall, an ugly business neatly pressed in a tough neighborhood, not exactly Clay's comfort zone, however he should not have expected anything less.

He analyzed the cast of characters standing in front of the establishment, four in all, unshaven, and their expressions vacant. Certainly some of Rebel's finest, drawn from its vast gene pool.

So how do I walk in there with a tire iron?

Without warning, Clay's driver's side window was smashed into a thousand pieces. A pair of paws larger than a grizzly pulled him out through the window then a fist drove through Clay's cheekbone sending him staggering across the street. The second blow to the stomach lifted him onto the sidewalk and now a pool cue was at his throat. Clearly someone was tipped off. Clay was firm against the brick wall, reeling from the attack and hurting everywhere. His gaze landed on his attacker's neck, which was wrapped in a snake tattoo. Clay thought back to Rebecca's description of the man she'd seen at the Black and White.

He was still regaining his senses from the first assault when a fist was closing in on his face. Elite athletes have lightning reflexes, and those in the top ninety-ninth percentile were blessed with something instinctively faster. The fist was within an inch of his eye when he shifted no more than necessary to miss the blow.

The giant man crushed his bare knuckles on the brick, breaking two fingers and his wrist. It was a good thing Clay moved, that blow would have killed him. All attention was directed to the antics of the injured as he cursed and jumped up and down, then doubled over his right arm.

Clay grabbed the pool cue that had him pinned and with a firm grip he popped it into the temple of the drunk to his right, and then sent his head backwards with a blow to the chin. The second participant took the heavier end of the cue in the groin, then an uppercut to the face. Clay drove his fist into the barfly's cheekbone, the recipient received the full impact, as his head had nowhere to go but against the brick wall. He fell unconscious.

Clay now faced his nemesis again. Blood was pulsing through the giant's face and neck, turning his sailor green tattoo a throbbing purple. This had to be the guy Clay was looking for. As the monster approached, the rage built between both men.

Kate didn't stand a chance with this guy. What kind of human being would do such a thing?

Max and Clay traded a few blows, but that wasn't going so well for Clay, even though he was only defending against Max's left. After each punch thrown by Clay, Max would simply shake his head back and forth and advance with a devastating one of his own, almost causing Clay to black out. Clay was tiring and his opponent seemed to be gaining strength.

Four spectators became seven as the racket outside of the hall was a comforting sound to the patrons. It could only be one thing, a street brawl. The combined IQ of twelve began to cheer on their fearless leader.

Clay was becoming a punching bag for the giant and was now backed up against his own car. A blow to the face, then the stomach, back to the face: Max was setting up between punches, reloading if you will. One of the geniuses on the sidewalk called to the Max, "Finish him off," as he slid a gun and a chunk of scrap lumber across the street.

"Beat him then shoot him." They called for blood.

Max only had to turn slightly, lifting his foot and stopping the pistol under his right heel.

Clay's right eye was closing shut and the pounding to his torso was only sustained through his good physical shape, however it was just a matter of time before he would be beaten to a pulp and sustain life-altering injuries. Clay could back up no further as he was pushed up against his rental car. He reached backwards into his front seat rummaged around and took a devastating blow to his stomach. The fist driving into Clay's mid-section was painful, knocking the wind from him. While doubled over writhing in pain, he spotted the lumber and grabbed the two-by-four from below the car. He grimaced, grit his teeth, and made full extension with his arms, generating incredible major league baseball club speed.

Meanwhile, Max picked up the gun from under his foot, set aim at Clay, and pulled the trigger; the two-by-four exploded into the side of Max's jaw, sending his teeth across the street, blood splashed like a bucket of red paint. He crashed to the street lifeless, his face visibly deformed.

Clay looked down at the primate, then picked up the gun threw it in the air and sent it to left field with what was left of his lumber. This sent everyone running back into the bar. He glanced at the shredded wood that remained in his hand. The bullet that was meant for Clay's head had entered the raw end of the two-by-four and traveled eighteen inches up the core of the barrel, pulverizing the pine in its wake.

Good luck.

Clay dislocated his opponent's knee with a vicious kick before struggling back into his own vehicle leaving a wake of destruction in his rear-view mirror as he pulled away. Once Clay was a safe distance from the debris, he adjusted the mirror towards himself, his face stung, and it hurt to breathe. What he saw shocked him. His white t-shirt was now red from the collar to his chest, his right eye puffed shut, and a shard of glass was glimmering in his neck, and that was at first glance. The plane boarded in less than two hours and he was at least forty minutes to the airport but knew that he could not be seen in public in this condition. He pulled into the hospital and went straight to the third floor. On more than one occasion he was directed to the emergency department but ignored the goodwill.

There he found Nurse Karen, the ice-woman he had an affinity with. She showed immediate concern as he winced, his right hand protecting his ribs as he continued to stagger towards her. She shuffled Clay into an empty waiting room.

"My God, boy, what did you do to yourself now?" she asked severely, although the concern was evident in her voice.

"Nothing I didn't deserve, I'm sure," he muttered, and then winced as the nurse touched some disinfectant to his bleeding brow.

"You're sure turning Rebel into a soap opera," she muttered. "I hate to think who's going to be next."

Once again, Clay felt immediately guilty for all the pain he brought onto so many innocent people in this town.

"How is Sheila, anyways? And how's her dad?"

The nurse tut-tutted. "They'll be okay. Sheila's back at home, resting, and her dad's been moved to a bed in the non- critical ward... he could go home if he wanted to, but I think he likes the food here. And the nurses." Clay smiled in spite of his pain.

Clay got his parade that day. A parade of nurses, who cleaned the glass from his cheek and neck, stitched a gash under his chin and iced his swollen eye. Big news in a small town travels quickly, and the donnybrook on the other side of the tracks had the nursing staff buzzing. They lined up just to get a glimpse of 'William Wallace' that righted two wrongs in their small town. A fresh white t-shirt was donated. Two young nurses volunteered to carefully cut off his old one, and then indulged him with a sponge bath. It was a good thing there were no sick patients in need of care for thirty minutes. He thanked Nurse Karen and limped to the airport with only minutes to spare.

19

June 19

By the end of her first full day at Philadelphia General Hospital, Rebecca had a good sense of the lay of the land. The best coffee was on the third floor, a small kiosk tucked close to a series of doctor's offices, the best salad bar was on the eighth floor, and home of the administrative offices and the best Chinese was the kiosk at the main entrance.

Clay caught up with Rebecca in the hallway just outside of Kate's room just prior to four in the afternoon.

"Jesus Christ, Clay. What does the other guy look like?" Rebecca touched his cheek. "You know she's going to kill you right?"

"I was just thinking the same thing so... I'm thinking that maybe a car accident excuse would suffice, at least until she's a little stronger."

"You're on your own on this one... besides; she'll know you're full of shit." Rebecca smiled from the side of her mouth.

She examined his eye a little closer. "Didn't know he was a lefty huh? What did you do to him?"

"He will be reminded of what he did to Kate each and every time he looks in the mirror. That's assuming he comes out of intensive care." He rolled his good eye towards Rebecca. "How is she?" he asked, his voice suddenly somber. It was a rhetorical question as the constant texts back and forth kept him well informed.

"No change. Tomorrow's supposed to be the big day."

"So they say."

They went into Kate's room, the nurse was sitting in the corner, and everyone smiled politely. Clay and Rebecca sat in silence one on each side of Kate's bed and there they remained well into the small hours of the morning. Rebecca was nodding off, so she bid Kate adieu and retired to the hotel. Clay never left her side that night.

***

Rebecca's alarm was redundant, but it went off nevertheless, so she arose from a sleepless night, grabbed a quick shower, and a few steps later she was on the main floor of the hospital.

She trundled up to the coffee kiosk then to Kate's room, waking Clay with the aroma of fresh coffee at around six a.m. He agreed to slip back to his hotel room and freshen up under the condition that she would call him the second the doctors arrived.

By all accounts, day three was to be the critical turning point for Kate. The nurses suggested they would no longer be required twenty-four hours once the medications were fully drawn down and Kate was slowly allowed to regain consciousness; however, they still remained by her side that morning.

Two doctors entered Kate's room just minutes after Clay returned. Rebecca and Clay exchanged glances, when they were asked to step out for a few moments, but complied without argument. After ten agonizing minutes the doctors emerged with brows furrowed.

"Follow us."

They walked in silence to a 'quiet room'.

Not a good sign.

"Please sit."

Clay lost all color as he steadied his hands on his knees.

This can't be good.

"Tell us straight up. What is going on?"

"Three days ago, we suggested cautious optimism as we needed to watch Kate's recovery from the significant trauma. Our CT scan suggests swelling of the brain. Mr. Stoppa, there is no easy way to say this, your wife has lapsed into a coma."

Clay's shoulders dropped; the words ripped his heart out and crushed it.

Take us back, Kate.

Rebecca whispered to herself, "The Lord hasn't been around much lately." She closed her eyes and shook her head no.

"At this point in time we do not know the depth of her coma, however it's not good," the doctor continued with more wonderful news. "She does not respond with any body movement to pain, no verbal response, and no eye opening."

Clay sat motionless as if he didn't understand what was being said.

"Furthermore, unless the pressure is relieved, her brain will continue to swell and push down on the brain stem which affects breathing and blood pressure."

"Does she have any permanent brain damage?" Rebecca wasn't sure where her question came from or whether it was even relevant.

"The effect of trauma to the brain is not predictable. It may or may not cause significant injury."

Could you be more vague?

"Now what?" Clay wanted to unload on the doctor.

"Now we do a procedure to reduce the swelling and we wait."

"Wait? How long do we wait?" Clay stood up and raised his voice; he was a little intimidating with the fresh scars on his face. Rebecca tried to calm him however the doctors reacted as if they were expecting his outburst.

"Mr. Stoppa, we are hopeful her coma does not last for more than a few weeks. Many recover fully, while others require forms of therapy."

"Some never recover." Clay spoke under his breath and ran his hands through his hair.

"We have to be patient. All of her vital signs are strong. We need to relieve the swelling. I wish we could tell you more."

"When will the surgery be?" Rebecca was anxious.

"Ten a.m. There will be papers to sign."

Clay closed his eyes.

Tell me I will wake up from this fucking nightmare.

His good eye welled up as he stumbled towards a chair beside Rebecca. She was in a state. "Around our house, Rebecca, we stand straight. We will get through this."

Could I sound less convincing?

He then put his arm out. She laid her head on his shoulder. They both closed their eyes, exhausted by the turn of events. Clay glanced one more time at the clock. It would be a long couple of hours.

The papers were signed and Kate was whisked off in a gurney. Clay and Rebecca meandered back to the waiting room. Hours upon hours of worrying was completely counterproductive; it was crucial to shift his mindset and reflect on happier times.

Clay's thoughts drifted back to a spring break, a couple of months before their tragedy. They had packed Wednesday night and when the school bell rang on Friday, they jumped in Clay's VW, threw on some Van Morrison, and headed down the coast to Myrtle Beach for some days of golf, sun and sand, a couple of steak dinners and long walks on the pier.

During the first full day they walked the shoreline after a glorious day full of golf, sunshine and fresh air. The winds were high and the waves crashed one after another. Kate looked amazing in her bikini, showing the beginning stages of a baby bump; Clay couldn't take his eyes from her as they chased each other into the first set of waves. He laughed, Kate screamed, and the undercurrents threw her to the ground. Clay dove towards her and came up in her arms. They kissed, but were interrupted when the constant series of waves knocked them off balance pushing them closer to shore. Kate shrieked with pleasure as they rolled to the water's edge.

She rested on her back, the final inertia of a wave tickling her arm. Clay leaned over her, their eyes transfixed on one another. Kate lifted her leg out of the sand and Clay pulled her closer running his hand up her shapely thigh. She leaned into him feeling each breath he took. How lucky they were.

"You are my everything, Kate, I am nothing without you. So mushy, aren't I?"

"No, it's sweet that you tell me these things. You come across as this macho jock, but I know the truth." She smiled. "You're as soft as a marshmallow."

They laughed and rolled around in the sand.

A larger wave splashed them again and Clay rolled to his back. Kate sat up and looked out to the horizon screening the sun with her hand. She pointed at what she thought were dolphins. He sat up, forcing his abs to naturally tense, much to Kate's liking. He agreed that they were in fact dolphins so he grabbed Kate's hand and they ran to the longest pier on the eastern seaboard only minutes away. "Grab your sandals and come with me. I am going to rock your world."

Clay caught Kate's hand with his right and the cooler with his left. All day he hid its contents. They ran to the pier, threw on their flip-flops, and bolted until there was nowhere left to run.

"Make a wish." They were out of breath. Clay pulled some bait from the cooler and threw it overboard.

"Make a wish?" she queried.

"Yah, the dolphins are coming."

"How do you know that?" Just as she finished her sentence, they appeared at the bottom of the pier thirty feet below. There had to be ten or twelve of them, staring up at Kate and Clay. Kate couldn't wipe the smile from her face. She had seen them in captivity, but never in their natural domain; somehow, they seemed happier, laughing and playing with one another.

"I don't believe it, they are so cute, and they're calling for us."

Clay pulled out two bread sticks that had been baked into circles about twelve inches in diameter. "Here."

He handed one to Kate.

"My parents brought me here as a kid and my dad said if you can get one of the bread rings on the fin of a dolphin then all your wishes will come true.

"Did you ever get a ringer?"

"No, but we sure had fun trying. We had some good times here as a family."

Kate went first, her ring spun like a Frisbee into the ocean, well beyond the dolphins below. One swam over and snapped it up, and they both laughed.

Clay acted out some calisthenics, making them both chuckle. Kate pushed him off balance then pulled him close and they kissed again. Clay grabbed his bread ring, shrugged his shoulders to loosen up, and then tossed his bread ring in a tight spin and it floated to the base of the pier. They both stood in disbelief, his ring landed on a dolphin's fin.

"Did you make a wish?"

He nodded.

"What did you wish for?"

"I can't tell you that." They walked hand in hand back to the sand.

The temperature remained in the low eighties as the sun was giving way to the horizon.

"Let's go for a swim and chase the dolphins." Kate pulled Clay to start running.

"Kate, come over here first."

Clay had a carving knife in the cooler and scratched off some barnacles on a foundation of the pier.

"This is the twelfth row, right?"

Kate counted the rows of telephone poles that were the supports for the giant boardwalk above. "Yes, twelfth row, why?"

"It was my dad's number in ball."

"And yours."

"Yah, and I watched him carve his and my mom's initials into this very pole when I was a kid. We would come to this pole every time we visited Myrtle Beach, and he would carve over the old initials. My dad would carve the initials and then I would run to my mom and tell her what he did, and she would say he didn't do it. I would jump up and down and tell her he did it, then finally she would come with me over here. Same routine every year I always fell for her antics." Clay smiled sadly.

"This pole?"

"Yes, this very pole." He carved CS loves KS and surrounded it with a heart.

A wave washed up and over the fresh artwork, the incremental eroding had begun.

"We will make a point of carrying on the tradition."

They swam out beyond the pier, Kate drifted in Clay's direction.

"Oh, what was that?" she was pushed forward. "I think a dolphin just brushed my legs."

"Don't be ridiculous." He smiled.

Kate wasn't smiling. "Oh my God it just happened again. Clay, I just got knocked from behind and it hurt. Help me get out of here."

Clay began to take her seriously and shifted from the sidestroke to a front crawl.

"CLAY, CLAY! Help me, I can't feel my legs! Oh my God my legs, Clay, I can't feel them, Clay, help me."

Clay awoke in a cold sweat, knocking his head against the waiting room wall behind him. Exactly what he needed, another shot to the head. He was disoriented for a very short time. Rebecca remained on his shoulder.

What the hell happened?

It was closing in on ten o'clock and a nurse came to get them. They were escorted to pre-op to spend a few minutes with Kate before the surgery. What a contrast from a few moments ago. Clay shook his head, took deep breaths, and then held Kate's hand. He hated the prep for surgery; it only reminded him of his father in his later years. Kate's face was relaxed, too relaxed, no emotion at all; the woman lying in the gurney didn't look at all like his wife.

Clay squeezed Kate's hand and whispered in her ear, "Don't let this be our last dance, Kate."

Rebecca couldn't bear to watch.

Kate had a number of hurdles still to cross if she was to survive, and they weren't likely to get any easier.

***

June 21

Kate remained comatose. After three days in Philadelphia, it was determined she could be transported home to Groves Memorial Hospital, a ten-minute walk along Union Street from the Stoppas' residence.

Clay drove back. It was the eeriest drive, following a paramedic transport unit with Kate lying on a gurney and Rebecca by her side. After signing more papers at Groves, Clay and Rebecca drove the short distance to their home and staggered into the kitchen, Clay throwing down his keys.

Not one thing had been touched during their absence: the morning paper from a week ago, the breakfast dishes, but nothing was right. He walked from one room to the next. Without Kate's presence, the house belonged to a stranger. Its aura was sucked up and splashed into a raging wind, dispersed across Gremlin. Their home had reverted back to a house. A house with no soul, its inhabitants without reason to believe: One Forty-Two Union had seen better days.

Clay called Tubs for an update on all fronts. Trevor Franklin disappeared off the map after the asylum, but he had good news on the Max character that laid the vicious attack on Kate. Based on eyewitnesses in the early a.m. he was a key suspect and they expected an arrest anytime. He was found in very rough shape in the hospital in Rebel.

Clay relayed this information to Rebecca.

"Well, that's good," said Rebecca, referring to Max's arrest. "What about the other Max?" Clay could tell from her voice that she still felt just as unsatisfied about the whole thing as he did. "And what about Allan Boyles? He's the one who set the Maxes on her, right? Isn't there going to be any justice for *him*?"

Clay just shrugged. "I'm not sure there's going to be any 'justice' in any of this."

"And Franklin? He's still out there, just roaming free. He's still out there; after all he's done to your family. And to me." She said this last part quietly, under her breath.

"Rebecca, you are part of our family now. What he did, he did to all of us. But we're going to stick together. We're going to heal together..."

Rebecca closed her eyes and shook her head. "It's times like this that I miss an elixir the most."

"We'll still catch the bastard, Rebecca," Clay promised. "We've just got to concentrate on getting Kate better first."

"Are you up to trading shifts?" Clay leaned on the kitchen island; Rebecca jumped up and sat on the counter on the other side about twelve feet away. "I'd just like to be with her now."

"Of course, anything."

"You have been a Godsend throughout all of this, Rebecca."

"I am here for both of you, you know that. We will get through this together, you said it best."

Clay walked into the study, a truly regal room, two walls floor to ceiling bookshelves and a cozy leather chair to curl up in. Clay could visualize Kate all snuggled up wrapped in an afghan his mother had crocheted, reading a favorite novel. He scanned floor to ceiling; different titles reminded him of better days, however there was one book he searched for, one that she kept by her bedside when they were first married. He would come home late from a ball practice and find Kate curled up under a blanket, sitting by the fire biting her fingernails enrapt with every page. He found what he was looking for.

"I'll take the first shift." He blew his nose and refrained from tearing up once again.

Kate was moved into a private room on the second floor. Her window overlooked Parsons Street, which paralleled their own. It was a gorgeous late summer's afternoon, a light breeze turned the maple tree leaves over, revealing their silver underside, and a sign that rain was not far away.

Clay made his way up to her room, and noticed the hushed tones as he passed the nursing station, everyone staring at their feet as he passed by. The scuttlebutt ran rampant in Gremlin after the accident in Alora.

Clay Stoppa killed a guy and this was his brother's revenge.

Clay Stoppa caught the guy who shot his wife and the CIA wanted the case to disappear.

Clay Stoppa blackmailed the Tigers manager who had him cut from the team and the Detroit mafia got involved.

Clay Stoppa owed some guys some serious money and wouldn't pay so they intended to take her ransom, but it went wrong.

Clay would learn to ignore the rumors; he'd gotten good at that over the years. Besides, he had energy for only one thing.

He pulled up a chair and held Kate's hand, adjusted his reading glasses to the end of his nose and pulled out the book *The Mists of Avalon* by Marion Zimmer Bradley. Clay got himself all choked up then cleared his throat. How many times had she read this book, and how many times did she share this book with friends as a gift? He figured she had purchased probably six copies to date, including one for his own mother when she was hospitalized.

He began reading aloud "'Book One, Mistress of Magic'. Even in high summer, Tintagel was a haunted place: Igraine, Lady of Duke Gorlois, looked out over the sea from the headland…"

And so it began, Clay was determined to provide Kate stimulation twenty-four hours each and every day. Rebecca would carry on while he caught a few hours of rest and then trade shifts again in between her shifts at the B&W. Stimulation was paramount. He was of the opinion that her mind was working hard to understand the King Arthur legend and this in turn would spark her to reach out of the coma and re-join him. This hope kept him alive.

The last person Rebecca had any concern for on the dreary Tuesday morning was herself. However, the calendar on her dresser had the date clearly circled and Dr. McLeod ten a.m. penciled in. Rebecca rubbed the date with her thumb as if erasing the appointment would make it go away. With a large sigh, and a childish huff of her breath she made her way to the shower, then Chuck's, and finally the waiting room.

Dr. McLeod greeted her with his warm grandfather-like smile and a huge paw that wrapped around her tiny hand with a gentle handshake.

"You are healthy as a horse, Rebecca, a term I don't fully understand. However, you fit the bill. Apart from highish blood pressure, which could be a result of the anxiety of the testing itself, your numbers look good. Now,"—the doctor leaned forward—"I am fully aware of Kate's accident and will be monitoring her, but today this is about you. You can't help Kate if you are not well."

They both nodded and smiled; Rebecca remained on the edge of her seat.

"Besides the obvious concern for Kate, have you had any restless nights as a result of your reoccurring nightmare?"

"No, not at all."

"How are you sleeping?"

"I'm not."

"Kate?"

"Yup." Her eyes watered a little.

"You likely aren't getting through a sleep cycle," the doctor half mumbled. "When I asked you to give me some info on yourself, you were quick to choose this dream, so I'm guessing this weighs heavily on your mind."

"It has for years, yes."

"Any idea what it's about?"

"No, it never makes sense, it's just numbers spiraling out of control. I feel like I am being lifted and tossed myself, then I wake up."

"How long have you had these dreams?"

"Since…" Rebecca stopped herself, "since as long as I can remember really. I can't really put a date in when I had my first one."

"Would it go back to your childhood?"

"No. I don't remember anything like that as a kid."

"A teenager perhaps?"

"Um..." Rebecca reflected, "yah... maybe." Rebecca took a sip from her coffee. "I'm not much help, am I?"

"Rebecca, nonsense, you are doing fine. I am just trying to establish a starting point here. Can you recall anything outside of the chaos of the numbers?"

"A room in a room, but that's about it."

"Okay, well do this for me, keep a pencil and notepad at your bedside and the next time you are startled by this nightmare just write down whatever comes to your mind. Can you do this for me, Rebecca?" The doctor raised his formidable eyebrows and smiled.

Rebecca smiled back and nodded.

"Right then, let's move on."

They chatted about Kate for a few moments then agreed to meet in a month unless she had a reoccurrence. "I am likely getting ahead of myself here, Rebecca, but in a couple of months' time the district psychiatrist is in our community, she uses my facility here. We should discuss the opportunity of working with you if we both see fit."

"Am I that messed up?"

"No, I don't mean it that way at all, but it would be nice to get to the bottom of this and maybe rid you of the reoccurring nightmares."

"Fair enough." Rebecca saluted the doctor and laughed. On her way out she shook her head, *what a stupid thing to agree to.*

20

October 30

Clay's gait was best described as melancholy. He ambled along Union Street towards the hospital after taking a short rest back at the house. Late October and the leaves were all but finished, the only color that remained were the red berries bursting to life on the hawthorn bushes, and the evergreen shrubs protecting the perennial gardens from the harsh winds of a long cold winter looming in the not so distant future. For the most part, Union Street had digressed to various shades of gray, stark and glum. In two hours, Kate would officially be in her fourth month of her coma, disheartening to say the least.

Clay touched base with Duvall, specifically the head of his department, and suggested his leave would be until Christmas and would drop by and sign all of the forms. The college was completely supportive, something that did weigh on his mind.

He reached for his phone and pressed Tubs, a call he knew would frustrate him. Trevor Franklin's investigation remained at a total standstill, no credit card trail, no debts, no mortgage, not even a speeding ticket, nothing; he was MIA.

Clay opened the door to Kate's room, Rebecca smiled meekly as their eyes met, she pursed her lips, folded today's newspaper that she was reading to Kate then stood up stretched and ambled over to her bedside and held her hand.

"How is she?"

"No change."

"Go home and get some rest. And thank you."

"Stop thanking me, and you're welcome." They both managed a smile.

Rebecca grabbed the cold Chinese that Chuck had sent over hours ago from the B&W. "It's still tasty." She offered the leftovers to Clay.

He waved no thanks.

"I think I'm officially addicted to the chicken balls." She said this jokingly.

"How are you doing anyways?"

"Good... well, no." She suddenly looked over at Kate as if she felt guilty for saying the words. "What I mean is, I am glad to help out instead of being the case study. Speaking of which I have a meeting at ten tomorrow, do you think..."

Clay waved, "Don't give it a second thought, I will be here. How is that going anyway?" Their eyes met again.

"Good actually, the group is strong and Kate's referral to Dr. McLeod has been a Godsend. I haven't had a drink since I got here. I guess I'm finally casting out my demons; it's good, one day and one step at a time... work's been good... and the meetings have been good... I feel like I am reclaiming my life again, for the first time since Boylston Street. And I have you two to thank for it."

Clay brushed the comment off. "You're the one who's changing your life around, Rebecca. You have no one to thank but yourself."

Rebecca's shook her head adamantly. "You and Kate have given me hope for the first time... ever. I was talking to my doctor about this earlier in the week, and I asked him if our relationship was possible, or was I living a dream of being necessary and cared for and secure. He said it was real and I was very fortunate, but had earned it through my goodness." She frowned. "Goodness," she repeated and shook her head as another wave of guilt fell upon her. "I need you guys more than you need me, that's for sure." She continued to hold Kate's hand then rested her head on Kate's chest, tears immediately started to stream from her eyes. "I just hope I can tell her that one day."

"She knows you're upset, Rebecca, and she knows you're close."

"If I could only stop with these." She pulled out the cigarettes.

"We all have our vices."

"You don't?"

"Maybe my vice is my own ego, my need to make everything about me and stir shit up. I started a hurricane, and in the eye of it is Franklin and Boyles, oblivious to how far their damage reached. What a fuck-up I am." He looked down at Kate.

They both sat down, Clay in a relaxed posture, Rebecca more upright as if she would up and leave any second.

"Clay, it's not as if you planned all of this or went into this knowing the risks. You walked into Rebel, inadvertently set off a grenade and the shrapnel landed here. I'm not being flippant, this is the way it is."

It was as if Clay didn't hear her. "I beat myself up every day. Kate said enough is enough, but I didn't listen. I had to be the hero. Always the fucking hero, well this isn't fucking baseball and this isn't a game." He ran his hands through Kate's hair and looked down at her.

Kate lay in her own pajamas, wrapped in his mother's multi-colored afghan. Clay's mom would make a blanket like this every few years with scraps of wool left over from some of her masterpieces. This was far from her best work, but it was Kate's favorite, probably because it was under the tree marked 'To Kate, Love Santa' the first time she met his parents. The gift was even a surprise to Clay, but that was the way his mother was. They had not been dating long, but Clay's mom's kindness and consideration towards others always shone through.

"So how do we bring our Kate back, Rebecca?" Clay tried to refocus their attention and pull back the tears.

"I think we keep stimulating her, keep reading, talking, blowing our noses in her ear." They both laughed. "Including her in the conversations just like we are now?"

Clay nodded. "Yeah. Especially that."

"And some good celebrity gossip never hurts, either," Rebecca joked, motioning towards the newspaper lying open at the end of the bed.

"You read her the paper?"

"Yah, I pick it up every day."

"I don't remember the last time I even listened to the news." They both knew what was being left unsaid: they had abandoned their research on Rickey Boyles and his baseball career.

They sat in silence and felt comfortable in Kate's room. "Clay, your greatest attribute, the one that sets you apart from the rest, is your unconditional love for Kate, and it is what I admire the most about you."

"Well it sure has worked out for Kate, hasn't it?" He shook his head. "Rebecca, we will stay on course, stimulate and you're right, we will bring Kate back to us."

They set their schedule for the next couple of days. Clay walked

Rebecca to the end of the hall and said their goodbyes.

After a short absence, Clay sat back in his newly familiar chair and shared the events of the last few hours with Kate.

Tubs knocked on Kate's door then entered. "Oh, hi, boss."

"Hey, Tubs, sit down." Clay moved to the end of the Kate's bed.

"How is our darling?" Tubs found her hand.

"Not much to report I'm afraid."

"Kinda like my investigation on Franklin. One thing's for sure though, if he uses any form of personal ID, credit card, or even gets pulled over for littering, the National Guard will close in."

Both men smiled and turned their attention to Kate, chatted for a bit and then bid one another adieu.

Days turned to weeks and this was the new normal, however, it was no easier for Clay. He often went out to the old property to vent his frustration by throwing some balls. He cried himself to sleep every night, and the nights he couldn't sleep, he would wander down to the hospital and sit with Kate and just hold her hand.

Clay leaned over Kate and held one of the colored squares of the afghan. He began pushing his index finger in and out of the holes in the blanket then released it and started over again. He turned to Kate and looked into her eyes that remained closed. Clay smiled. The room was quiet and there was very little commotion in the hallway. He kept playing with the afghan, his index finger turning blue.

"I'm wearing that sweater you got me for my birthday; it fits well. I still can't believe you got me into baby blue, or 'Columbus blue' as you like to call it."

Clay brushed her cheek and ran his fingers down her neck. The bruising was all but healed and her color, now only pale, not that sickly yellow after the surgery. The scarring on her shoulder was not as raised now and the bump on her collar bone not quite as pronounced. Clay too had healed; he now had matching scars on his eyebrows, the one on the left he would have to explain to Kate.

"Kate… do you remember the first Christmas?" Clay held up the corner of the blanket. "We were so young. I'm not sure what got me on the topic, probably this afghan. We came to my place for Christmas dinner; you had never met my parents. Remember how nervous you were? My dad met you at the door and gave you a big handshake and my mom shook her head at Dad and gave you a hug then offered you eggnog. I'll never forget the look on your face, she poured you this monster tumbler of the stuff and your eyes went as large as saucers. God, you were beautiful. Are beautiful, I didn't mean it like that."

Clay continued. "When they left the room, I asked what the matter was, were you allergic to eggs or something, and you said that your mother used to give you eggnog on Christmas Eve in these tiny sherry glasses and you would sip it because it was such a special treat."

Clay laughed. "God, you were so innocent. Twenty-three years old and still thought eggnog was for grand occasions."

He laughed again. "Then we stayed over and you were the last one down the next morning and we were waiting for you. I'll never forget, you had a mop of loose curls and a big colorful eighties sweater over your shoulders. We were in the kitchen and I said we are going out for breakfast when you're ready. My parents walked ahead to the car and I felt this tug on my sleeve, and you turned to me and said, 'well, aren't we going to eat first?' I laughed and laughed until I realized you were serious. You said that this was the first time in your life you had ever stepped out of the house in the morning without having something in your tummy." Clay laughed again.

"I brought in a photo of us from our wedding day, it's right beside your bed stand. I found some old negatives and had a couple developed and this is my favorite." It was a photo of Kate in her dress under a train trestle and Clay kneeling beside her. Clay picked up Kate's brush and began stroking her hair, which was fanned out behind her head.

"I'll never forget the day I was doing the dishes in the old kitchen. We were married only a couple of months and I was picturing you in your wedding dress. I was so wrapped up in my thoughts and then you walked into the room and called me. I turned and all I could see was you in that dress walking towards me. I swore I was looking at a ghost. The image lasted so long, and you kept moving towards me and I could not catch my breath. Kate, I have never had that experience before or since that time. It was truly farfetched. I guess you really did take my breath away."

Clay sat in silence for a spell just stroking Kate's hair. "It's the simple things, isn't it, Kate, the things we do from day to day, the acts of kindness, the random joke, the spontaneous laughter. Those are the things that have bonded us all of these years later. And respect of course, I think it's our respect for one another that is the glue.

"You know I thought a baby would make us stronger... but that wasn't true. I used to use our daughter as an excuse to put distance between myself and you—I can see that now... fine time to reflect and confess all my sins, huh?

"I believe someone once said, 'living is what we are doing when we are making other plans.' It went something like that. I often wonder what our lives would have been like had I let go of this before now. Would we have been happier? That's a stupid question... of course you would have been. I know how excruciating it was for you to lose the baby—to lose all hope of ever becoming a mother. But still, you got over it to a degree. How did you have the strength to move on? You always said you were given the choice, wallow in self-pity, or get on with life. You said you tried the self-pity route and found it too depressing, so you moved on. I wish I had been as strong as you." He paused in thought.

"I think I continued my search because I was living in denial or maybe I always had to be the hero. I catch the guy and everything gets better. What a crock that is.

"I have been selfish, Kate. I made you wait for me while I was out there trying to catch the bastard." He wiped her brow. "I chased him for me, not for you and now I've got you in this mess. But I still maintain if I don't catch Franklin, no one will, and his destruction might never stop. And I'll be damned if he gets away with ruining another family."

Clay was suddenly hyper aware of his wallet in his back pocket—the wallet that still housed the composite drawing of the shooter after all those years. He recalled the sketch of the face he knew so well. Not for the first time, he realized that his hatred was now fractured. Yes, a lot of it was still directed at the man he now knew as Trevor Franklin, the shooter. But some was also held back for a person Clay had never even been in the same square mile as: Allan Boyles.

"They will pay for this, Kate, all of them."

And with that, Clay picked up the copy of Ayn Rand's *Atlas Shrugged*.

"This is such light reading, Kate, I'm not sure if it meets my intellectual standards." Clay spoke with his tongue firmly implanted in cheek and then settled into chapter four.

***

Clay read aloud for a couple of hours, when a burst of energy shot through Kate's door sending him through the roof. It was Julie Hook and she was something pissed.

"So, when did you intend to tell me about this catastrophe, you fuck-up?" Julie was mincing words again. She walked straight to Kate's side.

"How long has she been in a coma? How did this happen? Jesus Christ, Clay, she's like a sister to me, she's all I've got."

Twenty years ago, you were teammates and she's like a sister.

"Julie, I'm sorry…"

"Sorry my ass, how could you do this, and who did this?"

"The doctors suggested it might only be a couple of weeks, but time passed and we were wrapped up in this day in and day out. How did you find out?"

"Rebecca texted. It seems that you didn't have the balls."

"I guess that's true. You know Julie; I was really looking forward to the day you would walk in here. I need you here like a fucking hole in the head." Clay stood up, casting a very threatening shadow. "We are both dying here, Julie."

"You and your vigilante heroics." Julie did not back down.

"Then who rights this, Julie?" Clay was red in the face raising his voice.

"No one. We accept it like Kate did and move on."

"Yah, Julie, you sit in that fucking chair for thirteen years after having a child, our child, ripped out of your womb. She has never accepted this, Julie; you don't know the first thing about her." Now he was vindictive.

"I resent that. I have known Kate for almost twenty years."

"You see, Julie, that's where you're wrong, you knew Kate twenty years ago and for a very short period of time. We shared our wedding vows, we married for better or for worse, and I have never taken anything more seriously in my fucking life. We married through sickness and through health, till death. She is my fucking life, Julie, no one, and I mean no one, will ever matter to me the way my wife does, so I am bursting apart inside here each and every moment of each and every fucking day."

They unlocked horns temporarily.

"I know. So did that Franklin guy send this guy to do this?"

Rebecca must have caught Julie up on some things, but not everything. There was so much more to the story than a text could ever convey.

"No, ironically we have a common enemy."

"And I suppose you're planning to go after him now too?" Julie asked, still a little confrontational.

Clay decided to ignore the tone and its implications. "No, I'm thinking of taking your advice for once and letting it go. Well, at least for the time being."

Julie gave Clay a rare half-smile. She moved to the other side of the bed and began to play with Kate's hair. After a few moments a newly purchased copy of *The Mists of Avalon* was pulled from her suitcase.

"We have finished that one."

"It's her favorite, she'll hear it again, and it will make her feel better."

"I'll grab you a coffee then."

***

November 2, Present Day

"A one-run lead and only five outs left. The crowd is going nuts. There is no sense in trying to figure this guy out. Rickey is determined to finish this game, even if we move into a rain delay."

"Well the tarps are ready to be pulled over. Our meteorologists are suggesting this will be a short one, maybe twenty minutes tops."

"I can't see Boyles emerging from the dugout again."

***

"There was room for both of us in the Major Leagues you know that?" Franklin spoke from within his own shadow.

Allan simply nodded.

"Starting the State Finals was not going to prevent your son from standing where he is today."

Allan nodded again.

"You have ruined my life."

"Take mine, spare my son." His voice was weak.

"I have suffered seventeen years. Did your son tell you I was alive?" A rhetorical question indeed.

***

"The tarps are lifted and, once again, I am resolved to being a broadcaster as Boyles proves me wrong. After seven and two thirds innings, in this weather, he has just thrown his last warm-up pitch. He nods to the dugout, then to the umpire. The batter, left fielder Riggs, steps in and swings at a fast ball, pops it up to short, and with one pitch we move to the final inning."

***

"Why did you never call the police over the years? I was tormenting your beloved son and you called for your own hired help. Oh, how'd that work out for you? No police or private investigators. Oh, I know… it's the secret. What did you call it, an 'accident'?"

"What do you want from us? It's me that did it. Why can't you leave Rickey out of it?" The left side of Allan's heavy woolen coat was saturated with his own thick syrupy blood.

"Let me use an analogy." Franklin turned to Allan. "A man kills his wife and kid, and then turns the gun on himself. The ultimate coward, no opportunity to lock him up, and make sure he becomes someone's bitch. If he had lived and gone to jail, the victims' family might draw some twisted satisfaction each day knowing that bastard is taking it up the ass every night. You and your son are my bitches."

"Enough… enough, you have me now, you tortured us for years, tracking my son down in town after town, game after game. End it now, let me die, spare my boy." Allan looked out towards the pitching mound.

"I did follow your boy around."

"You left Rebel though."

"Yes, I made myself pretty scarce. After leaving the asylum, I turned my headlights south and looked up in the metropolis of Ramon, New Mexico. I rented the only home in the town, a dark sinister heap without a soul. It reminded me of me so I just could not resist."

"You sent me the notes."

"Of course. You wouldn't do squat with them. God, I followed your son everywhere for years. Crossed the great divide, as they refer to it."

"And then?"

"Back to Ramon and my clapboard facade, no heat, and no hydro, just an empty shell. Twenty-eight hours south of Rebel."

"Sorry, I missed that one."

"It was as remote as a psychopath sitting in club seats at game seven."

"Ahh, fuck me." Allan wanted anything but this.

"It was there I studied your son, his Ivy League status at Princeton that I paid so dearly for and then the draft and the 'perfect fit' with the Texas Rangers, a beleaguered franchise that could now pin its hopes on the 'Boy Wonder.'"

"So what made you send me all the letters, the threats, the photos?"

"My original plan was short and sweet really. When Rickey was to start his first ever game on that Monday in Arlington—"

"Yah, I remember it well."

"Then he got moved forward to Fenway."

"Third game of the year, a Saturday in Boston." Allan mumbled as he was drawn back in time.

"Too last minute. I was set for Arlington and then I messed up. But then I thought two birds with one stone?"

"Two birds?"

"Yah, I had other reasons to be in Boston. Clean up some other loose ends, but…" Franklin paused and faced forward not paying attention to the game. "It's a shame really; I didn't want you to see him play one game."

"How considerate… you prick."

"An hour or so before game time I pulled into a Burger King on Boylston Street close to Fenway. I ended up in the drive-thru lane."

"You fucked up."

"No that was intentional."

"I got to the kiosk and I snapped. You should have seen the look on her face when she saw me with a gun; then I snapped. Pow." Franklin raised his thumb and pointed his index finger emulating a gun. "Two shots, the first hit her and the second ricocheted somewhere."

"I remember it well." Allan thought for a moment then mumbled, "Somehow I knew it was you."

Franklin ignored Allan's response. "My foot slipped off the brake when I shot a second time. The bullet ricocheted off the steel pillar. I panicked and squealed onto the street, bodies were scattering everywhere. I do however have this vivid memory of a man leaning over a woman on the sidewalk. In all the chaos that day, I have that memory, so vivid, very odd."

"You know you've made your point. Why don't we come to some kind of arrangement and you and I just walk away?"

"Walk away—hilarious."

"I can provide you heaven on earth."

"Heaven on earth?" Franklin seethed, "You are so myopic."

"Money, I will make your life comfortable."

"Of course."

"Maybe so?" Allan begged pathetically. The two men sat with their thoughts.

"Well, how about it?" Allan bargained, "An ambulance for million dollars?"

"Ha. A dollar amount. Interesting."

"There is always…" Allan's side was piercing "There is always a price."

"Oh, there's a price all right, and many… too many of us paid it."

"Are you referring to the drive-thru wake you left in your path?"

"I am indeed." Franklin smiled as he followed a foul ball over his head. "For days, I waited for the shoe to drop, but nothing happened after what I did. I'm down in Ramon, listening to the news; I picked up the national papers, read local police reports, but nothing. Months passed and I started to convince myself that I got away with the crime. I guess maybe that makes us kindred spirits, huh, Allan?"

"In what sense?"

"In the sense that you ripped my ten-million-dollar shoulder off."

"Oh, okay, so we have a number now... ten million."

"The number is a hundred million. Not plausible."

"So then what..."

"As it turns out the drive-thru incident was a blessing in disguise for me. As I later discovered, the Governor for the State of Massachusetts and his wife were in attendance at Fenway that day. I would have been nabbed for sure."

"Bad luck for me." Allan took deep breaths.

"Didn't you read about it in the newspaper article I sent you, Allan? That was your first victim. Because you made me do that to her, you see..."

"As if I would give a fuck... and yes, I read your letters, all of them."

"You looked for me."

"Yah, holed up in Godforsaken Ramon, as if anyone would find you there."

"I opted to live as a virtual recluse for years and years. No one would believe someone actually lived in the dwelling I inhabited; therefore, no attention would be given to me. Over the course of that first winter I made the decision, use the same philosophy I used in getting out of the asylum... patience. Take as much time as necessary and yield control of your son's life and ultimately your destiny." Franklin stared into Allan's foggy eyes.

"Rickey was predictable," Allan conceded.

Franklin sat back in a semi-relaxed posture and stared out onto the field. "He lacked any self-esteem."

"Yup, and had full rein with his income."

"An enormous amount of money, no proper guidance, and a below average IQ, so that implied disaster, it was only a question of when."

"Easy." Allan still had some resilience.

"I mused about my direction all winter."

"Mused, did you? Lah-di-dah."

"The demise of the 'Boyles duo' would be a long and drawn out affair and once I convinced myself of this scenario I became 'selective impulsive', that is, I could carefully weigh the costs and benefits of my plan, its punishment, if caught, and the ability to carefully contrive every last detail."

"A pat on the back for sure… you fuck."

"I decided to follow your son everywhere."

"I know, I got the notes, enough already." Allan coughed and the jarring had him almost pass out.

"My off seasons were my time to regroup in the Godforsaken." Franklin almost cracked a smile. "In the winter darkness, I had complete silence, no breeze, cool, and not a star in the sky; I was alone. I chose this haven for hibernation extremely well; in fact, a cave-dweller would likely have more interruptions. I was soul searching, which is saying a lot for a man with no soul."

"Jesus Christ, I'm done, aren't I?" Allan glanced around desperate to catch someone's eye.

Franklin sat in silence thinking about more peaceful times in Ramon.

In the springtime the screen door would slam, my ball cap fluttered as I walked across the porch in my well-worn cowboy boots and a ragged sweater. I turned on the small transistor radio, Travis Tritt. The insignificant flame of my lighter broke the darkness; I always cherished the first drag the best. I set myself in an old rocking chair, its cadence was consistent; the floorboards creaked under the stress. I was free of all concern; my thoughts were crisp and pure. Rickey Boyles' second season was about to begin in Texas and all coats hung on his newel post. I rocked back and forth, reviewed the overall game plan, and was satisfied. Mental torture was my plan of attack, a much more satisfying retribution. It would begin after spring training, but there was no agenda as to when it would wind up.

"See what you made me do, Allan? See what you made me do?"

"Yes, but…" Allan caught himself, why antagonize?

"Over the next thirteen years, I would hold your son, Boyles, like a marionette, manipulating the strings one at a time, taking control of his life, one incident at a time."

"You chased him everywhere."

"I did, Baltimore early in the second season. I drew up my first of many letters that would become oh so familiar to you. You remember my artwork, Allan?"

"Clearly; the cut-out words from a magazine, going as far as to using the same Crowne Plaza letterhead."

"Did you look for fingerprints?"

"No."

"Of course, you did but you needn't 've bothered; you knew it was me."

"The incident on Washington Boulevard? That surely conjured up some memories from the State Finals and Rebel."

"It did."

"The drive-thru shooting was all over the morning headlines, emergency vehicles at Toni's Grill. Rickey lost that game."

"You were relentless."

"I followed your son, I rattled both of you with my drive-thrus, the personal letters, the taunts, and suggestions. Without fail, he blew up in the games after the letters and the drive-thru events."

"I know, I know."

"And was it all worth it, Allan? Was all the fame and fortune worth it for you and your son? Sure, you've got your mansions in Texas and New York, but your son is the laughing stock of the sports world… such a personal fuck-up, what with his public indiscretions… his life's like a soap opera, Allan. You know, I think you both might be getting what you deserve." With that Franklin stuck the knife in deeper.

Allan's eyes bulged; he was speechless with the all-consuming pain.

"There were more letters to you, Detroit, Cleveland, the mid-west, the coast; it didn't matter, over the years I was there, creating terror in towns and ball parks alike. Rickey's kids came along and then the disastrous mainstream coverage of the affairs and the divorce, which I am proud to have played a role in.

"Did you want to kill me, Allan? Did you want to finish me off? Well, the jokes on you, because our roles have reversed."

Franklin watched Rickey warm up on the mound, the tension in Yankee stadium thick. "That boy of yours is something else, Allan."

"Yes." Allan was still shuddering from the most recent attack.

"'The Rat' as he was referred to in the dressing room is an embarrassment to his ball club and major league baseball."

"Okay, I get it, now get me some help."

Franklin ignored his pleas. "He publicly embarrassed his wife, a classless act, and further separated the athlete and all of his elegance from the man with all of his social equality. Just another example for the youth to admire the athlete, but not the person."

"Enough," Allan pleaded.

"By the end of the season, he lost half his fortune in an uncontested divorce and won a second Cy Young Award as the top pitcher in major league baseball. Ha."

"Quite a feat. Not as grand as yours."

"I would have to agree. The shootings at the various drive-thrus strewn across America: Boston, Seattle, Oakland, Chicago, Detroit, Baltimore, Arlington, Cleveland and most recently Philadelphia. The late trade to New York threw me for a loop though."

***

October 31

"Fuck her." Clay was still steaming and had no intention of returning with a coffee; it would be a form of apology. He had no desire to follow up on their semi-set truce. Julie stirred up the demons of guilt that were never far from the surface. He was hopping mad and found himself just strolling aimlessly street after street after street, until his adrenalin shifted from a boil to a simmer, calm enough now to step into his own house.

Clay moved swiftly through the kitchen into the dining room and closed in on the study, with the intention of restacking the Rand book he had been clutching for hours. No need to take the novel to and fro, one thing was for sure; Kate was destined to listen to *The Mists of Avalon* at least one more time.

As he passed through the doorway, he caught sight of Rebecca curled up in one of the den's wing-backed chairs, her bare legs sweeping over the side. Clay stopped dead in his tracks.

She jumped up in surprise as he entered the room, then spun around and sat down. She was wearing nothing but an oversized t-shirt. Her cheeks were on fire, as embarrassment flushed her face.

"I am so sorry, I didn't see you." Clay was equally embarrassed. He tried to avert his eyes to the ground.

"I thought you'd still be at the hospital."

"I left. Julie showed up." His voice still reflected his anger.

"Oh, right. I meant to mention that. Sorry." She stood up, and then tugged at the bottom hem of the t-shirt, unsuccessfully attempting more coverage.

Clay waved the apology away. "No, you were right to tell her. It's just she makes me so mad. I can't help it. She always just makes me feel so... so..."

"Mad?" she repeated with a joking tone, trying to ease the embarrassment they were both feeling.

Rebecca stood before Clay, she looked vulnerable, and seductive at the same time, her curves defined, in a t-shirt clinging to her breasts then brushing her thin but shapely hips. Her legs were also thin and many years of walking made them flawless and strong.

Clay had never notice Rebecca's figure; he was always aware of her natural beauty, but never had the inclination to notice her striking form. He immediately apologized then turned to put away the book. When he turned around Rebecca remained standing in front of him even though he gave her ample time to walk away.

They stared at one another.

Clay shook his head. "Once again, sorry."

"Me too, I am walking away now." Rebecca bowed her head.

"Me too."

They both started towards the stairs, and then stopped. "This is a little awkward."

"You think?"

They both smiled.

"You first, I'll catch up on some scores." Clay pointed at the games room.

"Good idea. I've got the early hospital shift tomorrow, so I'd better hit the hay."

Clay walked into the games room, and pulled a throw blanket over himself. He flicked between stations paying no attention to the screen as he tried to erase the incident in the study from his mind. Adultery comes in many forms and in his opinion the standoff between the bookcases was certainly one of them. He stayed on the couch all night, hesitant to return to the hospital in case Julie was still there—as she was the absolute last person he wanted to see. Clay tossed and turned on the pullout, his thoughts bouncing between Kate and Rebecca, but mostly occupied with Kate. He awoke just before seven, and estimated five or six hours of restless sleep. His first instinct was to look for messages on his cell phone. There was one from Rebecca sent just moments ago.

I'm at the hospital with your bf Jules ☺. *No change with Kate, but come ASAP. There's news.*

Glad that their uncomfortable moment the night before seemed to have passed, Clay bound upstairs and jumped in the shower for a thirty-second rinse. His curiosity was beyond piqued, and he was down to the hospital by seven twenty, and for the first time in over a month his gait had some purpose.

He skipped by his usual coffee stop and went directly to Kate's room. Clay acknowledged no one as he picked up speed upon the final turn through the hallway. He was surprised to see Tubs' oversized boots temporarily blocking the door to Kate's room; after a couple of attempts Clay managed to get into the room.

"Tubs! What's up?"

Tubs was dressed in uniform looking very official; a giant of a man dwarfing everyone. Julie, sitting beside Kate's bedside, looked like she had not slept, which pleased Clay. Rebecca looked surprisingly fresh, almost cocky as she stood with a newspaper smiling.

"Today is why I read the paper, each and every day." She spoke up handing the paper to Clay, pleased as punch.

Clay accepted the folded newsprint and read the headline. He looked over at Tubs. "Are you thinking what I'm thinking?"

Tubs took no time to digest Rebecca's discovery. "For sure, boss."

Clay kept reading.

***

Trevor Franklin's trek from Ramon New Mexico to New York City had a detour. After thirty-two hours behind the wheel, he was exhausted, numb, and stiff as hell, as he had only stopped long enough to put gas in the tank and relieve himself. Typically, he chose an 'off the beaten track' gas bar and would hole himself up in their washroom to do some push-ups and sit-ups, fill up with gas, and be on his way. He always traveled the speed limit, checked all headlights and taillights, abiding by all traffic laws, indicating, shoulder checks, complete stops, just like a kid on his on his driver's test. The last thing he wanted was to attract the wrong attention.

The last leg of his marathon drive and just prior to entering Philadelphia, Franklin turned inland one hour to the quaint town of Gremlin, Pennsylvania. This was a stop by design. It would be a quick stop, just in and out, check out their hotshot chief of police, and see if there was any truth to the fact that someone in this fairy-tale town was onto him. Franklin wasn't about why; he was just looking for the facts.

The crisp, still morning air certainly suggested that the fall sun had little time to raise the temperature much above freezing.

Following the street signs towards the town's police department, Franklin drifted down a series of hills to the main street. He sat at a red light, his indicator blinking right as instructed by the sign above. To his right, the Black and White restaurant, and his left a gas station. He changed signals as he thought it best to fill up before the final push. He waited for a slender woman with two large coffees to pass by, and then completed his left, pulled into the station and filled with gas. Cash payments were made inside, and while waiting at the till he noticed a composite of himself on the exit door. Franklin raised his eyebrow, a sure sign of surprise and likely his grandest outburst of emotion in months. The likeness was extraordinary. He wondered how it came about; this detective here in Gremlin was really on to something. He pulled his hoody over his head also drawing his sunglasses over his eyes then handed over the exact change.

Impressive.

He grabbed the likeness and pulled it off the glass door exit; this would be a souvenir for his living room, he thought. Franklin was ambling to his vehicle when two young high school students stopped him at his car.

"Excuse me, sir, we are just gathering signatures for Mrs.—"

"Stop." He wanted nothing to do with the girls. He held out his left hand and the girls jumped back. Rather than make a scene he changed his tone. "I would gladly sign." He grabbed the corner of the rolled-up poster and steadied it on the hood of his car. He struggled to hold the pen; his fine motor skills had never recovered. After a shaky start, he managed to sign the scroll for the two companions.

They thanked him and ran off.

Franklin was back in his car moseying down Main Street. He saw the same woman who crossed in front of him earlier, this time she was talking to a huge police officer who was presumably sipping on one of the coffees she carried earlier. They were leaning up against his cruiser sharing a laugh.

Big dude.

Franklin carried on and pulled into the police station, went straight to the photos on the wall and studied Police Chief Michael Campbell's mug, and quickly realized that it was him that he just passed.

This guy is smarter than he looks.

He had seen enough and was not about to take any more risks; this guy was definitely onto him.

I might have to revisit this quaint little town, we will see.

Off to Manhattan. Now was not the time for Franklin to concern himself with the extent of Chief Campbell's manhunt.

***

Clay remained with Kate as Julie had slipped back to the Stoppas' to freshen up. Tubs was off to clean up some files then grab an overnight bag, then back to the rendezvous point for the hastily prepared plan. Rebecca re-joined Clay who sat reading the article once more. They were interrupted by a tiny knock at Kate's door, so tiny, both Rebecca and Clay waited to hear if there would be second one. Sure enough a few seconds later came more taps on the door. Rebecca rose first.

"Are you a friend of Mrs. Stoppa?" A young Asian girl not more than fourteen and not yet five feet tall stood in the doorway, dressed in a peach dress, white tights, and black shoes, her hair in two ponytails arching over her tiny ears. She stood beside an East-Indian girl also in a dress, hers covered in roses. She too had on white tights and black shoes. She wore a rose above one ear and stood just a little taller than her friend. The two girls were smiling ear-to-ear; striking images, intelligent sparkles in their eyes.

"I am her friend, yes."

"Then you're lucky," the Asian girl piped up.

"Yes, I am." Rebecca couldn't help but smile.

"Are you Mr. Stoppa?" By now Clay stood over Rebecca's shoulder.

"I am, yes." Both Clay and Rebecca smiled at the two stunning young faces greeting them at the door.

The Asian girl began, "I am Sally Jackson, and this is Sonya Manpreete, and we were in… no we ARE in Mrs. Stoppa's grade nine math class. We made a poster for her and everyone signed it."

"And we mean *everyone*." The girls were so excited; Sally held her end of the scroll and Sonya allowed the poster to unveil as she walked down the hall. The collage of the school was truly extraordinary; it would have taken weeks to color. Sally stopped walking once she was ten feet away from Sonya, a three-by-ten patchwork jammed with signatures and well wishes.

Clay was speechless.

"By everyone? How many did sign this?" Rebecca's voice was one of bewilderment.

"Everyone." Sally smiled ear-to-ear she bounced up and down in her little shoes.

"Yah, we made our way around the whole town and I figure we got over two thousand signatures wishing Mrs. Stoppa to get well."

"I still have blisters on my feet." Sonya smiled; her multi-color braces sparkled in the hall lighting.

"You see, Mr. Stoppa, and ma'am, Mrs. Stoppa is the best teacher in the world, and I know she would have done this for one of us if we were sick, even in her wheelchair she would have got the job done."

"Come in, girls. She is sleeping, but she can hear you so if you want to say something." Rebecca motioned for the girls to enter.

The girls handed the poster to Clay; he was mesmerized by the thought and effort rolled out before his eyes and began to read some of the well wishes, all the while admiring the artwork underneath the signatures.

The girls stood silent.

"It's okay, girls, she is listening." Rebecca put a hand on each of their backs.

"Mrs. Stoppa," Sonya's voice was tiny and sweet, "we really miss you at the school, it just isn't the same, and we need you back."

"And we miss your wheelchair exhibitions."

"Her what?" Rebecca spoke up.

"Oh, Mrs. Stoppa can balance on two wheels around the whole school and can spin on both front and back wheels."

"Yah, and because of her, we beat the junior boys basketball team, because she played on our team. She's a wicked basketball player; she made the boy's look stupid. Do you remember, Tommy turned to you and said it's not fair she has a wheelchair? I think even Mrs. Stoppa laughed at him. We just love Mrs. Stoppa." Sonya held Kate's hand.

"Get her out of this coma, please." She directed her command to Rebecca.

Rebecca swallowed hard. "We are working on that every hour."

"May we come back?"

Rebecca couldn't respond she was so choked up.

"Any time, girls." Clay smiled. "When did you start this?"

"Twenty-one days ago. We went door to door after school."

"Every day?"

"Yeah, and on weekends too."

"I can't wait for Mrs. Stoppa to wake up and see the poster. Girls you have touched my heart." Clay looked into both girls' eyes.

"We will come back soon."

They saluted each other then gave a light hug to Rebecca and Clay and vanished down the hall, and like two angels they swooped in and touched the lives of Rebecca and Clay and just as quickly disappeared.

Rebecca and Clay hung the poster the best they could and sat back staring at the beautiful gesture, there were sketches of the school, basketball, Kate in her chair smiling, there were flowers and gardens and school buses, and on top of it all, well wishes and signatures.

Clay had a funny habit of looking at the extreme four corners of everything, from the big screen motion picture to fine art in a museum. He always studied the corners, the ultimate attention to detail. The poster in front of him was no exception. The top right-hand corner caught Clay's attention. He stared at it for the longest time then stood up to get a closer look.

It was a message from a student that read, 'what I wish for' and under it was a sketch of Kate standing in front of her classroom the wheelchair was folded in the corner.

Clay shook his head and began to turn away from the poster when his head shot back to that same corner. A signature of 'Trevor Franklin' was scrolled not far from the Kate's chair. There was no mistaking it.

It sent shivers down Clay's back as he took a couple of steps backward. "The girls in all their innocence had the signature of the devil himself."

"What are you talking about?" Rebecca followed Clay's line of sight then narrowed her eyes. "Are you fucking kidding me?"

So many unanswered questions lie in that signature, too many to comprehend.

"He was, or is, in our town, snooping around, Clay."

"We have his attention, but how did we get it?" After ten or fifteen seconds, of just staring, Rebecca broke the silence. "Do you think he is still here?"

"Gremlin, no I doubt it, not with the posters. It would be like hiding in plain sight. Tubs will be here soon. We will see what he wants to do."

***

Franklin left his vehicle at a 'park and fly' in Newark and then caught a bus to the Island and finally a taxi to the East Village and Alphabet City, not exactly the most welcoming neighborhood in Manhattan. Franklin had an innate sense of finding the cesspool in every community. It was there he found his hostel, a gross excuse for a rooming house, certainly a place where no one wants to know your name. He passed by a street person with a sign 'Castrate all the Pedophiles' and a jar with a dollar sign. Franklin thought back to Mulliganskull and one inmate in particular. He turned on his heels and threw a fifty in the jar. Even psychopaths have their moments.

At precisely two a.m. he sealed an envelope with his usual style of context and made his way over to the Hotel, walked through the posh lobby, nodded and smiled at the sharply dressed bellhop then straight to the elevator. Franklin always had a hard time smiling. He did it so rarely and, through the years, it just wasn't a natural expression for him. Only when it was absolutely necessary did he mask his snarl.

The grand puppeteer slid a final letter under the door to the room of Boyles Sr. then he slipped onto the elevator and disappeared out the back.

Boyles Sr. awoke early and stumbled to his entranceway, casually glanced for the morning paper turned away but just as quickly spun around.

He scooped up the familiar envelope, read it and fell back onto his bed closed his eyes and contemplated his next move.

***

Fifteen hours later, a city frenzied with anticipation was temporarily pacified as the Yankees clipped the wings of their National League counterparts and won game six with four runs in three separate innings, running roughshod over the hapless Padres. The evening was one giant celebration, and game seven could not have been scripted any better as the two aces of the league would match up in the pinnacle, baseball's ultimate spotlight.

Players left their respective dressing rooms feeding the press fodder for the evening news. Conspicuous by his absence however was Rickey Boyles. The stars were lined up for the 'Boy Wonder', as it was his time to shine, the starter in a one game showdown, winners take all.

Rickey hid in the showers until most players had left then started a conversation with the team physiotherapist and convinced him he needed a rub down. By the time they were done, only training staff and custodial remained in the hallways. Rather than risk a straggler from the newsroom, Rickey sat in front of his locker and phoned his dad again.

"Well?"

"You don't have any choice, son. I am sorry."

Boyles hung up without saying goodbye. He dialed another number.

***

The Commissioner of Major League Baseball sat behind his mahogany desk on the thirty-third floor of his Park Avenue office, staring down at the lone sheet of paper on his desk. It was now the small hours of the morning; game six was a thing of the past, old news. He looked over the top of his glasses at the five men in his presence.

"Are we sure about this rescheduling?" The commissioner looked over top of his bifocals that sat precariously perched on the tip of his nose and then made eye contact with each person in the room. "Because if you're wrong about this and the weather turns out to be fine, I look like an idiot and I am not big on looking like an idiot."

Meteorologists predicted an early winter storm would strike and strike hard in the next couple of hours, one that would paralyze the city. They were one hundred percent sure of the prognostication. The commissioner turned in his chair, his back now to his audience and looked out the window, the snow had already started. According to the prognosticators this freak snowstorm would pass by at noon the following day and the temperatures would rise to more seasonal levels by evening, however the hours leading to the calm were tenuous at best.

"When do we announce this?"

"Now, sir."

"Fine."

If you include old Yankee Stadium, the two cathedrals have hosted more championship finals than any other, but it would have to wait one more day to be in the limelight. Game Seven was given a twenty-four-hour reprieve due to the insurgence of inclement weather not suitable for the game of baseball.

***

"Okay, let's be sure of this everybody." Clay looked up at Rebecca, Julie, and Tubs. He read the article aloud. "'Boyles has announced he is retiring, and there is a press conference scheduled for tonight in New York,'" Clay continued, "'Rickey Boyles has 'one upped' the mighty Yankees and has stolen the thunder leading into tomorrow night's game seven. The two-time Cy Young winner, twenty-seven outs away from his first World Series, and pitching his best in five years has suddenly announced that this will be his final start and he is set to retire.'" Clay looked at his audience then continued. "'So many unanswered questions, and on the surface, nothing makes sense, especially the timing. The Yankees organization would make no comment, but it is safe to say that ownership that paid a hefty price to acquire the ace will be livid to say the least. The press conference scheduled tonight is arguably the hottest ticket in town, hotter than game seven.'"

"If he is retiring, Trevor Franklin will be at that game." Rebecca looked around the room. "Are we in complete agreement?"

Everyone nodded.

Clay looked around the room, first at Kate, then Julie, and back to Rebecca then to the corner of the mural on the wall. "I will need a press pass for this evening, but I think I can get one. Tubs are you up for this road trip?"

"Of course, boss, we have some work to do."

Clay looked at Rebecca and then back at Julie. Their eyes locked in a match of wills, who would blink first.

"Go… I know you need my blessing, so you have it, now go, before I change my mind!" Julie looked over at Kate for her approval. She made eye contact with Clay once again, her expression uncharacteristically soft. "Clay, for God's sake be careful."

"Catch the bastard." Rebecca smirked out the side of her mouth.

Clay leaned over his wife and gave her a long tender kiss.

"I love you so much, Kate. Maybe after tomorrow, I'll be able to love you the way you need me to." Clay kissed her again. A tear dropped from his cheek onto hers.

***

Franklin reconsidered the finished letter addressed to Boyle's Sr. then let out a sigh and leaned back in his chair. The sigh was not one of sadness, nor was it one of relief; it was more like a sigh suggesting the end was near. So much had happened so many trials and tribulations. The tragedy, the master plan, its execution, and now finally all wrapped up in a note, and the instructions carefully sent to Boyle's Sr.

The letter from Franklin was simple.

'Retire; announce it today or I kill both you and your father. Retire and we both retire.'

Patience was Franklin's virtue, and the might of Daddy
Boyles held no candle to Franklin's flame.

Daddy never fixed Rickey's problem and the decision not to go to the authorities was painfully obvious, so Franklin's threat would be adhered to; retire, and then deal with the consequences on another day.

21

November 1

"My story for a pass... you have a deal." Clay's eyes were on the road and his expression was a mix of defeat and annoyance as he ended the call. He then turned to Tubs. "I will have a pass for both the press conference tonight and the game tomorrow night. We'll get you in as my special assistant, just remember the camera for validity."

Clay still had some pull in the professional ranks. A press pass for Boyle's official retirement announcement and a game day pass for the following evening, two hottest items in the Northeast States. With one phone call and a side deal, Clay had both. Tubs just shook his head at his comrade.

Clay then dialed Rebecca's number. "Hey, we need to find Allan Boyles at the Yankees game tomorrow tonight. Presumably he will need to secure his own ticket, as I suspect his Yankee connections are a little tenuous ever since sonny boy left the team in the lurch. We find him and Franklin isn't far away."

Rebecca and Julie sat with coffees in Kate's room. "I'm putting you on speaker ... where do we start?"

"We will start with a call to his office, his agent, his son's agent, see who gets him tickets," Julie began barking out orders in quick succession, taking the reins as the unspoken leader. Clay rolled his eyes as Julie continued. "We can look at companies he is affiliated with; maybe they have a corporate box. I guess he won't be welcome in the Yankee box?"

"That's for sure; the Yankees spent a fortune to acquire Rickey, at the expense of packing their roster with young talent to grow on." Clay paused. "I read the papers this morning just like you, but none have suggestions as to why. Clearly there is something else working here, someone else is pulling his strings."

"Someone," Rebecca's voice cut in quietly.

"So, we're sure he won't be sitting in the assigned seats that are reserved for players' family members?" Tubs spoke up.

"It would not surprise me if that perk was pulled this morning, but I guess it can't be ignored," Clay interjected.

"We will do some digging from here," Julie said. "We'll try to locate Rickey Boyles' reserved seating and let you know what we come up with." Without another word, she disconnected.

"I guess we were done," Clay muttered.

"I love a woman in power," Tubs said with a lascivious grin.

"There's the old Tubs... I was wondering where my old friend had gotten to..."

Tubs brushed off the comment. "Yah, I've been having some personal troubles, but things are turning around..."

"Good." Clay automated. It was a shame he wasn't paying better attention to his oldest and dearest friend.

Clay glanced at the dashboard clock. His meeting was scheduled at the Barkley on Madison Avenue, so he used his hands-free to call ahead for a couple of rooms.

"How exactly did you swing that press pass?" Tubs was curious.

"Let's just say I have something a reporter wants, so we are making a trade so to speak. I'm meeting up with him this afternoon to get the pass."

"What exactly is it that he wants from you?"

"Long story."

Tubs knew enough from the tone in his friend's voice not to pry.

Clay changed the topic. "So, I am still a little confused, how did you spot Kate that morning? What were you doing at the look out at dawn on a Monday?"

"Long story."

"Touché."

A few minutes of silence hung between them.

Clay was the next to speak. "Well, you saved Kate's life, and I just hope you know how much it means to me. Whether you want to come clean or not." Clay tried to keep his voice light, but his concern was evident.

"Okay, I'll tell you, come to think of it... I actually have to... it's part of my therapy."

"Therapy? What are you talking about... like *shrink* therapy?"

Over the next forty miles, Tubs came clean to Clay... the gambling and the booze. After a six-month downward spiral, Tubs and Sally Campbell had a net worth of negative three quarters of a million dollars, including a first, a second, and a third mortgage totaling over fifty thousand dollars higher than the current market value of their home. Between the mortgages, the private loan, the credit cards, and the economy, they were in a financial quagmire. He talked about his desperation and the gun in his mouth at the lookout.

Clay was stunned, speechless. He kept looking over at Tubs, who continued his story without expression, all the while staring out the window.

"I saw it as my only option; she would collect the insurance and at least come out of it with the house free and clear, but not much more."

"And your son and Sally?" Clay was scared; he was coming to the quick realization that his dearest friend in the world was in a very dark place.

"Sally didn't quite see it that way."

"I guess not."

"You can well imagine the horror; first her husband is about to off himself and secondly we can't afford groceries. She isn't saying much to me yet, but we are still under the same roof. We have met with a bankruptcy firm, and as of now we have a six-month plan to see where we are before applying for insolvency. There is a chance we will climb back out, but it will take years. One day at a time."

"What the hell were you thinking, Tubs?" Clay couldn't keep the hurt from his voice. The thought of potentially having lost his best friend on the same day he'd nearly lost his wife was unbearable. "Had you killed yourself she would have been devastated, and your son with no father, incomprehensible. You're a local hero to many in our parts, chief of police and whatnot. It would have got out eventually, your cause of death; your son would be devastated and scarred for life."

"I suggest, Clay, I wasn't of sound mind."

"I'm sorry, shit, I don't know what I'm talking about. I have never walked a mile in your shoes."

"Well, that's why I am in therapy. With someone Rebecca recommended—Doctor McLeod. But it's all on the down low. I can't be deemed suicidal and carry a firearm, and I need an income, to say the least."

They sat silent.

"How did I miss all of this?" Clay thought back to all of the warning signs he should have caught, but didn't. "Why didn't you come to me? Shit, man, I'm your best friend!"

"Embarrassed mostly, if it's any consolation, you couldn't have stopped it. I needed to reach the bottom and seek professional help. If it wasn't for seeing Kate, I'd be…" He didn't finish that sentence.

Clay felt like shit and said what everyone says, but few mean. "Well if there is anything we can do to help, we will… I mean it."

"I know."

"I mean it."

"I know."

"You said McLeod's your doctor?" Clay asked, trying to inch onto firmer ground. "He's really good. Kate saw him after the incident. Maybe I'll be seeing him too; by the time this all comes to a head. Special rates for a four pack?"

The two men managed feeble smiles.

They drove in silence for a while; the closer they got to Philly and the coast, the worse the weather conditions. It was the beginning of November and it looked like mid-February, blowing snow and white outs. Thirty minutes later, they were crawling in the late morning rush hour, and had covered maybe two miles, the snow still falling. The weather channel suggested it would end by noon and then a sharp rise in temperature, which could cause flooding in certain areas. Even the weather network commended the baseball commissioner for shifting the game to Saturday night. The playing conditions would be cold and damp, but at least the night time temperature would be above freezing.

Clay looked for the first commuter train exit to Manhattan and pulled off the highway. It was the only way they would make their appointment.

Tubs grabbed their luggage—and laughed at Clay's choice of a bat bag for his carry on.

***

The Barclay on Madison was brimming with excitement partially due to a Friday in the 'Big Apple', tourists and business people weaving in and out, money flowing like a never-ending fountain. Fashion, limousines, billboards, and jewelry, the surroundings and crowds all larger than life; a state of exuberance only made possible by the catalyst they call Manhattan, the epicenter of self-indulgence, each and every upper-class citizen brimming with self-importance.

Tubs shook his head at the general pace of the public and gestured to Clay the same.

Clay found a printed settee in the main lobby, looked at his watch for the twentieth time, and waited. "Wait till you meet this guy, Tubs."

A small man in his mid-sixties, sharply dressed, with a full head of shocking white hair, slapped Clay over the head with his folded newspaper.

"Stoppa will be our stopper," the small man bellowed, his smile still lighting up a room and his eyes as blue as a Caribbean Sea would melt even the hardest of souls.

Clay stood up and gave the little man a big genuine hug. "Bugs, you look great."

He was known as Bugs in the industry, because when he had a story to write, he bugged the hell out of the individual until he got his exclusive.

"Age has agreed with you, Stoppa, you have kept yourself fit as a fiddle." Bugs looked him over like a father would his own son. "God, you look like you could still take the mound."

"Thanks, Bugs, you look great too. Listen, meet Tubs, a childhood friend, he's up here helping me out."

"Tubs? Now that must carry a story."

"Yah, I carry most of that story in my gut." Tubs rubbed his robust stomach, laughing.

"Tubs," Clay jumped in, full of enthusiasm. "Meet one of the greats. Alden Hooper. He's winding down a legendary career as a journalist for the *Detroit Free Press*."

"Over forty years in the industry, but who's counting." Hooper shook Tubs' hand almost rattling it off his arm.

"The man could have retired years ago, but he was just having too much fun." Clay put his arm around the bundle of energy.

Bugs had legendary status with sports columnists and it gave him a certain amount of slack in his later years. He only covered sporting events close to his heart and no longer had to chase the 'up and comers' across the four corners of the US. The World Series was his baby... that and boxing were his two favorites. He was very close to Joe Louis on his way up; he covered the Tigers' World Series victories in 1968 and '84. He was fortunate to be in a city where reporting on hockey mattered, and his repertoire included interviews with one of the greatest to ever 'lace 'em up', someone he referred to as a close friend, Mr. Gordie Howe, Mr. Hockey.

Clay knew that every flattering word he spoke was the truth. Hooper was one of the most esteemed journalists in the industry, thanks mostly to his uncompromising respect for the story and the player. If the information he received from a celebrity was meant to stay off the record, then it did. The players had always trusted Hooper, and in his line of work, it catapulted him to the top of his vocation.

"It's been a long time, Bugs."

"I've waited longer for stories; it's only been seventeen or eighteen years for this one."

"Bugs, after all this time no one will be interested in my story. I was just one of thousands of arms coming up through the system."

Tubs looked back and forth between the two men, his curiosity piqued. Clay had told no one but Kate the truth about why he'd left the majors so prematurely; he hadn't even told his best friend.

"I'm at the stage in my life that the important stories are now the ones I am interested in. This is one of them."

"I see." Clay crossed his arms over his chest and pondered his response.

"So, surely I don't need to remind you of our little deal? A story for a badge." Hooper flicked his press pass that hung around his neck.

"Let's grab a coffee." Clay knew he wouldn't find a bistro that was to his liking so they strolled over to the hotel breakfast bar.

"Why are you so interested in Clay's story?" Tubs asked the reporter as they weaved by an energetic passerby. "I've known him since he was a kid, and he's never struck me as being all that interesting."

Clay rolled his eyes and punched his friend in the stomach.

"In all my years covering the game, I believed Clay Stoppa was going to be the best Detroit had ever seen," Bugs answered, ignoring Tubs' joking jab. "He had the arm and that intuitive savvy, game sense, call it what you want. He was a great college pitcher, but a better shortstop, and he was smart. The smartest I had seen. Christ with his IQ you could have become a brain surgeon." He paused. "Did you become a brain surgeon?"

The three laughed and sat at a tall four-top table.

"There are the hardened fans who still ask about you, but this is really for me," Bugs told Clay. "I always liked you, son."

Clay didn't know what to say. He felt genuinely moved by the man's kind words. "Thanks, Bugs, you deserved better from me."

As a waitress came and took their coffee orders, Bugs looked at the boy who was now a man. "I remember the day you got that scar." He pointed at the one over his left eyebrow.

"That was in Triple A. You didn't cover that."

"I was there because Toledo was putting the future arm of the Tigers in at shortstop for defensive purposes. Imagine that, a pitcher thrown into the key defensive position because you were the best. You went two for three, walked, hit two in, turned two double plays and slit your head open sliding head first into second on the cleats of Harman Killebrew's great-nephew."

"I was safe."

"You were... and they called you out in a heap of dust."

The waitress returned and put three poor excuses for mugs in front of them.

"Exactly, Linstrom called me out because I gave him a hard time the night before when he was behind the plate."

Clay stirred his overpriced coffee. "Was he actually related to Killebrew or are you making that up?"

Bugs just smiled and shrugged his shoulders.

"So where do I begin? You ask questions? How do you want to do this?" Clay sipped on his coffee.

"Okay, why do you need the pass?"

Clay and Tubs exchanged a quick glance.

"I told you on the phone, Bugs, nothing means more to me so, trust me on this and I may have a real story for you sooner than later."

"Fair enough, the last time I pushed you it took what, eighteen years to get the answer?

"About that, yah."

"Okay, then just start talking." Bugs crossed his legs and got comfortable. Tubs leaned forward, anxious to be let in on something he'd been wondering about for years.

Clay looked into his eyes, everyone else in the room just faded away. "It was a grand illusion, Bugs, one that started in my final year of college. I was unstoppable in my third year, the year the Tigers showed interest in me, but while I was throwing missiles, I was tearing my shoulder apart. At first, they said it was tendonitis, but rest and rehab didn't fix it. It was all the soft tissue; it was ripping apart so my stabilization was out of sorts. The school sent me away, for surgery."

Clay looked for a reaction; he knew this was something Hooper had never heard. The reporter didn't flinch, however. Surely he was used to hearing sob sports stories.

"It was kept a secret. They did arthroscopy surgery, anterior capsular plication it was called, to tighten the anterior portion of my shoulder capsule to reduce the looseness." Clay grabbed his shoulder and moved it in a circular motion. "Fourth year, the year after surgery, we didn't have much of a team, and the pitching coach knew where I was heading so he rested me, watched my pitch count, and never taxed my shoulder. I threw well, but not great. I certainly didn't take any chances, since I was so close to 'the show'."

"Exciting times, so few get the chance."

"I signed the deal with Detroit, and they didn't want to rush me, so I was relegated to Toledo. I pitched well down there, but I could feel it, Bugs. Nothing you could see from the outside and likely not a lot could be explained from an x-ray, but it was like…" Clay stirred a coffee that did not need stirring. "It was like…"

"Waiting for the other shoe." Bugs interjected.

"Yes, exactly." Clay set down his spoon. "I got the call up in the fall when the roster was expanded to forty and traveled with the Tigers. They wanted me to get a feel for the big leagues, the life, and the distractions and eventually get me some innings." Clay paused, asked for more coffee and waited for the server to leave.

Bugs and Tubs sat in silence.

"It was the end of the season; we were at the old Tiger stadium, Minnesota was in town and the game meant absolutely nothing to either franchise. If you recall, Minnesota was out of the race weeks ago, and we were done by the all-star break."

Bugs nodded, "You were thirty-four games out of first and Minnesota not much better."

"The night was freezing cold."

"It was a Tuesday night." Bugs added.

Tubs was nodding. "It was on my and Sally's two-year anniversary. We spent the night glued to the screen in our little walk-up."

"There were probably three thousand of us in the ballpark, and I'm including everybody from staff to ball players, custodial and culinary staff, everyone." They both shook their heads and laughed. "What a miserable night. The call came to the bullpen in the sixth and they told me to warm up. We were losing six to three, and our starter, Reggie, was done for the night."

"They announced my name and I came running onto the field from the right bullpen for the very first time. By then there were probably five hundred left in a stadium that held forty thousand. But I heard the cheers as I was stepping into uncharted territory. I still remember how lush the grass was beneath my feet, everything was grander in the bigs."

"What no one knew was that my arm was ripping apart from the inside. I felt it in the summer, but forged ahead. I had to be a call up to the Tigers in the fall and I needed to make any sacrifice necessary to get there."

"Why? What was the rush, especially if you were injuring yourself? I just don't get it!"

"I'm getting to that."

Tubs nodded when the waitress came by with the coffee pot and then emptied three packets of sugar into his cup.

"I threw two or three warm-up pitches," Clay continued.

"You threw four."

"Okay, I threw four." Clay smiled. "I waved Rodrigo, my battery mate, off and told the umpire I was ready. I figured I had about twenty pitches in me that night and nine outs to get, so you do the math."

"Well you only used five in the seventh."

"Yes ... and six in the eighth. But my shoulder was on fire, and I couldn't touch it. Any signs of aggravation and they would have pulled me. To complicate matters, by the time I stepped onto the mound in the ninth, we were winning and I was the pitcher of record. I stood to win my first major league game."

"Only in baseball," Tubs interjected. "No clocks, no time outs."

"It is a pure part of the game, and that's why the boys step on the field for all nine innings no matter the score," Bugs added, and all three nodded at his wisdom.

"The first batter of the ninth was a pinch hitter from their farm system."

"Michael Jonis, never amounted to much." Bugs thought nothing of his commentary. "You blew three fastballs down the heart of the plate. He couldn't catch up with any of them."

"Martinez was next."

"He was batting over .300 for the season, on a team that gave him no support. He was a formidable opponent to say the least." Bugs kept a straight face.

"He stepped in there and looked me straight in the eyes. Such a professional, it didn't matter that it was pouring rain, and his team sucked, and we sucked, and the game meant nothing. He was being paid a small fortune to play ball for his franchise and he gave it one hundred and ten percent every time."

"He was the best, no doubt."

"I remember what I was thinking before stepping up to pitch. I have got seven up and seven down and now I face my first legitimate major league batter."

"I remember thinking the same thing, God's truth." Bugs raised his hands and looked back and forth between them.

"I just kept shaking Rodo off, he was looking for my breaking ball, maybe a slider, but no, they would have hurt too much so he got the heat.

After the third pitch I heard something tear in my arm and I buckled on the mound trying to catch my breath. I had never felt something hurt that bad in my life."

"Yah, everyone came out to the mound and you are pointing at the ground. It was pouring by this point." Bugs shared more commentary.

"Yah, I was pointing at the side of the mound and the mud on the infield."

"It was meant to be that night, Stoppa, because if I recall Morrison was calling the balls and strikes."

"What would that matter?" Tubs was confused.

"Funny you should say that." Clay was excited and he looked over at Tubs. "So, the umpire came to the mound and my manager Millar asked him to call the game, but it was Morrison, and he went by the books. I'll never forget what he said." Clay put on a deep growly voice. "'I will send this into a rain delay, and we will finish the two outs at midnight if you wish. I suspect by then no one will be left here to watch, except us fools. This is the Major Leagues boys, not some minor peewee tournament in Bismarck, North Dakota. We are here to play ball, and play ball we will.'"

The men laughed in unison at the table.

"So, my arm is dangling at my side, I haven't moved it since I heard the tearing sound. We stared each other down, Rodo called for some junk, but I shook him off and threw a ninety-seven mile an hour fast ball in the freezing rain that he tattooed, just foul."

"I still think that ball landed in Canada." Bugs added.

"I was hunched over watching the ball travel and I couldn't breathe my arm hurt that much. Now I had to throw the junk Rodo was asking for."

"Which of course twists and pulls your arm some more."

"Twelve pitches from hell." Clay agreed.

"Thirteen because he popped the fourteenth to shallow right."

"Your memory, Bugs."

"It mattered to me."

"I could barely catch my breath between pitches."

"Two out, one to go."

"They brought in another pinch hitter from the minors."

"Carson was his name."

"Thank you, yes... I rattled the ball in my hand but couldn't feel it. I figured I had one, maybe two, pitches, tops, left in me. I remember thinking he needed something to swing at and hopefully a ground ball or a pop up would seal the deal." Clay took another sip of coffee.

"Here she comes, one of the best pitches you will ever witness." Bugs sat on the edge of his chair.

Clay blushed slightly. "I wound up and tossed what turned out to be my fastball, but at change up speed."

"The ball came in at seventy-two miles per hour."

"Yah, but my form would suggest one hundred and two miles per hour."

Bugs cut in. "I was in the press box and I remarked that I had never seen such a big league changeup from a rookie."

"Well, it wasn't a changeup."

"No?"

"My shoulder popped out of the socket and ripped every piece of cartilage, ligament, soft tissue, hard tissue, you name it, and it was torn to shreds."

"It's amazing the pitch made it to the plate." Tubs quipped.

"I looked at the ground after I threw it and expected to see my arm just lying there." They all smiled.

"What happened?" Tubs had no recollection.

"Well the kid was so far in front of the pitch he just nubbed it to first and was out." Bugs spoke like an announcer.

"You got the win," Tubs added.

"So why ruin a career for that win?" Bugs looked into his eyes.

Clay's voice cracked slightly. "I got the win all right and as the team gathered around me, I looked into the section right behind the dugout." Clay paused. "Mom helped Dad to his feet and there they stood. They gave me a standing ovation and I tipped my cap to my father." Clay's eyes glazed over.

Bugs and Tubs looked at one another.

"You see, guys, my father had terminal cancer and wouldn't see Christmas. This was the only chance to see me in 'the show'." Clay stirred what was left of his coffee. "I could pitch for twenty years, Bugs, in front of millions of baseball fans, make millions of dollars, but they weren't the ones I played for. My dad was there for me every step of the way. He drove me to the park, he practiced with me, he gave me instruction, and he watched me. He took his holidays around my baseball; they spent every penny they had to make sure I played the game. When I got that phone call that summer and Mom told me the news, I knew I couldn't say anything about my shoulder. I had to get the call up and I had to pitch for my folks. That game on that cold rainy night meant everything to me, and if I had the chance to change anything, I wouldn't."

They sat in silence for a moment.

"I blew my arm out, had irreparable damage and never threw again. So that's the story, Bugs. For the longest time, only my wife knew the truth. Now you and my best friend do too."

"It will stay that way," Bugs assured him. "That's one hell of a story, son, one for the ages." Clay stared into his coffee cup as Bugs reached in his pocket and pulled out the press pass.

"Here. A deal's a deal."

"You trust me, Bugs?"

"I do."

"I will give you another story of another major leaguer and how his father influenced his career, but I need to complete some unfinished business that has been lingering for the past thirteen years."

"I can wait. I am a patient man."

"That you are." And with that, the two men shook hands then hugged. "I will see you at the press conference tonight, but don't stand anywhere near me. You'll be the first to get the real story. Tonight, I am just rattling some chains."

"What a day for a press conference, that Rickey Boyles is the type of player that embarrasses such a beautiful game." And with that Bugs disappeared into the lobby.

They never make the press conference rooms large enough. Maybe it's to create more of a buzz, generate the crazed ambiance they are looking for, however in the case of Rickey Boyle's retirement, maybe they just didn't have enough time to prepare. The final game of the World Series was set, it's game seven and someone goes home with the hardware; that in itself gives the media enough fodder to feed a pack of wolves. Combine the season's finale with an extra day in-between games and now you have time to dig deeper into the nuances of the game, its players, the management, and the strategies. Now add the sudden retirement announcement from the central figure, the lead actor, the maestro, the game seven, larger than life pitcher extraordinaire Rickey Boyles, and you have 'the perfect storm'.

The room was packed. Cameras flashed, media jostled for position, microphones were strategically placed around the three tables set up at the front of the conference room. Reporters were shouting out questions and craning their necks to see the front of the room. And this is before Rickey even arrived.

More reporters spilled into the hallway and others stood in front of the closed-circuit TV, preparing to do their piece for the newsrooms they represented. The big boys got the front row, in fact, only the large market media were in the room, other smaller markets were relegated outside of the main circus. ESPN had the backdrop to the front table, a one hundred-thousand-dollar price tag, and payable to the Yankees organization. If they were going to lose their 'great hope' then they were also going to cash in on his every step towards obscurity.

Clay managed to elbow his way into the main room pushing a rather large and exuberant individual out of his way, much to the liking of the regulars at these events. He adjusted the Yankees ball cap he had just purchased, pulling it down low over his eyes.

Clicking cameras and the loud drown of voices, one hundred different conversations at the exact same time filled the room, and finally the lights intensified to live camera levels, Boyles was set to make his entrance.

Three men in suits entered to a barrage of flashes, and then came Rickey Boyles with his million-dollar smile, waving to the media. Following him into the room was another suit and then BAM. When the older man, who Clay knew to be his father, Allan, walked in with his smug demeanor, Clay lurched forward ever so slightly, a lump forming in his throat and then twangs of nausea. Clay felt heat run across his forehead.

How can you stand there so smug; after all the damage you have caused. You have no fucking idea.

Clay wasn't expecting to get so angry upon the sight of Rickey's dad, Kate's voice screamed terror in his head, as he watched her wheelchair spin out of control. He was bursting inside and could feel his heart pounding in his chest.

The lights continued to flash, verbal darts were thrown, and the microphones adjusted into place.

Rickey's agent was hard to take seriously; probably the three gold bangles, the heavy-linked neck chain, and the thin gold watch did not help. He ran both hands through his head of heavily jelled, slicked back, jet-black hair and announced the obvious; one of the greatest pitchers of modern day, with an illustrious career, was retiring for personal reasons.

I'll bet, maybe advanced herpes.

Clay cleared his throat, but held back.

"I will read a prepared statement, then Rickey will answer a few questions."

The statement rambled on about his career, his dedication to family, friends, his team, and the game of baseball itself.

Maybe he mixed up his clients?

Clay shifted slightly for a better view, his eyes boring in on Allan. Clay leaned forward, wondering if Allan knows how many lives he ruined.

He spoke ad nauseam about Rickey's stats and the professional manner that he approached the game and life.

Yah, he definitely had the wrong speech.

"A few questions for Rickey?"

The room erupted, and the audience of reporters pushed forward like the influx of passengers at the most popular subway stop during rush hour. Questions flew from all directions; it was showtime.

"Why now, Rickey? How did your teammates react? How upset is Yankee ownership, as they gave up some incredible prospects to Texas? Will all be forgiven if you win tomorrow night? Is your decision final?"

"DID TREVOR FRANKLIN HAVE ANYTHING TO DO WITH YOUR DECISION?"

Confusion buzzed through the room. Everyone seemed to have the same question: who the hell was Trevor Franklin?

They'll find out soon enough, Clay thought. Of that he had no doubt. Allan Boyles almost had a coronary on stage.

Who the fuck was that? Did he actually say Trevor Franklin? WHO THE FUCK WAS THAT?

Rickey adjusted his microphone and cleared his throat.

Daddy?

Reporters looked at one another then started asking the obvious question; who is Trevor Franklin? some reporters started jotting in their little notepads. The men at the front of the room whispered into Rickey's ear and he whispered back shaking his head no.

Rickey leaned into the microphone. "Next question." There were no more smiles from the 'Boy Wonder'.

The *Washington Post* jumped in and the noise level increased as if nothing was said. "A lot of legendary players have taken the high road and retired, but reneged and come out of retirement shortly afterwards, is this a ploy you have considered?"

"It really hasn't entered my mind; I have a number of people to consult with before making those kinds of decisions."

Franklin smirked from the back of the hallway as he watched the events on closed caption; his bellhop uniform blended right in.

That is very true.

Franklin glared in the general direction of Clay; however, it was difficult for him to pinpoint the exact location of the 'Franklin' question. One thing he knew for sure was that someone was onto him. He'd need to be sure to cover his tracks from here on in.

Clay returned his attention to Rickey.

Boy is he rattled!

Still, Rickey couldn't shake the outburst from Clay and he motioned that it was time to get up to leave. The second he shifted his chair back the decibel level increased once again and more questions rang out.

Clay's was the loudest. "DO YOU KNOW HOW MANY LIVES HAVE BEEN RUINED DURING YOUR RISE TO THE TOP? DO YOU EVEN CARE?"

And then the room went silent.

What a terrific question, straight to the point.

Franklin chuckled to himself.

With no thought of where he was or who he was, Rickey jumped the table like a hockey player jumping the boards. Clay didn't waste any time and lunged in the direction of Rickey and his cronies. Boyles Sr. wasn't far behind his son, and now bodyguards and police dove into the melee. Clay figured he would only get in one swing so the decision was easy. And with a spectacular right, Allan Boyles had never been struck so hard and so flush in his life. Clay was getting good with his new-found athleticism and Allan's left eye would prove that fact for at least the next six weeks.

Franklin was outright laughing for the first time in years.

God, I couldn't have scripted this scene any better.

Clay pulled away from the donnybrook and of course all the attention was thrown on Rickey. Clay cleared the room, but not before Boyles Sr. flipped open his phone. Clay pushed his way out to the back exit and disappeared into a taxi. He was most certainly followed. With everything transpiring over the weekend, he figured it was clear sailing to game time and it was time to focus on the event that lay ahead.

That was a major miscalculation.

22

November 2, Present Day

"Do you think they had any luck last night?" Tubs cut into his formidable stack of pancakes laced in butter and syrup. He was referring to the sleuth exercise Julie and Rebecca were immersed in for the best part of yesterday.

"I'll give them another hour, it's only seven." Clay looked for a refill of his coffee and rubbed his knuckles. "Knowing Rebecca, she worked all night."

"Oh, there it is again, this time it's on CNN." Both men looked up from their breakfast and viewed the press conference and the punch.

"Man, that was solid, are you sure you didn't break a knuckle or something? They really caught that one from all angles." Tubs was not going to let this one go for years.

"I can't believe the coverage this is getting." Clay shook his head in disbelief.

Clay and Tubs strained to hear the report as the anchor of the news brief suggested the *Detroit Free Press* had no idea who the reporter was and how he got in the room. As for the questions that set Boyles off, everyone was baffled as to who Trevor Franklin was.

"Well, if nothing else, Trevor Franklin's name is out there," Clay quipped.

"Did you see how pissed Boyles looked?" Tubs asked.

"Which one?" Clay smirked.

"Seems to be no love lost between the Yankees and their 'Boy Wonder', huh?" Tubs noted as he watched another replay of the punch.

"Nope. And I think the lack of Yankee ownership at the press conference definitely confirms that Boyles will be on his own for a ticket tonight."

"I wonder how the ladies are getting along on that front," Tubs said through a mouthful of breakfast, eyeing Clay's phone.

Clay couldn't wait any longer and he pulled out his phone and dialed Rebecca. "Good morning, how is Kate?" His voice was strong but slightly anxious.

"No change, a quiet night." Rebecca's tone brightened perceptibly. "Nice punch by the way." The smirk was visible in her inflection. "It got our mojo going here on the continuing care unit. Julie on the other hand, she's something pissed. I think it's the pickle up her ass."

Clay's spontaneous laugh was a welcomed break on the other end of the line. "You could tell it was me, huh?"

"Of course. A wolf in a Yankees cap is still a wolf, or however the saying goes."

"Did you have any luck last night with tickets or leads?"

"I called Allan Boyles Holdings, and got an answering service. I suggested I had tickets for tonight's game if he needed them. I just said I was with Unijoist Corp. Julie's idea; it's a company he has something to do with. His 'personal assistant' actually called me back late last night. She said that he was looked after for tonight and appreciated the offer. When I suggested the executives of Unipir wanted to get together for drinks so could I have his section number, she said the offer would be passed on and if he wanted company, we would be the first to know."

"That's a load."

"Yup."

"Did you get anything else?"

"I went out on a limb and suggested the two seats we had were 'in the action' the best in the house, but she said he had already arranged for a seat this evening."

"A seat, singular."

"Well I asked the same. I said I had a pair. She said that he only required the one tonight, so offered them to another client."

"Julie actually called the Simmone and left him a message suggesting she had an extra ticket hoping it might be better than his and maybe get his seat choice that way, but no one has responded."

"The Simmone? How did you know that Boyles Sr. is staying there?"

"He and his dad live in that hotel in Manhattan; I read it in some glamour magazine. He was on the cover. It's a five-star luxury hotel at 5th and 63rd Street? The gossip rags are good for something after all."

Clay rolled his eyes. "Whatever you say. Anything else?"

"We called various ticket agencies, the Yankees organization, Will Call at Yankee Stadium, a host of other companies he is affiliated with… on and on and on, but no results."

"Good work."

"We are no closer."

"I think we are. Did you look for single seat sale since the Yankee box office opened after game six?"

"Yes, but I doubt he would purchase it, he would go through corporate channels, ticket companies, that sort of thing."

"Or his hotel," Clay interrupted. "Bugs, last night, said the rich are catered to and come to expect it, so Boyles probably just called the concierge for the best seat in the house."

"Everything would be last minute, so that would make perfect sense," Rebecca noted.

"Well, keep digging, mine is only a hunch."

"Hey listen, about the pickle…"

Clay grinned. "You're on your own there, Rebecca. Just steer clear when she gets in her moods. Now, I gotta go. And tell Kate… tell her I'll see her soon."

***

It was Saturday in Manhattan, a city large enough to conceal the excitement of a World Series game seven. There were fans mingling in Yankees jerseys, but for the most part, the city of eight million had a lot more to offer on this cold and dreary morning. The snow was melting and would continue to do so all day; however, the pedestrians now had dirt and slush to contend with. Clay chuckled thinking about, Rebecca's take on rain and the comical reactions from passers-by.

Nothing paralyzes New York City like a good snowstorm, particularly a freak one on the first weekend of November, so as the city dug its way out of this one, the town embraced itself for another busy day.

After a twenty-five-minute taxi ride from the Madison to the Simmone, Clay and Tubs jumped out.

In a city where first class and 'five-star' encase you, it takes something extraordinary to really stand out. The Simmone Hotel stood out, arguably the finest accommodation on the island, the view of Central Park breathtaking and the neighborhood, midtown Manhattan, legendary.

Rickey Boyles was residing in a grand one-bedroom suite at the Simmone listed at $3,500.00 per night. The price did not include room and spa service, or the added amenities that he had grown to expect: women, drugs, and alcohol all at his beck and call. All together Boyles Jr. paid approximately five thousand dollars per night, every night since becoming a member of the New York Yankees baseball organization. The hotel did not offer any leniency in the 'going rate' even though the room sat empty night after night when the team was out of town.

Decadence, frivolity, and stupidity all wrapped in one tidy package named Rickey Boyles. Wonders never cease. His father was 'slumming it' in an executive suite at $1,500.00 per night in the same hotel. His dad checked in three days ago. At least, that's what the doorman told Tubs and Clay in exchange for a fifty.

After hauling on the substantial brass doors, Clay skipped up the lobby stairs two at a time with Tubs hot on his heels. It was hard not to be impressed with the main lobby, the marble wainscoting, and the ceramic floor bordered in mahogany framed in ornate trim on the walls and ceilings. Clay was sickened that a person the likes of Boyles could afford this, night after night after night.

The floor transformed to a checkerboard in the main lobby, on one wall three kiosks for check in, opposite that, the baggage control, and, finally, the concierge. Clay waved off the advancing bellhop, his white gloves preparing to handle all luggage and tips. He then ignored the series of greetings and good mornings from the hotel staff and headed straight to the concierge desk.

Tubs circled the lobby looking for either Boyles or someone resembling Franklin then settled within earshot of Clay and the concierge.

Clay approached the pedestal and read his lapel. "Jean, my name is

Clay Stoppa and I am looking for some information."

"Not a problem, sir, what room number are you."

"I am not a guest here."

"Maybe reception would be of more assistance."

Clay hated the arrogance; he always got his back up in these situations, maybe Tubs would have been better to make the initial meeting. "And how would you know reception would better serve my needs, when you don't know my needs, because you haven't asked me of my needs."

"I look after guest services, Mr. Stoppa, and you are not a guest." Jean's smile was smug.

Clay advanced in a manner that could be interpreted as slightly hostile and certainly intimidating. He was face to face with Jean the much shorter and slighter built man. "I'm just asking for a little help here, man to man."

Clay noticed the concierge's right arm reach below his pedestal.

"Wait," said Tubs, coming up behind them. He flashed his badge.

The concierge's arm stopped in mid-air. "So, you're a cop," he said, his voice ringing with contempt.

"Allan Boyles. He is expecting a package, correct?" Clay was hedging his bets.

"There is such thing as client confidentiality—"

"There's such thing as obstruction of justice, too. Now, Allan Boyles. Is he expecting a package or not?"

Jean nodded.

Clay could not believe their luck. He concealed his enthusiasm.

"Tickets to tonight's game?" Tubs demanded.

"One, he only ordered one."

"I have a message for him, where is his seat."

"Just leave your message with me; I see him coming and going."

Tubs stepped forward and leaned his full weight on the desk, dwarfing the spindly concierge. "You really don't want to get involved, but you may have information that will lead us to a second dangerous individual." He was fingering his badge as he spoke.

"What do you mean *second* dangerous individual?" Jean brought his hand to his throat and gasped in alarm. "*Mon adieu!* Am I in danger?"

Tubs let out an exasperated breath and leaned over the counter. "Were you the one who ordered the ticket?"

Jean nodded.

"What seat?"

"I don't know; they never told me. They just said that they'd send over the best ticket they had. All I know is that it must be good... great actually, judging by the price he paid."

"What agency?" Clay demanded.

"The Ticket Agency on 5th and 42nd." Tubs noted that down in his little notebook.

"Why is everyone so interested in Allan Boyles, anyways? His son is the man of the hour, not him."

"Why... who else is interested in Allan Boyles?" Clay backed off slightly.

"There was a guy here less than half an hour ago also asking about his seat for tonight."

Clay's insides clenched in his gut, was he standing where Franklin had been not even an hour before?

Tubs pulled out the aged composite. "Does this look like the man that was here?"

"It looks similar. I couldn't be certain."

"What did he want?"

"He wanted to know which ticket agency I used to order the ticket for Mr. Boyles, same as you."

"And did you tell him?"

Jean nodded, looking slightly guilty.

"What about *client confidentiality*?" Clay mocked.

"He seemed quite pleasant. Very polite," Jean defended.

Tubs leaned over Jean. "Murderers come in all shapes and sizes. Now what else did you tell him?"

Jean gasped again. "Oh, my. Well, he asked when it was ordered and also if it was a single or multiple order. I said single and that was it."

"Call the Ticket Agency and ask which seat is reserved for Allan Boyles."

Jean complied and spoke into the phone for a few moments. Judging by his reaction, it was clear to Clay and Tubs he was at a dead end.

Not waiting any longer, Tubs took the phone and introduced himself as a chief of police. "Now explain to me why you cannot tell me which seat is Allan Boyles."

Clay leaned in closer to Tubs to hear the voice droning on the other end of the line. "I can't tell you who is getting which ticket, they are purchased for clients, often by a third party, rarely is it done in person, besides, its private information and I don't have to disclose to you without a warrant."

"All right, tell me this. How many single seats are you delivering or having picked up?"

"Hang on."

Tubs heard typing in the background. "One hundred and twenty-five single tickets."

"How many are being picked up?"

"Zero, we deliver its part of the service."

"How many are dropped at the Simmone?"

"We actually pass that side of Central Park to a different delivery service. It's a logistics service, it's quite complicated, and we break our deliveries into various sectors to keep the costs down. So, I really couldn't say—"

Tubs was growing frustrated. "Fine. Can I at least get a list of the single seats?"

"That I can do, I will email it to the Simmone right now."

"Good. And one last question: based on the list, how many of the seats, in your opinion would be suitable for a VIP, like the father of one of the star players."

"Oh, that's easy... all of them."

"Why do you say that?"

"Because we're a premiere service, sir. Some are private boxes, some in the Legends Section, some in the action, some platinum plus, you see sir, every seat we sold for tonight costs each client over ten thousand dollars."

Tubs swallowed hard. "That includes delivery, right."

"Of course."

"When is delivery scheduled for this hotel?"

"Let's see."—more typing—"Oh, that location, and the service we

325

use guaranteed delivery, but I can't say when. It could be a late one. I show four doubles and one single to the Simmone, but like I said the delivery of which tickets is not sorted through us."

"Who is the courier, maybe we can reach them."

"We contract out to three couriers. Let me see… The company 'Q' is who we use to that particular area. But they likely have subbed out to other couriers in the district."

Tubs groaned.

"Anything else?"

"Give me Q's number please, maybe I can reach them and see if they subbed out your delivery." After jotting down the ten-digit code Tubs was just shaking his head and he passed the phone back to the concierge.

Clay looked at his watch; it was shortly after nine a.m. "One of us has to wait here all day or at least until the ticket arrives." Clay looked up at Tubs, who nodded.

Clay leaned towards the concierge. "When that envelope arrives, we need to know the seat number of the single ticket, without Mr. Boyles knowledge. I am going to pay you in advance. Remember, my partner could run around gathering a warrant, but with you being a good citizen and all…" Clay waited.

"Five hundred."

"One hundred, you pimp."

"Two fifty."

"One fifty, you leach," Tubs interjected.

He accepted the money.

"This is a really simple operation, if it gets fucked up; you get fucked up, are we clear." Tubs six-foot, seven-inch frame came in handy once in a while.

The concierge just nodded.

The boys moved to chairs across from the concierge and didn't let Jean out of their sight as they contemplated the next move.

Clay went first. "Do you think the guy asking about the tickets an hour ago was Franklin?"

"Yes."

"He only wanted the name of the ticket company. How does he use that info? Why wouldn't he wait around like us?" He glanced over his shoulder, taking in the whole lobby, but saw nothing suspicious. "He must have a plan." Clay pondered, and then jumped to his feet. "I'll be back in an hour."

***

Franklin dropped a thousand dollars on the lap of the hugely overweight smelly individual who referred only to himself as Milo.

"So, you need nothing else." His fat chubby fingers were poised on one of the four keyboards that sat in front of various sized flat screens. The obese man reached into a bag of Doritos then rolled his chair to a keyboard and monitor directly to his left.

"After I do this no one is getting info from this network for a while."

"Good. Go ahead." Franklin adjusted his hood and stepped out into the wind.

***

Clay traveled by taxi south on 5th to 42nd then west to an old house transformed into one of the many small businesses in the area, the lime green neon sign flashing 'TICKETS' gave away his set destination. After paying the taxi driver, Clay broke into a jog. He turned under the flashing neon sign then entered a small room, with simple office décor. A distraught middle-aged woman was sitting at a computer, both elbows on the table, her head resting between her hands.

"I can't help you, sir, my system is down." Her voice was monotone and sounded defeated. She didn't look over towards the potential customer; her attention was on the monitor. "I can't believe this happened, of all days," she mumbled

"What do you mean? Everything was running twenty minutes ago."

The woman just shrugged. "Someone just hacked into my mainframe and damaged some of my files."

"How do you know it's not just a glitch?" Clay jumped in.

"A glitch?" She looked over top her monitor. "We pay thousands a month for safeguards so glitches like this do not occur. This is a hack, that's for sure; we have had the odd one. Dammit!"

"The corrupted files wouldn't happen to be tonight's ball game?"

She looked over her glasses. "Among other events on tonight, but yes the ball game is our biggest happening this evening."

"Shit." Clay adjusted his plan. "Can you tell me when the Q courier is scheduled to get to the Simmone?" Clay took a stab in the dark. Her colleague hadn't been any help on this front over the phone, but maybe she would be.

"Are you kidding? This is Game Seven of the World Series. More merchandise is being shipped around the city today than presents on the week before Christmas. Calling would be a joke at this stage."

Clay groaned inwardly. "Where are they located?"

"Probably rent space from a bike shop, not exactly high tech."

Clay lowered his head and sighed. He stepped outside again without the courtesy of a goodbye or thanks.

***

Clay went back to the hotel and met up with Tubs.

"I got the list of single ticket seats," Tubs said, waving an email print out. "What'd you get?"

"I got a lesson about underestimating our friend Franklin. He just hacked into the agency, probably found Boyles seat somehow then corrupted the system."

"Do you think he's onto us?" Tubs wondered.

"Maybe he saw the press conference last night," Clay said, suddenly fearing the consequences of his knee-jerk actions. "Shit!" He pounded his knees with his fists; what if he had just ruined any chance they had of catching the bastard? "Stupid," Clay muttered under his breath.

"That means we definitely have no way of tracking Boyles down until the ticket arrives," Tubs deduced.

"It also means Franklin has no reason to arrive early to the game and certainly no reason to come back here."

"For all we know, he's some kind of computer freak and he is a hundred steps ahead of us," Tubs said, keeping his eyes on Jean. He rested his torso in the chair closest to him in order to remain in earshot.

"Hard to say about the game though, if he intends to make a

statement tonight, he may be checking his vantage points thus an early arrival." Clay opened a coffee he grabbed at the corner then handed one to his friend. "How do you get a firearm into Yankee Stadium?" Clay continued to stare at the main entrance if by some miracle.

"Whoa, Clay, let's not get carried away—"

"Not me, Tubs. HIM."

"Oh." Tubs thought about it for a second. "Plenty of ways, maybe an inside job, pay someone to plant the gun and you retrieve it during the game. Kinda like in the Godfather, stick it under a toilet."

"I guess if he really wanted a firearm in that building, he will figure it out."

"For sure."

"As much as I've hated Franklin for years, Allan Boyles is the root of this evil. Franklin will be close to Allan tonight. I know it. I'm going over there… to the stadium." He was already out of his seat and reaching for the list of seats.

Tubs didn't argue. "I'll stay with our man here and wait for the ticket."

"Okay, buddy. Thanks." Clay paused mid-stride and turned back to his friend. "I mean it, Tubs. Thank you. For everything."

"Sure thing, buddy. Sure thing."

Clay stepped outside; the day was warming up as predicted, however they did call for showers on and off all day.

Nothing but limos lined the entrance to the hotel. Clay flagged down a taxi across the street and negotiated a price to Yankee Stadium. The hotel was only seven miles from the ballpark, but New York Traffic could turn the short hop into an all-day affair, as it turns out the twenty-minute drive took approximately forty.

Clay jumped out of the cab close to the main entrance to the new Yankee Stadium. He had only seen pictures, and even though he was completely preoccupied, he couldn't help but be overwhelmed by the size of the structure.

He waved his press pass at the security his thumb partially obstructing his name and photo ID. Clay was also careful not to make eye contact, and acted nonchalant, as this was just supposed to be a job he did day in and day out. He wondered if the Detroit Free Press would be flagged upon his arrival, but he was okay for now. The more he thought about his antics yesterday, the more he realized it was a stupid thing to do. Drawing attention to him over a punch and a little tension release was a stupid move. He looked down at his swollen knuckles and shook his head. As Clay scanned and passed through metal detectors his thoughts turned to the Godfather.

He was surprised how many people were already arriving for the game. A line-up was forming outside, with the gates not opening until three o'clock, the wait was five hours. Clay spent the next couple of hours consulting his list and checking out the one hundred and twenty-five, ten-thousand-dollar seats around the stadium. He would await Tubs' call of course, but had eliminated at least seventy of the seats primarily based on the proximity to the pitcher's mound and the home team dugout. Clay assumed that Boyles would want to be close to his son's final game, and if it was Franklin's intention to be there, he would want to be close to both father and son.

Clay stopped in his tracks.

How many single ticket sales were side by side?

Clay flipped to his floor layout again and counted twelve.

What if Franklin was able to purchase beside Boyles?

It was certainly a possibility, one that would be ideal for Franklin. Clay found his way around to the various seats.

Clay sat in a seat near the Yankees bullpen, watching some of the stretching and instruction for the visiting Padres. Clay was in constant contact with both Tubs and Rebecca via text, but nothing was advancing in their favor. Clay sat in the twelve seats that were designated as single ticket holders and created a probability chart on the seating map he held in his hand. He knew it would be almost impossible to move from section to section once the crowds settled in so a 'most likely to least likely' list made the most sense.

Clay's attention was diverted to the main concourse as a trickle of hardcore Yankee faithful began to pour into the bowl from every nook and cranny. It was five past three in the afternoon.

Clay sat back in one of the high-priced seats and shook his head. He found himself daydreaming about Kate; his level of guilt was peaking again. He had to get this right—for her sake as well as his.

Shake it off, not now.

Clay had to get his game face on and start looking for Allan Boyles, the guy with the shiner, and of course, Trevor Franklin, not such an easy person to pick out.

Two more hours had passed and the stadium was beginning to buzz. Half the seats were now occupied and the energy was increasing. Clay called Tubs for an update, but he had nothing to report. He called Rebecca as well and she too had nothing. Kate remained peaceful.

Earlier in the day, Clay asked Rebecca to keep trying to purchase tickets through the agency, but all day she was denied due to technical difficulties. Franklin, he assumed, really did a number on their system.

The aisles were filling up thus making Clay's movement between sections more and more difficult, fans young and old, picking up pretzels, dogs, beer, souvenirs, and programs. Now the cathedral was louder by the minute, a steady stream of fans washed into the seating as if the stadium was submerged and the fans were the water. The groundskeepers were on the field now, there had to be two hundred of them, preparing for a long battle against the elements, and the players were warming up in full uniform covered in heavy jackets and sweatpants, and toques or earmuffs, they looked more like a team preparing for the grid iron as opposed to the field of dreams.

Clay began checking his watch every couple of minutes; he was anxious.

***

Tubs checked his watch. It was 5:10 and still no sign of the delivery service. Tubs read the same magazine for the tenth time; he now had a suitable understanding of the various qualities in diamond rings and that carat size was not the only important consideration when purchasing. Tubs and luxury magazines seemed to have a way of finding one another.

Finally, a bike courier dressed for Everest jogged to the concierge, and Jean signed for the envelope. With a wink of an eye, Jean directed his attention to Tubs, who jumped up, grabbed the envelope from the pedestal, and broke through the layers of plastic and computer-generated labels. He found the single ticket and pulled it out just far enough to read the section row and seat.

Tubs turned and reached for his phone, his heart pounding.

Took you long enough.

Two shadows approached Tubs. The gun was concealed so well, only Tubs and the assailant knew it was in his ribs. Tubs froze, while his gun and phone were confiscated. Tubs lowered his head. He had been duped. All of his attention was set on Jean, the concierge, and he didn't have the street sense to consider an assailant.

Tubs lowered his head.

How could he be so stupid… his personal involvement overcame his professional training.

The two men who stood eye to eye with Tubs turned him towards the elevator using the gun as an indicator of direction.

The formidable wall of three strolled towards the bank of elevators at the rear of the lobby. Tubs looked towards the concierge desk, desperately hoping to catch Jean's eye, but the snooty Frenchman was busy resealing the envelope and calling up to the Allan Boyles and in turn hailing his limousine. He didn't look up as Tubs walked away.

***

Ten past six, Clay was growing restless, the game started at eight. He speed-dialed Tubs once more but got no answer.

A trashcan by the elevator doors at the Simmone vibrated ever so softly.

***

"This guy is a fucking cop, what now?" One of the giant's rifled through Tubs' identification.

"Just call and see what he wants us to do."

The men exited the elevator three levels below the lobby and stepped into a nondescript hallway. Tubs was hit hard, first a blow to the stomach that caught him completely off guard and consequently winded him, and then a crack to the face with his own gun knocking him out cold.

A few moments later he awoke dazed and confused, his right temple was pounding. It was only after attempting to stand did he notice his hands were bound behind his back and his ankles duct taped together and tied to the cross beam of a chair. He looked at the three walls he faced; it seemed to be some sort of maintenance room, filled with furnaces, hot water heaters, and air conditioning units. His sudden gyration tipped the chair, and he lay helpless on the floor.

"I don't think he should hear this call."

One of the two interrogators laid a marker with his heel on Tubs' already wounded temple and knocked him out again.

Allan Boyles was in the back of a limousine on his way to the game when he took the call.

"A cop?" He thought for a moment. "No change of plans."

***

Clay stopped counting the number of times he pressed send on his mobile. Why wasn't Tubs answering? His gut told him something had gone terribly wrong. He looked around the stadium. Now it was packed and he hadn't a clue where to look next. The atmosphere was a lot more overwhelming than he had anticipated for with his own growing anxiety; Clay was doing nothing with any purpose. He made the decision to go back to the hotel and hoped the hell he would hear from Tubs before exiting the stadium.

Yankee Stadium expected a capacity crowd of fifty-three thousand fans. The corridors, bars, food, and souvenir stands were all packed. Even the Great Hall, a foyer between the exterior and interior wall of the building, was extremely congested. Clay was having a very difficult time getting past the throngs of patrons, so at certain points he just had to slow it down and go with the flow. Back to front, shoulder to shoulder, he filed toward Gate Four, the main entrance.

Unexpectedly, Clay's wrist was squeezed tight and pulled up behind his back causing him to reach onto his toes to relieve the pain, a gun grinded into his lower spine. Tubs wasn't the only one under surveillance all day.

Judging by the size of the paw that held him firmly, Clay figured he had another linebacker on his hands.

"Just keep walking; we will go to the hotel together."

The jostling in the Great Hall was like a dance everyone was performing as the patrons were filing to their seats for the national anthem. Clay was being steered to the right; the gunman continued his relentless armlock while trying to remain incognito. They guided by the sushi bar and Clay deftly swooped up a chopstick with his free right hand, then with no hesitation, lodged it into the thigh of the assailant. With a shriek of pain, he released Clay instantaneously. The pain in Clay's left shoulder immediately subsided, allowing him to lower the boom on the assailant's shin with his heel and then wheeled around with a knee to the groin, followed with one to the head.

Clay gritted his teeth. Another couple of shots to the head and the groin, and the man was laid out. Some of the crowd gathered for the spectacle, others scattered. There was no doubt in Clay's mind that Tubs was in trouble.

Police were running to the commotion and Clay slipped into the food court, disappearing into the restrooms and a toilet stall. He gathered his composure, wiped his brow and caught his breath.

Normal, relaxed, calm, but excited for the game.

Clay came out of the stall his jacket folded over his arm, the press pass hidden under his shirt, a smile painted on his face. He struck up a conversation with a guy in his mid-twenties who was dressed in complete Yankee paraphernalia, and they strolled past the police that were in full force searching for the perpetrator. Clay glanced over the shoulder of the eager fan in time to witness the Boyles' goon with the chopstick lodged in his leg, seething in pain. Three paramedics and no less than six officers were escorting him.

Clay continued to nod and laugh at the appropriate times when the fan maniac spewed out more stats about his beloved Yanks. They shared one another's enthusiasm until Gate Four, the main entrance, where they parted ways.

Outside the stadium, Clay paused at a souvenir booth. "Give me those two Yankee's bats there." He pointed at the regulation sized hardball bats painted in Yankee pinstripes.

"Standard or the souvenir size?"

"The real ones."

"One hundred forty, but they each come with a ball."

Clay threw down the money, and grabbed the two bats with one hand. The merchant handed him the first ball, which Clay deftly pocketed before beginning to walk away.

"Hey, you get another ball, buddy," the souvenir seller called after him.

"Give it to some kid," Clay called over his shoulder as he headed towards the line of yellow limos, and with no fanfare, he slid into the back seat of a waiting car. Clay pulled the wrappers off the bats and stuffed the ball in his leather jacket. The taxi driver caught Clay's eye in the back as he was inspecting the quality of his new weapon.

"Had enough baseball?" the cabbie asked, referring to Clay's early exit from the game.

"That's one way of putting it."

***

Alex Ruby and John Harley were the defensive right guard and the offensive center respectively for the NCAA Texas Longhorns three years ago. Broken knees, shredded hamstrings, overuse of steroids, and just plain stupidity were the main reasons their careers came to a grinding halt after their third and final appearance in the Cotton Bowl. It was time for a career change. Since each of these men weighed at least fifty pounds heavier than their playing weight, it meant that approximately seven hundred and fifty pounds of muscle and fat where pounding on Tubs' face.

"Let me guess," Tubs wheezed between blows. "Are you the Maxes? Or the Maxes' cousins?" A particularly vicious left uppercut stole his breath before he could say anything else.

"You're lucky the Maxes aren't here, or you'd be dead already," the taller of the two thugs spat.

"Yeah," chimed in his shadow. "As it is, thanks to your *friend*, Max Bentley will never walk again and the other Max is still in traction."

Tubs felt his own knee kicked out from under him and had visions of traction in his own future. *I get it*, his thoughts swam, *an eye for an eye.*

After a torturous twenty minutes, the custodial room in the basement of the Simmone looked like a butcher shop, meat tenderizing with each blow to Tub's torso. His face looked like a barbequed sausage from the constant pounding. Tubs sat helpless to each blow as his hands and feet remained bound to a chair. Between each punishing crack his head hung lifeless as he swayed from side to side. Occasionally he would whimper, but each shot brought an increased level of numbness. His auditory senses were growing dim partially from the beating and partially because his ears had swollen up like cauliflowers.

Frick and Frack were no closer to knowing why he and Clay were in town and why they knew about Franklin.

***

Clay finally arrived at the hotel after what felt like an eternity. After slow and steady movement in the constant traffic he jumped from the cab, as it had barely rolled to a stop then walked into the lobby with both bats in one hand.

Clay waved at the bellhop. "Souvenirs for the kids."

Clay looked like he was ready to rip Jean's head off when he reached his pedestal.

"Where's my partner?"

Clay was seething angry his face so intense.

The concierge was visibly intimidated. "He opened the envelope and then they left."

"They?" Clay was a little too loud, drawing attention to him. He toned it down. "Who are they?"

"I really wasn't paying much attention, he really ripped the envelope and I had to get it back together. They walked towards the elevators over there."

"There?" He pointed at the room elevators.

"No, the one to the right, the service one."

Clay bolted to the right; he was no longer concerned about drawing attention to himself. He glanced at the floor choices above the elevator; they included M1, M2, M3, P1, P2, and P3. Clay took the stairs to M1. If they went to the parking garage it was all over.

He opened the heavy metal door quietly. In front of him was a relatively narrow nondescript hallway, doors leading off to the right and left, three on each side. An identical door to the one he just walked through was at the opposite end of the corridor. No doors had windows. Clay walked gingerly with a bat in each hand, almost tiptoeing. He stopped at the first door on his right and listened intently, all that could be heard was a gentle humming of a generator. The second door he came to was on his left, marked custodial. Clay lowered his head and listened, but then jerked away as he heard voices. Clay moved in once again, the voices much more discernable. He carefully, set one of the bats by the entrance and took a firm grip on the second, waggling it in a small circular pattern as if preparing to face a fastball. He listened.

"We are wasting our time; we won't get squat from him now that he's like pulp. No one can take that without squealing."

"Call him, see if he wants us to finish him off and show him to Mr. Hudson, or are we to cut off his fingers and see if that gets us anywhere. These brass knuckles hurt like hell."

"I don't think he can talk anyway; his brain is probably scrambled."

"Look at him, no one can take a beating like that, we really fucked him up." They both laughed.

Clay closed his eyes and prepared himself.

Go for the knees, not the head. One, two, three...

Clay twisted the knob and kicked the door open. Two shadows turned and automatically reached for their sidearms but before either of them could, Clay's incredible speed and accuracy with a bat snapped the wrist of the man on his right, and with his follow through he nailed the second gangster in the side of the head.

Knees, moron.

Not a lot of people knew Clay was as strong from both sides of the plate. This came in handy. He lowered his right hand to the knob of the bat and took an equally productive swing from the left side and buckled the left knee of one of the tyrants, turning his leg into an 'L' shape. The mammoth crumpled to the ground in agony. It was then that Clay made his first mistake. He took another swing at the same hoodlum, crushing his other kneecap, hyper extending the appendage and likely crippling him for life. In the meantime, the second heavy laid a right fist into Clay's cheek, cracking his orbital bone and sending him backwards into the hallway. He had never been hit that hard in his life, this one worse than any of the shots he took in Rebel. One could only imagine what his friend had just endured. The impact sent his bat spiraling into the corner. Clay lay on the floor trying to shake off the assault and prevent himself from blacking out. He looked through the doorway and a man he did not recognize stared back at him. Tubs' face was disfigured like someone suffering from lionitis, his jaw hung down, his skin, deep purple, and his shirt saturated in blood. It was the first opportunity Clay had to look at his partner.

Clay was blind with anger, he gritted his teeth as the second assailant appeared in the doorway, not with a gun, but with his bat. Clay crouched like a back catcher, bouncing on the balls of his feet and waited.

This guy has never held a bat in his life; go ahead telegraph your attack.

He raised the bat over his head as if hitting something with his back swing, then came down with all his might as if taking a swing with an axe, his face contorted like a madman with a hot pepper shoved up his ass. Clay waited; the bat was wired for his head. It seemed like his opponent's motions were in slow motion. Clay waited, and waited to the point that it seemed humanly impossible not to get clobbered by the upcoming deluge, and then at the last second sprung to his right rolling towards his other bat lying against the door. The scoundrel's bat smashed against the cement floor busting in two just above his grip.

Clay's first assault was to the ribs, his victim took a step sideways, and the second cracked his shin in two pieces. Clay paused and looked at his dearest friend sitting lifeless in his chair. Clay was once again filled with rage then turned and knocked most of the aggressor's teeth out snapping his jaw into a thousand pieces. He lay unconscious.

The second stooge dragged himself into the hallway and lifted his gun. In an almost cocky fashion, Clay waggled his bat and sent the firearm airborne into the stairwell door, following up with a shot to the jaw busting both his bat and the goon's face permanently.

Clay ran to his friend and released his feet and hands from the chair. Tubs collapsed into Clays arms; it was all he could do to steady the massive man as he leaned into him. Tubs were mumbling something, but his words were not discernable. "Oh my God, Tubs… okay, be strong for Sally and Harper."

Clay dialed 911, left Tubs temporarily and waited at the main entrance to the hotel. The paramedics arrived quickly—likely due to the upscale address of the emergency—and Clay escorted them to the service elevator. The patrons were giddy with excitement… so much activity. Clay waited for the doors to close, hit the M1 button, then immediately hit the emergency button freezing the elevator between floors. Lights flashed, bells rang, and Clay ignored all of the distractions.

He turned to the startled paramedics. "When we get down here three men are in dire need of your help, however, only one deserves it. He is a cop and my friend. Get us to a hospital; let the fire and rescue services that are on their way deal the other two." Clay looked the young paramedic in the eyes, then uttered one final plea. "Just get Michael to the hospital, I beg you."

"We can't do that, sir, we must stabilize each individual."

Clay stopped him in his tracks. "I am not asking you."

They looked at one another. "He's a cop?"

"He's a cop."

"At least let us make sure the other two are stabilized."

"Fair enough."

Clay rushed the emergency crew along.

***

Clay jumped in the back of the ambulance with Tubs.

The ambulance jostled back and forth, Clay used his legs and arms for balance. "How is he?"

"He is responsive, which is good, considering the beating he must have taken. They will likely do a CT scan and monitor his vitals. It will move things along if we can prove he is a cop."

"Sure." Clay gave them all the information to plug into the computer and sure enough his name popped up, Michael Cornelius Campbell, Chief of Police, Town of Gremlin, Pennsylvania.

"That's him." They had to trust Clay because a physical identification was not an option.

"He's trying to hold your hand."

"Huh?" The paramedic's words took Clay by surprise.

"Look." He pointed.

Sure enough, Tubs was reaching for Clay. He swallowed hard and held his hand out to Tubs. He wasn't looking to hold his hand at all; he was delivering a piece of paper. It was moist and pressed into a small square. Clay opened it. Tubs had traced some numbers and letters over and over again using his own blood.

Unbelievable.

While Tubs was getting the pulp beaten out of him, he was giving Clay the gate, section and seat number for Allan Boyles.

The back doors opened and Tubs was wheeled into the emergency.

***

Franklin stood at the entrance marked Gate Four and awaited the arrival of a man known only as 'the Colt'.

The Colt was instructed to wear a florescent green sweater.

Franklin spotted him from a distance, which was no surprise, and cut him off in a small alcove. Franklin's right hand clutched a billfold of fourteen thousand, three hundred twenty dollars, all of the money he had in his jeans for SEC 17B, Row 8, Seat 7, of the Legends Section of the stadium, a seat just to the right, of the Yankee dugout, and seven rows above, the playing field.

Franklin grabbed his arm, causing the Colt to wince then raise his voice in anger. "Can't be too sure, come with me." Franklin walked his short-term business partner to the wicket and waited for the authorization to be confirmed, before releasing his grip on the professional scalper.

This wasn't just any seat; this was a seat of a lifetime.

***

Clay sat in a hospital waiting room… again. He rested his head on a fist but that didn't last, his cracked orbital bone was more painful than he had thought. Clay reached into his pocket and removed the still damp piece of paper, unfolded it and went to the triage nurse to borrow a pencil. He lightly shaded over the fingernail bloody imprints. 1788. He turned to the nurse and interrupted her chart work.

"Could you pull something up on your Internet?"

She examined Clay's look of desperation. "In two minutes, I am on a break; you can walk with me to the café, I can look up your site down there."

They walked down to the cafeteria together and Clay bought her a coffee while she logged on to the Internet.

"These numbers represent a seat at Yankee Stadium," he said, pointing to the piece of paper.

"This is what your buddy lost his mind over? A seat at a baseball game?"

"Lost his mind?"

"Got a severe concussion for sure."

Clay shook off the comment. He had to believe that Tubs was going to be okay. "We're here for more than just a seat, that's for sure. We're here to..." Clay paused. What exactly where they there for, anyways? "We're here to right a wrong that's been going on for, far too long."

This answer seemed to satisfy the nurse. "It goes section, row, seat, is that right?"

Clay nodded, "Usually, yah."

"Yah, I've been to a few games, but my granddaddy and my daddy were Dodgers fans from way back." The nurse chatted as the machine searched for results.

"Brooklyn, nice." Clay was trying hard to hold himself together.

"I think this is the seat you are looking for." She pointed at a seat in the Legends Section directly behind the dugout.

They walked back to emerge together. "So, are you going to let this slip by?"

"What do you mean?"

"You can sit here and do nothing or you can go do whatever you and your mate were here to do, and then come back."

Clay didn't know what to do. He didn't want to leave Tubs, but he didn't want to let this opportunity pass, either. If he did, Tubs' suffering would have been for nothing.

"Give me your cell number," the nurse urged. "I promise I will call you back if I think it's that important."

"You will call? You promise?"

"I promise. I'm on till dawn, honey."

Clay didn't hesitate and ran out the door. He hailed the first taxi. A Sikh in a Yankees turban picked him up.

"Yankee Stadium."

"You're not serious."

"Yes; and turn on the game. What inning are they in?"

"Rain delays, two of them so they are just heading into the eighth, the game is taking forever."

Clay's stomach turned. "Who's on the mound?"

"Not sure, I think Boyles is coming back out."

"God, I hope so."

"Yeah me too, we need to get the job done."

You're telling me.

"How fast can you get me there?"

"Half hour."

"How about ten minutes." Clay waved five large in his rear-view sight.

The driver's U-turn was not subtle at all, especially now that he was driving the wrong way on a one-way. Gurmez Sukvinder, the drivers name officially inscribed on the dashboard, was no longer comfortable squeezing by the oncoming traffic so he pounded the cab up onto the sidewalk. There he increased his speed, narrowly avoiding mailboxes, planters and garbage containers. Clay hung on to the 'Oh my God bar' above his right arm; his shoulder with a slight twinge.

Gurmez jumped back onto the street; traffic seemed to be moving in his direction now. He laid on the horn, slammed on the brakes as he approached a red light then sped on through. The driver did this time and time again, sped up, look both ways and forged ahead, honking, weaving, braking and accelerating, his eyes darting back and forth, one second on the road, the next his rear view and then the side view. He was calm and confident, a master of his craft, braking, merging, and accelerating as if it was an everyday occurrence, but then came an engineering feat, so simple, so important and so frustrating; a bridge, the narrowing of the hourglass, measured, deliberate, and unhurried, the structure thwarting all their efforts. In a word, Clay was losing the race against time.

***

"What has to be going on in the mind of Lacoste managing this epic game? He has arguably the best pitcher to don a Yankees' uniform in my lifetime ready to go back out there, and the strongest closer in the league, fresh and ready to pounce."

"I know what you mean. Three outs away from his first, and I guess only, World Series ring, Boyles looks completely poised, unlike his condition after the announcement in the turmoil yesterday at that press conference."

"Yes, for those of you that didn't read about it or see it on TV…"

***

"This is how it works, Allan. This is hell. Right here, right now. And when you are called to heaven, you will go up there, but not be allowed to stay. You will be sent back down here to hell and do it all over again, until you get it right. The way I see it, you have been one fuck-up after another in this lifetime. Maybe you were worse in the last go around, maybe you were Attila the Hun or someone like that. I will send you to heaven, but hell waits." Franklin was whispering in Allan's ear.

Allan turned to Franklin and mouthed some words. Franklin leaned in. "What was that, I missed it?"

"At least my son amounted to something."

***

"So here we go, his warm-up pitches complete, and now faces the top of the order. Boyles is back."

***

Clay dropped the five one-hundred-dollar bills on the front passenger seat, jumped out of the cab and sprinted across the Franklin Bridge, his lungs caving in and the lactic acid burning in his legs; each step jarred his fractured cheekbone causing great pain up the side of his head. It had been years since he sprinted, his form was strong at first, but he was showing fatigue after only a hundred or so steps. He pumped hard with his arms, generating better speed from his legs when he felt the fatigue; the arms moved higher and harder pushing his legs to do the same. He came to the end of the bridge and hailed down another taxi.

Clay couldn't give him his destination as he was completely winded, a fire running through his chest, so he pointed at the press pass around his neck. The driver did not need to be encouraged to make time, any one working that hard had a goal in mind.

***

"We have a code blue, grab the crash cart." The intensity of the Emergency wing increased a couple of octaves. The already frantic staff were now running to Michael Campbell's aid.

***

"Right here." Clay jumped out and bolted across the expansive sidewalk leading to Gate Four. After hurdling the turnstile, he waved his pass at the police and security, turned right in the Great Hall and dodged by the odd straggler that wasn't in the bowl riveted to the tense ninth inning. Section 17, he took a hard left and jumped up six stairs in two steps.

***

Franklin turned to Boyles and nudged him. Allan was coming in and out of consciousness; his shirt was blood soaked the wool coat he wore now saturated, blood dripping to the concrete below.

"Are you paying attention here, your son is in the world's spotlight, and this should be your proudest moment. Is this what you were working towards since Rebel?"

"What I did to you," Allan raised his eyebrows and looked at the crowd then smiled. "I wouldn't have changed a thing."

***

The nurse stopped manual CPR just long enough for the paddles to be set. "Clear!"

The paddles jolted Campbell's large frame in the hospital gurney. They turned to the monitor, but it remained a flat line.

"Clear!"

***

Clay stood at the top of the Legends Section, just steps from the field and the Yankees dugout. He squatted due to the overwhelming attention he was receiving, and then counted up eight rows. He then counted across the row but it was difficult to see because of the umbrellas still being tossed around, and fans scrambling back and forth in their seats.

Clay's eyes focused in on the back of a fan's head, a black hoody and an older gentleman in a fedora and brown woolen coat to his right. He vaguely recognized the older man from the night before, but something about him at the moment seemed waxy and unnatural. Then Clay caught sight of the purple shiner visible just beneath the fedora's brim.

That has to be them.

They sat still; an anomaly surrounded by screaming fans.

***

"That's a pop up to short center and the short stop, Rodriguez has a beat on it. He has caught it; the crowd rises and that's one away."

***

Clay lost sight of them in the pandemonium.

***

"Two hundred and twenty volts." The paddles were rubbed together. "Clear!"

***

"A grounder to second and a throw to first, two down, we are just one out away from crowning a World Champion. You can hear this crowd in Jersey, man."

***

The stadium was deafening, the cathedral was shaking, and in the bedlam, Franklin pulled out his gun and set in on Allan's lap. Franklin put his hand on Boyles left shoulder and pressed down.

"Your son will go out in a blaze of glory." Franklin's sinister smile was directed at Allan.

"Bastard." Allan feebly reached for the gun. The crowd jumped up and down, fanatics standing, and weaving, surrounding the two men on all sides.

***

Clay kept his eyes focused in the direction of row eight. He too was trapped, as the aisles were filled with fans working their way down to the field.

Clay's phone vibrated, but it was imperceptible to him amidst the surging crowd.

***

Franklin pulled out his knife one last time and ripped it into Allan's side. He looked him in the eyes and the knife plunged into a rib. Allan screamed in horror and the crowd screamed along. Franklin laughed.

Oh, the sweet justice; I have prepared so long for this day. Keep looking into my eyes, Allan; I will be your last vision on this earth.

He plunged the knife in five or six more times until Allan sat lifeless in his seat.

***

"Boyles leans in for the signal, stares at the third base coach, and starts his wind up. Here comes the pitch. Just outside and the count is full. The walls are pounding again as the crowd's drumming reaches a crescendo for the next pitch."

"Man, what a night."

"Here's the wind up, and that's ball four. Boyles picks up the rosin bag and takes a few steps towards the mound. Fifty-three thousand umpires would have called that one differently, including Boyles."

"That puts a whole new perspective on the inning with the tying run on first. The walked batsman has been replaced with Smith, the speedy replacement. The Yankees skipper is on the way to the mound; he has not signaled to the bullpen for a reliever, my guess is he will have a chat with Boyles first, give the bullpen some valuable extra seconds on such frosty evening."

"Not only that, he will wait to see if the Padres go with a pinch hitter before he chooses a righty or a lefty from the pen."

"That's always a critical point in this chess game we like to refer to as baseball."

"That ball four sure took the wind out of the sails of this hometown crowd. They were one strike away from another World Series victory, and now they have to ramp it up again."

***

The crowd settled to their seats during the break in the action and Clay once again had a visual on Franklin and Boyles. Clay remained pinned against the rail, the crowd no longer attached to any seating arrangements.

A relative hush came over the crowd as they waited out the time delay. Clay watched Franklin shift slightly then rise.

In a deep hollow voice, Franklin yelled over the hum of the crowd. "You just threw your last pitch ever, Boyles."

With that, Clay watched as Franklin reached down and pulled his gun from Allan's lap and steadied it with both hands. Franklin extended his right arm and steadied his wrist with his left.

Clay was pinned in a frenzy of fans and stood helpless. Franklin bent his knees and shifted his right leg in front of his left.

A fan yelled 'gun' and the crowd went into hysterics scrambling and ducking.

Rickey heard the disruption from the mound, it was a different excitement from that of a radical fan and he turned in the general direction of the dugout.

The manager continued the longest stroll in baseball.

Clay saw the gun, but was in no position to do anything. In seconds, the aisles had become jammed with a paranoid crowd clambering in all directions and he had nowhere to go. A police officer was scrambling for his weapon, but he was in a precarious position. Truly, no shot could be fired.

Clay rubbed his wrist against his right pocket then remembered the souvenir shop.

With the gun steadied, Franklin cocked his head slightly, for better aim.

Clay reached into his leather coat pocket, and pulled out the ball he picked up a few hours ago. He pushed some fans to the side and gave himself just enough room to set up to throw.

This one is for you, Kate.

Clay took a deep breath and released it slowly, then focused on Franklin's head. He pictured the bullseye on the old shed and thought of all the pent-up anger that target had come to represent for him. Clay wound up and threw a bullet two-seamed fastball as hard as he could. His shoulder ripped apart; a painful reminder of his past heroics. He watched the line of the ball closing in on the side of Franklin's head.

Impact.

Franklin didn't know what hit him. The gun flew from his hand and he fell forward into the empty seat below. He shook his head and righted himself then staggered to his left raising his jaw. Blood poured down the side of his face.

"Noooooo!" he screamed in a hollow screech that reverberated onto the field. Franklin shook his head, blood sprayed on those closest to him, as his actions had fans diving for cover, diving to be far away from this madman.

Franklin spit out blood, stepped onto the top of the seat in front of him and dove towards the field, his arms waving in the air as he screamed for Rickey's death. Police surrounded the paranoid man and no less than six cops dove on the fuming, raging spectacle.

***

"Something just happened to the left of the Yankees bull pen, the crowd dispersed and police have gathered, and by the looks of things, not just one or two officers."

"The skipper has made up his mind and he will go to the bullpen. Rickey Boyles is done for the night and possibly forever. He is receiving a standing ovation as he tips his cap to the crowd."

"Listen to that crowd."

***

Clay fell back into the great foyer landing against the wall. Police continued to run towards Section 17, against the crowds running in the opposite direction. Clay dropped to the floor and sat with his back against the concrete. For the time being he was left alone. His phone vibrated, and this time he felt it.

Jesus Christ. Tubs.

"Hello." He lifted his left hand and with his index finger, plugged his other ear. "Hello," he repeated, his stomach was flipping.

"Clay, its Julie." There was silence after that.

"Julie?" Clay's stomach dropped to a new all-time low. A phone call from Julie could only mean one thing. "Oh my God, is it Kate? Is she okay? Speak up, Julie, I can barely hear you."

Silence.

Jesus Christ.

Clay stood up and fought his way to the closest exit expecting stronger reception. "Julie?"

She had passed the phone to Rebecca. "Clay? It's Rebecca." Her voice was shaky she held her breath in order to gain composure and then continued.

This is the end I can't listen to this... Jesus Christ don't say it... Fuck.

Clay's eyes filled with tears.

Rebecca called out. "Clay, there is so much noise, but Clay I hope you can hear me... Kate wants to know if you caught the bad guy?"

Clay came to an abrupt stop. He was stunned. It took a good few seconds for it to sink in. "Are you serious?" He began crying uncontrollably. He slid himself into a food kiosk, and skulked into a back entry, the crowd noise muffled considerably.

"Yes, here she is." Rebecca could barely get the words out.

A quiet voice whispered. "Clay?"

"Oh my God, Kate, it's you, oh my God. I can't believe it's you. I love you." Clay fell back and slid down the wall and bowed his head.

"I love you too. Come home soon, okay."

"As soon as I can," he promised.

Rebecca came back on the line. "The doctors are in with here now, Clay. Come home as soon as you can." Rebecca's voice caught in her throat. "Okay, I'm gonna let you go now." Before she hung up, she said incredulously, "Kate's come back to us, Clay. Our time in the woods is over."

Clay gulped down the lump that was forming in his throat. "Yes," he whispered into the cool New York air. "It's finally over."

They hung up and the phone vibrated again. This time it was a NYC number...

Tubs, shit.

***

"I don't think I will live to see a more bizarre World Series ending like that."

"Who would believe that a top of the tenth, extra inning, two out home run that would ultimately end a franchise-long drought for the Padres would be the secondary story."

"After the arrest in the section beside the Yankee dugout, and the hour and the half game delay, the players were allowed back onto the field and I think every on duty and off duty cop was called in. The field was lined three-deep with a sea of blue just to allow the inning and a half."

"Man."

***

Coach Riggins leaned over and switched off the radio set he had been listening to on his porch and then start whistling to himself as he paced down the veranda steps and turned the sprinkler onto his rose garden.

Coach Riggins one of the *true* adversaries—the bystander who stood back and did nothing—was still going about his business, whistling a merry tune.

23

Eight months later

Clay would not share his weekend plans with Kate. His only instructions were to pack for five days; the weather would be warmer than home, but only slightly so. He also mentioned to dress casual and bring lots of sunscreen.

Clay paused by the house, gathered the luggage then glanced at his watch and hurried out. He was running late but would meet Kate and the others at the Black and White as agreed.

Rebecca was the first to arrive. A bell chimed as she made her entrance. She waved at Chuck. He sat reading the local horse racing results on a stool that was covered in newspaper. The stool, as old as the restaurant itself, remained tucked in the corner by the cash register and front window. Chuck's attention was drawn away from his successes just long enough to peer at the opening door, his eyes smiled as he recognized Rebecca then gave a little bow as per usual.

Thursday at four thirty in the afternoon, just prior to the long weekend wasn't exactly prime time at Chuck's so Rebecca had her choice of booths. Before she had her jacket on the hanger, a cup of steaming hot black coffee was set in place. She slid across the red, cracking vinyl and wrapped her hands around the white porcelain. Rebecca was in a contemplative frame of mind and stared into the black liquid, watching the ripples undulate to the cup's edge.

What a year.

So many bumps along the way, the highest of highs and the lowest of lows, she had to reach the bottom in order to push off, and that fateful evening in Boston was when it occurred. For the first time in her life she felt loved and necessary. Weekly therapy continued to steer her in the right direction, clear precise thinking, living in the present and for the first time, planning for the future. The waves of guilt subdued substantially when Kate's health took a turn for the better.

Kate arrived about five minutes later; she had a meeting with council downtown that ran a little late, no fault but her own. She looked beautiful, dressed in all black: her favorite color. The low neckline showed off her perfect complexion, shining in the late afternoon sun.

Rebecca waved, as did Chuck. She ordered an orange juice on her way past the counter, wheeled to the booth and then shifted from her chair to the red vinyl with great ease. She had not been in such good shape in years. It began with therapy to increase the mobility in her shoulder, and then the strength-building program. Atrophy in her legs was the norm, but the eight weeks in bed made her whole body shrivel. After four weeks of physiotherapy, she took it upon herself to get into the gym each and every day. At first her routine was simple and short, but as time went by, she gained momentum and a rigorous workout became the norm.

Rebecca drove her everywhere and eventually agreed to join the fitness facility herself. Although she never pushed herself, it was the first time she had ever done anything athletic. Rebecca even cut down on the smoking. The workouts were therapeutic for both women, and essential for Kate if she was to live a long life.

"Did you see the sports section?" Kate asked Rebecca, tossing the *New York Times* on the table. "We got a two-page spread."

Rebecca grabbed for the paper and flipped to the right section. "The Dark Side of the Diamond, by: Alden Hooper," she read. Her eyes skimmed the article, stopping for a brief moment on the description of the shooting at the Burger King in Boston nearly fourteen years ago. "Do you think Franklin will ever get out of the asylum?"

Kate was thoughtful. "Either way, it will never matter to us. His beef was with Rickey's dad, and he tidied that up."

"Won't he be pissed that Rickey's pitching again?"

"Not as pissed as the Yankees." They both laughed.

Just then Clay arrived; he was full of smiles and jubilation, not just because of the article, more for his and Kate's impending weekend away.

Kate greeted him with a kiss meant more for the privacy of the bedroom. He then playfully pushed her towards the edge of the booth to make room for himself. Coffee soon arrived and Chuck smiled then toddled off.

Clay was rarely without a smile these days and always in good spirits. He put some weight back on and with the baseball season just underway he too was training hard. Kate thought he looked buffed and said so, mostly to embarrass him, but also because she knew it was true.

Tubs was the last to arrive, he walked from the police station as he was still without a car and now the proud owner of a brass tipped walking cane. After the heart failure, he had a series of small strokes leaving him slightly numb on his right side. He was improving, and the doctors suggested full recovery if he was careful with diet and daily exercise. Needless to say, the cane was still around, and the recovery was a little behind schedule, one battle at a time for Tubs.

Chuck brought more coffee and juice.

Kate started things off. "Okay, thank you, Rebecca and Tubs, for meeting us here tonight. Happy Birthday to you…" She started to sing, and then Clay and Tubs jumped in. Chuck scampered over to make it a quartet.

Rebecca went scarlet. "How did you know?"

"I got curious… and your wallet was just sitting on the counter one day, so…" Kate grinned mischievously.

Rebecca shook her head and chuckled.

Kate continued. "Clay and I have something to share with both of you, but before we do, the birthday girl needs to order."

Chuck jumped in. "I know Becky's favorite." They all agreed to have that, and off he went again.

"Fair enough," Kate continued. "I just want to say that, Rebecca, you are like an angel who appeared from nowhere. I really don't know what I would have done without you. Not only did you help to catch the bastard, you have been at my side every step of the way in my recovery. A year ago, you were a person in a file on Clay's desk and now you're my closest friend." Rebecca's eyes were glazed with tears, as were Kate's. "Here, this is for you."

Kate handed Rebecca a beautifully wrapped box. Clay sat forward in his seat. Rebecca began to cry.

"Oh my God, Rebecca. Please don't cry."

"Tears of joy, I haven't had a present since I was seventeen."

"Oh, Rebecca." Kate ran her hand through her hair. "Well, we will never let that happen again."

Rebecca gathered herself the best she could and she carefully unwrapped the cheery birthday-themed paper and painstakingly opened the box one slice of tape at a time. She removed the wrapping paper and looked at the sweatshirt for a second and then it sank in. She dropped the box to her lap and covered her face with her hands.

"I cannot believe you had this done, this is the most thoughtful..." Rebecca stared at a deep navy sweatshirt with heavy multi-dimensional embroidery, emblazed in official script. The font was 'collegiate' making the presentation so real and so official. The shirt read 'University of Public Boston'.

"Wear it proud, Rebecca, you are a true graduate," Clay piped up.

"We have something else," Kate called out.

Kate continued, "As you know, Clay and I had the property in the country and we finally sold it." She handed each of them an envelope. Tubs, this should give you and Sally some breathing room, and, Rebecca, we hope you decide to buy that little bungalow you have been eyeing up on Tower Street."

Clay spoke up before either Rebecca or Tubs could jump in. "Now before you say no, you have no choice, Kate and I want this, and this is non-negotiable."

Chuck arrived with platters of Chinese food, mounded to feed a kingdom.

The dinner club laughed and hugged for over an hour, eating copious amounts. Even Tubs was reaching his limit.

"So, when are you two leaving?" Rebecca threw her eyes back and forth between Clay and Kate.

"Well, Clay won't exactly tell me where we are going, but we are packed, and the stuff is in the van." Kate raised her eyebrows and set her head on his shoulder.

"Clay?" Rebecca pried.

"No. Kate will give you all the details Tuesday."

"We need to get on the road, so thank you for meeting so early." Clay spoke up after a third or fourth coffee refill.

They hugged and wished the happy couple a fun weekend. Once out the door, Tubs and Rebecca stared at one another.

"Well, we have to open them at some point."

"For sure."

Rebecca was the first to open her envelope. "Holy shit, Tubs, open yours." It was too late to catch Clay and Kate, so Rebecca dialed Kate's cell.

In the meantime, Tubs did as he was told and nearly fell over. "Holy shit, they must have just split the proceeds in two. This is way out of line."

Kate recognized Rebecca's number and answered. "Yesss."

"You two are nuts, this is insane."

"No, it isn't, and this in non-negotiable and we love both of you, see you Tuesday." She hung up and smiled. "They didn't wait long... so, Clay Stoppa, where are you taking me?"

"You figure it out."

They entered onto the 495 South and eventually merged onto I-95. Kate guessed Washington, then when they past the cut off, she picked Richmond, then Nashville, Raleigh and Atlanta.

They never shut up the whole drive, solving world issues, talking about problem students, and their relationship with Rebecca and Tubs, eight hours later and a second tank of gas, they crossed into South Carolina and exited onto Highway 501 East. By now it was two a.m., neither one tired, everything serene.

Kate went quiet on the exit. "Oh, Clay, I know now." She turned towards the window and began crying.

"Kate this is supposed to make you happy."

"Happy tears, Clay." She pointed at her eyes. "Can't you see the difference."

Clay smiled. "I'm getting better at seeing that lately."

They arrived in Myrtle Beach a few hours before dawn and Clay asked if they could go straight to the pier before checking in. Kate smiled and nodded.

The entrance to the pier was a glorified arcade with cheap food and fishing tackle. Clay recognized a photo of the owner operator hanging on the wall from some forty years ago, a time when his parents brought him down here. It was like walking into a time capsule.

The building lead onto the pier. Kate entered the 24-hour shop and wheeled straight outside. The ocean breeze was warm and constant; only the white wave breaks could be seen under the moonlight. Kate closed her eyes for a moment and concentrated on the smell of the sea and sounds of waves folding below. Clay stopped part way and counted the pillars below. "This one, Kate, this is the one we signed."

"We will go down there tomorrow and carve our initials again."

They reached the end and stared out into the distance. "Did you bring you bread rings, Clay? Do you think we will see any dolphins?" Kate playfully laughed.

"We can do that tomorrow as well." Clay sat on the bench beside Kate and stared to the horizon, the stars infinite. After a few moments he looked over at Kate, she was smiling ear-to-ear, her hair blowing in the wind.

Clay reached into his pocket and went down on one knee. "What are you doing?" Kate looked at his hand and then into his eyes.

"Kate?" Clay opened a ring box exposing a diamond surrounded in sapphires. "Kate, will you marry me all over again?"

She could only nod and they hugged.

Clay wiped away her tears. "Well that's good, because I have booked us a second honeymoon this summer in Italy."

They sat in silence until the sun began to brighten the horizon.

"Thank you for being my best friend." They held hands as Clay pushed them back to the shoreline.

Epilogue

Three months later

Rebecca didn't leave herself a lot of time. Had she been thinking, the wiser approach would be straight off to McLeod's office from the Black and White, but she just had to squeeze in some groceries and drop them off at her house. After glancing at her watch, she stepped out to the curb, squinting six driveways south towards Kate and Clay's place, but to no avail, the driveway was empty, so she called a taxi.

The seven-dollar fare put Rebecca in a foul mood. She could count the number of times on one hand she paid for transportation. She thought it a complete waste of money, the result of poor planning. Such a short bloody walk she thought as she rudely dropped the cash on the front seat. She opened the door to Dr. McLeod's.

"Good afternoon, Rebecca, they are running about fifteen minutes behind, so just take a seat."

"Ha." Rebecca shook her head in disgust. "I could have walked here twice."

The familiar face of Dr. McLeod led Rebecca into his office. She was introduced to Dr. McVittie, the psychiatrist.

"Rebecca, hi…" She stood to greet Rebecca. Her height and terrific posture always caught Rebecca off guard. Standing over six feet tall, shoulders pushed back, and her torso arched, caused Rebecca to back up a pace upon shaking hands. "Thanks for seeing me again, Rebecca, please have a seat."

"Thanks." Rebecca crossed her legs away from the psychiatrist.

"I have reviewed Dr. McLeod's observations over the past year and I have predispositions, however before I draw any professional conclusions on your traumas and their effect on you today, I have some questions."

"Shoot."

"Do you understand doctor client privileges?"

"I believe so... it stays in this room."

"Essentially yes, so I want to cover off some sensitive issues, but this will only help you if you cooperate completely." Dr. McVittie crossed her legs and looked into Rebecca's eyes. "Can you do this for me?"

"Yes."

McVittie stared intently in silence. "Okay, so I want to focus on the reoccurring dream."

"Fine." Rebecca squirmed in the chair.

"I know this is not your favorite subject, so bear with me." Rebecca smiled politely.

"This test you are writing in a private kiosk, the room in a room; does it seem odd to you that it would be so noisy in a testing room?"

"Yah, I've never thought of that but I guess so."

"Did you ever write exams in a noisy auditorium?"

"Outside of shuffling paper, not that I recall."

"Did you write applications or do testing for anything extracurricular that may have rattled you?"

"Not that I can think of."

"Did you have any issues in a class where maybe you failed a test and you were centered out and embarrassed to the point of cruelty?"

"No."

"How about kiosks, what is your recollection of them?"

"The library."

"Go ahead."

"I spent months, arguably years, in the Boston Public Library."

"Did you study or read in the kiosks?"

"No, I would just pass by them for the most part."

"Okay, we'll move on."

"The spinning out of control, what is causing the panic?"

"Numbers, I can't make sense of them and I have no control as I fall into a darkness, then I wake up."

"Is there an end when you fall? Is there something that jolts you awake?"

"No, I don't think so, nothing that I remember."

"Okay, Rebecca, let's move on here." Dr. McVittie looked at her notes and tapped her fingers. "You have changed your name from Abby Lee Haason?"

Rebecca bowed her head. "Yes, I did it legally. How did you find that?" She had an edge to her inflection.

"Well, it was through medical records that transferred with the name change." McVitte looked up. "Are we good to continue here, Rebecca?"

She only nodded.

"Do you remember the car accident?" Rebecca nodded again.

"Can you take me through it?"

Rebecca fell back in the chair and closed her eyes and shook her head no.

"Rebecca, did you write a test just before the accident?"

She opened her eyes, reached forward and took a tissue from the table. She nodded then dabbed the side of her eye with the corner of the tissue.

"What test did you complete?"

"My driver's test."

"Was that a written test?"

"Yes, the first step to your license."

"Where was the test?"

"In a mall."

"A shopping mall?"

"Yah, in the back, behind all of the license registration area."

"What was the weather like that day?"

"Horrible."

"Rainy?"

"No. Snow, a blizzard, high winds."

"So, why that day? Why could you not wait a day?"

"It was my birthday, my sixteenth and I was promised my license on that day."

"So, your mom drove you?"

"Yes, after a screaming match and I basically pushed her into the car."

"And you passed?" Rebecca nodded.

"Then what?"

"I drove."

"Your mom let you drive for the first time in a raging storm?"

"I lied to her."

"What do you mean?"

"I said I would only drive to the end of the parking lot, since it was basically empty and she could drive us home."

"And?"

"And we came to the end of the parking lot and I floored it out onto the street."

"And then?"

"The truck hit us broadside, and my mom…"